Fools and Villains

Fred Coppenhall

'A fool and knave are plants of every soil'
Robert Burns

© Fred Coppenhall, 2008

Published by Quoin Publishing

November 2008

ISBN 978-0-9560761-0-6

Cover images © Caraman | Dreamstime.com

Cover design by Clare Brayshaw

Prepared and printed by:
York Publishing Services Ltd
64 Hallfield Road
Layerthorpe
York YO31 7ZQ
Tel: 01904 431213
Website: www.yps-publishing.co.uk

CONTENTS

Chapter One

A Sad Beginning

Who are a little wise, the best fools be.
(John Donne)

The dictionary tells us that a fool is one wanting in wisdom, judgement or sense. What it misses out is the everyday fact that fools are often the nicest people.

The tale that follows begins with a sad episode. It is, unhappily, an integral part of the plot so I thought it best to get it over with in the first chapter. Conveniently, it fits historically at the beginning, too.

Should the reader skip the sad part, an important element of the plot would be missed so I suggest that you plough bravely through, gently wipe your eyes and proceed with the lighter hearted section.

The meaning of bittersweet is softened by its latter part. So, constructed on that model, a tale with a sad beginning and a happy ending should leave the reader in a good mood rather than pensive, merry rather than morose.

This has been my aim while writing it.

Mostly, anyway.

* * *

Henry Pym was sitting in the library of his parents' home, a large, careworn house called Cabley Hall which hid in the flat countryside of North-Western England. Henry was dealing with the morning delivery of mail.

To an observant person, Henry's military background was evident in his dress, his confident bearing and his air of unquestionable authority. It would have taken an act of supreme self-assurance to disagree with or to provoke him in any way for, even on those occasions when he was wrong, Henry went wrong in the correct manner. His dark hair which surrounded the crown it had gradually abandoned was interspersed with white and kept as neatly trimmed as his moustache. A small paunch made his cummerbund, worn at the annual regimental reunion, a rather more obvious part of his evening dress than it used to be.

The envelope which lay on the table in front of him bore his full title, Lord Henry Pym Hughes and was written in a decorative, feminine hand. What the envelope had held and which Henry was now reading was a letter from Angela Poindexter, the wife of an old friend, Robert, whom he had known from his public school days and whose friendship had continued through military service and beyond.

Henry looked through the large windows of the library, past the open green of the grounds of the house and beyond, over the tops of the scratchy conifers which crowded around two sides of the property like eager spectators and let his mind drift back to when he had last seen the Poindexters. It had been just two years ago at the funeral of their daughter, Regina. She had been thrown from her horse while out riding and snapped her neck on the top rail of a field gate. Her death had come shockingly soon after the diagnosis of Robert's illness, an inoperable cancer of the stomach.

Henry had felt that, in Robert's place, he couldn't have coped with such misfortune and found it impossible to convey effectively his sympathies to the bereaved parents as they stood at Regina's graveside under a beautiful summer sun which poured warmth and light wastefully into the hole where her coffin lay.

Illnesses and their sufferers are often described directionally; they turn corners, they undergo reverses or go into a decline. After Regina died, Robert's illness fell off a cliff. No sooner was she buried than Robert took to his death-bed. The family which he had nurtured with devotion and selflessness was shattered and broken. Angela grew fearful, life had taken on a threatening tone.

Henry had had a smaller problem of his own: the relationship with his wife Sophia had crumbled, they had separated and his preoccupation with this had meant that he had overlooked or ignored opportunities to spend time with friends, Robert and Angela in particular. It had been difficult to maintain links with any of his acquaintances while Sophia was slowly and determinedly pulling herself out of the social circle. Now, according to Angela's letter, there wasn't much time to see his friend before he died. Robert had missed the last regimental reunion and would be missed at the next.

Angela lived over in the next county, near the east coast, where Robert had settled at the end of his army career and it took some four hours of driving before Henry arrived at Robert's house. He had brought with him an overnight bag whose contents would be sufficient to last him several more nights if circumstances required it.

The house was large and grey and stood in its own private acre, looking away from the road as though ashamed of something. Its view was uninspiring, overlooking undulating fields with just distant farm buildings to mar a feeling of solitude.

It had been built in the early part of the twentieth century by the man responsible for the nearby ribbon development of Cranby Steeple, a manufactory town. The isolation of the house suggested that its builder had no wish to live anywhere near those for whom he built houses.

There were no domestic animals in the limited grounds of the house, no dogs, no laughing children. Trimmed, silent lawns with, here and there, clumps of ordered, ornamental bushes surrounding the house like mourners but, with all its curtains drawn against sound, the house was blind to the tedium of its environment.

Henry rolled respectfully up the drive and parked near to the porticoed doorway and, before he had chance to knock, Angela opened the door and greeted him warmly and, it seemed, gratefully. She took him upstairs immediately to see Robert, as though she expected death to snatch him away at any second.

As he followed her, Henry noticed the subdued look of the house inside; there was nothing which was white, no brightness and even the lights appeared muted. There was a sepia tone to everything he looked at. It couldn't really be like this, could it? Surely it was the mood of the household which had cast this overall gloom and not the way things had been meant to look. The air seemed neither warm nor cold, the atmosphere neither welcoming nor unfriendly, almost as if the house no longer cared who came or went.

There was an ominous quiet which sat heavily on the stairs.

In contrast, Robert's room was alarmingly bright, it was like stepping from cloud into sunshine. Robert lay on his bed, gaunt, waxen and completely oblivious to both his pain and his surroundings. It was a shock for Henry to see how much his friend had deteriorated. There was very little left of the man he once knew. Others in that situation would have given up the battle for life long ago but Robert was always a fighter, never conceding a point if possible. It hurt Henry to see that what Robert was striving against now was unconquerable.

It's odd that when someone of your acquaintance leaves, either for pastures new or just simply dies, it's then that you can think of all sorts of things that you had wanted to say to them. Henry wanted so much to be able to speak to Robert but could not find appropriate words.

Angela was tearful and, inside, very frightened. She had been emotionally dependent on Robert after Regina had died. Her relationship with Robert's parent's was poor – they thought that their son had married beneath him and had no warm feelings for their daughter-in-law. They had had plans for Robert to marry a girl who was the daughter of friends of theirs, someone with connections. This one would never do. Angela was not connected.

Angela's own parents were both in their eighties and too frail for her to lean on in times of crisis. Neither she nor Robert had brothers or sisters, leaving her no-one to whom she could look to for support. She was frightened of having to stand alone, and unsure whether she could manage it.

Robert was being cared for professionally around the clock, care which was paid for assertively by his parents. A doctor called twice a day to monitor his condition and a team of nurses was on duty around the clock. Robert's lucid moments, free from both drugs and pain had become less frequent as his condition grew worse and these, his final days, were spent unconscious.

The pain which was killing him, and his efforts to surmount it and continue to draw breath, had become Robert's only remaining fixation in life. In contrast, Angela's pain was, at least, bearable; a constant distress constructed from grief. In the last few weeks, her life had been reduced to rubble and she felt the need to pull out the happy moments, spread them out to dry in whatever sun would shine and show them to whomever would take the time to look.

Most days, Angela had the company of Georgina Clegg, a near neighbour and friend of hers. Georgina was a practical and emotional help-mate but even her efforts could not calm Angela's fear of her future – a ragged black flapping flag inside her mind which seemed to invite her to shrug off her cares and join her husband and daughter. Georgina had remained with Angela for as long as she could but the day before Henry arrived, she had been obliged to return home to see to her own affairs and Angela was relieved to see someone else, someone to help prevent the loneliness.

"I'm really grateful you could get over to see Robert." Angela said as she and Henry looked helplessly at Robert lying in unawareness, constricted into a tiny, one-man world, waiting for the end.

Henry understood that she meant it was she who was glad of his presence, of his shoulder, ready for her to cry on.

Robert's room, hitherto shared with Angela, had been changed into a replica hospital ward. There was an electronic monitor to constantly check his life-signs, an oxygen bottle to one side of the bed and the table-top on the other side was cluttered with containers for the drugs on which Robert depended. Overall there was a smell more easily associated with an operating theatre than a bedroom and it stripped the atmosphere of any hope.

As Henry turned to leave Robert's room, his eye was drawn to a beautiful oval miniature in a rosewood frame which hung on the wall overlooking the bed.

"That's remarkable, that's you to life and yet, it looks quite old." he said to Angela. He moved closer to see it better. "Who painted it?"

"Come downstairs for coffee and I'll tell you about it."

Across the long pine table which dominated the quarry-tiled kitchen, Angela told Henry about the painting.

"When Robert first took me home to meet his parents — they weren't very impressed by me and our relationship has hardly flourished since — he showed me around the place. In one room, one they referred to as the music room – it contained a grand piano – hung several portraits of Robert's ancestors. One he was particularly eager to show me was of his great-grandmother, Rosalind, and I was quite taken aback with its resemblance to myself. It was exquisite and I fell in love with the painting. It sounds vain, I know but I can't explain the feelings I had. It was this resemblance which had first drawn Robert to me, the day we first met. He had spotted me at a party given by mutual friends and could not believe the similarity I bore to his dead relative. I found him a little intense at first; I couldn't understand why he seemed so obsessed with me. Robert's persistence paid off because I found myself gradually falling for him. And when he showed me the painting on my first visit to his parents' home to introduce me to them, I was thrilled. Afterwards, when we married, Robert gave me the miniature as a wedding present. It was his to give as it had been willed to him when Rosalind's daughter, Robert's grandmother, died. His mother was very upset by its removal from the family to which it belonged and tried to persuade Robert to take it back. In her eyes, I was not a family member, I was an outsider. She refused, even, to acknowledge the resemblance. She has been extremely resentful of me ever since."

During this account, Angela's eyes had looked down into her coffee cup as though she were describing scenes she could discern in the gleam from the china. Now she looked up at Henry, her face pummeled by fatigue and tears growing from her eyes and added, "It will be all I have left of our marriage apart from the memories."

Later that afternoon, the doctor, a chubby faced, friendly looking Asian man, arrived to check Robert's condition. After a slightly longer period than was usual for his visit, he came downstairs with a grim look on his face.

"Mrs Poindexter, I'm afraid that your husband's condition has worsened noticeably since this morning. He is extremely weak and slipping, I feel, into a final coma and I cannot give you any more hope. It may be over quite quickly. I'm sorry, I've done all I can." His shoulders and arms sagged with sorrow as he spoke.

Angela muffled a squeal with her handkerchief and began to cry. The doctor seemed reluctant to leave her in this freshly tearful state but Henry reassured the doctor that he would care for Angela and would call him should his services be required.

Before leaving, the doctor handed a packet to Henry, "These are sedatives. Use your judgement and give just one if you feel that she needs it but, remember, no more than two in any twenty four hour period."

Henry shook hands with the doctor and showed him out.

Angela was sitting on the bottom step of the stairs weeping, with neither the will to go up to see her husband nor to seek somewhere where she might cry in more comfort. Henry led her gently to the drawing room and made her sit in an easy-chair.

"Would you like something to drink? Coffee, perhaps" he asked.

"No, thank you." she sniffed.

"Would you like to talk?"

"That might help."

They talked for some time about mutual acquaintances touching once on Henry's sister, Antonia who Angela knew and liked from their encounters at regimental dinners. It was unimportant chat with the sole purpose of allowing the doctor's prognosis to sink in slowly. A little mental padding for her bruised emotions. Suddenly, becoming firm and resolved, Angela said, "I must phone Robert's parents. They have to be informed and I have no doubt that they will want to be with Robert now."

"Would you like me to call them?" Henry offered.

"No, I shall do it but thank you anyway." Angela clutched Henry's hand warmly and seemed reluctant to let it go.

Hilary and Aubrey Poindexter received the bad news of their son's deterioration; she with outspoken, demonstrative grief, he with the self-possession of hearing that which he had expected to hear. Aubrey did not allow his emotions full freedom, it would have won disapproval from his wife. Together they prepared to go to their son's bedside.

Despite an invitation to do so, the Poindexters did not stay with Angela but booked into a nearby hotel in Cranby Steeple. When they arrived at the house to see Robert, Hilary explained to Angela that she hadn't wanted to inconvenience her in any way and that, at the hotel, they were close enough to come whenever bidden. She pointedly put a card with the hotel's telephone number onto the hall table.

Henry had formed quite quickly a dislike for the Poindexters despite their being his friend's parents. Mrs Poindexter, in particular, angered him with her unwarranted arrogance. Mr. Poindexter was almost a mouse. It seemed wrong that they were Robert's parents; they didn't appear qualified for the honour.

It was apparent to Angela that Hilary had refused out of spite to share her hospitality, and was reluctant even to spend one night under her roof notwithstanding the fact that her only son lay dying under it. Aubrey would have accepted the invitation but must accede to his wife's wishes. Aubrey did as he was told.

One morning, two days after Robert's parents arrived, the nurse came downstairs to inform Angela that Robert had died quietly. She did this in a calm, business-like manner which invited little hysteria and then went to telephone the doctor while Angela tumbled, frightened, up the stairs to see him. Henry felt sorry not to have seen his friend during a period of consciousness so that he could have said goodbye to him. Angela was freshly distraught, sitting by the bed and talking distractedly to her dead husband so Henry called Robert's parents with the news and they arrived half an hour later. Hilary had dressed to impress although who this effort was for was just not clear. She had on a fur coat with a matching fur hat and looked like a ferret with ideas above its station. She was tight-lipped and said nothing as Henry opened the door to them – she was fighting to maintain control of her emotions and the stress of doing so showed plainly on her face. Deep inside, the softer, pinker Hilary wanted to weep openly, to demonstrate her grief and to be hugged and sympathised with but she couldn't do that in front of strangers, it would be out of character and she most certainly could not break down in front of Angela or this friend of Robert's, it would be so many broken palings in the fence she had put around herself.

Aubrey looked worried, he was unable to deal with his wife in the state she was in and he did not know how he should behave after Robert's death. He accepted it, had grown used to the idea during the period of Robert's illness but something was missing, perhaps permission from his wife to grieve and, until it felt right, there could be none of that. Even then, the grief would have to be private, he couldn't share it with Hilary. Aubrey had no-one to turn to, either.

They went quietly upstairs to see Robert for the last time. Angela felt it politic to be downstairs while they were with their son and not intrude on their distress.

Hilary stood at the foot of the bed staring at a corpse which bore little resemblance to the son she had borne and loved. Her hands were crossed on her breast as though trying to retain her mixed feelings. Weaving between the sorrow and the anguish, there was anger. It was born of the resentment she felt for this woman who had stolen her son from her. Illogically, the anger shifted a little of the blame for Robert's death to her daughter-in-law and increased the ill-will she felt towards her.

"If Robert hadn't married this woman, I would still have a grandchild – perhaps even more than one – and Robert would still be alive!" she cried bitterly to no-one in particular.

Aubrey, who was sitting on the side of the bed with his son's cold hand in his and who had been thinking of times past which he had shared with him – his first bicycle – his rugby captaincy during his schooldays – was brought back to reality by this cruel remark of his wife's. Long used to her vinegar tongue and her dim view of the world, he was nevertheless disturbed by her statement.

"Don't be ridiculous, Hilary. You can't —" His exasperation refused to allow him to finish the sentence. Sadly, he rose and found himself weeping. "Goodbye, son." he said to Robert and left the room.

Hilary's tightly controlled emotions didn't allow for tears just yet. They would wait until the moment was more appropriate. A time more public, perhaps. She scanned with a critical eye the room which Robert and Angela had shared. None of it pleased her. Nowhere could draw a warm thought from that bleak mind. Her eye took in the miniature and her musings grew more venomous. She stared at it and remembered how she had felt when Robert had given it away to that woman. It had been plain jealousy which had twisted her heart although she would never have admitted as much. She moved around the bed to get closer to the portrait. Grief was trying to force its way out but she sniffed it back and let it be supplanted by her growing anger.

Who does she think she is?

She shan't keep it. She has no right to it. It belongs in my family.

By now, fully convinced that it would be neglectful, even wrong, for her to leave it where it was, she looked back at Robert as though he might catch her in the act and disapprove. Then she lifted the painting from its place on the wall and put it carefully into her bag. Hilary's motives for taking back this painting were more venial than sentimental; she was fully aware of the value of the thing. However, she had completely convinced herself that she what she was doing was honourable.

"It shouldn't be lost to us." she told her son as she kissed away her guilt on his cold forehead.

It was rightfully hers, she reasoned. It had belonged to her family and back to its bosom it must go.

She didn't tell Aubrey what she had done until long after Robert was buried. He was naturally angry but dared not insist that it was returned. He could even see some of his wife's reasons for taking it. Afterwards, whenever Aubrey looked upon the miniature, he felt pricked, unjustly in his opinion, by his conscience. There it hung, a reminder of a dead son and a lost granddaughter. He imagined he could feel the reproach which would be his if Robert were able to express it. It caused him enough discomfort to make him avoid the music room whenever possible.

Hilary, by contrast, felt nothing but pride and a triumph which made her stand taller and stiffer when she looked at the painting. She would enter the music room on the slightest provocation, music often furthest from her mind, and stand before this rosewood oval and exult. If the long departed Rosalind had any opinion on the matter, her picture didn't show it.

Henry paid his final respects to his friend after the Poindexters had quitted the house and after the doctor had been to officially pronounce Robert dead. The hospital smell still lingered but the nurse, the machinery and the concern had all gone. The room was more like a bedroom again, its occupant never more to wake. It was funny, Henry thought, in a detached way, that, although the room was lit in exactly the same way as before Robert's death, it seemed darker, somehow. It was as though his soul, at the point of departure, had taken with it some of the light.

The night of Robert's death, Henry and Angela, both robbed of the desire to sleep, sat talking well into the small hours. It was much needed mutual support and, although the news of his dying had been passed throughout Robert's family and close friends, that night only Henry and Angela were in the house.

They were again in the kitchen, seated face to face

across the table. On one side, a large black cast-iron stove was still burning slowly, its heat throwing a sympathetic blanket of warm air across the melancholy pair. A single light above the worktop in the far corner of the kitchen provided the only illumination, marking with stiff shadows the area where Henry and Angela sat. Angela had made coffee for them both – his stood cold and half-finished to one side, her cup was empty but she kept it on its saucer in front of her and occasionally rotated the cup thoughtfully. Then, in an attempt to wrench her mind away from Robert, she began to probe Henry's personal pain.

"Were you badly hurt by Sophia's leaving?"

Henry looked up from his own musings and hesitated before answering. He had been thinking, too, of Robert and he realised that Angela was deliberately trying to divert both their minds from their immediate grief.

"Initially, yes. My pride was injured but soon I realised that it had all been unavoidable. Tim Farron, the man she took off with – did you ever meet him?" Angela nodded and he went on, "He was the chap who introduced me to Sophia at a regimental dinner and, because of that, had been invited to be our best man when we married shortly afterwards. What I hadn't known at the time was that Tim and Sophia had something going between them before I arrived. He wasn't to know that Sophia would drop him in favour of me on the strength of an introduction. He must have been seething inside to lose her like that. He didn't show it, though. At least, not to me."

Henry became reflective again and Angela prodded him with another question.

"After all this time, whatever made her leave you to go back to Tim? It couldn't be caprice – not after all those years you have been together."

Henry humphed in an ironic way, "All those years Sophia and I spent together were the same years that Tim and Sophia spent together. She had been having an affair with him for almost the whole time, from what I gather. And now, with hindsight, I suspect that my daughter, Christina might be his, too."

There was anger in Henry's voice and it lifted the heavy, deathly atmosphere in the room with its power.

"Are you sure?" Angela's question was intended to keep the subject open rather than let Henry jam it back under his sub-conscious. He looked across to her, puzzled by her doubt.

"Would you like another coffee?" she asked.

"Please." He pushed his cup towards her.

While Angela made her way over to the worktop where the kettle stood, Henry explained, "I've considered the relevant dates and Christina's conception was very probably at a time when I was over in Germany. Two or three weeks later and I would have been back at home. Almost perfect timing and Sophia would have got away with it had we stayed together. I first began to harbour suspicions after she had gone off with Tim and it was that which led me to carefully compare Christina's facial features to us all. It's Tim she resembles most but I don't think I would have noticed without those doubts. I'm fairly sure that Christina is not aware of the truth and I won't be the one to tell her."

"Have you broken off all contact with her now?"

"No, no, we write to each other. We exchange the odd snapshot and try to maintain a sort of relationship under difficult circumstances. She's still my daughter, I still love her. I was present at her birth, I brought her up as mine. The fact that she is not genetically related to me seems to have little bearing on the matter."

"Do you still have any feelings for Sophia?" Angela had to raise her voice slightly as the kettle was coming to the boil.

"Not good ones. I used to love her and then — I still love the old Sophia, the one I was happy with. I hate the present version. Tim's a bloody fool, too. It's all very well having an

14

affair with a married woman but not to take her and marry her. She has already proved herself incapable of constancy and there's no guarantee that she'll remain faithful to him. Still, she's his problem, now."

Angela brought over two fresh cups of coffee and placed one in front of Henry. It was a small domestic duty she was happy to perform. There had been no call for her to pay such attention to anyone for a long time.

"Will you see Christina again?"

"Possibly. I'd like to. While she lives with her mother, she is likely to hear a biassed version of events and I may not come out of it very well. Later, when she's a little older and can think entirely for herself, we may be able to arrange something."

Angela sipped her coffee and shivered. It was an emotional reaction as the room was still quite warm. Henry felt the need to go to to her and put his arm around her shoulders but could not bring himself to do it. He was fearful of rejection and also not really sure how proper it would seem in the light of their present and separate situations.

"What will you do now?" Angela asked.

"Once the house is sold and the divorce settled, I plan to move back home with my parents and sister. That's where I've been since Sophia and I separated. It's a base from which to plan my future. I have no idea what is waiting for me but I'm thankful that there is nothing greatly worrisome. Have you any thoughts about yourself?"

"No – it's too soon. One thing at a time. In my future, there is only Robert's funeral. Afterwards, there will be time enough to wonder what to do."

When, finally, fatigue overcame her embattled emotions, Angela thanked Henry for his company and took herself off to bed; in the room next to the one in which her dead husband lay and where she had been sleeping during the final stages of his illness.

Henry helped himself to a contemplative brandy and

soda and, shortly afterwards, went to his room and dozed, deep sleep being very elusive to him.

The funeral was arranged very quickly and on a windy, worrisome Tuesday morning, watched by his wife, several of his friends and his mother and father, Robert was laid in a grave next to his only daughter in the graveyard of Cranby Steeple church.

Aubrey wept hidden tears, Angela cried openly and inconsolably, Hilary dabbed at imaginary tears with a miniscule handkerchief and pulled her face to look as though she were crying but her anger still prevented her from grieving. Henry was rigidly supportive of Angela, trying to comfort her without attracting the attention of Hilary for whom his dislike was now thoroughly entrenched.

The day afterwards, Henry went home, there was nothing more he could do and if he stayed longer with Angela, it might cause scandal. Even so, just under the sheeting of his current emotions, a new feeling for Angela was beginning to grow.

* * *

The day after Robert's interment, as Henry was driving home, there was a wedding at Cranby Steeple church. The tearful congregation had been replaced by a joyful one, mournful dirges were not heard that day but the sounds of sturdy, uplifting hymns floated over those resting in peace.

Elaine Merryweather became Mrs Leigh Purslipp and, after their honeymoon on the Costa Brava, the happy pair moved west to a new home and a new job for Leigh.

Elaine was the eldest of four sisters, the last two of whom she had helped her mother bring up, thus planting a strong maternal instinct in her breast. Her bridesmaid siblings were a little jealous and a little bit in love with this tall strong man who had come to take their big sister away.

* * *

16

It wasn't until after Henry's departure that Angela, alone and with a half-formed plan to go and stay with her parents for a little while, went back into the room where Robert had fought for his life against his pain and been finally vanquished. She stared at the empty bed, stripped of its linen and shivered at the cold which seemed to emanate from it. When she turned to leave the room and its memories, she noticed that the miniature was missing. She gripped the post at the foot of the bed for physical support, her legs felt that they might give way beneath her and tears filled her eyes. Who? — Hilary! Of course! Who else could have taken it? What a cruel, thoughtless bitch she must be to do a thing like that. What right had she? She stared at the space on the wall where the painting had hung and tried to understand what she was seeing.

Something, perhaps common sense, prevented Angela from confronting Hilary with the deed. The woman would deny it, of course, even manage to look offended at such an accusation and Aubrey would lie through his teeth to back her up. It would be pointless. And she lacked the inner strength to go through with it. She sat down on the bed and wept; crying for Robert; crying for their dead daughter and for herself, feeling robbed of everything that she loved.

A month later, having spent a much needed break with her parents, involving herself in their world and losing herself in their needs, Angela had almost recuperated. She was much stronger emotionally and now felt equal to shrugging off her old life and beginning a new one. Three things only would she take with her, three items of emotional baggage which she was willing to carry for the rest of her life; her memories of Regina, her memories of Robert and her hostility towards Hilary Poindexter for having robbed her.

Before taking leave of her parents, she had been thinking rather fondly of Henry and rang him to let him know how she was coping. Henry gave her an open invitation to stay at the family home with him and Toni whenever she felt the need. She promised to take up the invitation – there was a chink of light in her future now – the black flag seemed smaller and flew more weakly now.

It was time, now, to make a complete break and to this end, she sold the house which had held and lost her future and moved away, to the west coast, not conscious that the move took her closer to both Henry Pym and Robert's parents.

The passage of time demonstrated the truth of her feelings. The feelings which were merely nascent in Angela and Henry at the time of Robert's death had grown stronger. Strong enough to develop into love.

Chapter Two

GERRY

*If the heart of a man is deprest with cares, The mist is
dispell'd when a woman appears.*
(John Gay)

There is an estate on the east side of Wettenham which
sits on the site of a long-vanished farm and the fields which
adjoined it. The names of the roads hereabouts reflect that
agricultural background, a fact lost on most of the residents
but it did give the planners and developers an easy time
when it came to naming the estate's arteries and veins.

Just off Barn Road, there is a close called Bottomfield
Close. These houses are not privately owned like those
of the rest of the estate but belong to the police authority.
They let these houses out to married bobbies who find it
difficult to purchase accommodation in the area to which
they have been assigned.

At number 12A lives Elaine Purslipp, the attractive
twenty eight year-old wife of Police Constable Leigh
Purslipp. There were two men in Elaine's life despite being
an old-fashioned girl and of the opinion that one was really

the ideal number. One of these, the acceptable one, was her husband, Leigh.

Recently, a note of bitterness had crept into the relationship between Elaine and Leigh. She wanted a baby and was unable to conceive. She had suspected that Leigh was suffering from an extremely low sperm count but had no doubts in her own ability to produce off-spring. Leigh's opinion in the matter differed. He was positive that he was not lacking in that department, not with his family background. Five kids his Dad had. And his various and numerous Aunts and Uncles all had at least two off-spring to swell the family tree. No, her eggs must be bad. After a rather late night discussion on this matter which grew rather heated and resulted in Leigh sleeping in one of the spare bedrooms, Elaine and Leigh agreed to both visit a fertility clinic and to seek advice on how to optimise their chances of conception. And also, Elaine thought, to prove Leigh wrong.

The trouble was, she now found herself to be pregnant and fairly certain that Leigh could not claim paternity.

Boredom was one of the causes of her plight. Boredom caused by Leigh's night duties. She hated those evenings alone with no-one to talk to. There were neighbours, sure, but they had their own lives to lead and even if she was invited round to spend an evening with friends, she was always alone by bedtime.

Some months ago Leigh and she had celebrated Leigh's twenty ninth birthday with a barbecue on their front lawn. They had invited neighbours and friends round and one of the guests was a police colleague of Leigh's whose name was Trevor. Drinks had been drunk and sausages and burgers consumed in plenty and all of this must have affected Elaine's judgement because she consented to sex with Trevor in the upstairs loo. The morning after the barbecue, she had felt idiotic. It was stupid of her to engage in a fling, putting her marriage at risk just for a quicky. She had hoped she could put the whole thing behind her and trust that Leigh would not find out about it.

Trevor had read more into the incident and, feeling that she she fancied him, wanted to see her again. At first she refused his advances, telling him not to be silly – that it was just a one-night stand and let's just leave it at that. The trouble was, as Trevor persisted in his attempts to win her, she weakened and she found herself thinking more fondly of him than a married woman should and, eventually and unstoppably, it became a full-blown affair. The silly part had been not bothering with birth control. After not having used any form of contraception since she married, Elaine just plain forgot. Or was it, she often asked herself during the aftermath and after the baby was born, was it a subconscious desire to become pregnant at any cost?

She still loved Leigh but she loved Trevor, too and she meant to keep the baby that was to come. She had suffered far too many barren years to contemplate getting rid of it. Nor had she considered the idea of setting up home with Trevor. That would be unthinkable, wouldn't it? Two marriages down the drain would be a lot for her conscience to bear but something would have to be done soon. It must all come to a head. The important thing to remember, she told herself, was the baby.

Trevor had very red hair. She was blonde with very freckly skin.Leigh was dark-haired with an Iberian look about him. It would be stupid of her to try and pass off the child as Leigh's if the little mite came out ginger.

On the other hand, if the baby had Leigh's colouring, it would be acceptable. He would pleased and proud. Pleased to prove me wrong and proud of being a father – proud of his own bollocks. Was it worth the chance? Was it a good idea to hang around on the off-chance that the baby would be acceptable to Leigh? A blond baby or, even brown, would do. If it didn't turn out that way, she would then have to face the anguish and suspicion. It could still lead to rows and divorce. Best to make the break now.

It was six p.m. and time to shut up shop. Gerry Fledding was closing for the day the newsagency which he'd inherited when his father had died. It had never been an ambition of his to be a shopkeeper but then, Gerry's life had been fairly free of ambition. With no objectives, there can be no failures to achieve and therefore fewer disappointments in life. This was how he consoled himself. It should have suited a man of his make-up to work in the steady, undemanding atmosphere of a paper shop but perhaps the source of his dissatisfaction was an unrecognised ambition. Something burned within him which he had persistently ignored.

It was the day after All Fools' Day and Gerry was slightly unhappy because it was his birthday. He hadn't bothered for some years to celebrate the passing of the years and tried to forget the date. A newspaper shop is one place in which this is difficult to do and he had been reminded that today he was fifty and that there was no-one to share that with.

Gerry was a compact looking man, somewhat shorter than average and very slightly overweight. His dark hair, kept well trimmed, was only just beginning to recede. Never a man who paid attention to the whims of fashion, he had reached an age where dressing comfortably suited him best. He favoured checked, open-necked shirts beneath dark v-necked sweaters; either dark slacks or jeans and soft leather slip-on shoes of the moccasin type. He pushed across the bolts on the front door, turned the key in the lock and turned the window sign from 'Open' to 'Closed'. He was in no rush yet to go home; there was no-one waiting there for him and he had no fixed idea how he was going to pass the evening. At the back of the shop, in the little kitchenette which his staff used for meal breaks, he made himself a cup of coffee and sat down at the little formica topped table.

There were ring-shaped stains on its top, crumbs and

an ashtray filled with screwed up crisp packets and biscuit wrappers. That's a metaphor for my life, he thought. Well, nearly. It's a bloody mess. I'm in a job I don't like, there's no romance in my life and no bright horizon to look towards. I shall have to do something about it. And I shall have to have a word with the staff about keeping this tea-room tidy.

Gerry's staff consisted of Mr. and Mrs. Jamieson who ran the shop from 8 a.m. to 4 p.m. while Gerry covered the two hour periods either side of their times. It suited him to work like that; four unsocial hours a day which didn't matter as he was rather unsociable himself.

No, not so much unsociable as needing to be alone. Gerry's principal way of beguiling an evening at home in his flat was writing for an hour or two. He had always enjoyed mystery novels and had read enough of them to form the opinion that he could write one just as entertaining as any author he had read and had managed to produce his first novel. Novella, really, it wasn't quite novel length, more of a longish short story. It remained unpublished but he'd found a creative kick in writing and it remained, by and large, a harmless hobby. His evening often ended with a film on the television and a glass of wine at his side. The inspiration for his writing regularly came when he was walking between his shop and his house and in his jacket he carried a pencil and a notebook in which he would hurriedly scribble barely legible notes: scenes which could be enlarged upon at leisure, conversation fragments which seemed to pop up in his head as he walked and character sketches of people he met, some of whom were customers in his shop. Sunday mornings, especially in Spring or Summer, were firm favourites because then, the world was his. Wettenham on a Sunday morning at half past five was a ghost town. The only things moving were litter in the breeze and the odd, cat-stressed pigeon. Those times, Gerry felt that he owned Wettenham and everything in it.

Occasionally Gerry would visit his local pub, taking his

notebook with him and interestedly watch the interactions of the clientele, sip from his pint and make furtive notes.

All of these past-times were solitary and required no help although, from time to time when Dave Belloe, an acquaintance from his school days, peered into the pub Gerry would forget the notepad and spend an hour or so in Dave's undemanding company. Their friendship did not extend outside the pub doors although each knew a lot about the other's family life. Gerry would forget his writing and sit with Dave, setting the political world straight from the bar or listen to Dave recreating the last night's football match.

Normally, when enmeshed in the construction of a story, company was to be avoided, especially when out walking; a conversation with a neighbour, for instance, could destroy a fragile mental scenario if it couldn't be quickly written down before it evaporated.

Company wasn't even appreciated when stretched out in front of the telly with a drink. He liked the sort of police/detective drama which drew him in and engaged him in the action. Any type would do as long as it was good at drawing him in. He did not want a source of flippant comments on whatever the actors were wearing or on the credibility of the action. Women who were unable to watch in silence were not welcome. Also, at least in Gerry's experience, they had a maddening habit of figuring out the identity of the baddie in any mystery play and, long before he could pick a suspect for himself, would sit, visibly overflowing with the need to tell just whodunnit.

Mr. and Mrs. Jamieson were a couple in their late fifties. Bob was a native of Port Regis, a maritime city about twenty miles away from Harnserlea where he now lived. He hadn't lost either the accent or the dry sense of humour the Port's natives were renowned for.

Bob's wife, Meera, came from Lancashire and of Indian parents. She was completely anglicised in accent and dress and had become gradually alienated from her parents and family because of her refusal to embrace their culture. She had fled the influence of her family, as soon as she was able, and moved to Port Regis where she got a job in a branch of a nationwide chain of chemist's shops.

Mr. Jamieson had gone into the shop where Meera worked to purchase an electric razor. He had been persuaded by some advertisements he had seen to change from the bothersome and, sometimes, bloody routine of wet shaving and to try the modern dry shaving technique which, if those adverts were to be believed, were not only bloodless and smoother, not only more convenient and comfortable but would attract women who were keen to feel the result. While pondering the choice available with absolutely no idea which kind was best, he heard a voice ask, "Can I help you, sir?"

He looked to his left and saw a warm, brown smile gazing at him. He smiled back, immediately attracted. On such insignificant foundations are great romances built. (Someone has probably already said that.)

Meera, for her part, saw Bob as soon as he entered the shop doorway and watched him as he looked around for the area which sold men's grooming products. She quite fancied the young man. Nothing in particular seemed to speak to her, nothing about him was outstanding enough to remark upon, it was just that first, favourable impression. She used her position as a salesperson to make contact.

Courtship was careful, private. Bob's parents made it clear that they disapproved of mixed marriages. Babies resulting from such unions were always at a disadvantage in life, they claimed, being scorned by both white and coloured people. Bob had listened to them but formed his own opinions.

Meera's parents would have disapproved for similar reasons had they known.

There were common passions; Bob and Meera liked to garden, especially the raising of vegetables for home consumption for they both loved good food. Neither were great readers but loved films and the cinema was the usual place to spend their courting time together. Later, when films came to be shown more regularly on the television, they had no further need for the cinema and watched their favourites at home. They preferred musicals of the sort that Hollywood was so good at churning out.

The sparsely attended registry office wedding was held eight months after that first meeting. Bob's brother was the reluctant best man, having told his and Bob's parents that he was attending an away football match with Bob. The happy pair left to honeymoon in a caravan in Rhyl. It was only afterwards that Bob informed his parents of the marriage and found himself their least favourite son.

Twelve months afterwards, a son, Roger, was born. Meera was happy with Bob's choice of name because it sounded to her like an English version of Rajah which is how she pronounced her son's name.

Bad luck enters into people's lives in differing ways and it can sometimes alter a person's perspective on life, depending on how much they must bear at one time. Some people stumble through their allotted span with little more than minor disasters to worry them; a car breakdown, a minor accident in the home, a lost purse or wallet or the like. Others seem to get their share all in one go. At three and a half years, Roger developed meningitis and died. Meera and Bob were inconsolable and it was along time before their grief grew thin enough to carry easily. Meera never made it all the way through the mourning. She turned Roger's room into a sort of shrine, kept beautifully clean, the walls decorated with many of the photographs they had taken of their child together with some pictures of the gods she had left behind with her abandoned background but which Roger had seemed attracted by; Shiva in classic, four-armed dancing pose; his son, the elephant-headed Ganesh and another of Indra riding a richly decorated elephant.

There, on the neatly made-up bed were some of the soft toys Roger had played with. In the drawers of the dresser were piles of neatly pressed clothes and, from time to time, when she felt sad, Meera would sit on the end of the bed and talk to her son or pray for him.

Bob indulged this behaviour of his wife, odd though it seemed to him. He carried a picture of Roger in his wallet and it was tucked away where he would only find it when searching for a little used card or carefully stowed ticket. Then a brief sadness would fall over him.

There were no more children. Meera saw to that and, although they had never discussed the subject, Bob would have agreed with her decision.

Bob called his wife 'Em' as though the two syllables of Meera were too foreign for his tongue to get around.

One aspect of her background which Mrs. Jamieson, nee Chandra, had not forsaken was its cuisine. It had given her an Indian outlook on British cookery and occasionally she would present Gerry with a jar of her highly spiced rhubarb chutney or one of her special curried steak and kidney pies. They were surprisingly good and Bob often talked with a shine in his eye of the meals that Meera put in front of him.

Drinking his tea, Gerry's mind turned slowly on his future or, at least, the possibilities which were latent in his future. Where would he be in, say, five years time? Would there be any one there to share his life? Did he really need anyone? After all, he was independent – a free spirit – at liberty to go anywhere. But where was there to go and why? And would there be any more point to a life shared with another woman? People, usually women, had pointed out to him that his solitary life was selfish. Well, yes! That was the whole bloody point. Living on your own not only allowed you to be selfish, it was de rigueur for some of your actions. Doing what you wanted and when you wanted to was the upside; not being able to tell anyone about it was the obverse, the flip-side and the least attractive aspect. And anyway, you can fart whenever you want to. And leave the toilet seat up. Those secrets he was happy to leave unshared.

The following morning, after the early rush had dwindled to just a few customers, Gerry found himself with time to reflect on this idea of another partner. He had just built himself a nice, dream log-cabin whose sole occupant, besides himself, was a smiling, buxom blonde with, occasionally, a dog which might join them to decorate the mental fireside scene when the door jangled loudly open with the entrance of another regular customer. Gerry didn't even need to look up, he knew that it was Constable Leigh Purslipp. It was a custom of Leigh's to bombard him with the latest jokes in an effort to make him laugh. Leigh's sense of humour and Gerry's were not quite on the same plane and so far, Leigh had failed to raise more than a smile.

"Mornin', Gerry. Have you heard about the three nuns and the sailor? This is a good one, I nearly wet meself when the sergeant told us it."

Leigh whose flat, dark hair always looked as though it had been painted onto his scalp had the build of a rugby player despite disdaining strenuous sports. It was a very impressive physique. He leaned over the counter and delivered the rest of the joke. Gerry smiled out of politeness for, even though Leigh's exuberance lent the story some interest, as usual it hadn't amused him.

"How's the missus, Leigh? Still keeping fine?" asked Gerry in order to avoid comment.

"Still bloody nagging – still broody. Wants a babby bad and it's my fault of course that she's not had one. She reckons me sperm aren't functioning proper. She wants me to have a test. That's a bit of a sticking point, that one. I do not fancy pulling my pudding for a doctor just to prove her point. How's yours?"

"Still gone, thankfully but I am seriously considering a replacement."

Leigh laughed. "You single buggers don't know when you're well off. You're best off without one, take my word."

"How's Ellis?" Gerry wanted to change the subject.

"Oh, he's fine. He's looking after the squad car, making sure no-one nicks it." Leigh grinned, "Twenty fags and these, please."

He laid two newspapers and a selection of crisps and snack bars onto the counter. These were his usual purchases for both himself and his partner, Ellis.

"Anything happening?" asked Gerry as money changed hands.

"Nah. Quiet. Sergeant's a bastard, still. And I'm still waiting for something to happen." he looked up at the ceiling as though looking for what he sought, "The big job, the breakthrough, you know?"

Leigh had a dream of busting a gang or smashing a drugs ring. Something which might impress his bosses and give him a leg up the ladder of promotion. He was currently finding the first rung set just a bit too high for him.

"Yeah, one day." Gerry sympathised.

Leigh had only been gone ten minutes when the Jamiesons stormed excitedly in.

They're a bit early, was Gerry's first thought before realising that perhaps they were thrilled by something; some news which they wanted to convey – to everyone and not just to him. Meera was waving a small piece of paper above her head and doing an impromptu dance up the aisle as she made her way towards the counter and Bob, all false teeth and bonhomie, having chosen a more direct route, was already leaning on the counter and about to burst.

"We've won – we've won!" he told Gerry.

Pleased for his friend and employee, Gerry nevertheless felt entitled to a little more information regarding this win. "Won what?" he asked.

"The bloody lottery!" Bob said, beaming ever more broadly.

Meera, meanwhile, had collared one of the customers, a middle-aged lady whom she knew and was giving her what was probably the selfsame news.

"That's brilliant." remarked Gerry, a little enviously, "How much?"

"Oh, we didn't get the jackpot or first prize or anything but we did win two hundred thousand pounds."

Gerry was impressed. "Two hundred grand!"

Even as a minor lottery prize, that much money was not to be sneered at. Then he realised that he might be losing his staff; after all, what need had they now of his wages?

"So, I suppose you're here to tell me to stuff the job, are you? I wouldn't blame you, I'd do the same in your place."

"No, no!" insisted Meera who had by this time reached the counter and finished her dancing and was merely bouncing on the spot, "We like working here and we both said we didn't want to give up the job." She grinned happily and Gerry looked back to Bob with a query in his eyebrows.

"Yes, we want to stop on." Bob confirmed, "The best part about a job like this is the socialising. You get to talk to all sorts of people and get friendly with them without the inconvenience of having to take them home. In fact, I'd just as easy work for nothing now I've got money behind me."

"I couldn't let you do that – I'd still pay you, of course. I suppose it's a relief not having to start new people, that would really be a bind so I'm grateful that you're stopping on. So, what are you going to do with all this money?"

"Oh – spend, save – pay off the mortgage – new car, that sort of thing. We haven't made any proper plans yet. It'll go,

I've no doubt." Bob explained.

Then another thought hit Gerry, "Hey! A bit of publicity for me, too. This is the newsagency which sold you the winning ticket. They'll come in droves just to buy a ticket here – as if that made any difference."

"Er – sorry, Gerry. We didn't buy the ticket here." Bob said.

"Oh – where, then?" Gerry felt a vague sense of disloyalty on the part of his staff.

"From the convenience store at the end of our street. He's made up, Maxie is – he's doing a poster to put in his window."

Ah, well, thought Gerry, I haven't gained by this but then – I haven't lost anything, either.

I suppose; maybe another woman might be a good idea, Gerry thought, the next morning, as he reflected on his life while he shaved and washed. The morning routine in the bathroom tended to make him contemplative and he sometimes found himself staring at his own reflection as though it was some sort of oracle. I'm managing O.K. I don't cook so well but with fresh fruit, supermarket microwaveables and the odd Sunday lunch at the pub, I eat well enough. Maybe the house isn't as clean as it could be but no-one could accuse me of being a slob. It's not that much different from when she was here.

'She' was Carol Davies, Gerry's ex-partner. They'd never got around to actual marriage. Not that legalising the situation would have altered things. They would still have split up. Irreconcileable samenesses. They had become indifferent to each other.

Carol had been Gerry's only and rather late endeavour to establish a long-term relationship with a woman.

As soon as Gerry had finished his formal education and with a single certificate for English Literature to show for it, he had joined his father in the running of the newsagency. It was inevitable, he knew, that this was to be his fate and he accepted it without a hint of rebellion but rather with resignation. He had no difficulty during his teens in picking up girls for quick flings. Whether it was his lacklustre job or some other thing which was missing, either from his personality or theirs, the affairs were always brief. He never broke with these girls; before he became tired of them, they would find someone else. Gerry never regretted their going, there is never, he often thought, a spark in any of these girls which lights my fire. Something is missing.

Love was not turning out to be all it was alleged to be. The pop-songs of his teen-age years promised eternal bliss and everlasting love. It was lies; all lies.

And no-one gave advice on how to recognise the initial stages of true love, it was generally understood that you would know.

Gerry's working life didn't interfere too greatly with his social life in those days. Once he'd learned the various functions of a newsagency, the day was split between him and his father, alternating shifts, morning or afternoon, on a weekly basis. Early morning starts, when it was Gerry's turn to open up, rather ruled out very late nights on the town but then, Gerry had never seen the point of being up and about after midnight. He was more of a lark than an owl.

Girls were usually met with at the local discotheque where Gerry and Mark Drew, an old classmate of his, would turn up in a hopeful frame of mind to see if anything fresh was gracing the dance floor. Girls invariably arrived in pairs. Sometimes a pretty one with a plain one which could be a disadvantage if the boys were also hunting in pairs as they could never agree whose turn it was to get the ugly one.

Mark eventually struck lucky and met his future wife. His girl hunting days were over and this marked the beginning of the end of Gerry's disco days. Hunting alone didn't have the same appeal. On nights when neither was lucky, Mark and Gerry could at least console each other over a pint. Sitting alone in a rapidly emptying discotheque, watching newly formed pairs leaving hand-in-hand and him with just a pint of lager for company struck Gerry as very, very sad.

I'm fishing in too small a pond, he thought, I'll never meet the girl of my dreams in that place.

Even so, futile hope continued to drag him back there for far too many weeks. Sometimes he was able to take the odd minnow home.

He met Carol in his father's shop. She was dark-haired, petite and moved in a way which demonstrated that she took a great pleasure in life. The way she walked tended to provoke a good deal of interest from passing males who saw her. That Gerry and Carol both felt something was undeniable. Eyes locked as she made her purchase of a local newspaper, hand lingered upon hand as the purchase was paid for and a short conversation later, they had a date to look forward to.

Later, Gerry was convinced that this was the real thing. The one true love as promised on acres of spiral-tracked vinyl all over the world. He had met his life-partner at last.

It was a perfectly ordinary romance. Later, they shopped around and leased a flat on the second floor of a three storey block. Then they moved in together. No-one mentioned marriage, there was no need. There were no older women to prod them into legalising the relationship. Gerry's mother had died a year before Carol came into his life and she was estranged from her parents. They lived in grumpy isolation on Anglesey and avoided contact with Carol because of her refusal to attend an uncle's funeral.

So, with just one parent between them, and no-one at all bothered about the lack of formality in their union, there was no pressure upon them to marry.

Slowly and simultaneously Gerry and Carol discovered something about male-female relationships. After the early stage where passion is still feverish, things begin to cool. You start to take each other more and more for granted. The impetus which carried them both out on rainy evenings, laughing together, for a drink and a curry had gone. The sun no longer seemed to shine enough to draw them out on those hand-held country walks where an afternoon could slip away blissfully unnoticed.

They ate the same meals together, watched the same television programmes and, sharing the same interest in this area, read the same books. It slowly began to dawn on both of them that these past-times of a mundane life could just as easily be pursued alone. They began, deliberately if unconsciously, to snipe at each other; picking rows needlessly as though to create some sort of emotional energy between them even if it was negative. Even if it hurt. A hollow tree will quickly die and, to the regret of neither, Carol one day packed her bags and left. There had been no argument; Carol had said, "This relationship isn't working, is it?"

Flustered, Gerry had answered, "Er, no, I don't suppose, really, it's, er." Gerry wasn't good at being articulate when flustered.

"Would you like me to leave, then?" she'd asked.

"Er, yes."

Gerry had almost sought this split but, lacking the courage to face any sort of emotional outburst from Carol, he had put the matter to one side, reluctant to force the issue. Carol's way was so quiet. So civilised. He almost loved her for it. That was the way to go. Well, the way for her to go.

Although the parting was painless and probably foreseeable, Gerry managed to miss Carol quite a lot after she had gone. Their sex life, even though it had been running on automatic, was still a habit which was difficult to break. There was a Carol-shaped hole in his life which took a long while to fill itself. An empty wine bottle sitting on a table is a constant reminder that there is no more wine left for as long as you neglect to bin it. Then it's forgotten. In a similar way, Carol was eventually binned.

Since then, he'd enjoyed his solitude, his lack of responsibilities, his freedom from women. There had been neither the time nor the motive for seeking a replacement.

Finished with his toilet, Gerry dutifully cleaned the basin and tidied everything away while busily pondering this new idea.

Another woman. He reviewed his image in the bathroom mirror, flattened his hair fussily and thought, I don't look too bad. I could still attract a woman. If I could find one.

After all, there were loads out there; he could have his pick. More variety than second-hand cars.

Downstairs, he pushed it to the back of his mind as he went to continue the story he was working on. He re-read the last two paragraphs to bring his thoughts back into this tiny, fictional world he'd created, to point it in the direction he wanted the plot to go then he picked up his pen and wrote:

Danny Craven liked being a policeman. It wasn't, though, his favourite job in all the world. Given the option, he would become a detective like a shot. Detective Constable would be fine for starters, it would be a step onto the bottom rung of the ladder which he yearned to climb and up there, in the clouds, was the summit of the profession – Detective Superintendent. His current job was a possible way in. It needed some hard work, some study and some luck.

Tall, as you would expect a policeman to be, sandy-haired and, as yet, still a bachelor, Danny patrolled his beat – watching over the manor – as he liked to think of it and dreamed of detective-hood. Solving crimes with dedication, logic and the assiduous observance of a shit-house rat; that was the object, the aim, the direction of his career. D.I. Danny Craven. Nice ring to it.

* * *

At the bottom of the page, he dried up. He could take it no further but, no matter, leave it brewing and inspiration will come. It occurred to him that he might have a good character in Danny Craven and, provided he could get them published, he could appear in a series of books like – Maigret or Poirot – only English, of course. Sort of charting his career as he rose through the ranks of the detectives. Hmm, Craven of the Yard, maybe.

This writing lark is like being on a roller-coaster, he thought, On a high and you can write like a demon and when you review what you've written, you think it's great. You think that you could give Mickey Spillane or Agatha Christie pointers. Or you could if they weren't both dead.

His mind flatly refused to supply him with the name of a living writer of that genre. His genre.

Then comes a low, you enter that pit where lie writers' block, depression and the notion – Why don't you just pack it all in?

Meanwhile, another idea was beginning to take shape. A new story; one based on his situation, about someone who advertises for a woman in a Lonely Hearts page. He leaned back in his chair and let the new thoughts develop. Make it different. O.K., he puts in a ridiculous advert – the man wants to find out what the reaction would be to a ludicrous demand. Would there be responses and would the applicants bother to be truthful or maybe they'd just take a chance? Make the ad. amusing – that would indicate a good sense of humour.

He sat up straight, moved by a second idea overlaying

the first. I'll send one in for real. Could even get a woman out of it. If not, it's down to research. Brilliant! All I need now is a silly ad.

It took several days before a suitable advert occured to him. It formed in his mind as he was walking to the shop and so he wrote it down as soon as he could and then left it to stew for a few days more.

It read:

Wanted; Intelligent woman 38 – 45 years. Must have spent lonely spinsterhood nursing aged parents, the last of whom has sadly and recently passed away, bequeathing a large and extensive library of books and music. A large and extensive bank account would be a welcome bonus.

Occasionally, since the idea of a new partner had occurred to him, Gerry entertained a niggling doubt, a reservation. He needed support, a little encouragement that he was on the right path. So far, everyone he'd asked had envied him his freedom.

Early one morning, while Gerry was on duty in the shop, a regular customer, a Mr. Gaines, came in for his usual purchases, a newspaper and a packet of cigarettes.

Gerry was not on first name terms with all of his old customers, his father had always maintained a respectful distance between himself and those that used his shop no matter how well known they became and Gerry saw no reason to veer from his father's way.

"Morning, Mr. Gaines. It's looking a bit threatening outside, isn't it?" Gerry nodded towards the bank of heavy, grey cloud which was hove to outside and above the shop.

"It'll not rain – he said so on the radio. What's new? Owt?" Mr. Gaines asked as he dropped the money for his purchases onto the counter.

"I've been thinking about taking on another woman." Gerry said, "I'm a bit fed up with being on my own and I think it might be a good idea if I was in a relationship."

Mr. Gaines was not so much unhappily married as dissatisfactorily encumbered. He was aware that he would find life difficult without the aid of a woman so he understood the necessity of having one about his house but he wasn't prepared to enjoy the experience. He viewed his wife in much the same, jaundiced way as a person with a broken leg would view their crutches.

"Damned silly if you ask me. If you've managed to survive for as long as you have without a woman, you should avoid the buggers strenuously. They're a bloody nuisance. Get a dog. Much better idea."

He picked up his cigarettes and paper from the counter and walked out, leaving Gerry unencouraged but not deterred. He didn't really fancy a dog, anyway.

It's funny, Gerry thought, if you ask a woman about getting married, she'll egg you on, make out that your life is impoverished without a woman to share it with you. Ask a bloke the same question, whether he's married or not, and he'll tell you to forget it. He would persuade you to join a Foreign Legion Death Squad rather than entangle yourself with a woman.

Four days later, the advertisement still read well. It was supposed to give the impression of creativity, humour and originality without spelling it out with those awful initials.

Gerry spent part of the next morning in his shop, looking for a suitable periodical to which he might send the advert. There were two; a local newspaper and a current events magazine with national distibution and he sent a copy of his advertisement to both.

Chapter Three

FINDING THE LADY

Be wise with speed; a fool at forty is a fool indeed.
(Edward Young)

It was the second of May. Spring had sprung and, having performed this remarkable feat, was resting on her laurels while Summer figured out a way to follow it. The morning was still, the peace embroidered with birdsong and lightly hemmed with the buzz of insects. The woodland was green and had been chopped into irregular rectangles for firebreaks, flooded with sunlight, some of which were kept relatively free from attempts at re-colonisation by the struggling plant-life with the frequent passage of horses, cyclists and walkers. They were known and used by the equestrian clique as gallops.

On one of these gallops stood a brown horse whose face was made strange by two oddly shaped white patches, giving it a lob-sided, maddened expression. Seated on this horse, looking around her appreciatively was a rider. No woodland nymph atop elfin steed was she but a middle-aged woman whose unadorned face proclaimed the benefits of an outdoor life. If you were inclined to be critical, you might remark that her nose was a little too large for the features it dominated but the overall impression was that of an honest woman who could be very determined should circumstances require it. Her eyes were of an ever-changing shade of blue, as though they changed to accommodate her mood and it would have been impossible for any two men to agree on their exact colour. She wore no hat on the mess of blonde curls; a man's green quilted shirt, its tails hanging over black jodhpurs which were tucked into scuffed riding boots which ensemble formed her riding habit. She breathed in, loving the smell of the place; the horsey, sandy, piney aroma on which the season had sprinkled a bouquet of bluebell, wood anemone and ramsons.

A middle aged man walking a spaniel approached and broke the peace with a polite 'Good morning'. He looked at her as she acknowledged his greeting. She was his own age and he felt qualified to judge her attractiveness. He approved of what he saw. The rider urged the horse on, the magic of the morning fragmented by the man and his dog but with the perverse feeling of regret that there was no-one to share the moment with her. A face tried to push its way through the folds of her memory; a smiling, young man's face but she pushed it back with practised sadness. Even so, it made her wistful and she wanted wildly to communicate her thoughts about this place, how she loved what she saw and experienced and it seemed selfish that she seemed to be the only one with this sense of joy.

The man watched her ride on and continued his walk. "I wouldn't kick that out of bed, Chubby." he said, addressing his dog. There was a half twitch in the dog's left ear as it acknowledged the voice of its master then the ear flopped back to its customary position.

As the man strode on, he noticed the piles of horse droppings on the sandy ground. "How come they don't have to clean up after their horses, eh?" Then he smiled as his imagination supplied him with the image of a horse with two full supermarket shopping bags slung athwart the horse behind the rider like some surreal pony express.

The rider, Toni Pym, sister of Henry Pym, was 47 and had never married – it was one of those things she had never got round to, like learning to swim or being waved at by the Pope. Marriage is not, on the whole, an ad hoc thing. One needs a willing partner and things must be arranged. Generally, family and friends like to be informed of the impending union and are often keen on joining in the fun. They might also welcome the suggestion of a do afterwards where the nuptials might be celebrated. Really, it all takes time and money and, when you consider the effort required, it's understandable when you hear of someone putting it off sine die or even avoiding the issue altogether.

Circumstances had worked together to prevent Toni's entry into matrimony: she was a member of the aristocracy although not a willing one and while this in itself was not a barrier to marriage, her poor opinion of her peer males was. There had been an exception; there always is. He had been Richard Marsh, an army lieutenant whom she had met at Ascot one beautiful summer. He had quite casually robbed her of her free will and she had fallen irretrievably in love with him. Marriage had been discussed and parents dutifully consulted. They approved. His family was well known in the county and he had been utterly charming to her mother and had impressed her father. That November he went over to Northern Ireland, his regiment about to relieve one whose tour was at an end and a road-side bomb had ensured that he would not be able to keep his promises to her.

So now, she deliberately avoided those functions where one of these peer males might be thrust upon her, her dislike based on their insularity, the way they surrounded themselves with each other, building a barrier between themselves and anyone perceived to be an outsider. Their world was one of artificially shrunken social horizons, a world peopled only by

41

class equals. In order to distance herself from those events which would involve mingling with these social pygmies, she occupied herself with those activities which interested her, chiefly equine and canine. The second reason for continued spinsterhood was that the care of and occasional breeding from her horses and dogs had filled her life to such an extent that the need for a husband had rarely made itself felt. It had never occured to her that her own brand of insularity was more severe than the one she avoided. Now, feeling that perhaps some aspects of life had been missed, she had run down the horse-breeding activities and there remained just two mounts; Moss Trooper, a twelve-year old, which she rode today and Ezekiel who was a mere eight years old. Of her two dogs; Sally was the last of her breeding bitches, too old for motherhood now and Grundy, a three-year old dog whelped by Sally.

The house in which she had been born and brought up was a magnificent and extensive building called Cabley Hall and splendidly isolated in a rural part of the county. It backed onto an extensive area of woodland owned and managed by the Forestry Commision and was surrounded on the other three sides by farm land which had once been the demesne of an ancestor until a combination of gambling debts and death duties had forced the sale of the land. This rather beautiful environment gave Toni all the room she neded for riding and dog walking, both of which activities allowed her to appreciate her world.

The only connection the house had with the outside world was a narrow, tarmacadamed lane which ran at right angles to its front entrance, sternly overlooked by two stone griffons perched on tall, sandstone gateposts from which hung the great pair of black, cast-iron gates which creaked loudly as they were opened. The lane led in one direction to the village of Cabley, once a source of labour for the estate and now dwindled into shrunken unwantedness. In the other direction, the lane lost itself in a bewildering network of farm accesses and linking lanes one, and only one, of which was connected to the main highway. It took the unwary stranger to those parts a great deal of familiarisation before he could reach his objective without taking at least one wrong turning. Navigation was made more difficult because the fingerposts which once had indicated the various hamlets and farmsteads had been removed some time ago to baffle the invading Third Reich and few of them had been replaced.

Until recently, the other members of the family occupying the house had been Toni and Henry's newly deceased parents. They had died when her seventy year old father got into difficulties while swimming off a Bermuda beach and her mother had gone to the bottom with him in an heroic but failed attempt to save him.

Henry's share in the parental will were his father's stock portfolio and ownership of a nearby tenanted farm while Toni inherited the big house.

Henry had moved back into the family home after the break-up of his marriage to Sophie but was presently to move out again once his plans to marry Angela Poindexter were complete. However, he was rather concerned for his sister's welfare, having to live alone in this huge house and, having been previously encouraged to do so by Angela, broached the subject with her.

"Toni?"

His sister was sitting in the library reading and, as she did when absorbed in a book or magazine, pushing her fingers through the curls of her unruly hair.

She looked up from the copy of 'Stable Management' which she held, quizzically raising her eyebrows.

"You know I don't like the idea of your being alone after I've gone. You need a man about the house. Would you consider marriage or even living in sin just to reassure me?" Henry said.

Toni smiled at her brother's awkward phrasing but she knew what he meant. " I've been giving it some thought myself." she said, laying her reading glasses down on top of the book and leaning back in the armchair. "I hadn't relished the thought of being the last one in, as it were, but I'm not at all sure how one goes about it at my age. I get the awful feeling that I may have left it too late. Do you have any suggestions?"

"Not a one. You don't really make yourself available to any of the unattached chaps who are circulating the county. Still, it is encouraging to know that we are thinking along the same lines. If I get any ideas, I'll let you know." A thought occured to him. "I'll give Angela a ring and see what she has to say."

Brightened by this idea, he went off to telephone his betrothed, the confident, able and very honourable Angela Poindexter. Some minutes later he returned.

"I had a short chat with Angela – she's fine, by the way, –" Henry cut short the question his sister had been about to ask, " – and she suggests the Lonely Hearts route."

Toni had broken off her reading again to listen to Henry. He sat down in the armchair opposite her and told her what Angela had suggested.

"You can pick yourself a man from one of those Lonely Hearts columns. It wouldn't do to advertise for yourself. If hoi polloi get wind of a titled lady up for the asking, you won't be able to see the end of the drive for daffodils. Pick carefully one or two men from the lovelorn and then make your selection from those that reply. It's a bit of a shot in the dark but you might get lucky. Angela says she knows dozens of people who are doing this sort of thing all the time."

Toni was not impressed by the lack of permanence implied by this last sentence but didn't say so.

"I'll give it a try – it can't hurt to see what's on offer." she said and resumed reading. Part of her mind wasn't concentrating on the text, it was busily constructing a castle in the air complete with mail-order squire.

The following morning, Henry found Toni in the stables, seeing to her horses. Their care and exercise along with responsibility for her two black labradors went a long way to filling her day. Henry had a bundle of periodicals with him and a grin on his round, friendly face which left Toni feeling a little apprehensive. Henry had been shopping.

"Leave them in the library, I'll look at them later." Toni said after Henry had explained why they'd been bought.

It wasn't until late afternoon that Toni found free time enough to look through all that Henry had brought her. And what a motley collection of men seemed to present itself. All proclaimed themselves fit, sociable, solvent, lovers of theatre and possessors of a good sense of humour. Toni privately thought that credibility was being stretched to some degree but she also harboured a feeling, a sort of intuition, that if the right advertisement came along, she would know it. She went off to the kitchen to make some coffee, feeling that a hot drink might help her wade through these humorous, cultured and provident single men.

It didn't take long to check each magazine – glancing through the column or two of assorted availables until her eye was caught by one particular advert. It stood out from all the others with its sheer cheek, its attitude of – 'this is what I want and if you can't make the grade, don't even bother to reply.'

"Ha! That's the one for me." and pointed a finger to the advertisement to show Henry, despite his inability to read it from where he was sitting.

"No, Toni dear, it's not like a hat shop, you must choose several, on approval, as it were, then you have the opportunity to separate the wheat from the chaff; or the idiots from the gentlemen. A much better chance of netting Mr. Right."

"Oh, the others sound very boring and ordinary and this man obviously isn't. At least, what he's written says he isn't. — Here." She thrust it towards him to read and continued, "I don't care what you say, I'm going to write to this man and find out what he's like. Anyway, if I don't like him, I can always try again."

Henry's view after reading what had been stabbed by his sister's forefinger was more critical. "You don't meet all of the criteria – you're too –." Henry had been about to point out that she was too old but realising in time that it would be unwise to insult her, amended it to, "You're much too good for this man!"

Discouragement, he realised, would be unproductive. He wasn't even going to mention that he thought the man must be distinctly odd for writing an advertisement like that in the first place.

Toni, oblivious to her brother's presence, had already seated herself at the writing desk and was composing a letter of introduction to a box. An unknown gentleman would pick this up and read it. And think about her. She chose her first words to him very carefully. This prodding of the future gave her an excited tingle.

***

In the large village of Wettenham, just a few miles across country from where Toni and Henry lived, there was a cluster of recently built houses, referred to locally as the estate. If you were to stare in at the front window of one of these houses without calling unnecessary attention to yourself, you might notice that the television was switched on.

This particular television was glaring maliciously from the corner of the room at the single female occupant. It was vainly trying to attract her notice with the latest antics from a popular soap opera and it was failing. Its aim in life, the raison d'être of any self-respecting television, was to be the centre of attention and it felt, if televisions could be said to feel, dissatisfied with its owner. She was seated in the opposite corner reading a magazine. Her favourite section of the magazine, 'Mate Match' was what held her gaze. She read every word keenly, each lonely man was figured in her mind quite vividly and each of them hungry for her, Monica Prough. Presently she uttered an involuntary but quiet 'ooh!' and circled one of the advertisements.

She made a habit of reading the personal columns of the local newspaper and various magazines. It ranked higher in importance to reading anything else, even the horoscopes were ignored until the lovelorn columns had been scanned. It was always the first section she turned to of every periodical she bought. Monica was 46 and divorced and had been looking for a man for the five years since Alan, her ex-husband had left her. There had been short relationships with men met through the personal columns or even at dinner-parties but they never lasted long. She was picky, she knew, and not just any man would do. He had to be special. Sense of humour, lively intelligence, honesty and an interesting outlook on life were the criteria she insisted upon and consistently failed to find in a man. Frequently, she would reject a prospective beau because he wan't a good listener or because all that he seemed to want to do was talk to her about football, not a subject high on the list of her interests. But she understood that time was running out; she must find that man soon or drop her standards and she hated the idea of settling for just any old bloke who might turn up.

Alan Prough was presently experiencing none of these problems. He had met Monica at an office party when he was on the lower slopes of the management mountain. His intention had been, and still was, to climb that mountain as high as possible. When he and Monica first met, he had found her constant girlish chatter endearing in an indulgent sort of way. One of the things Monica most loved to do was talk. She loved the art of conversation although her style was didactic rather than dialectic. She could hold both ends of a conversation and frequently did. Feeling that one of her principal purposes of life was to impart information, she was over-enthusiastic in this aim and was difficult to stop. But there had to be an audience and it was first her partially deaf father (who really could turn a deaf ear) and then Alan who were the city gates to her verbal battering ram. Now that they were both gone, she needed a replacement. On her own, she spoke rarely, mostly to chide herself if she found fault in her own actions and she greatly missed having a target at which to direct her remarks.

Monica was also an enthusiastic bed-partner so, shortly after their first meeting, she and Alan married. A few years later, the only result of their energetic sex-lives was born and they called him Wayne. There was no particular reason for this choice other than that it was quite a popular name among the young mothers of the country. It was round about this time that Monica's chatter had started to grate. Alan had begun to find it tiresome rather than endearing and it was with relief that he was relegated to second place in Monica's affections with a concomitant loss of attention. The infant Wayne seemed to love the unending prattle coming from his mother and would lie for hours in his cot or pram with a silly grin on his drooly face, watching and listening. Alan, meanwhile, found someone else. A silent partner, as he liked to think of her. She was Susan, a temp. both in employment and Alan's life. Most women, in fact were satisfyingly mute when compared to Monica. There were several more partners for Alan after he and Susan broke up following a quarrel about commitment. The last, with whom he set up home away from Monica had been a woman he'd met at a speed dating session. Alan had seen the advertisement which said "We need more Men!"

along with a telephone number and the address and date of the venue. Intrigued, he phoned and offered them his services. There was an introduction charge but by the end of the evening, Alan knew that it was money well spent. Rhianna was the girl of his dreams. This wasn't strictly true as Racquel Welch figured largely in Alan's daydreams and occasionally those of his sleep and Rhianna bore no resemblance to that object of a million desires but Alan was willing to stretch a point. He left Monica very shortly afterwards and let her file for divorce. This took rather a long time as Monica procrastinated for a year being convinced that Alan would eventually see the error of his ways and come back to her. She told herself that she would forgive him, of course. In time. But Alan didn't come back for his forgiveness. He didn't care, he was happy with Rhianna.

Another of the compelling reasons for Monica to have a man in her life was in order to satisfy a deep-felt need to look after someone. Wayne only went part way to fulfilling this yen because, although he loved his mum, he soon grew into an independent lad who looked on the family home as a convenient base; somewhere to lay his head, to eat and to get his washing done. Entertainment was looked for elsewhere.

Monica's need stemmed from girlhood. When she was twelve, her mother, a solidly built, dark-haired woman, abandoned the family and ran away with the tally-man. Not everyone thought Monica's mother a desirable woman but the tally-man did. Monica still had the occasional telephone conversation with her mother despite not having seen her since the elopement and all these years later and contrary to form, she and the tally-man were still together in a house in Swansea.

So Monica shouldered the responsibilities that her mother had relinquished and looked after the house and her father. Where her relationship with her mother had been distant but friendly as it, indeed, remains to this day, she loved her father mightily. He could do no wrong in her eyes. He was not a lazy man, he regularly brought home his pay-packet and he did the manly sort of jobs around the house; decorating, shelf fixing and the like. Monica happily assumed the mantle of the lady of the house. Her proficiency in both cooking and housework satisfied her father to such an extent that he never bothered to find a substitute for his long-gone wife.

Monica enjoyed her new role and often spoiled her father by feeding him dishes which might have caused his doctor to shake his head in disapproval. Thus, when Monica was just twenty, her beloved father died of a heart attack brought on, the doctor said, by an unhealthy lifestyle. She was heart-broken and the hole he had left in her life seemed so difficult to fill.

Scanning the 'Men searching for Women' column didn't take Monica long and rarely was there anyone worthy of consideration but this week was different. The sort of man who would put in an advertisement like the one she had just spotted must be special. She admitted to herself that she didn't match any of the requirements but, surely it was a joke, wasn't it? He couldn't possibly want exactly what he'd asked for. She could still pass for forty-five, she owned a library which, admittedly, consisted of only a dozen or so paperbacks by various women authors writing solely on romantic subjects and she loved music, she thought, looking at an old transistor radio which sat on the window ledge and which was her only source of that commodity. And she felt intelligent. Hadn't she just got eight out of ten in that general knowledge quiz in the paper? What was it called? It'll come in a minute. Anyway, she must be intelligent to do that well. Determined to answer, she composed an introductory letter and posted it that very afternoon. Then Monica sat back to wait.

She waited for a reply from someone who just had to be Mr. Right and she waited for her son, Wayne, to come home from work so she could cook his tea. She had no idea what Wayne did for a living, it had never occurred to her to ask; no matter, he put money on the table every Friday to cover his keep and sometimes he bought her things. A lovely boy who loved his mum and so she felt disinclined to inquire as to the source of his wage and where it was he went in the evenings straight after his tea. In fact, tea-time was the only part of the day she was likely to see Wayne. Still, a hard-working lad like that deserves time to play.

Wayne was an unprepossessing young man whose ambition in life was still unformed in his mind. He liked an easy, informal and comfortable income derived from dubious sources but which kept a roof over his head, clothes on his back and supported his only hobby. Wayne loved films. Nothing cultish or demanding; his were the popular action and adventure variety. He was not so much a movie buff, rather a sponge. He watched his films, either on video or at the cinema, with a keen eye and rarely wanted to see a film twice. The plot of each film and any important dialogue heard in it were stored away for future reference in a sort of mental projection room. Ask Wayne the name of a producer or director of a film and you would be met with a blank stare. Ask for the name of the principle actor and it would be a difficult question for him. Anything you needed to know about the characters, what they did or said and what the film was about and you could not stump him.

At about this time, Wayne, Monica's beloved son and heir, the light of her life and rapidly ripening fruit of her loins was giving his whole-hearted attention to his young lady friend, the dark-haired Kerry-Ann Graves. She worked in a chemist's shop on the Wettenham High Street and, occasionally, when it suited him, Wayne would meet Kerry-Ann from work and escort her home.

Kerry-Ann was almost attractive but very unpolished. Without any idea of how to capitalise on her looks, she aped popular celebrities and not always with good effect. She had thin, unkissable lips which she smeared with a pale lipstick, completely camouflaging the lip-line, making her look lipless and her face habitually wore a cocky, couldn't-give-a-shit look barely enhanced by the lively brown eyes which were constantly watching all that went on around her. Her voice had the flat, tired vowels of that part of the county, imbuing her speech with a degree of tedium despite her spirited manner.

These walks were often a time to discuss their future, to make little plans and to air their hopes and dreams for engagement had been mentioned as a possibility. Today, however, the mood was somewhat bleaker because Wayne, arriving a little before the shop was due to close, had gone in to chat to Kerry-Ann and succumbed to temptation. Now he was being punished for this sin.

"I think you were very lucky that Mr. Bentley didn't press charges. He could've called the police, you know."

Wayne was aware that if Mr. Bentley had called the police, no-one would have got home on time and, in fact, they would all be still in the shop waiting for them to arrive but, as this was a poor argument in his defence, he stuck to lying about the incident.

"They couldn't have done me, it was pure accident – a slip of my memory. I've got – you know – what'sit – where your memory slips?"

Kerry-Ann couldn't help him with the name for this ailment and besides, she didn't actually believe him.

"He seen you on the camera. And he'll have the tape so they could've played it back to the police. What do you want bathroom scales for anyway?"

"It's my mum's birthday soon, I thought I'd better get her something. I was going to pay for them but my memory slipped."

"But you didn't even have any sodding money! So what would you pay for it with?"

Caught out, Wayne was slow to react to this last argument from prosecuting council. Then an idea came.

"Ah! – see. I thought I had got money with me. It was another – what'sit – memory slip, wasn't it?"

"Yeah, pull the other one Wayne. Listen, we're supposed to be getting engaged soon. I don't want a feller that's always in trouble with the police or always nicking stuff. I want an honest feller, right? I mean it Wayne – anymore from you and I'm chucking you. You and me will be finished. Do you understand?"

Part way through Kerry-Ann's last delivery, Wayne had become fed up of being nagged so he stopped listening. He was being – what? – victimised. That was it. He was a victim and he was having to suffer for it. Eventually, a nudge from Kerry-Ann made him realise that she was waiting for some comment from him.

"Oh – yes." Her tone had seemed to require agreement of some sort so this was a shot in the dark. Happily, Kerry-Ann was satisfied and the prosecution rested.

"Are we going to the chippy, tonight?" asked Wayne, anxious to change the subject.

"No, my mum's doing something special tonight so I've got to go home for my tea."

"What're you having?"

"I dunno, chicken and chips, I think."

On a motorway slip-road, some miles east of port Regis, sat a police patrol car. In it were Leigh Purslipp and Ellis Clough, on motorway duty. They tended to treat the quiet parts of their watch, the parts where they weren't actually required to investigate something or to chase someone, as legitimate break times. After all, there were those duties which had been too busy to allow a break and they always felt that they were owed a few. They had a cup of coffee each from a communal flask, Leigh was slowly emptying a bag of smokey-bacon flavoured crisps and Ellis was gnawing on a snack-bar while they chatted as friends do.

Ellis' maternal grandparents had come over from Jamaica on the S.S. Windrush while his father's family, also coloured, could trace their British roots back some two hundred years. Ellis had served with the Army for four years and then, when his time was up, joined the police, a job which he loved but in which he had no ambitions. He wanted to continue as he was, an ordinary copper, as far away from the management level as he could be, he just wanted to float through to an early retirement with the minimum effort and the minimum commitment.

Ellis liked Leigh. They had been thrown together two years ago and become firm friends although they didn't socialise much out of work. They did, however, know about each other's backgrounds and family from long nocturnal conversations while on duty.

"I don't understand why you don't want to get on in the force, El. I don't want this job for the rest of my time. I fancy getting behind a desk when I'm a bit older. Quiet life and a fat paypacket, that's me." Leigh munched another crisp.

"We've got a quiet life, now. Provided these pillocks," a wave at the passing motorists, "continue to drive without actually ploughing into one another, we should have yet another undisturbed shift. We're getting paid for this! Easy money." Ellis appreciated the good parts of his job. When things were going right, you wouldn't hear him complain. Not Ellis.

"Nah, it's all right, I suppose but I want to discover a murder or bust up a drugs operation." Leigh leaned forward to wipe the inside of windscreen where his coffee had fogged it.

"What? Catch them?"

"No. Nothing dangerous. You could spot a drugs

operation, hand it over to the Squad and still get a bit of credit. And I couldn't solve a murder. I don't think I'd want to do that. Just discover the body, like." Leigh looked up towards the top of the windscreen and gesticulated with his free hand to indicate the scene in his mind's eye, "Gruesomely hacked up, put in bin-bags and dumped somewhere out of the way, where the killer thinks no-one would find it – but I do, see?"

"Where, like?" Ellis enquired, not being able to imagine such a place with any ease.

From Leigh's reply, one could fairly deduce that he, too, was unable to think up a situation with the correct criteria.

"I don't know, could be anywhere. Not necessarily a special place, just where I'm first on the scene, first to make the discovery."

"You wouldn't like it, seeing a body. You'd honk your ring up if you saw something like that. I've seen a dead body and it wasn't pretty."

Leigh turned towards Ellis, impressed with the news, "Really, when was this?"

"Well, it was my gran. She'd just died. Mind, she wasn't pretty when she was alive but she looked terrible when she was dead." Ellis shuddered at the memory, "Gives me the creeps just thinking about it. Believe me, mate, you wouldn't like it. No, if you take my advice, forget murders. Stick to the bad lads, the thieves. Much better idea. Any thief is better looking than my gran."

Leigh screwed up the empty crisp packet and stuffed it into the pocket of the passenger door. He looked thoughtful. "Breaking up a gang – drug pushers, thieves, whatever, might do. Not as much whatsit, cachet, as a blood-soaked corpse but it'd do."

They relaxed in silence for a minute or so until they were summoned by the radio to report to the next motorway exit where an accident had occurred.

"Here we go, break over. Belt up, mate." Ellis said as he pulled out of the slip road.

Ellis and his wife Sandra had bought themselves a house in a leafier part of Brundon, a suburb of Port Regis. They didn't want the constraints of renting a police house and they felt able to afford the prices asked for houses in that area. One of the criteria of purchase, as far as Ellis was concerned, was the amount of garden it afforded for he was a keen vegetable gardener. Fruit, too, but the useless side of gardening, the showy flowers, held no appeal for him. "You can't eat flowers." he would say.

There was enough room at the back for a small play area for their daughter, Leanne, who was born just two years after they first moved in and who was now an active three.

Daddy had to make sure that Leanne couldn't wander about the cultivated part and had erected a low chicken-wire fence to separate Daddy's play area from Leanne's.

So proud and diligent was Ellis in his past-time that the produce was too great for their needs and Ellis took an immense amount of pleasure from giving the excess away to family and friends.

Included on this list was Mr. and Mrs. Dickenson from next door, pensioners who were both well into their seventies.

Mr. Dickenson was disabled but willing, when he could get out, to offer criticism of Ellis' gardening methods over the garden fence which divided the properties. He considered Ellis' success to be pure beginner's luck.

Mrs. Dickenson was a spry, hen of a woman kept constantly active with housework and gossip. So used had she become to this bounty from next door that she had come to expect it as a right. Should any vegetable not reach the standard to which she was accustomed, she would march round to Ellis' house and demand a replacement.

Fortunately, Ellis was not offended by her behaviour and found it funny instead. He would even apologise to Mrs. Dickenson as he exchanged the offending vegetable.

"I shall replace it free of charge, madam." Ellis would say in jest.

Mrs. Dickenson had had a humour by-pass at some time in her distant past and could never see the joke. "I should think so, too." she would snort, disgusted with the service.

This short conversation would take place every time Mrs. Dickenson came round and she never seemed to remember that they had said all that before. There may have been goldfish in her family somewhere.

Sandra didn't see the funny side. "Why don't you just tell her to piss off with her moaning?", she asked Ellis.

All that considered, you might expect Ellis' life to be blissful. He had a job he liked, a wife and child he loved and a pleasant neighbourhood to live in but there is a smudge on his horizon, a cloud in his sky, a blight on his joy. Someone was breaking into his garden and nicking stuff. It had started about a year ago when the odd carrot, lettuce or whatever would go A.W.O.L. and it had puzzled Ellis but not worried him too much. Such was his output that no-one had to do without their usual bag of Ellis' vegetables.

Now things had stepped up a notch and some bastard had nicked all his early rhubarb. Every pink and luscious stem had gone. Even the crowns had been damaged by malice or haste. Then the cabbage started to disappear at an alarming rate and Mrs. Dickenson had been round to complain that she'd not had her usual delivery. Such was her distress that Ellis had almost been moved to buy her some cabbage from the fruiterer's shop in the precinct. Almost but not quite.

What to do? He could call the police but he knew exactly what would happen: a constable, likely one of his mates, would call round and wearily take a statement, issue him with an incident number and, like as not, make a joke about it. And that would be probably the last he would hear of the matter.

But he was the police! It was up to him to sort the matter. To action, Ellis.

Chapter Four

MONICA

All women born are so perverse no man
need boast their love possessing.
(Robert Bridges)

Leigh Purslipp and Ellis Clough were preparing to go on an early morning shift. This was Leigh's least favourite time of the day and, added to his normal, early-morning grumpiness were his worries about his home life. He was not best suited for company. Seeing his friend's demeanour, Ellis tried to deflect Leigh's problem by throwing his own at him and broached the perplexing problem of his disappearing vegetables.

"They've not only pinched all my rhubarb – and damaged the crowns – but nicked a load of Spring cabbage. No idea who's doing it but I'd love to catch 'em at it." Ellis sounded astonished at the perpetrator's gall.

"Have you reported it to the police?" Leigh loved making joking references to the police as though he had no connection with them whatsoever.

"Don't piss about, mate. This is serious. You know

what'd happen if I did. Sod all. I need an idea which might help me catch whoever it is."

"Get yourself one of those cheap camera thingies. You can put them anywhere nowadays. Connect it to a video recorder and set it before you go to bed. You've got six hours coverage of what's going on in your garden. If you miss them first time, have another go."

Ellis looked thoughtful. It was evident that he approved of Leigh's idea. It was sensible, too, and this was quite uncharacteristic.

"I'll try that, mate. Thanks."

* * *

It was dark – black – almost subterranean. A cold, soft drizzle filled the air and the only interesting thing in view was a blonde girl draped languidly over the hand-rail by the entrance to the public library. She was either dead or very, very uncomfortable.

Danny Craven walked slowly closer, scanning the surrounding area for anything – anyone – suspicious and considering the options. He whistled. The blonde didn't move. She must be dead, he thought and wandered over to assess the situation. He walked carefully, looking around him for anything which might help explain the girl's current predicament. There seemed to be no clues, not even on the body itself or, at least, on the parts he could see. The girl wore a light brown raincoat beneath which protruded a dark blue skirt. Tights and heel-less slingbacks finished the lower end off. The upper end was hatless. Danny touched her neck with his fingertips the way he had seen doctors do in films. He thought that they probably did it to check for a pulse but he could not feel one. She just felt cold – very cold.

'She must have been dead for at least – oh, a good while.' he said aloud. Then, into his lapel radio he called, 'Sarge, I've found a body near the library, a young woman. Could be foul play.'

'Just don't touch it!' came the scratchy, irritable voice of the duty desk segeant, 'We'll send the squad round.' The sergeant, like the stereotypical man of his station, was experienced, cynical, and, what's more, knew of Danny's ambitions.

Danny backed off, looked around him and then continued with a local search. Excitement at the thought of detective work, albeit unofficial and unasked for, filled him. Mentally, he ran through the rules for dealing with a situation like this. Here he was, Danny Craven, first on the scene of a real murder case – maybe murder – it didn't look to him like any sort of accidental death. Touch nothing, notice everything, try to reconstruct the events which led up to the killing.

He saw a watch lying against the base of the wall and close enough to the body to be significant. Its strap had been broken. Danny darted forward excitedly to pick it up but stopped himself in time. He would leave it for the C.I.D. when they came but he would point it out for them. That was his duty. They would take the credit. Meanwhile, he had a few minutes to make some notes and form his own theories.

* * *

Gerry put down his pen and pushed his chair back. He was happy with what had been written but now he was stuck. He had run out of steam and could not see yet where this story was taking him. The idea was sound; a young policeman who solves the murder mystery which has had the best detectives baffled for months. He'd read advice in books written by top authors who claimed not to know what would happen at the end of any novel that they were writing until they reached it. Surely that couldn't be true. You need to have an objective. An end towards which you aim while you write. He couldn't imagine how anyone could pick up a pen or sit in front of a typewriter and just write, presumably letting it all flow from some cerebral well of fantasy. His method was to figure out a plot; beginning, middle and end. Then, with characters gathered along the way, he could people the plot and develop it in a planned way. But now, he could write no further. That was his lot for the day. He picked up the letter which had arrived with the morning's mail and re-read it.

Dear Sir,

I was very much interested in your advert when I saw it in a magazine I can't believe that you would insist on an exact match to your requirements so I'm replying in the hope that we'll be right for each other anyhow, I couldn't believe it when I saw it, I just knew that this could be the right man for me, I am the right age and just love music and reading but most of all, I love to care for a man, to love him, to look after him and to cook wonderful meals for him so I'm sure that you and I would get along like a house on fire once we meet and I am so looking forward to that day.

But first, I suppose you will want to exchange letters and get to know me a little better that way before we meet and I shall want to get to know you a little better too, I can't believe that you would want an exact match to what you said in your advert although I did look after my Dad who is no longer with us (God rest him) and my mum's in Swansea and I don't suppose that counts.

Anyway, I don't think you're going to get any better than me, I am enclosing a photograph so that you can see what I mean (and what you'll get Ha Ha), I must go now, I have some shopping to do,

Love and kisses,
Monica Prough.

Gerry stopped reading and looked at the photograph again. An attractive, dark-haired woman with a close-lipped smile looked back. In Gerry's mind, photographs were not a great deal of help in forming an opinion of someone you don't know but at least there was no obvious negative aspect in the image. He continued reading.

This Monica had little going for her as far as Gerry could see but still, it was a reply and, if nothing else, would supply material for his story which hadn't progressed very well of late. He had set himself a deadline, a date by which he would finish this novel but it was looking unachievable; too many evenings had been spent staring at blank pieces of A4 with nothing appearing on them but sad looking coffee rings. Maybe a meeting with this Monica would rouse the muse. She may even turn out to be the woman he was searching for. A long shot but worth a go.

Her address was in Wettenham which wasn't far from where Gerry lived and she'd even provided her telephone number. Well, we'll bypass the courtship by letter and I'll give her a ring and find out what the woman is like.

Gerry spent the day thinking about this next step with Monica and decided to go for broke. As soon as he returned home from the shop that evening, he called her.

The voice that answered seemed surprised to find her telephone ringing. At the end of the call, some twenty minutes later, Gerry found that he had a sore ear from holding the phone to it for too long and a date to meet Monica just two days away, on the Friday evening. Things had happened a tiny bit too quickly for him. Monica's method of chatting up a man was a sort of verbal avalanche. He had agreed to her arrangements in a mild panic; a way to end the phone call by going along with her plans. He would have preferred, with hindsight, to have eased into the relationship gradually; slowly getting to know this woman first before making the commitment of actually meeting her. This way had something of the scaffold's trapdoor about it.

* * *

Ellis had taken a few days off work and had some shopping to do. In Port Regis city centre was a shop which sold all kinds of electronic goods and in this place, Ellis sought advice.

"So." The assistant began, "How big is this garden of yours so I can tell how many cameras you'll need and do you think that you'll want motion sensors?"

Ellis described his garden and explained that, as he would tape over a six hour period continuously, he didn't feel that the added expense of a motion sensor was justified.

Satisfied, the assistant disappeared into the room behind the counter and came back shortly with four boxes and a small roll of signal cable.

"Right, you set these cameras up where they can see the garden, feed the signals into this box here, this will send a composite picture of what the cameras see. Basically, your telly screen will be split up into four, one bit will be blank and the other three will show camera output. O.K. on that?"

"Yes, thanks." said Ellis as he handed over his credit card to pay for the purchases. He was quite excited. He had a new toy to play with, an acquisition which affects all men in a happy sort of way, and he had a means of thwarting the phantom veggie-nicker as he'd come to think of him.

When he had outlined his plan to Sandra, she had suggested that it might be cheaper to get a dog. Ellis had been about to accept Sandra's plan as a better one than his when he saw several loop-holes.

"First, we'd have to get a pup and they stay in the house so that's not effective. Second, if we got a full-grown guard dog, it might be a danger to Leanne and third, what would we do with it once the thief has been caught? Nice try, though."

Sandra was disappointed. The kind of dog she had had in mind wasn't really a good guard dog, anyway. She fancied something fluffy which she and Leanne could cuddle. Oh, well, give a man a gadget to play with and it will keep him happy for hours.

Once back home, Ellis positioned one camera on the rear corner of the house which covered the garden at the side and the other two fixed to fence posts in the two far corners of the back garden, pointing back towards the house. He buried the signal and power leads for these two shallowly in the soil and then took leads from all three into the house via a hole which he drilled in the wall and connected the three cameras to the splitter box. Finally, this box was connected to the video recorder.

He switched on the television to check the signals and after a couple of adjustments to the cameras outside, he was satisfied. All he needed do now was to set the timer on his video recorder from midnight to six and he would have six hours of surveillance.

The next morning, full of anticipation, Ellis sat down to watch the footage. He soon became bored because nothing was happening and then it occurred to him that if he went to check the garden first, it would tell him whether he needed to watch the tape.

It was a frosty morning and Ellis shivered as he inspected his vegetable patch. Nothing had been touched but he thought he should check everything more closely later, when it warmed up, in case the frost had done any damage. He went back in to stop the tape running and switch the television off, just in time to see a neighbour's cat wander across the screen.

Later, while in the front garden checking to see if the previous evening's frost had caused any problems, three small children aged probably between six and eight years old approached the gate.

"Ello mister." said one who had possibly been elected spokesman for the group.

"Are you a policeman?" asked a second child from slightly behind the spokesman as though using him for protection.

"Yes," said Ellis, "and who are you three?"

Ignoring the question, the spokesman got straight to the point, "We've seen a ghost."

"At night-time." added the second. The third child remained uncommunicative but interested in the interchange.

Ellis was intrigued and stood up to better speak to the children. Encouraged by this adult interest, the spokesman expanded his theme.

"Yes, we were watching it through the curtains in the bedroom and we seen it in your garden."

The third child nodded vigorously and wiped its nose across a dirty coat sleeve in confirmation.

"So, what did this ghost look like?" asked Ellis.

"A bit like Caspar only bigger." There were two confirmatory nodding heads.

"Well thank you for the information, I'll see what I can do about it."

"Will you catch it and put it in jail?" asked number two.

"I don't know whether you can put a ghost in jail. Wouldn't he slip through the bars and escape?"

The children giggled. They liked adults who were silly.

"I shall try to catch him anyway." continued Ellis.

After that promise from Ellis, the children lapsed into an unintelligible and private interchange which included punching each other, laughing and running down the street.

The following morning, Ellis checked the garden first. The row of spinach which he'd planted and which was almost ready had been pulled. Not all the plants had been taken but those remaining had been destroyed. Ellis was angry and rushed back in to check his video footage. He had already worked out how to watch it. He rewound the tape about ten minutes and checked the spinach bed. Wrecked. Then doing the same in half hour rewinds, he found where the bed was undisturbed. Running forwards a few minutes at the time he eventually found the culprit at work. It was some little sod in a sheet! Dressed up like a party ghost he worked quickly, pulling up plants and looking frequently back at the house in case he was being watched. It was weird to see, this Ku Klux Klan wannabe running around in his garden. He stopped the tape, made himself a coffee and figured out a plan.

* * *

Friday found Gerry feeling extremely nervous and beginning to regret what he'd done. He felt with ever increasing strength that Monica was not for him, she didn't seem to have any of the qualifications he would expect of a life partner. He tried to shrug the feeling off, telling himself that he didn't know her well enough to discount her and that it was all down to pre-match nerves. He would go through with it, he was not the type to break promises or stand anyone up.

The arranged venue was a restaurant in Wettenham; one of those establishments which had begun life as a public house and progressed through pickled eggs and ploughman's to full restaurant service via an expensive and ill-advised refurbishment. It had been renamed The Arbroath Smokie and the Scottish theme had been stamped onto every aspect inside. Its menu consisted of traditional and faux Scottish food served by young people who wore tams; the female staff sported kilts and the males wore plaid waistcoats to impress their Scottishness upon the clientele. There were panels all round the walls depicting the various tartans and between these, reproduction claymores were thrust behind ersatz shields screwed to the wall. There wasn't a Scottish accent in evidence anywhere. Gerry, mildly amused, took a seat by the bar and asked for a pint of heavy.

The youth behind the bar looked confused and asked him to repeat the order and Gerry, rather than pursue it, changed the order to half a pint of bitter. Then he sat with his back to the bar surveying the customers. He regretted having forgotten his notebook in which he would often write short character sketches of people he saw but it was of little consequence for nervousness had robbed him of the concentration needed to do this.

Before long, a woman so like the photograph he'd brought that it had to be Monica arrived and Gerry warily stood up to be identified and to greet her. She was easily recognisable but he asked nonetheless.

Her reaction was a little unexpected for she treated him like a long-lost friend and hugged and kissed him with an enthusiasm which completely shattered Gerry's reserve. He waved vaguely to an empty table with a freshly freed arm and Monica, understanding the gesture, grabbed the other one with both of hers in a very proprietorial fashion and, instead of allowing Gerry to lead her there, steered him forcefully in that direction all the while asking him how he was and did he find it difficult to get here and isn't this place nice? This flustered him but he managed to remember to ask her whether she would like a drink after he had disentangled himself from her grasp and she was seated and, for the present, silent.

When he returned, clutching her drink, the remains of his half of bitter and feeling a little calmer, he had time to study his date for the night. She had removed her coat and arranged it round the back of her chair, her gloves and handbag were placed on the table to her right. Her hair was black enough to suggest artificial means had been used to maintain the colour and it framed deep blue eyes. She was stockily built and very tastefully dressed, making for a quite fanciable woman. It was her teeth which detracted from the whole. They were large, white and there seemed to be a lot of them, arranged in a predatory and regimented order. The top set described a larger arc than the bottom and when she spoke, it was as though she was trying to keep them in. She must have had a vivid mental image of their flying out uncontrollably judging by the efforts her top lip made trying to restrain them.

Gerry felt overwhelmed by her volubility. He had made a mental note before coming out not to hog the conversation with fascinating facts about his life and to politely prompt the lady to talk about herself with a few prepared questions. It was unnecessary. Monica managed the conversation completely. Her monologue of her life and loves was broken only occasionally by rapid bursts of questions directed at Gerry which he could only half answer before she thundered on to the next subject dear to her.

Gerry ordered and ate his meal automatically, watching fascinatedly as food disappeared down Monica's throat with barely a break in her prattle. For an experiment, Gerry thought of a silly statement for that brief period when she was silent. It was to be "I ran over an aardvark on the way here."

This sort of remark has an arresting quality. Even when a person is in full didactic flow, some small part of the brain is listening, waiting for incoming data such as an approaching enemy or even interested questions. In Monica's case, this part of the brain wasn't active in that respect. It had gone missing, become atrophied or been seconded to other duties and so it wasn't surprising that Gerry's remark went unheard. He only managed to get half way through the sentence before, ostrich-like, her food was swallowed and she continued talking. Gerry's dead aardvark remained unmourned.

The evening whirled on and, at its close, as the conversational dust was settling and they prepared to leave, Gerry had come to the conclusion that this woman was nowhere near to being Mrs Right. He paid the bill and rejoined her, in his gallant fashion, to walk her to the car. There had been a brief moment when he had entertained the idea of escape via the men's toilet window.

"Listen, you must come to dinner tomorrow night – my treat this time – you know my address, don't you?" Gerry nodded dumbly in between words. "Be there for half past seven. I shall see you then." she said quickly and then pulled Gerry towards her with her hands on his arms and rewarded him with a full-on kiss before getting into her car. The rather mundane fact that her car was a yellow Nissan Micra was one of those pieces of data that Gerry's brain normally would have rejected as trivial and wasteful of memory space. Whether noting the fact would have been of any help later on is just conjecture. Right now, all he could think of was the end of the evening.

During Monica's farewell, Gerry had said nothing. Some part of his mind was away plotting how to get rid of her and the remaining part couldn't cope with what was happening to him. His lower face felt mashed. She'd put a lot of power, masquerading as passion, into that kiss and his lower lip was bleeding slightly. He was very thoughtful as he went to find his car and as he climbed in and switched on the ignition, turned off the radio to appreciate the silence.

He sat in the car wondering what to do and sucking his bottom lip. Should he just not turn up? Could he feign illness? No, that wasn't like him and besides, that damned woman had wheedled his address and telephone number from him – he'd seen her write them down in a notebook produced from her handbag – so she'd want to know why he hadn't come. She might even appear on his doorstep if he failed to find hers. He'd have to go as arranged. He would break it to her then and she would have to accept it. It was a crap time to pick for a break-up, immediately after what was no doubt intended as a romantic dinner but perhaps, at least, she wouldn't feel that he'd taken an instant dislike to her. It had been quick – but not instant. Sod it, he would have to go tomorrow and maybe something would occur to him on the spur of the moment. He could pick an argument with her, be really disagreeable so that she would fall out with him and throw him out. Feeling a little better, Gerry put the car into first gear, reached automatically for the radio switch, had second thoughts and drove home in tranquility.

Monica's trip home was brighter than Gerry's. She was jubilant; this was the man for her. Even after such a brief acquaintance, she knew. Women's intuition. This man was going to be her next husband. O.K. so he was a little shy at first but she'd soon got him chatting to her. And that kiss when they'd parted. She felt a warm tingle inside as she remembered it. She fell to thinking about dinner the following night. Something special so she could impress him with her cooking skills. And a bottle of posh wine. Then – who knows what might happen? She smiled to herself as she parked her car in front of her house.

The following evening found Gerry on the doorstep of Monica's address feeling even more nervous than the previous night. What seemed to be worse than the unknown was the knowledge that he now had of Monica. He had tried to write a character sketch of her earlier in the day, thinking that perhaps a personality as strong as Monica's could find its way into his writing somewhere. Possibly there was a short story somewhere with her as the central figure. But nothing would come except for one word: fearsome. A short story of a murdering housewife might be suitable. Or one about a murdering husband, driven mad by her non-stop talking and desperate for some peace and quiet. Justifiable homicide, the judge would call it. He pressed the bell, still undecided whether he had done the right thing by coming empty-handed. He thought that if he turned up bearing wine, chocolate or flowers, it might encourage her and that would never do.

The door opened abruptly, almost as soon as his finger came off the bell-push. She must have been lying in wait.

He was greeted with another face-masher of a kiss but he managed to turn slightly and take the brunt of it on his cheek. He did not want the cut on his bottom lip opening up again. He put his arms around her as though there was some positive feeling on his part. It felt nice. How odd, he thought, I could probably stomach the idea of casual sex with this woman yet not a prolonged relationship. The idea of using her in that way until something better turned up was bravely pushed away.

Monica ushered him into the living room which was one of only two rooms on the ground floor, the other being her kitchen. It was a very feminine room, a strong floral smell, pastel coloured furnishings and an overall fluffiness. The keynote of all this was a stuffed pink rabbit standing on top of the television on a large doily which overflowed down the front and obscured part of the screen. The rabbit leered at him. There was no evidence of books or music in the room, a feature which would have sparked Gerry's interest. Even the grubby little transistor radio on the window sill was switched off.

Monica had disappeared into the kitchen, no doubt to attend to whatever it was which spewed out delicious smells of the meal to come. Gerry felt hungry already.

"Would you like something to drink?" Monica shouted, unseen, "Dinner will be half an hour yet."

"Er, tea, please." he called back, "Milk and no sugar."

A few minutes later, she reappeared clutching the mug of tea and wearing what seemed to Gerry a raptorial smile.

He sat down on one of the fluffy, beige armchairs and held his mug defensively in front of him.

"Oh, I'm so pleased you came, I've been rushed off my feet today getting things ready, making sure everything was right for you, did you get here all right? I hope you like chicken, that's what I've done for tonight and do you like wine? You'd never guess the trouble I had in the butcher's today, I wanted to do duck, you know? Something posh, maybe some orange sauce to go with it, do you like duck? but he'd got none in, some woman who's putting on a dinner party or something had been in and bought the lot and I couldn't go to the supermarket, there wasn't the time what with the cooking time and everything so I had to settle for chicken, well, what can you do? Still, I prefer chicken anyway, it's not as greasy as duck and you can have cranberry sauce with it if you like, do you like cranberry sauce? Or you can have redcurrant jelly if we've got any in, I'll just go and check the potatoes."

Gerry reeled from this verbal bombardment. The tea had been no defence against that. He looked at the mug's contents, suspicious now and put it down on the table next to his armchair. On a doily.

He now felt mildly worried. He really was not looking forward to further exposure to this woman. Part of his mind, the sensible part, screamed, "Run!" The stupid part of his mind which appeared to be in charge of motor control this evening either refused to listen or couldn't decide quickly enough and then Gerry's chance was gone as Monica reappeared with a glass of wine in her hand. As soon as she hove into view, the wittering began again.

"You don't mind if I start before you, I know you have to be careful if you're driving so I won't push you to a drink. I do love a glass of wine at home, so much better than what they serve you in pubs. The white is usually too warm and sweet and the red is too thin and quite sour. Now, this one I like. I get it from the supermarket you know. It's very reasonable You can get it in boxes now, did you know? Fancy putting wine into a cardboard box. Well, call me a traditionalist if you like but I prefer my wine in bottles – or out of them." She giggled to indicate the joke and Gerry wondered whether she employed that circular breathing which well-known didgeridoo players employ in the pursuit of their craft, the woman certainly didn't appear to take breaths.

"Well, you can see what you're getting – well – almost, anyway." she continued

There seemed to be some subliminal message in what Monica told him which increased the worrying feeling which Gerry had. Too much had been said for recall and analysis but a warning bell had sounded deep in his brain and Gerry didn't know what it was for. He was, however, developing an ability to screen out whatever it was she said. It didn't seem to matter what she was talking about, there was never enough time to answer or comment before she'd re-ranged her guns and recommenced the attack from a different quarter. She was sitting on the arm of the sofa, facing him and unable to get any closer without actually sitting on his lap. She was still talking.

Sometimes sentences would force themselves into Gerry's conscious if they sparked some interest in him such as, on the subject of her departed husband, " He even went to a speed-dating session and didn't take me!" It would have been foolish of him to ask her to expand any of these statements. Gerry spent some time trying to make sense of the account and let imagination supply an explanation. He was getting the impression that Monica's ex-husband put some effort into separating himself from her. He did not feel surprised. He felt a sort of comradeship with this unknown hero who had married Monica and then escaped alive.

After what seemed like an age later, there was a noise from the kitchen, a ping which announced that something in there had completed its function.

"Dinner's ready." she said brightly, "Sit yourself at the table." and waved her empty glass at the dining table in the centre of the room on which had been set two places.

Well, at least I'm ready to eat, thought Gerry as he arranged a napkin on his knees.

She brought in two meals, ready dished and placed one in front of Gerry.

"Dig in." she said and rushed back into the kitchen bringing back the bottle of wine and two glasses.

"You'll have one, it's all right to have just one glass, it won't put you over the limit and I know how nice it is to have a glass of wine with a meal." she gabbled and placed a full glass by his elbow and re-filled her own.

"Here's to us." she pledged, forcing Gerry to drink a toast he could not approve of. Despite his misgivings, he enjoyed the meal. There was no doubt but that the woman was a proficient cook. Even the wine, a fruity Sauvignon Blanc, suited his palate.

Monica talked the whole time, pausing only for forkfuls of food or to sip her wine. Gerry didn't feel in the mood to repeat his restaurant experiment, he was looking forward to going home. He occasionally nodded towards her or forced a half smile but without the slightest intention of encouragement. Monica's glass was now on its third helping. Gerry knew everything he needed and more besides about Monica. She was divorced (on grounds of the mental cruelty inflicted on her husband?), had a grown son, Wayne, who still lived with her but was out for the evening, she was forty seven and worked in the offices of the local council. The important facts done with long ago, those of lesser value were surfacing and Monica was currently regaling him with details of an elderly aunt's recent operation to fit a new hip and Gerry had become mentally agile enough to switch in and out of her conversation.

Wonder if her ex-husband could do that? Probably. I've only been at it a day or so and he had a good few years of it. If I ever meet the poor sod, I'll stand him a pint. And let him talk to me. I bet his voice sounds rusty. Probably never needed it for all that time with her. Just nod and smile; that's all I need do to keep up my end of the conversation.

"Sweet or cheese?"

Gerry's listening had switched in a little too late to understand what she'd asked. Her face had that hopeful look which indicated that an answer of some sort was required of him.

"Pardon?"

"I said, would you like sweet or cheese?"

"Er, cheese would be fine – I think a sweet might be just a little filling." Gerry patted his stomach.

She felt disappointed that he had passed up the opportunity of sampling her lemon meringue pie for both Wayne and her husband had frequently complimented her on her meringues. she beamed at him toothily and left to fetch the cheese board.

Gerry looked up at the clock, wondering when it would be civil to leave. An opportunity to pick a quarrel with her didn't seem likely to present itself, he couldn't get a word in. He would have to write. How do you provoke a quarrel by letter?

Freshly brewed coffee followed the cheese and Monica rambled on. Her next-door neighbour was being heavily criticised for failing to control a cat and Gerry's thoughts wandered again. He was inwardly composing a goodbye letter to her. Saying goodbye to Monica from a safe distance appealed to him a little more than direct confrontation.

"Well, sit yourself down and I'll clean up." Monica announced. The ritual feeding was at an end and a feeling of mild terror nudged Gerry as he wondered how the rest of the evening would be passed. Monica cleared the table, chatting as she went, commenting on the awful behaviour of the local youth and how the parents were entirely to blame. Gerry waited. She perched again on the end of the sofa and asked for opinions on the meal. Gerry could only answer truthfully but hesitantly; he didn't want to offer any words which might foster the illusion that he was keen. Nevertheless, Monica was heartened. Inside she thrilled that the dinner had been such a huge success and she had evidently made an impact on Gerry with her cooking skills. She hoped that he was just as struck with everything else, too. She had a lot to offer a man like this. Someone who would appreciate her. She was now half way through her fourth glass of wine and the cumulative effect of the alcohol had allowed the idea of taking the evening's proceedings onto a higher plane unwisely to present itself. Her good judgement had been swamped by supermarket Sauvignon and she said suddenly to Gerry, "Sha'n't be a minute."

Then she went upstairs.

Her bedroom was at the top of the stairs to the left, directly opposite the spare bedroom in which was a freshly made-up bed. Just in case.

She went into her room and began to undress. It was very evidently a woman's room. Pink wallpaper with a pattern of climbing roses, Heavy red curtains dominated the broad window. One wall had its length covered by a fitted wardrobe with mirrored doors which reflected the double bed backed by a white padded headboard and topped by a rose patterned coverlet. The floor was covered wall to wall in imitation lambs' wool.

Had Gerry seen this room, he would have drawn parallels with the web of a black widow spider although, to be fair, there were really no obvious comparisons. No, not visually, Gerry would have argued, but for purpose there were several.

She left on her underwear and put on a black, silk dressing gown which she neglected to fasten and then stood in front of the array of mirrors, the outer doors of the wardrobe open to add depth to her image. She wanted to gauge the effect she might have on Gerry. She was pleased. Quickly she patted and primped her hair and went back down, one hand holding her gown closed in front. As she reached the bottom of the stairs, she said, "Another coffee, Gerry or would you prefer a glass of brandy?"

Gerry turned to answer and as he did, she let the gown fall open. Her intentions were clear; Gerry was horrified.

He stood up. "Er." he said and dropped the mug he'd

been holding which broke its handle off as it hit the carpet. "Oh, sorry, er, look, I don't think things are working out. Erm, it's late – I have to go – I'm sorry." He bent to pick up the broken mug, placed it on the table, dropping the handle inside and dashed for the front door. He fumbled for catch and let himself out into the welcome cool of the evening.

Inside the house, Monica watched him go and two big, warm, salty tears carried mascara down the length of her face. She sat sadly on the bottom stair and sniffed. "Never even gave me a goodnight kiss." she said to the pink rabbit which leered unsympathetically, "Perhaps I had a little too much wine." Then she went to fetch the bottle which still had another glassful inside it. She drank it slowly, sniffily and thought about her next move.

The following morning Monica sat and composed a letter of apology to Gerry, owning the fault as hers and asking for another meeting to make amends. She was careful not to make specific reference to the incident which had broken up the evening.

Gerry spent the day in a haze, flustered and unsure of himself. He let his work in the shop take his mind from Monica and even sent Bob and Meera home on full pay while he finished the morning in the shop. At twelve o'clock, it being Sunday, he closed up and went to his local for a beer and lunch. Here he could feel comparitively safe.

They'd found another corpse or, at least, the street cleaners had. A brunette this time; the body just left where it could be easily found. Danny had leaned on his friend, Charley Kinsman to gain access to the files on both women. Funny choice of initials, Danny mused as he made his way to Charley's office, parents not thinking there. Mind you, how were they to know that he would become a Detective Inspector. Danny studied both files and made copious notes. He wanted to see if he could draw parallels. No-one was saying anything but it looked as though the killer of both these women was the same man. The same careless dumping of the body, an arrogant gesture because, as there was no attempt made to hide the killing, it was as though someone wanted to put out a warning – or did they want to get caught quickly?

The second victim was a dark-haired woman, well-dressed and found sitting in the doorway of Woolworths clutching a pink, stuffed rabbit.

Like the blonde, she had been killed by a single stab wound to the heart by a stiletto or similar weapon. There had been no sign of any struggle so maybe both the victims knew the murderer. Charley was planning to check out the acquaintances of both women right now, looking for the common denominator.

Chapter Five

CORRESPONDENCE

It seemed good to me also... to write unto thee
(St. Luke)

As normal, when Gerry arrived home from his Monday morning stint purveying newspapers and tobacco to the inhabitants of Wettenham, there was a large pile of mail behind the door. Usually, it consisted of junk mail or bills and rarely anything interesting but, today, in amongst the offers for cheap motor insurance and music club memberships was a long, pale-blue envelope in an elegant hand. Curious, Gerry dropped the rest of his correspondence on the hall table while he investigated this one. Its return address was c/o the Post Office, Cabley, a village he knew of but had never visited as it was buried in the countryside somewhere nearby. Cabley, in Gerry's mind, was a place to go provided there was a specific reason: if you lived there, for instance. It had no architectural or historical features which might attract a tourist.

He sniffed at the envelope which had only a papery smell and gave him no clue to its provenance. He felt it without knowing why and something told him that it could be special, important, even. He opened it.

The letter was another reply to his advertisement and it read:

'I was intrigued by your plea in a certain periodical to the extent that I now find myself replying. My name is Toni (short for Antonia) and it seems that, despite the strangeness of your criteria, I am quite a good match although the likelihood that we are made for each other may be stretching the limits of coincidence.

However, I would like us to correspond, at least, until such time that one of us finds the other not to their taste.

Nothing further until I hear from you.'

There was just a 'T' as a signature and no address on the top of the page, just c/o Cabley Post Office. Now it was Gerry's turn to be intrigued. A strange and slightly unfriendly letter. He took it into the kitchen to re-read while he made himself a coffee, the rest of the morning's mail, like Monica, temporarily forgotten.

After an hour's thought during which he pottered around the flat doing a little necessary housework, sometimes stopping in his tracks to concentrate better, Gerry sat down to write his first letter to this odd-sounding lady.

'Dear Toni,

I'm delighted to have received your letter. I must own to a little subterfuge here. While it's true that I'm looking for a partner, I do so in a dilatory fashion because the one that I need must be special and my lack of optimism keeps me from searching in what might be a more productive manner, there is an ulterior motive for placing that advertisement.

It might be logical to presume that anyone who answers an ad. like mine must be special to some degree but whatever the outcome, I would like to hear of your reactions to and reasons for answering it.

That motive, the hidden facet, stems from my literary

ambitions; the wording for the ad. came to me while working on a short story and so I posted it to see what sort of response it might elicit both for research and for personal reasons.

Thus, not only are you a prospective candidate for my heart, you might also become a character in an unpublished story.'

After revealing his reasons, Gerry then went on to introduce himself to Toni. He had no idea how she might take the first part of the letter but at least he was letting her know that he was no ordinary bloke and that he could be counted on to be open and honest with her.

Later, after the letter had been posted, a thought occurred to Gerry which, at first, seemed quite profound. He wrote this in his journal: ' Women love an honest man, and not surprisingly, men like an honest woman and, according to gender, it's always your sex which gets the shitty end of the stick'

Then he read what he had written and decided that it was fatuous bilge but wouldn't cross it out because it would make the journal look untidy.

* * *

It was evening in the Clough household and Ellis, with an open bottle of beer at his side, Sandra, with an empty tea-cup by hers, were watching television. The programme showing was not engaging Ellis' full attention and he found his mind wandering.

Leanne was playing in that barely understandable way; a sort of proto-motherhood that little girls demonstrate. She would pick up a doll or a soft toy animal, cuddle it for a while, talking hushed gibberish to it and then, seeming to become annoyed with the toy, she would hurl it from her. She would move from toy to scattered toy in this manner and, at intervals, squeeze into the gap by the side of her mother and suck her thumb until it was time to resume the game.

Ellis had noted the time that the apparition had appeared in his garden and he felt it likely that, should the culprit re-appear, it would be at a similar time. A criminal can become regular in his habits and ultimately predictable. That was how some of them are caught. It was worth his while to stay up late tonight and try to catch the thief red-handed.

Musing on this and on the strange garb which his man had elected to wear, his funny bone was struck by a passing thought and he laughed out loud.

Leanne stopped what she was doing and smiled shyly, thinking that her actions were the cause of Daddy's laughter. Sandra, knowing that the television hadn't amused him, looked over and asked, "So what's funny?"

"Have we got any old sheets?" Ellis asked back.

"What for?"

"Can I borrow one?"

So far, none of the questions was being answered. Each provoked a return question. Then Sandra realised why her husband needed an old sheet and joined in the laughter. Leanne dropped the toy donkey which was taking its turn as pretend off-spring and clapped her hands.

"I'll get you one." said Sandra, getting up.

"I won't try it on till the baby's in bed. She might get nightmares."

Later, Leanne tucked into bed in her bedroom and with the dolly most in favour that night, Ellis donned the sheet.

"Can't bloody see!" he exclaimed but Sandra was there with a pair of scissors and cut him a pair of eyeholes.

At midnight, sheet at the ready, Ellis sat in the darkened living room watching the monitor which he had turned away from the window. The curtains remained open.

Soon, a sheeted figure was spotted strolling confidently

up the garden path and making for the back of the garden where Ellis had planted broccoli and leeks. Ellis put on his sheet and followed out through the back door which he'd left unlatched so as not to make any noise.

The ghost had its back to Ellis as it busied itself pulling up the young leeks and wasn't aware of being watched until it heard a loud BOO!! It jumped.

The apparition turned quickly towards the source of the noise, saw what had made it and squealed. Then it made to flee but Ellis was prepared and caught the ghost's neck in a tight grip.

"Not only boo but you're under arrest for knackering my garden, mate."

With one hand he whipped away the thief's sheet and deftly cuffed him to his own wrist.

"Let's go and see if the duty desk sergeant is in a good mood, shall we?"

There was no resistance, the ghost had had all its spirit blown away.

Down at the police station, Ellis handed him over to the duty segeant and asked that he be charged with aggravated trespass. During the journey, Ellis had discovered only the lad's name: Darren Stillwater.

Stripped of his sheet, Darren turned out to be an unprepossessing, undeveloped youth with a surprisingly clear complexion. In someone of his age and gender, you might expect a large area of face to be given over to acne but there was not a single blemish. This was a result of pure fortune rather than an exemplary diet.

He had a sleazy look which made one conjecture that perhaps he suffered none of those scruples which might limit his activities. He also suffered from poor self-image and the conjecturing person might remark, 'Quite rightly so'. There are those who feel that the likes of Darren deserve more sympathy and understanding but most of them either work for the Social Services or practise psychotherapy.

The desk sergeant took out a form on which to write Darren's personal details, took a pen from his pocket and, having been given his charge's name by Ellis, wrote, saying, "Name: Darren Stillwater, Address?"

"Piss off! I'm telling you nothing. I want my phone call and a solicitor."

This, perhaps, was not a remark to make if you wanted to get off on the right foot with the desk sergeant. He was a patient man, an asset in his job which involved meeting some of the least nice people of the area and so was not angry with Darren. He could achieve his aim calmly and satisfyingly, he was a policeman.

"Well, since we can't run you home because you won't tell us where you live, we'll have to put you up for the night."

"Guest in number three!" he shouted and a young constable came in and led a protesting Darren to the cells. He was unimpressed with Darren's avowed familiarity with his rights.

* * *

The following morning, there was just the one letter lying among the less attractive mail on Gerry's mat. It was from Monica and Gerry felt uneasy as he looked at the envelope. He opened it wishing that he'd never met the damned woman and his wish grew more fervent as he read what she'd written.

She apologised for her rather forward behaviour and promised that, if Gerry could feel it in his heart to forgive her, she would never do anything so silly again. She was sure that there was ground firm enough on which to establish a relationship between them and she hoped that Gerry would see things in that same, optimistic light. Meanwhile, she would wait to hear from him.

She'll wait a bloody long time, thought Gerry, I can't seem to get through to her that I'm not interested so I am not going to write to tell her what she should already know. He screwed the letter up and threw it in the waste bin which was kept by the hall table for the reception of junk-mail. He missed. The letter was left on the floor while Gerry went to find some activity which would take his mind from Monica. In the kitchen, his stomach reminded him that he was hungry and that it was time to eat. Gerry's odd working hours led often to odd meal times and, despite its not being quite mid-morning, he fancied a curry.

"Meat!" he said to himself. There was some minced beef in the fridge and he dropped that into a pan and put the pan on the cooker.

"Spices!" He opened the cupboard above the fridge and took out a container of curry powder, a small pot of chili powder and a jar of mango chutney. Teaspoonfuls of each joined the mince.

He chopped an onion, a carrot and a garlic clove and these, with a splash of water from the kettle, went in also. Putting the pan on to heat and humming an irritating tune to himself, he went to look for some rice.

Now, if you had chosen that moment to stop and interrogate him on the subject of Monica, you would have noticed an annoyed look clouding his face because that simple activity in the kitchen had driven her, albeit temporarily, from his mind and he would not have been grateful to you for having mentioned her foul name.

* * *

The very same morning that Gerry received his letter from Monica, Darren Stillwater was regretting his strategy of non-co-operation with the police. He had spent a very uncomfortable night in the cell and his breakfast had been a cold bacon sandwich and a tepid cup of stewed tea. Now he very much wanted to go home. If they asked him any more questions, he was going to answer them, probably truthfully.

It was Segeant Watham who let him out shortly after nine o'clock and led him to an interview room, sat him down with a fresh cup of tea and lit him a cigarette.

The sergeant, an old hand with reluctant interviewees, proffered a cigarette and opened on an informal note, "What's that on your teeshirt?"

"Probably a bit of breakfast." answered Darren sullenly, taking the cigarette.

"No, the writing, what's it say?"

Darren was proud of this teeshirt, it was a souvenir from a gig where he saw his favourite band and he wore it proudly, thinking perhaps that passers-by might read it and admire his musical taste. He brightened.

"Borborygmus." he informed the sergeant.

The sergeant was not a fan of modern music and so could be excused for not knowing what the word meant, "What's it mean, then?"

"They're a group from round here. They're brilliant. I've got all their records."

The latter claim was truthful, Borborygmus had issued just one C.D., a limited, private pressing and Darren had bought a copy. It had the wonderful effect of thrilling his auditory nerves while irritating the shit out of his next-door neighbour.

"Right, let's get some details down. Name?"

"Darren Stillwater. Do I not get a lawyer?"

"I wouldn't advise it. It'll just mean that you'll be kept here that much longer. Just give us all your details, we'll send you home and later you'll probably be called in front of the magistrates soon and be told you're a naughty boy."

That didn't sound too bad a prospect and so Darren told sergeant Watham everything; it turned out that Darren's father ran a fruiterer's shop and was a little upset by Ellis giving fruit and vegetables away to potential customers of his, thereby losing him trade. He had paid Darren to go and trash Ellis' garden so his customers would return. Darren had chosen his strange costume to frighten off anyone who saw him and prevent recognition.

* * *

Toni liked Gerry's letter enough to reply. She had shown it to Henry who pronounced Gerry, out loud this time, distinctly odd but that did nothing to douse her interest. Though piqued, a little consideration would not go amiss before she wrote her response and, since there was work to do in the stables, she headed for the horses; thinking of what Gerry had said and mentally preparing answers to his questions. This chap, she thought, sounded genuine enough. Interesting and intelligent, too, in all probability. And he'd called her special. Well, sort of. Meanwhile, there was yet no need to reveal her full identity or address. A character in a story, perhaps. Now that sounded exciting. Wonder what sort of books he writes?

Henry had his forthcoming marriage to worry about. There were so many things to remember and Toni's latest interest began to slip from his mind. He drove over to see Angela who was at her home compiling a guest list and writing the invitations. Even in her company, Henry felt restless and was of little help and was sent to the kitchen to make coffee for the both of them.

As he returned, he asked, "Have you any single males on your side of the family, close enough to invite without suspicion and old enough to interest Toni?"

"Why darling? Do you think she might not enjoy herself unless she has a man to lean on?"

"Partly. I'm quite concerned about her remaining alone in the hall, a spinster for the rest of her life. I'd love to see her finally hitched to the right sort of man and I'm clutching at straws, here. If there was a loose male at the wedding, there's an outside chance that she could go for him. What do you think?"

"I don't share your optimism. If Toni really wanted to marry someone, I feel sure that she could manage the process alone. However, I have a cousin, David, who is divorced and scouting around for a second wife. I could ask him along, is that all right?"

Henry humphed his acceptance. It was worth a bash, anyway.

"You won't forget to invite Christina, will you?"

"Already done, darling." she said, waving an envelope at him.

Angela continued writing the invitation cards. Henry watched her appreciatively as men in love sometimes do. Her face, in profile, reminded him of the missing portrait and he felt, strongly then, the wish that he could return the painting to her as a wedding gift. It irked him that she had been robbed in such a callous way. Robert would have done something, he wouldn't have sat here fretting about it.

* * *

Monica left it about a week before she let herself accept that Gerry was not going to reply. Every morning she had pattered down stairs to her breakfast and looked at the doormat in a hopeful way. If there was correspondence lying there, her pace and her heart would quicken but each morning she was disappointed.

She felt sad but kept finding excuses for the lapse. Perhaps he has gone away for a while and her letter still lay on the mat at his home, awaiting his return. He might even be too ill to write. Then she admitted to herself that he had just not bothered to write back. Letters are too easily ignored, she would go and see him personally and they could talk about it. She had no idea where or at what he worked and so did not know when he would most likely be at home. She eventually decided, after a little thought, that Sunday afternoon would be a good time.

Gerry came to the door on the second ring of the

bell. He didn't look pleased to see her but invited her in nonetheless. The house was a little too untidy, Monica thought, a little dirty and quite obviously in need of a woman's touch. Those curtains can't have been washed for twelve months at least.

He brought her a cup of tea and listened politely to what she had to say. He accepted her apology, he was sure that it wasn't typical behaviour and that she would never do anything like it again and then he told her that there was nothing more to discuss. No, there wasn't another woman, as yet.

'As yet!' Monica had stopped listening to him. The talent that Gerry had developed slowly was innate in Monica, a part of her feminine weaponry and used instinctively whenever someone was about to say anything she didn't want to hear. The poor man was evidently in need of a woman's strength and here he was, trying to pretend that he wasn't interested in her when she had warmth, tenderness and support to give him. Maybe, given a little time, he would change his mind.

She could feel her eyes growing hot as a prelude to tears and she mustn't let him see her cry. Weeping would gain nothing – Monica was astute enough always to use the right weapon in her emotional armoury.

"I'll go now." she said curtly and got up to leave.

Gerry said nothing, he got up and walked with her to the front door, opening it for her to go out. The idea of being so courteous as to escort her to her car didn't enter his mind. For all Gerry knew, she might have arrived in a pony and trap or a pushbike.

"Goodbye, Monica." But it was mostly said as he closed the door on her. Monica didn't hear it.

As she drove home, she felt more lonely than she had felt for a long time. It was a painful, sinking sensation that drained the strength from her and messed up her thinking. Some perverse mental imp told her that it was pity she was feeling. Pity for the poor, poor man who was crying out for the love of a good woman and yet could not see it. Perhaps she could help him to see. She needed to think of a way to open his eyes.

* * *

It was getting serious, now. Three murders so close to one another were unusual. The words 'serial killer' were being bandied around the police station. Talk in the locker room had been about nothing else. Football had faded into the background, mentioned in passing by the odd die-hard fan and ignored by everyone else. This third murder had been savage. Another brunette just battered to death and left for someone to find. An old man walking his dog, taking it out for one last opportunity to void its bowels and bladder before being shut in for the night had been the first on the scene. The man had vomited all over the pavement at the sight of her and then had a panic attack as he caught his dog licking from a pool of blood. Danny felt sympathy for the old man after he'd seen the photographs. It was a shocking, sickening sight. Whoever had done this had gone berserk – wild with temper.

"I'm not supposed to show you these, they're strictly for the investigating team." Charley said as he laid the photographs on Danny's desk.

"You've done wonders letting me get to see these shots of the crime scene," Danny said, gratefully as he leafed through the shots, "I owe you one."

A picture was gradually building of what was happening although there was doubt whether the perpetrator was the same person this third time. The other two had seemed more casual; not as violent, somehow.

This victim had been smacked more than once in the mouth with the murder weapon. Several teeth were missing, probably swallowed. Still, the 'doc would find those when he did the post-mortem. There was one big, black thread running right through all these killings. Background checks showed that each of these women was a lesbian. They had all frequented a gay bar near the railway station, The Roseate Kitty. Big clue. Now, perhaps they could get somewhere.

* * *

Darren duly appeared in front of the magistrates. It wasn't his first appearance: he had met with them twice previously; once for shop-lifting and once for vandalising a wheelie bin. The three justices, two men and a lady who all seemed incredibly old to Darren, spoke to him of the improvement which was required in his behaviour and how a young man like himself should be thinking of settling down and becoming a solid citizen and not misbehaving in such a childish manner. Darren listened dutifully but with every intention of forgetting each word. Then they awarded him thirty hours of community service. Darren grinned. This had the effect of making two of the magistrates wish that they had opted for a harsher sentence. Take a leer, a smirk, a sly grin and a grimace. Mix them together and you have what Darren did with his mouth when he attempted to smile. It was a facial contortion more fitted for the music-hall than polite society, a member of which, Darren would never count himself

* * *

Toni wrote to Gerry just before the extensive preparations began for Henry's wedding. She had asked Henry if he would consider leaving her name off the guest list but Henry explained that both he and Angela would expect her to be there. For Toni, it would mean a trip to the shops to buy an outfit which was possibly fashionable and chic enough to hold its own at an event of this nature. She certainly didn't own one. Perhaps Marisa might be of some help. All the females attending the wedding, with the exception of the bridesmaids who would wear what the bride told them to, would be engaged in competitive dressing and Toni hated to do that. And no doubt some well-meaning prodnose would see to it that there was at least one unattached male who would be set on her like a terrier to a badger. She would, unhappily, have to buy a new hat.

Still, there was time yet. She would concentrate on her budding pen-friendship with Gerry a while longer before facing the problems that would arise from attending her brother's wedding.

The correspondence between Toni and Gerry moved from tentative to voluminous. He liked the feel of these letters and, more particularly, the luxurious scent which emanated from them. No matter what became of this affair, he would always keep the pages in their respective envelopes and tied up in a rubber band so that he could re-read them and relive the joyful optimism that each brought him now.

They had exchanged photographs. Gerry had sent his best photograph to Monica and could hardly ask for it back and the negative, of course, could not be found so Toni got the second best ones which were all rubbish. He could make out little from the head and shoulders shot which Toni had sent to him. There was a vague, leafy sort of background so it had probably been taken in her back garden. Indeed, she looked dressed for gardening and, judging by her hair, had likely indulged in that activity for an hour or so before that picture was taken. No glamour queen, she. That suited Gerry, a narcissistic woman who would spend an hour in front of a mirror, scraping and painting before going out of an evening was not the partner for him. He noted that both her parents were dead and was gratified to discover that her tastes in music and literature were as catholic as his and that she had a library of both.

Wow! some of my criteria are actually being met, he thought gleefully. Then he realised how the loss of her parents wasn't for his benefit and, as though she could hear him thinking, tried to convince himself that he hadn't been really serious about everything in the advert.

Discussions on those subjects which interested them both had filled a lot of writing paper and would give them plenty to talk about when they finally met. This all sounded very promising; they had another thing in common, neither of them could cook very well. And yet, despite this burgeoning relationship, she was still having her letters directed to Cabley Post Office.

I suppose I'm still potentially a pervert until we actually meet and she would find out for herself, Gerry thought.

* * *

Toni pulled out three snapshots from Gerry's letter. All were of poor quality; either badly focussed or over exposed. One of them had been cut in half, presumably to remove a second person from the picture. Even so, it was just possible mentally to form a composite image of the subject. He seemed quite pleasant looking, almost attractive and with no obvious bits missing. The time is fast approaching, Toni thought, when we must meet. The thought of it made her feel sort of chewy inside – nervous or excited? She couldn't decide. She put the snapshots in a drawer, none of them was suitable for a bedside frame.

* * *

Monica waited. Sometimes she waited outside Gerry's flat. She spent one Friday, having taken time off work for the purpose, from eight in the morning until just after five in the evening. She saw Gerry arrive from somewhere at a quarter past eight and leave again at a quarter past five. These movements were regular and he rarely went out during the day. Monica was curious about the trips he was making at either end of the day. There wasn't reason enough to suspect that he had another woman.

In contrast to her son, Monica's means were wholly legitimate. She worked as a receptionist in the local council offices, on the front desk. This, for Monica, was an ideal job for it enabled her to talk and to get paid for it. She particularly looked forward to the arrival of regular customers with whom she could gossip. One of her favourites was old Mr. Blitterworth; he was such a good listener. The reason for this was that Mr. Blitterworth, knowing Monica of old and being quite deaf, turned off his hearing aid whenever he came in to pay his council tax and spent the time ogling Monica's breasts. This did not give Mr. Blitterworth an erection, that old thing had retired long ago but it was still an enjoyable experience for him. Entertainment, at his time of life, was to be taken wherever and whenever it occurred.

Monica's superior, the oppressive and, to her, dislikeable Mrs. Wardle, disapproved of chatter and had the unique talent of being able to stem Monica's flow with a simple glare. Currently, Mrs. Wardle was concerned by the amount of time that Monica was having off work.

One evening, she parked near Gerry's house at five. She wore a black tracksuit, red trainers and a pair of sunglasses in readiness for what she hoped might be a bit of sleuthing. Not long after, Gerry came out, walking along with his head down as though deep in thought.

Monica got out of her car, locking the door behind her and followed him. Twenty minutes of stalking her prey, sometimes dodging into alleys or deep shadow; unnecessarily as Gerry had no idea that he was being followed, and Monica saw him disappear into a newsagent's shop. She waited outside for half an hour and when it became apparent that he had not gone in there to buy an evening newspaper, she sidled up to the shop and peered in at the window. Gerry was behind the counter talking to a customer. Monica realised, with a flash of what sometimes passes for intuition, that he must work there. Without thinking, she glanced up at the board above the shop front and read: 'Fledding's Newsagency'. Monica put two and two together. He owns the shop! A great discovery. She noted the shop's telephone number and made her way back to her car. As she drove home, it occured to her that his arrivals home must have been from that shop. This was easy enough to check but where did he go during the day? That might take time. Watching Gerry interested Monica. It had awakened something within her that, hitherto, she'd been unaware of. Something of the hunter or the tracker, one of those types who tirelessly follows a target until it was run to ground.

'Get to know your prey' That was a line from something she'd read somewhere. One of those unused quotations that had accidentally stuck to the fabric of her memory like a burr to a hiker's sock. It was appropriate, though. She was getting to know Gerry better and better now that she was watching over him. It gave her a comfortable feeling which raised her spirits a good deal.

Chapter Six

THE MEETING

What need a man forestall his date of grief and run to meet what he would most avoid.
(John Milton)

Gerry was first to suggest that he and Toni should meet. He felt that they had got to know one another quite well and that they must meet face to face for the relationship to go further. He wrote and asked whether she would make the arrangements to rendezvous somewhere on neutral ground, date and time to be whatever would be convenient for her. A pub lunch, an evening meal in a restaurant, whichever suited her.

"Would you like me to come with you?" Henry asked as he watched Toni putting her enthusiastic reply to Gerry into an envelope. He felt a little concerned for his sister, almost parental.

"Why? So you can play gooseberry?", Her smile indicated that she found Henry's suggestion a little ridiculous.

"No, I wouldn't be with you, I'd seat myself at another

table and sort of keep my eye on things. That way, if needed, I could be at your elbow in seconds. You might even find my presence reassuring."

Toni laughed, "Gerry would probably spot you very quickly and ask me whether I knew the suspicious looking person spying on us from behind a newspaper. Don't be silly, Henry. Everything will be perfectly all right. But thank you for thinking of me."

Henry grunted his unhappiness, he felt entitled to watch over his sister.

"Well, take a mobile telephone with you – and some pepper spray. It's as well to be prepared for anything."

An indulgent smile met his recommendations.

Toni had complete confidence in the arrangements she had made with Gerry. She had asked him not to dress to impress, mentioning that it was to be quite informal and also open for either of them to walk away if the other was becoming a disappointment. The venue suggested was a pub in Demsbury, a country village which Gerry did not know. He decided to reconnoitre so that there was less chance of getting lost on the day and he would know what sort of place it was.

Monica spotted him coming out of the house and getting into his car.

Aha!, she thought, something is happening. Where is he off to, now? She started her car and followed him.

Demsbury, Gerry discovered, like Cabley, was an out of the way agricultural village which was rarely visited by strangers other than ramblers. There were farm complexes at either end of the lane which ran through the village, a village hall cum infants' school set back from the lane with a sort of green in front of it and from which the faint sounds of children floated in through the open car window sounding like dream chatter. Nearby was an untidy scatter of cottages, some of which were thatched. Gerry had managed to get lost just once but as there was no time constraint, he didn't panic. Concentrating on finding his way, he didn't notice the yellow Nissan Micra which would have appeared in his rear-view mirror from time to time. The Demsbury Arms stood prominently at the western end of the village, the last building of all. Gerry parked in the pub's car-park and walked inside to check it out.

There was no-one to be seen when he walked into the single, large room with its central bar. There were neither customers nor bar-staff. He looked around him in a vaguely appreciative manner. The room was elevated at one side, that part forming the dining area. The lower part was where the serious drinking was done and where bar meals were available. Stuffing his hands into his pockets, Gerry walked over to the bar, leaned on it and coughed loudly towards an open door which led into the private section behind the bar. An appetising smell wafted through the gap, indicating that some sort of food preparation was going on in the kitchen. The clip-clop of a pair of high heels announced the arrival of a member of staff and there was a profound silence as Gerry looked at the new arrival and she, in turn, looked at him. Recognition, on both sides, was instant, it was surprise which caused delay.

"Carol!" Gerry said.

"What on earth are you doing here?" she asked him.

Monica had parked in front of the village hall and hurried to the pub to see what Gerry was up to. She attempted to walk up to it in a casual manner, as though she might be a customer but merely succeeded in looking very suspicious. Fortunately, no-one happened to see her. A stealthy glance through the window showed just two people inside, one of which was a woman who, thankfully, was behind the bar. She watched for ten minutes while Gerry chatted to the woman behind the bar. He didn't appear to be expecting anyone so, feeling reassured, she made her way back to the car to wait for Gerry to come out.

Strangely, Gerry felt no recognisable emotion surfacing as he looked at Carol; it was as though she was a casual acquaintance rather than an ex-lover. This lack of feeling boosted his confidence and removed any impulse he may have had not to be truthful with her.

"I'm just checking this place out; I'm to meet a woman here tomorrow for lunch – a date, sort of – and you know my talent for getting lost in strange places. I thought I'd better familiarise myself with the route so that tomorrow there's less chance of arriving late because of a missed turning."

Carol remembered Gerry's inability to find his way around. He had the directional capabilities of a mouse in a cocoa tin. At least, until he'd learned where to go. She felt no jealousy on learning Gerry's news, he had long been replaced in her affections by Sammy Fox, a divorced horse vetinarian who held her in high esteem, exactly where she liked to be.

"So, who is it? Do I know her?" she asked with genuine interest.

"Her name's Toni, with an i, Toni Pym, that's all I know. I don't even know where she lives yet. All my letters go to Cabley Post Office. Er, can I have a bitter shandy and a meat pie, please. I might as well behave like a real customer."

"Well, you may rely on me to be the soul of discretion. I won't let on that you and I have a history. I shall behave like the perfect stranger."

As Carol poured his drink he asked, "Is it always this empty in here? I thought there might at least be one or two people in having lunch."

"You picked a bad day, almost everyone local has gone to the farmers' market at Steadmore. We'll be back to normal tomorrow."

Gerry continued to chat to Carol while he drank his

shandy, discovering in the process about Sammy the vet., Carol's new partner, and how she came to be working behind the bar of the Demsbury Arms. Gerry was pleasantly surprised at how well he and Carol were getting on together now that they were no longer lovers. She seemed genuinely nice and almost sisterly. Later, he took his leave, made his way back to the car and, after a minute or two spent trying to remember which way he had entered the village, set off for home. As he left, he noticed the yellow Nissan parked by the village hall, it made the village seem not quite so deserted. He failed to recognise the driver.

* * *

A realisation that the arranged meeting was not only very close but had the potential to change her life a great deal hit Toni quite suddenly. It produced within her a palpable feeling of insecurity very much similar to that sensation you get when the bicycle beneath you starts to wobble. She grew contemplative. There were no regrets for having begun this affair with Gerry but there were unidentifiable nagging doubts which tended to damp the enthusiasm she should feel for what was to come. One of these doubts, she knew, was engendered by her station in life. She had made no mention of it in her letters to Gerry in case it should either put him off or, worse, encourage him for the wrong reasons. She would tell him when it became necessary, when he had come to know her better. First, they must meet as equals and, if there was reason to continue and build on the relationship, then it would have to come out. So: she must begin with that all-important first impression. How to dress? Whatever she chose, it must not appear expensive, showy or give any indication of her class. She was reminded of the fairy tale, 'The Prince and the Pauper' and how the prince dressed like a peasant in order to woo the girl he'd met one day while out hunting. There were parallels with her case but much of the detail of the fairy-story had been clouded by time so that she could not remember whether it had a happy ending or not. Probably did, she reflected, most fairy-tales do. The problem was, this particular one missed the point of the class thing. No doubt the peasant girl was really a princess captured in infancy by the gypsies and sold to the old forester in exchange for a bundle of firewood or something. That discovery would have made it all right for them to marry. No class boundaries breached there. Can't have royal blood mingling with that of the peasantry, wouldn't do at all. Bloody snobs. What shall I wear? Wonder if the old woodcutter was invited to wedding?

Outside her room, there was the sound of a vacuum cleaner being switched on and this gave Toni an idea. Marisa will be able to help me choose something. Marisa was Toni's daily help, a married girl in her mid-thirties who had a young son. She lived in Cabley and came in to help around the house whenever the boy was in school. Marisa was as much a friend as an employee and Toni valued her opinions. She looked out of the room and called Marisa in.

"I'd like you to help me, Marisa, if you would. I have a lunch date tomorrow with a gentleman who I haven't met yet."

Marisa's hand flew to her mouth to hide the smile which was rapidly growing into a grin. Then she dropped the pretence and admitted through her glee, "Sorry, I'm just a little surprised, that's all. Who is it?"

Toni wasn't offended by Marisa's amusement, she knew it was a friendly reaction to her news.

"His name isn't important. It is extremely important that I do not yet reveal my background. He doesn't know my title or even where I live and will not find out unless we become closer friends. So I must not wear anything which might give the game away and I need you to help me choose, if you would."

Marisa, after a little consideration, pulled out a pair of black slacks, a beige blouse and a brown two-button jacket and arranged them on the bed so that Toni could see the effect.

"But those slacks are ancient!" Toni protested.

"It's a good idea to mix old and new." Marisa explained, "If you wear all new, it looks as though you're trying too hard and all old as though you don't care."

Toni nodded slowly as she saw Marisa's point. It was a sound choice.

Gerry had no doubts about what to wear. He was going to dress to impress but without actually having to shop for anything new. Buying new clothes would be taking things too far. No woman, no matter how seemingly attractive, is worth going shopping for. Shopping was something that was done only when absolutely necessary. Such as for food.

Gerry's choice was a black, badgeless blazer which had been worn only once before, for the wedding of Carol's younger sister. This over blue corduroy trousers and a pale green shirt. No tie. No chance. Ties are too formal. He discovered that he didn't even feel very nervous about the meeting. He had adopted a philosophical approach, viewing the event as research and with one of two outcomes, each a winner in its own field. If Toni and he didn't get on, there would be a deal of material to use for his writing. Even if it all turned out a howling success and Toni fell for him in a big way, there would be material to use. He had decided not to take his notebook feeling that perhaps his date might not appreciate his scribbling away while she talked to him. She might get the impression that he wasn't paying her enough attention. So he must be attentive and retentive. Then he could go home and spend the rest of the evening writing his impressions of a wonderful or of a disastrous date with a strange woman.

Having found the 'Demsbury Arms' once, the second time was almost as easy and Gerry only lost his way once; this time in a different lane from the one he'd been lost in on his first visit. He had, however, allowed a little time for just that contingency and panic never got a chance to crumble his reserve. He remained confident of reaching his destination on time. He parked his car, at first unsure of his next step but went into the pub thinking that either Toni would be already here and inside or she would arrive to find him there. None of the cars in the car park gave him any clues that they might belong to a lady of her description. Assuming the lowish profile of the casual customer, Gerry wandered in, hands in pockets, his manner meandering between saunter and swagger and pulled up by the bar. Customers were scattered thinly about, one or two in the dining area and a small clump near the bar, swapping jokes and evidently at home in their surroundings. Looking to Carol whose familiar face was somehow reassuring, he beckoned her over. There was a mental flashback to a half-remembered film where the detective approaches the busty blonde working the bar, pulls a photograph out of his pocket as he slides onto a stool – at the same time picking up a glass of whisky which he hadn't been heard to order – and says, 'Have you seen this guy?' as Gerry showed Carol his photograph of Toni.

"This is my date for today, have you seen her?"

Carol took the snap, looked at it closely and shook her head. As she looked up to say no, the woman in the picture walked through the door. "She's here now." said Carol, handing the photograph back to Gerry. He turned quickly towards the door, staring.

Toni paused at the door and walked towards the bar.

"Toni?" asked Gerry.

"Yes. How are you Gerry? Can we sit down?"

"Sure.– Er, what would you like to drink?"

"Orange juice, please. I'm really pleased to meet you at last."

She held out her hand for Gerry to shake and he was struck by the firmness of her grip and how pleasant her hand felt. Too many women failed to return any grip in a hand shake and with the damp feel which their hands often have, it is often a little like holding a warm fish. Toni clasped his hand in friendship and Gerry felt inclined to contain her hand; to linger with the grasp and appreciate its warmth. Manners prevailed and he reluctantly let go, indicating an empty table. He was strangely impressed by how her eyes seemed to throw the sky at him. He was excited by the possibility of a future with her.

When they were seated, Carol removed herself from behind the bar and brought two menu cards and with a sincerity for which Gerry was unprepared, announced herself at their service.

Gerry relaxed, Toni tensed. Her natural defences were raised; she must not be inveigled by a smooth talking ladies' man – she must be wary of all but the peasant of princely birth.

"So what do you fancy?" As soon as the line was out, Gerry regretted it; a cliché, a double entendre and plain unimaginitive. He attempted to divert the scorn which his remark deserved by ordering the vegetarian lasagne. Toni donned reading glasses to read the menu. It was at this point that Gerry was smitten. She was one of those women whose features are enhanced by spectacles and Gerry was quite thrilled by the effect it had. It was also evident that make-up was minimal or absent, another point in her favour. There was a brown velvet ribbon which was used to tie her hair back. His attention made Toni glance at him, as though to reassure herself that his gaze was friendly and Gerry saw a carpet of bluebells looking back. Suddenly, he knew that she was the woman for him, that he had to make this thing work. Now he felt under pressure to impress. He was happy with what he had but would she be happy with him after tonight?

Having chosen salad, Toni placed her elbows on the table and rested her chin on her clasped hands. She looked at Gerry with a smile, a warm, friendly one which dissipated the apprehension which Gerry could feel building up inside him.

"It's a little nerve-wracking, this initial contact, isn't it?" she said, trying to put both him and herself more at ease.

Gerry noticed her refined accent. To him, this spoke of education and intelligence; two important factors in a woman where he was concerned. She seemed to be wearing a perfume which gave off a faint, barely detectable smell of violets. He breathed in heavily, savouring the air around her.

"Yes." he replied, "You're right. Maybe it will get easier from now on."

"How's the writing coming along? Can I read about me yet?"

"It's not coming on very well. There have been distractions." Gerry answered with a meaningful grin directed at Toni but with a mental image of Monica. A bloodier image, undoubtedly created by his recent writing, that of Monica spitting blood and teeth after a hefty blow, made its way into the forefront of his mind. He tried to push it down but fragments of it kept resurfacing.

"Well, what made you want to write? How does one go about it?"

Gerry siezed on this question to make Monica go away. "It was a gradual thing with me; almost an extension of my reading. There came a slow realisation that I, too, could produce a book. I've found that, in order to write a novel, I first need a plot. No, don't smile – not all writers start with that much. Sometimes a book will be written from nothing more concrete than just an idea. I need a solid outline of the whole book. Characters fall into place as and when they are needed for the purposes of the plot and I pick my characters out of everyday life. I suppose the innate talent, the thing that not everyone has, is the ability to describe a thing in words. I can't draw or paint for the life of me but I can write a picture. When I was in my youth, I wanted to be able to speak the way that characters in books and films do. I know, now, that it's not possible, they say whatever the writers want them to say and in reality, conversations are ad hoc – bitty. Ideas tumbling in, jostling, forming a disorderly queue. Really, the only way I can speak elegantly, smoothly is to let my characters do it for me."

" I think that you speak quite well when you talk to me, some of it must have rubbed off. How would you describe me, then?"

"I won't do that. I couldn't describe you true to life because I don't know you well enough but I will send you a written portrait when I feel qualified to. What I would do if I was here on my own is to look around for likely subjects. I would have brought my notepad and pen to jot things down. See the man over to your right? Dark suit and dark blue shirt."

Toni glanced quickly to the table indicated by Gerry.

"He's with his partner." Gerry went on, "And he's not paying her much attention; he's distracted in some way so I would make guesses to explain this behaviour. He's married to the woman he's with – if it was a date or someone else's wife, for instance, he'd be far more attentive – and he's in middle management and he has work related worries. Hence his distraction. From something just as mundane as that, you can build up a plot and it could make a whodunnit. And I'm hogging the conversation when I promised myself that I wouldn't. Your turn; there's one question you have avoided answering in your letters – what do you do for a living?"

Toni coloured a little and Gerry noticed her discomfort.

"I don't. I've never worked. I have – independent means." she admitted.

"How on earth do you fill your day?" asked Gerry who could not imagine living his life as one long holiday.

"I have a great deal to do with running a house and caring for my horses and dogs. And I love riding so I'm never at a loss for anything to occupy my mind. Do you like horses?"

Gerry winced mentally at a painful memory.

"I have to admit to a fear of horses. Not a phobia; I'm just very wary if in accidental proximity to one. A creature of that size and weight which can shy at the sight of a crisp packet does nothing to allay that fear. Not only that but I have a childhood memory of being put on horseback. It seemed gigantic to me and my abiding impression is one of pain. I felt as though I was being split up the middle."

"Poor you. That was misguided of someone. A full grown horse is far too broad across the back for a small child. Perhaps there might be an opportunity of meeting my horses and I could help you to overcome your fear."

This sounded encouraging to Gerry. Now, there didn't seem much likelihood of her walking out halfway through this date and, since he felt quite drawn to her, he didn't want her to.

"So who looks after you?" Toni asked in an abrupt change of subject.

"I do." said Gerry a little indignantly, "I'm pretty much capable around the house. I'm by no means outstanding at anything, particularly cookery but I manage."

She smiled, "My cookery has been described as 'well-meaning'. I think that you can gather from that that we are probably at the same level in culinary skills."

Gerry laughed in a polite and restrained way and inwardly congratulated himself on how well things were going.

There was a short silence during which both of them paid a little attention to the food which they were eating and each made a private promise not to mention the food as a subject of conversation. For Toni it would have been untimely and for Gerry it would have been scraping the barrel of small-talk with only a discussion of the weather remaining, stuck grimly to one side.

Toni broke the short silence, "What is your ideal where a woman is concerned? What would be the sort of woman who would normally appeal to you? And – please – no references to me – I'm not fishing for compliments and I do detest flattery. This is a genuine question."

Gerry checked himself because, already, his half-prepared answer included barely hidden flannel and her face showed that she meant it when she said that she would not tolerate it.

"I don't like prissy, pretty women who spend time and money trying to improve on their appearance when it would be more productively spent improving intellect and personality. So, now," said Gerry, waxing mathematical, "if we describe the set of women who do appeal, I think I'd find you in there somewhere."

"I said no compliments." she said rather ineffectually.

Gerry's brow did an impression of an apologetic look and he ignored her comment.

"What about family? Are there lots of you?" Toni asked. Subject changes, she saw, were almost unavoidable.

"No brothers, no sisters, a couple of aunts and uncles with whom I exchange Christmas cards and precious little else. And I'm an orphan."

Toni looked straight into his eyes, a little shocked at this last piece of news.

"Poor you. Where were you brought up? In one of those homes, then?"

"What homes?" asked Gerry, baffled.

"An orphanage."

Gerry smiled. "I only meant that both my parents are dead. They survived long enough to see me into adulthood. I didn't mean to mislead you. Or perhaps I did. What about your parents?"

Toni looked down at her plate to oversee the loading of her fork as she said, "Recently deceased."

It is thought that putting the hand in front of the mouth when shocked by something that someone has said or done is to prevent one saying anything inappropriate at a bad time. It is really to cover the fact that you have temporarily lost control of your lower jaw and you wish to deny the other party the opportunity to count your fillings. This was a gesture of politeness that Gerry was not familiar with and so both his hands gripped the table cloth while he gaped.

"Oh — I'm sorry — the advert — I never meant to — It was actually meant to be a joke. – It wasn't – I am sorry. How?"

Toni could not help smiling a little at Gerry's discomfiture even though she had not fully come to terms with her parents' accident.

"They were on holiday on Bermuda. They were both as fit as fiddles and tended to have active days rather than lazing around on the beach. Daddy was snorkelling and apparently got into some sort of difficulty, the authorities weren't absolutely sure of what the initial cause was. Mummy was swimming nearby and keeping half an eye on Daddy when she realised that something had gone wrong. She had no flippers or goggles with her but she attempted to save Daddy and couldn't. They both drowned." Toni's eyes had that shine which indicates nearby tears and this was not lost on Gerry.

"Oh, bloody hell! What a horrible thing to happen. When was this?"

"Just last Spring. I'm sorry if it's put a bit of a damper on the small-talk. You weren't to know."

"Yes, I couldn't have known, it just makes my advert seem very silly, now. Why on earth did you bother to answer it?"

"Because you sounded interesting. And nothing has happened to make me want to revise that. Put it down to coincidence, O.K.?"

By this time, Toni had decided that Gerry was at least tolerable. She was slowly beginning to appreciate him and, so far, there seemed to be no reason to dislike him. The meal had disappeared, a barely noticed prop on this particular stage, and had been replaced by coffee. The conversation washed back and forth with Gerry constantly aware of just how easy it was to hog it all and throwing questions back at Toni just as soon as he could. It was a wonderful contrast to the experience with Monica. The time had passed very pleasurably for both of them and just two short hours after that first meeting, Toni stood up.

" I must go, I have really enjoyed my time with you today and I promise that shall be in touch. Here's my telephone number." she said, handing Gerry a slip of paper, "May I have yours? I should like to see you again."

Gerry was at a loss for words. He patted his pockets for the notepaper and pen that normally he carried with him but had deliberately left at home. Toni handed him a slim, warm, gold-plated pen and a small address book open at a blank page. He scribbled down his home number, thought about adding the shop's number, changed his mind and handed it back reverently. He was so flustered with pleasure that he almost forgot his manners.

"I'll see you to your car." he said.

"No, it's fine, really. I'll ring. Bye."

She'd gone. Then it dawned on Gerry that she hadn't offered to pick up any part of the bill. Not that he would have wanted her to but modern women often insisted on paying their fair share. He went over to the bar to settle up.

"Wow! She's posh." said Carol as she made up Gerry's receipt, "Where did you get that from?"

"It's a long story. Still, she was nice, wasn't she?"

"Yes, she was – so tell me all about it."

Gerry told Carol about the ad and why he'd put it in. He mentioned the disaster with Monica which, for some reason, Carol found funny and finished with what he knew of his latest date.

"Well, I wish you luck with this one, she looks quite a catch."

"Thanks." Gerry said and turned to go home.

He drove home in a slightly dreamy state and wouldn't have noticed the yellow Nissan even if it had been there. This day, Mrs. Wardle had refused Monica leave to go to yet another family funeral. She felt that, if Monica wasn't lying, the family members were being exceptionally careless.

* * *

"Hey, Charley!" Danny was paying Charley a visit to his office. He wanted the latest information on the murders.

"Yo, Danny – they've got a suspect for these killings. A woman, would you believe? Here." Charley passed a photograph to Danny. It showed a blonde, tousle-haired woman, plainly dressed, probably aged thirty-five or so. She was quite attractive. Danny could fall for a woman like that. Dead easy. He handed the photograph back.

"She looks nice — you wouldn't think a woman like this could kill, would you?"

"You never know with women." Charley pointed out, "Butter wouldn't melt in their mouths because they're cold-hearted bitches, some of 'em."

"Have you got a file on her?"

"No, there's not much on her yet, we're holding her for as long as we can for questioning but then she's free to walk. She's only a suspect and we've got very little to go on. She lives in that old house up by the park."

"Yes, I know the one. So, what's the connection here?"

"She's gay like the others. The boss thinks there's some sort of sexual motive but I can't see it myself. Nothing's clear yet."

* * *

Gerry felt good about life. In this mood, writing was a joy and the words were coming easily but he stopped and saved the chapter he'd been working on, switched off the computer and reached for his journal. He always wrote in this with a fountain pen. It felt suitable for what felt like an old-fashioned habit, that of keeping a journal, even if this one was full of random entries and not kept like a diary. He just wrote what he felt he should, dated it if he could remember to and put it away on a shelf until the next time. It was to be read by posterity although just who that might be could not be imagined. An unknown grandchild was difficult to visualise, especially as there were no children to produce another generation. He could also see the day when he, old and withered and sitting in some home for the elderly, could read the thoughts of his younger self. Tonight he must tell his older self about his first date with Toni:

'After a disastrous date with Monica the mobile mouth (ooh! Alliteration!), it was a refreshing change to see a little culture waft into my life. She's not a striking looking woman, a lot of men wouldn't give her a second glance – myself included under different circumstances.'

Here he stopped with the weird idea that Toni herself could read what he had written if something should come of their meeting.

What if she and I got married and she moves in with me and, dusting the house through, she finds this and reads what I've just written about her? He hated to cross out what he had written, it would look untidy and ripping the page out to rewrite it wouldn't do. And it would be impossible to rewrite the whole damned journal. He would just have to find a good place to hide it.

'Meeting with Toni (Antonia) allowed me a peek under her skin and I really like her. And she likes me enough to agree to a second date! Maybe I'm on to something here.'

His future self, of course, would know how it all turned out.

Chapter Seven

ROBBIE THE BURGLAR

The dupe of folly or the slave of crime.
(Wordsworth)

Port Regis had once been a thriving city port on the west coast of Britain and stood facing America; or it would have done had Ireland not been in the way.

The once small fishing village had built a fortune on the export of slaves and emigrants and the import of raw sugar and bananas and, as a consequence, had grown grand and populous.

Now, its heyday over, the docks were largely idle, its grey cranes standing immobile and unwanted like ornamental herons, watching for the occasional cruise-liner – perhaps carrying descendants of those slaves and emigrants of long ago– and standing silent guard over the leisure marinas and the seamen's museum.

Behind and parallel to what remained of a forbidding dock wall ran a road called, naturally enough, Dock Road. The road was in a poor state of repair and litter drifted into the pot-holes and large stretches of the original duck-stone surface were laid bare. Along its length and facing the dock from the other side of the road were the few public houses which had survived the dearth of custom since the docks' demise and which now relied on local trade and the odd, curious visitor. They stood, sparsely spaced in wasteland flecked with litter, vulnerable, like the skittles that survived the first ball.

On Sunday mornings, a market would appear alongside the road, almost hiding the pubs from view. It was advertised as a car-boot sale which, inasmuch as the goods on sale arrived in the boots of cars, was an accurate description. Not that the registered owner of one or two of the cars was aware of the contents of his car boot – or even of the whereabouts of his car. Sometimes these misplaced vehicles were sold too, along with its contents. A browser in the market might hear this snippet of conversation;

"How much for the banger and everything in it?"

"Two grand."

"Bit much, fifteen."

"Eighteen."

"Deal."

Cash and ownership of the vehicle with its contents would change places and the browser would discover the stall to be under new management; the ex-stallholder having called a taxi and gone home, his work done for the day.

It was rumoured that, if you had been burgled on a Saturday night, it was possible to go to the Dock Road market on the following morning and buy your stuff back again, provided you were quick. The alternative, of course, having failed to find your property, was to buy someone else's at a knock-down price. This was not strictly illegal since it was only ugly rumour which insisted that the goods on sale that morning had been in the homes of their rightful owners as recently as the previous night. Thus was the Sunday market created and fuelled. Those on one side of the stalls created a demand and also supplied the wherewithal to satisfy that demand. The punters bought the stuff and took it home in a sort of renewal of the cycle.

Working on the supply side of this rather dark economy was a young lad known to his colleagues as 'Robbie the Burglar'. Partly because his real name was Robbie Benson and partly because burglary was his chosen trade.The two principle activities which occupied Robbie and provided his income were: good, old-fashioned burglary and stealing cars from stupid people. Winter mornings were easiest for finding unattended vehicles with a handy set of keys inside; their owners parked by the newsagent on their way to work and would leave their engines running to keep the heater going while they nipped in for a paper. Or a car might be found in front of a house coughing smoky fumes into the cold morning air and slowly warming while the owner breakfasted. A warm car is a lost car. In summer, in rural places, there was often the adult paper-boy who was just too careless to switch off his engine or a delivery van whose driver had grown complacent. There will always be sufficient stupid people to provide opportunities to make a thief's life easy.

Robbie's upbringing was very much middle class and by no means deprived. His parents lived in a large, three-storied town house in Brundon, an area south of Port Regis which was so thickly spread with trees as to be considered rural by townies. Robbie's mother and father had wanted him properly educated with a view to a degree from the university and a job of which they could boast. This sort of ambition while, no doubt, admirable, requires a certain amount of co-operation from the child and Robbie didn't give it. He rebelled, at first, in little ways; grumpy, secluded adolescence, smoking against advice, mixing with the wrong people until eventually he became alienated from his parents and drifted into crime. The influence for this choice of career came from a best friend, one of the wrong people, a certain Ronald Swyres. If you had known him from his deplorable childhood, it would have been a safe bet to have predicted that Ronald would go astray. Untrustworthy, shiftless and surly; these characteristics were reflected in the face and manner of Ronald who, disliking his given name, encouraged everyone to call him 'Wiry', a corruption of his surname. Every one, even the warders in his present place of involuntary abode called him Wiry. Robbie and Wiry had been parted as friends owing to Wiry having earned several years incarceration for armed robbery. Robbie disapproved of that sort of thing, it didn't seem fair play, somehow, waving a shotgun under someone's nose in order to get your own way. No, there are rules to observe, even in thieving.

For the purposes of burglary, Robbie, for preference, would select a rural area close to a motorway junction; the sort of place that comes under 'Location, location, location.' and is chosen by business types who like a house in the country with easy access to the city for work or for pleasure.

For transport, Robbie used a stately Transit van. The legend painted on the sides of the van proclaimed it to belong to a fictitious firm of builders. If you rang the telephone number printed underneath the company name, you would be informed by a recorded message that the number was no longer available. However, a builder's van raises no suspicions as it cruises country lanes, there was no way to know that its driver was looking for a target rather than a customer.

The van was cheap to run as it had been declared as kept off road which indeed it was when it wasn't in use. The tax-disc was a facsimile of a genuine disc which had been scanned into a computer, digitally altered and printed out. It would have taken a particularly vigilant policeman to spot that the disc wasn't real. Careful driving and attention to road-worthiness ensured that being pulled over remained unlikely.

What was thrown into the back after a night's raid was later fenced through someone Robbie knew back in the city.

Robbie was a friendly looking young man, not the sort of person you would guess to be a burglar if, say, there was occasion for you to speculate on his calling although, to be fair, you might hazard unemployed. His brown hair was cut short because a rapidly receding hair-line did not go with hair of any great length in Robbie's opinion. He favoured blue denim as a general rule with a shiny pair of brown Doc Martin boots, almost the old 'bovver-boy' uniform. The shine on his boots was a deep glow; that part was important, Robbie liked to look down and admire the shine as he walked.

He lived in a cramped and rather untidy flat near to the dock area which he shared with a girlfriend, Annie. A quiet tour of the premises would have revealed to an inquisitive stranger that one of the occupants was a great reader. In each of the living room and the bedroom was a small bookcase packed with paperbacks. Robbie was the reader, Annie claimed not to have the patience. Robbie kept quiet about his reading habits in case his reputation suffered for, in the bookcases were volumes by Dickens, Hardy, Eliot, Conrad and others, some of whom were poets. Annie liked Robbie to read some of the shorter, more romantic poems to her while they lay in bed but could not be persuaded to discover literature for herself.

Annie was aware of what Robbie did for a living but had slender hopes of one day making an honest man of him. She was a dark-haired, plumpish girl with the residue of a Welsh accent lurking within her speech and was dissatisfied with the amount of money coming into the flat.

She worked regular hours in a petrol filling station and had home-making ambitions which not only exceeded their combined income but might have caused Robbie to worry a little and perhaps view their shared future in a less kindly light. Currently, he was merely aware that Annie moaned a lot about money and that she might feel happier if he was making a great deal more than he did. Also, furniture and curtains never seemed to last very long before being replaced. This need to increase his wages without actually getting a job was at the back of his mind as he walked towards the market.

It was a Sunday with the market in full swing and Robbie was feeling somewhat resentful with the difference between what he earned from his fence on an item he'd stolen and what was asked for that same item on the market. He had stood beside a short, irritable man who was buying a D.V.D. recorder and had watched as he paid for the item. Then, the man had backed away from the stall, clutching his purchase and, spotting Robbie, had said, "This was in our 'ouse bloody Friday and some bastard nicked it. Now look, I'm 'avin' to buy it back! Cheaper than a new one, I suppose and it were never insured."

He tucked it under his arm and strode off.

That bastard could have been me, thought Robbie, an idea forming in his mind.

He wandered idly down the road, eyeing the items for sale and enjoying the banter between buyer and seller and presently encountered the man who bought from him those items which Robbie stole. Chevis Yardley, widely known as 'Miss' for obvious reasons, was walking in the opposite direction to Robbie but his was a proprietorial air. His camel-hair coat was unusual enough in this area to mark him as a man to be respected. He eschewed confidence and a small, half-chewed cigar protruded from a small, half-chewed face. It was the face of an impassioned

Pekinese. Chevis had started to lose his hair, too. Instead of the customary pattern of male baldness; a two pronged retreat from crown and brow, Chevis' loss was exclusively from the front giving a high forehead which, in Chevis' case, had reached a third of the way across the top of his skull while the remainder of his hair remained obstinately luxuriant. Since he favoured a thick, even style, the result was that from the side his hair looked like a toupee forced backwards by a strong headwind. Whatever your private opinions were of Chevis' personal appearance, it was best not to air them. Chevis demanded respect.

"Morning, Chev." said Robbie. He would never use the nick-name to his face, he hadn't the status. He would never climb high enough up the ladder to look down on Chev, the only position from which to call him 'Miss'.

Chevis looked Robbie over and smiled. "Anything for me, Robbie?" he asked.

"No, not yet, later in the week for definite. Can I ask a question, I'm just a bit curious?"

"As long as it's not a request for money, go ahead."

"If I flog you a video for a tenner, how come you can charge fifty on the stall? That's a big mark-up. It doesn't seem a fair share for me and I do all the heavy work."

"Overheads. It's the way the market works. Put a bit more time in, work hard and maybe one day you'll have the soft options, the lion's share of the loot and a posh car to go with it.", explained Chevis helpfully.

"Right.That's how it works, is it?" said Robbie in a disgruntled, off-hand way. Then, after a pause in which there seemed to be another query brewing, "See you soon, Chev."

"Yeah." said Chevis, waving his cigar at him.

Robbie continued his walk deep in thought.

What he'd heard about the handling fee was enough to unsettle him and make him unhappy with the arrangement. The mark up for more expensive items like jewellery must be even higher. The trouble was, he couldn't set up shop for himself; the whole system was so closely monitored by those it most benefitted that a newcomer could not blunder in, take a share of the proceeds and advantage of the carefully designed security system. This latter completely dispensed with the services of the police and worked rather like a Trades Union or a Guild. Disputes were settled, families of men unfortunate enough to fall foul of the law were given financial help and it was also a means of contacting specialised help should one require it. If Robbie were to strike out on his own; become an independent dealer as it were, he would need to operate far away from the market and not tread on anyone's toes. He knew how dangerous it was to upset the market traders.

Shit and destruction, if I can find another way I could get Annie off my back, Robbie thought as he pushed open the door of the 'Baltimore Oriole' and into the thick, noisy atmosphere of the dock-side pub. She'll maybe stop mithering me for more money, then.

Robbie was to meet Wilf Hevard in the pub, an old friend and accomplice and they were to discuss future plans.

Wilf was perpetually unemployed but busy at this and that. This was his chosen occupation. He liked to think of himself as an entrepreneur and he had few enough misgivings to make himself moderately successful in the low-lit world in which he lived. He had worked for a short but ultimately profitable time for a firm which specialised in the fitting and maintenance of domestic security systems. Wilf had shown a surprising talent for the job and had learned not only how to fit such systems but also how they might be circumvented. Nowadays, he felt it incumbent upon himself, for purely professional reasons, to keep this knowledge up to date. Such was his skill that, bearing in mind his lack of intellectual prowess, he might have been considered almost an idiot savant, were that phrase in common currency in the circles in which Wilf moved.

Wilf's father and mother had been a housebreaker and a shoplifter repectively. So Wilf grew up where crime was the norm and it was natural that he would drift into some illicit occupation when he attained adulthood. To Wilf, there was no right or wrong about thieving, it was what some people did for a living. Some drive buses, some work in offices and others steal stuff.

Wilf's mother had died in prison – a heart attack, they said – but neither Wilf nor his father held any grudge. Prison was part of the game; you only went if you got caught. Wilf occasionally visited his mother during her last incarceration. It was always a strange, unconventional experience – not because of what she was or why she was there – it was the place, the smell, the noise and all those bloody women, few of whom you could ever turn your back on. Wilf felt very intimidated. He vowed never to go to prison on the strength of these feelings he had but still, it's never a choice, it's what happens. Wilf had been quite lucky so far.

Wilf's dad ended up going straight although not through choice. A lifetime's addiction to full-strength tobacco had left him suffering from emphysema and living in a nursing home. His own final place of confinement. He was now, in his own hoarse wheeze, 'too knackered to nick 'owt.' Father and son rarely saw each other now; too busy was Wilf's permanent excuse but the real reason was because he could not bear to watch his father deteriorate into a shrivelled cough.

Wilf was married to Beryl, a plain looking, heavy-set woman who was aware that her husband was jobless – he was still drawing benefit – but the extra money which Wilf brought in from wherever he went to do whatever it was he did came in handy and she, like Monica Prough, was not one to question its provenance.

Wilf loved Beryl in that off-hand, uncommitted way that some men adopt. He always brought her tea in bed in the morning and they spent that quality time together sharing gossip from their separate worlds, hers about the customers of the pet shop where she worked and, with a more vicious note, about the neighbours she had fallen out with. Wilf's contribution was sparser and tended to cover those parts of his day which were legitimate.

Wilf also liked to think of himself as a musician although few genuine musicians would agree. He was a member of a band called 'Borborygmus', a name which Robbie had supplied at a time when the group was casting about for an identity and whose meaning appealed to all the band members. The group played music of the 'Death Metal' genre and Wilf was the growler. His role, similar to the chanteur or crooner, was to stand in front of the microphone and deliver the lyrics in the stylised way of the day. It was a throaty growl in which all comprehensibilty was lost.

Practice for the group was irregular (although anyone not a fan of this music might have said unnecessary) and wherever a tolerant venue could be found. Gigs were few and far between and therefore not a reliable source of income for Wilf. He did it because he loved it. It had a sort of glamour and a nebulous promise of greater things in the future. Practice was also rather informal for it never seemed to matter if one member or another of the group was missing, his place could be filled temporarily or just left vacant. Wilf's voice was naturally deep with a geological timbre, one of the reasons why he had been chosen to front the group. This mode of singing conferred many advantages over more traditional methods. Lyrics, such as they were, were easy to learn and occasional fluffs went unnoticed - - one might as well quibble over the words of a skat song. The disadvantage was the sore throat which could come quite quickly. Wilf found a wonderful restorative in Stout but this had added quite considerably to his waistline.

The group were on the books of Harvey Bredgold, a booking agent based in Port Regis although not many gigs were forthcoming from that direction. It seemed that the public at large had yet to come round to appreciating the music of 'Borborygmus'.

To be fair, Harvey had made some effort to promote the group. They had made a C.D. of their songs in a hired studio and one hundred copies of 'I Want to Eat Your Dog', decorated with some bilious artwork were available for sale. Twenty three had been sold so far. More successful were the 'T' shirts; black with the word 'BORBORYGMUS' written across the front in a strange, gothic, red script. They sold these at gigs and had shifted fifty of them.

During the day, Wilf had people to see. It was essential that he kept abreast of happenings on the street. That way, he could put himself up for the odd, lucrative job that might need a driver or an extra pair of eyes.

He took his lunch in 'The Baltimore Oriole'. People there knew who he was.

Robbie spotted Wilf's dirty blonde thatch and gleaming chrome earrings easily but went to the bar first to buy himself a pint of lager. Then he sat down at Wilf's table. Wilf was occupied with his mobile phone, something he did whenever he found himself alone for a few minutes. He was either sending text messages to Beryl or altering the profile of the machine just because the option was available. Right now he was listening to a selection of ring tones and barely acknowledged Robbie's arrival.

"Put that down, Wilf, you know that it winds me up."

Wilf looked up. "Hey up! You look a bit distracted, mate." Wilf said as he pushed the phone back into his pocket. His small, squirrely mouth hid between fat cheeks and had small, thin lips which would appear and disappear as he spoke, as if looking for a place to hide. His teeth were invisible; it was impossible to discern whether they were missing or not as his smiles were all tight-lipped. Even when he mispronounced the 'th' syllable as 'f'; rather than the top teeth appearing over the bottom lip, the latter would just vanish into his mouth.

"Yes, I am." Robbie explained, "I was looking at what the punter pays to buy back the gear we nick and how much I get for passing it to the market. It's a big difference. I'm trying to think of a way to cut out that side of things – you know – and get the money straight from the punter. That way we'd get more and work less."

"Can't do that, if you cut out them bastards like 'Miss' Chevis, you're going to wake up one morning with 'Heavy George' bouncing up and down on your skull."

Robbie winced at the image. Heavy George was both immense and belligerent. He was the muscle on the market and remarkably effective in maintaining order within the market by his presence only. Argumentative types had only to spy Heavy George as a puff of smoke on the horizon to become perfectly agreeable types. George favoured one weapon and that was his weight. He could throw it around with both agility and accuracy. There was a back-up baseball bat said to be buried deep in the folds of the grey herringbone overcoat which he normally wore but this was conjecture. George never seemed to need it. There were people who could claim to prefer being hit with a baseball bat than to be interviewed by George.

George had had, for most of his life, a pugilistic background. When George was just ten, his parents moved from mid-Wales into the Port Regis area and, at his new school, George was picked on for having a strange accent. The school bully, an unlikeable twelve-year old called Douglas, took particular delight in taking George by surprise and beating him to the ground. George's father explained to his tearful son just what he must do to stop the bully in his tracks. True to dad's prediction, Douglas fell harder than he had expected to and during the week that the ex-bully remained at home nursing his bruises, George dealt with those who still felt brave enough to ridicule him. Douglas came back as a nobody. As reigning school bully, George differed from the stereotype in that he picked on only those who were bigger than he was – this was partly due to his father's advice – and along the way, garnered a good deal of hero-worship from Douglas' former victims, some of whom were girls. Strangely, George never took advantage of the girls' attention.

Later, when he became old enough, he joined the local lads' club where he was schooled in the arts of boxing and wrestling by Mr. Cross, an enthusiastic instructor whose career as a professional wrestler had ended after an accident in, or, to be more accurate, just outside the ring. Quickly, under Mr. Cross' tutelage, George gained the club championship, district medium-weight championship and, finally, heavyweight championship of H.M. Prison, Wakefield where he had been sent after an unfortunate encounter with a taxi driver. At that time, George had owned a small, fluffy terrier of indistinct parentage and on whom he doted. He was accustomed to take Dandy, the dog, with him to the bookies and, while inside, tie Dandy to a no parking sign which was conveniently nearby. The sign had been placed on rather a narrow section of pavement and George had not calculated that the length of the dog's lead was somewhat greater than the width of the pavement. Dandy spent the time sniffing around, reading the canine signs and probably hoping for the tell-tale odour of a bitch on heat. He unwisely strayed onto the road-side where a taxi parked on top of him. The driver had failed to hear the squeak, squelch or bump which resulted from his front wheel hitting the dog and therefore was completely at a loss when a large angry man with tears streaming down his face dragged him from his cab and began hitting him with an unattractive degree of ferocity. George was upset. Very upset. The taxi driver would testify to that, indeed, did testify to that at the subsequent court hearing. George was convicted with Actual Bodily Harm and given three years custody. The taxi driver spent three weeks in hospital and seven more at home before he was fit to work again.

It was in prison that George enhanced his abilities with the additional skills which would not have gained the approval of those regulatory bodies concerned with wrestling and boxing. It was here, also, that he met Chevis Yardley, serving time for living off the proceeds of a prostitute, a woman who, to all intents and purposes, was Chevis' wife. Chevis felt that he was innocent since the money should have been counted as household income but he served eighteen months despite his protests. Chevis had already decided on a career change and George had seemed to him to be an ideal candidate to assist him in his new ventures.

George had a couple of secrets; a big one and a little one. The little one was that he loved the countryside and its flora and fauna and was more than averagely adept at identifying what he saw when out in the fields. This was one of those secrets which won't creep out no matter how careless you become. Mainly because it didn't fit with George's image. If you saw George out enjoying the countryside, you would dismiss it from your mind either because it was unbelievable or because you would assume that George was disposing of someone in a quiet spot.

The big secret was well kept because it would have destroyed George's credibility if it was let out into his working world. So he was very, very careful that not even a breath of a rumour should carry any part of this secret away. George was gay.

There were just four other people who were privy to this secret of Heavy George's. One was his mother who wouldn't have told anyone because she didn't quite believe it to be true. The second was his brother, Alfie, who was exceptionally loyal and who completely understood the foolhardiness of passing on such information. The third was George's current partner who thought along the same lines as Alfie.

There were two ex-boyfriends of George's who had known. One of these was dead and the other maintained a firm reticence because he wasn't quite sure just how his predecessor had died.

Robbie pushed the violent image of Heavy George to the back of his mind, "Yeah, but think about it, most people have stuff which isn't replaceable with insurance money - - records, paintings, that sort of stuff. If it's got sentimental value, you'd pay to get it back. On top of that, a lot of people don't even bother insuring half the stuff they've got so there'd be no pay out anyway. We just have to target the sort of things that they want back and would be willing to pay for. Any cash lying around is a bonus for us, they won't get that back. Sod the videos and tellies, you can replace them any time. We're going to specialise. But you're right, Wilf." Robbie conceded, "We'd have to keep well away from the market but it could be done."

Robbie took a thoughtful pull on his pint then asked, "Is there anything about?"

"Yes, Wayne Prough's got us a couple of smart houses to check out. We could try out this idea of yours starting this Friday night."

As if on cue, Wayne swaggered into the bar and made for their table. Wayne's public persona was that of a strutting, rambunctious roughie-toughie but, at heart and at home, he was a sweetie. He sat down, nodding at Robbie and Wilf and shook his hand to the barman, indicating that a drink was required.

"So what's the S.P., Wayne?" asked Robbie.

"Remember when I had to do that bit of, what's it, community service last week? After that bastard in the Drunken Monkey made a comment about Kerry-Ann and the landlord threw me out? Well, I got stuck with a couple of idiots paintin' a whatsit, a scout hut. More skivin' than paintin' but it all helps; that the main thing. Anyway, this lad called Darren and me got chattin' an' he tells me all about himself, most of which I forget. It's the important bits what count. Darren reckoned that he was done for robbery but really he got nicked for stealing vegetables from a copper's garden."

It was true that Wayne's mind was of the type which picks over the dross of casual conversation, only selecting choice pieces worth committing to memory. The fact that Darren had an uncle Leonard who lived in the Brundon area of Port Regis and who had a collection of antique shit, to borrow from Darren's phraseology, was stored carefully alongside the fact that, in a cupboard in the room where the antiques were kept, there was a tin box containing cash from which the young Darren had been used to filch the odd fiver. When Wayne was likely to use this information was never considered at the time, it was just worth remembering. It came to mind when Wilf had asked him to look out for a job in the near future. The telephone book told him just where uncle Leonard lived.

"How many's in the house?" Robbie asked when Wayne had finished describing the job and its possible fruits.

"He's on his own now his missis has kicked it." Wayne explained.

"Right, I'll pick you both up Friday, ten o'clock. Be sober." warned Robbie.

"Yes, but we can get pissed tonight if we want, right, Wayne?"

"Not for me, Wilf, I've got a video to watch round Kerry-Ann's place. Her dad's away somewhere and her mum don't mind me much if I behave so I'll be off after this." Wayne held up his half-finished pint as an indication.

"What are you watching?" Robbie asked, interestedly.

"Oh, it's an old one, black and white, even. It's about

this gentleman burglar called Raffles. He's brilliant. They never can catch him. And he's almost a goodie, you know? If you watched it, you'd be stickin' up for him, Raffles. And he cops for the women. They love him." Wayne sank half of what he had left in his glass, he was excited about the evening to come.

"Hey!" said Robbie, seizing upon Wayne's conversation, "Wayne as Raffles! We shall have to call him 'Waffles'" He laughed at his wit.

Wilf was either not concentrating or could not see Robbie's reasoning, "Why Waffles? What would you want to call him that for?"

Wayne ignored them both, downed the rest of his pint and bade them goodbye. His imagination was in command of the thinking part of his brain and he wandered round to Kerry-Ann's house on automatic pilot.

* * *

The room was in darkness, a small shaft of moonlight peering between the curtains made it possible to make out the form of a young girl asleep in the bed. She wore a white silk night gown which rustled against the peach-coloured silken sheets as she stirred in the midst of a dream.

The lower half of the sash window glided noiselessly open and a gentleman wearing evening dress with white kid gloves climbed in. He stood still for a moment, regaining his breath and taking in the details of the room.

He strode quickly and quietly to an ornate wooden box which was lying on the dressing table, opened it and removed a necklace and a pair of earrings. The diamonds in each caught tiny shafts of moonlight and threw their brilliance into the gentleman's eyes. He put the jewellery into a black velvet bag which he had taken from his jacket and put the bag back into his pocket. He walked over to the girl, bent and kissed her forehead tenderly and then left a small white pasteboard card on the bedside table. It bore just one word: Raffles.

The curtains stirred as though filled with a breeze and he was gone.

* * *

Bloody Waffles! Wayne pushed his hands into his pockets and whistled the image away.

Chapter Eight

OUR FIRST JOB

Heads I win, Tails you lose
(Croker)

Leonard Stillwater was sixty eight and a retired antiques dealer. He lived alone, as Wayne had rightly divined, in a three storey house, part of a 1920's ribbon developement, several of which fanned out along the Port Regis approach roads. His wife, Marie, to whom he had been married for thirty-three years had died from an unlucky combination of asthma and influenza. Since her death, Leonard had been unable to sleep in the bedroom he had shared with her for so long. He closed the door, effectively shutting the room up as he had done with two other bedrooms once their occupants, his children Rosemary and David, had left home to pursue their own paths through life.

Some fortunate people put on old age like a well-loved coat, it seems to suit them to the extent that they seem always to have been old and it would be difficult to imagine them being any younger. Leonard had avoided the crueller effects of age up to the point where Marie had died and then it had dropped on him like a concrete slab. Friends recalled how, just last week, he had looked twenty years younger. Leonard did not seem to notice what had happened to him. He quietly mourned his wife's passing and resumed bachelorhood. There was no question of his ever replacing Marie.

He bought a single bed and installed it in his erstwhile office on the top floor. This was his 'temple of contemplation' as he liked to think of it, where, during his working life, his paperwork was done and catalogues of up and coming auctions were browsed through in an oasis of quiet; insulated from all street noise by double glazing and from household noise by an intervening floor. Now, besides his bed, the room contained a bookcase full of Leonard's favourite reading matter; westerns and historical romance, an easy chair and a portable television.

There were two views from this room both of which Leonard enjoyed. One to the North-East was of Port Regis sitting in a haze of traffic fumes and dust with the sun glinting sometimes from the river. Traffic of all kinds was visible from this window and it was the boats, cars and aeroplanes which fascinated Leonard as he pondered the frenetic dashing from here to wherever and back of the occupants of those machines. Each of them compelled to rush through life in a way which Leonard no longer had to. It made him feel serene and content.

To the South-East, a window looked over houses interspersed with the greenery which latter tended towards predomination the further you looked, a promise of countryside beyond. In front of this window was a telescope mounted on a tripod. This was purchased once Leonard realised that, just a hundred yards away, the lady of the house was in the habit of preparing for bed without having first closed her curtains.

The lady in view was Jennifer Heaton, an attractive, albeit slightly overweight brunette on the shy side of forty although Leonard was not aware of either her name or age. Her physical attributes were what attracted his attention. Bored by her husband's frequent absences of an evening as he displayed his skills as a dart player in the local league, Jennifer had one evening stood naked in front of her bedroom window and pulled the curtains open and then, just as quickly closed them. It was this particular evening that Leonard, resting his eyes from reading by gazing through the window, felt an urge to buy a telescope.

"Taking up astronomy." he told the man who sold it to him although the man did not listen, customers were always giving him useless bits of information. Whether he might have showed more interest had Leonard been honest and admitted to buying it in order to stare into a woman's bedroom window is a matter of conjecture.

Jennifer had experienced a strange thrill at this first disclosure and had gradually developed her technique to a more natural undressing procedure, finishing off by closing the curtains and climbing into bed. She had no idea of whether anyone watched her or not. The thrill was felt with or without an audience. It was the naughtiness of her act which excited her She knew that Bernard, her husband would be mightily pissed off if he knew what she was doing and hoped that someone may be out there fantasising about her body.

Leonard got a kick out of it, too. Partly it was due to the reassurance he felt from actually getting an erection while watching Jennifer than any other aspect. He didn't always achieve a climax from self-stimulation during Jennifer's appearances but that didn't bother him. There was, at least, some sort of life left between his legs. It was nice to know that his penis was not the corpse it appeared to be when he saw it dangling over the toilet bowl of a morning.

Downstairs, Leonard had another special room where he kept his private collection of items acquired, one way

134

or another, during his working life. One of his proudest possessions was a collection of birds' eggs. The cabinet which contained them in a set of custom-made drawers had come his way quite legally. A widow had been selling off her late husband's impedimenta to realise the cash needed to enable her to join her daughter in Canada and live in comfort there until she finally went the way of her former mate. Leonard, in his role as an antiques dealer, bought some of her better furniture including the cabinet.

It had been offered for sale in Leonard's shop and sat in one corner occasionally peered at or inspected but never bought for over two years. During this time, Leonard grew quite fond of it and, in quiet periods, would open the drawers to examine their contents. There were single eggs and whole clutches artfully arranged and lying in nests of cotton wool in depressions carved into the thick wooden base of each drawer. The eggs were labelled with the name of the bird which had laid them, the date when the clutch was taken and the location from where they were taken. Eventually, realising that the cabinet would probably never be sold and that he would rather have it for himself, Leonard took it home and installed it in his front room. Marie made no comment on its arrival, she was used to strange things being brought home and dismissed it as another one of Leonard's quirks.

Leonard knew that such collections, when registered as this one had been, were legal but adding to them or starting new collections was definitely not. The authorities viewed egging as a very serious offence and had supplied deterrents to discourage anyone contemplating this activity as a new hobby.

Leonard had discovered two of the drawers to be only part full and, at the bottom of one of the cotton-wool nests, fragments of shell indicating that, of the missing eggs, some had been broken.

They could be easily replaced, thought Leonard. They had belonged to common enough birds. Although being long past fit for the activities indulged in by the average egger, Leonard had a nephew, Darren, who would do almost anything provided the wages were attractive enough. The niceties of British law seemed not to bother Darren very much and he had already done community service and forked out a hefty fine because of this lack of concern. He remained undeterred by his punishments because he felt he was unjustly singled out by the authorities whom he despised. It was Darren who had trespassed private woodland, shinned up trees and risked scrapes, scratches and falls as he collected the eggs which his uncle had requested of him. Darren didn't do it for the love of his aged relative nor for the furtherance of scientific endeavour. He did it purely for the money. Leonard paid well.

On the night that Robbie, Wilf and Wayne had set aside for their first job as an independent team, Leonard had spent twenty minutes before retiring watching Jennifer get ready for bed. This time he had no erection but he still enjoyed the show although there was a nagging doubt that perhaps he'd seen her go through the pantomime so many times that he was becoming jaded. He settled down with a Zane Grey and shortly afterwards, felt drowsy enough to switch off his reading lamp and drop into a sound sleep.

By the time Leonard was in his dreams, galloping across the purple sage with a naked Jennifer draped, unconscious across his saddle, Robbie and Wilf had gained illegal entry to the ground floor of Leonard's home.

Robbie didn't waste time with any other part of Leonard's house, he went straight to the front room where he knew the antique collection to be kept. First, he double checked that the heavy curtains across the window were drawn carefully enough to exclude any light from the streetlamps then switched on a battery-powered lamp and set it on a table in the middle of the room where it illuminated the entire room with a low level of light. Then he switched on a torch with which to inspect more closely the items he selected. Wilf was checking the many pictures on the walls both for value and also for evidence of a safe. There was no safe but two attractive prints were deposited in the sports bag which had been brought for the purpose.

In a sideboard which contained a small collection of assorted china items and some twee-looking teapots, Robbie found a tin box. No attempt had been made to hide it for it had been pushed carelessly behind a teapot shaped like a thatched cottage. It wasn't even locked so Robbie opened it.

"Two hundred quid." he whispered to Wilf.

"Petrol money." Wilf whispered back, "What else?"

"I'm lookin'." said Robbie.

Robbie didn't recognise the purpose of the cabinet in the corner despite the lack of depth which the many drawers showed. He pulled one out.

"Eggs!" he whispered again.

"What?" Wilf returned in his normal voice.

"Eggs." Robbie repeated, emulating Wilf in dropping the whisper.

"Don't be so bloody silly. We want valuable stuff, not soddin' groceries."

"No, come here and look. These birds' eggs are worth a few bob nowadays. Pity we can't nick the whole cabinet."

Wilf came over clutching the sports bag which, along with the paintings, now held some Japanese pottery and a ceramic orange which had rather taken his fancy.

"We'll just take a few drawers full at random. They're bound to be worth something to the old man. You carry 'em separate while I take the bag. I think we've probably got enough now, haven't we, Wilf?"

"You're the boss – let's go, then."

They made their way back to the van where Wayne was waiting, smoking nervously, his eyes flicking alternately forwards and to the van's mirrors to check for nosy dog walkers and sneaky police patrols.

"What you got?" asked Wayne as they clambered in, carefully stowing the trays of eggs on the shelf attached to the van's inside wall.

"Eggs." said Robbie.

"Eggs? Are we in for whatsit, omelette tonight?" asked Wayne, rather puzzled by Robbie's answer.

"No. Birds' eggs. Collector's junk. And Wilf's got some pictures and stuff. Could be two – three grands worth if we get it right. And I've left 'im – the customer – a little note explaining our motives and a method of contact."

"Brilliant." said Wayne with feeling as he started the van and moved off for home. He was relieved that everything had gone so smoothly.

"Brilliant." he repeated, throwing the still lit cigarette end out of the van window.

Leonard first realised that something was wrong when he came downstairs the following morning to make himself a cup of tea and noticed the front door slightly ajar. He went to it, puzzled, pulled it open to see if any one was outside, closed it carefully and then, on an impulse, decided to check his collection room.

A shock-wave of nausea travelled through him as he realised that someone must have broken in and stolen some of his antiques. His eye was drawn to the egg-cabinet in the corner, alerted by the missing drawers the way the eye is drawn to a person's missing front teeth. There was a pale, yellow piece of note paper stuck to the front with adhesive tape. He pulled it off and read it:

'We have your stuff. We will call you and arrange a meeting where you can have the option of buying it all back. Don't call the busies or you will force us to dispose of it elsewhere and you won't get it back at all.'

There was a pencilled over capital 'R' underneath where it seemed that the writer had begun to sign it and then stopped and crossed it out. Leonard noticed that, as he read, his hand was shaking. He sat down on the arm of one of the room's easy chairs, the note in his right hand which clutched his knee, and thought about what he might do.

First, if he called in the police and they recovered the stolen items, the providence of one or two of them, not excluding the eggs, might be called into question. It would be awkward to have to provide answers. There could even be charges levelled at him for possession of those eggs not listed as part of the original contents of the cabinet! That, if he was lucky, might result in just a heavy fine. Within ten minutes, Leonard had reached the conclusion that there was really only one way to go. He must pay the ransom to recover his goods. Even losing them altogether wasn't worth the risk – they might still be traced back to him, closely followed by another set of awkward questions.

Leonard spent the next few days fretting in the manner that porpentines are alleged to. Several times a day he went to check the front door in case some sort of communication had arrived, carrying further instructions.

When, at last, it did arrive, it was clear that it had done so under the cover of darkness for it was on the mat when he came down for his morning cup of tea, long before the postman was due. He read the directions which told him to meet with 'the team' in the car-park of Snow Edge railway station, a little used stop on the main line out of Port Regis. Its car-park was often used, at night, by the local youth who would gather there to consume specially brewed and cheap lager and to smoke cannabis. At that time, Friday, eleven o'clock at night, it would be deserted, the youths, by then, usually having gone on to a rave. The letter went on to reassure Leonard that everything would be conducted in a business-like manner provided he didn't try to involve anyone else and, on completion, there would be a personal guarantee from 'the team' that they would never visit his premises again.

Leonard felt far from reassured by the contents of the note. In fact, his state of nervousness had increased a great deal and he went off to find his bottle of rum with which to fortify his tea while he thought about the coming meeting.

That same morning, Leonard went to his bank and withdrew two thousand pounds in cash which he added to the one thousand which he usually kept in a tea-caddy in his bedroom as a sort of float in case a worthwhile purchase came his way. This was a habit formed when he had been active in the antiques trade and had found difficult to break since retiring. It was during this morning that Leonard discovered that the small float, the two hundred kept downstairs had also been taken. Somehow, that seemed but a slight annoyance compared to the other losses.

No matter how hard he thought about the matter, he could see no way round it. It seemed best to put a brave face on things and do as the note said.

He made a resolution to try to be as observant as possible during the transaction and pick up any clues which could lead to identifying any member of 'the team' but what he could possibly do with the information gained, there was no idea.

Friday evening oozed slowly into place and Leonard prepared to go. He put the money into a large, brown envelope which he pushed into the inside pocket of his overcoat. He was now talking to himself a great deal more than he had used to.

"Just nerves." he told himself.

"Close the front door properly." he reminded himself.

"Don't forget to check there's enough petrol." he warned himself as he fumbled for the keys to the car.

On arrival at the station car-park, Leonard began to worry that he was a: too early and b: in the wrong place because there was neither vehicle nor persons about. Then c:, that they might be waiting and watching somewhere to check whether he'd brought any assistance occured to him and utterly failed to calm him. His back felt terribly itchy. He tried to settle down and wait but in the end, just waited.

At length, a car arrived. Only its sidelights were on and it was impossible to make out any distiguishing feature of the vehicle in the gloom. It parked and the driver extinguished the lights. Leonard sat tight.

Then a figure stepped out from the passenger side of the car, walked forwards several paces and called, "Mr Stillwater?"

Leonard wound down his window all the way and answered, "Yes?"

"Out of the car and move towards the litter bin." the voice instructed and an arm pointed in the direction it wished him to go.

"Pardon?" Leonard asked, more from nervous stupidity than from any inability to hear or understand what he was being asked to do.

The instruction was repeated, an irritable note creeping into the voice of the unseen speaker and Leonard complied, closing his car door as he went.

The figure moved over to Leonard's car and flashed a torch to illuminate its interior, possibly to check for hidden occupants; unwanted witnesses.

"Got the money?", the voice asked.

"Yes." said Leonard, "Three thousand pounds."

The figure turned towards the darkened vehicle in which it had arrived and called, "Get the man's gear!"

Another dark shape pushed out from the rear doors, indicating that the vehicle was some sort of van. The figure was carrying a cardboard box and a plastic sack under one arm and took them over to the litter bin area where Leonard stood.

"Have a look, it's all there and hand over the cash while you're at it." the first figure instructed.

Leonard could barely see what was in the box or the bag but his fear of the situation made him blind to any possibility that they might attempt to rook him and he handed over the envelope containing the banknotes. They were snatched from his hand by the man who had brought his belongings but there was no glimpse of any feature which Leonard could later recall. He stood, uncertain, as the two men hurried back to their car which left immediately, the driver neglecting to switch on the lights until after they had left the car park.

Leonard stood for a while, shivering and unsure, then loaded first the bag and then the box into his car before driving slowly home.

Back in his house, Leonard discovered that everything had been returned to him with no damage. He wasn't sure whether it was relief he felt but he wept, nonetheless. Then he wiped his eyes on the sleeve of his coat and went to find the bottle of rum.

"Well, that was a piece of piss." cried Robbie ebulliently, hoisting his glass to toast 'the team'.

"The team." Wilf concurred, waving his glass vaguely at the other two.

"Here's to the next job!" Wayne said and took a huge draught by way of underlining his toast, banged the glass back on the table and added, "May they all be good 'uns."

The team' had met up in 'The Irish Hand', a pub in Port Regis which they did not normally use and where they were unlikely to be recognised. They had come to celebrate and to divide the cash. Robbie felt buoyant; a grand for one night's work. That was what it was all about. Maybe he could buy Annie something nice. Something to stop her mithering for a bit.

"We need to keep this quiet – first we don't want anyone

else muscling in on this game; it's our game and we don't need any help. Second, we don't want the fences to realise that they've been cut out."

"But they have, haven't they?" asked Wayne who tried to see things clearly.

"Yes, they have." Robbie answered, "But they musn't know. So, don't go splashing this around too quickly if you don't want anyone to get too nosy. And have a word with your Beryl, Wilf. Or rather, don't say a thing."

Wilf's dearly beloved was not a woman in whom you could confide with any safety. She believed in freedom of information.

"I shan't tell her. By the time I've paid off the bookie, bought myself a couple of ounces of skunk, there might be just enough to get her the new telly I promised her for her birfday. I fought I might have to lift one but I shall buy it, legit, from a shop. You get a cardboard box wiv it and everyfing. She'll be well chuffed wiv it."

"Well, I wouldn't dare say anything to Kerry-Ann. She's a bit sniffy about me nicking stuff. I'll probably put it in the building society. So – what's the next move?" Wayne asked while closely examining his pint as though to intimate to likely spies or earwigs that it was the quality of the ale which they were discussing rather than the doubly illicit activities of 'the team'.

"We'll meet back here in a week and meanwhile, Wayne, keep your eyes open for another easy mark. Last night's one was a blinder." Robbie announced.

Wayne almost blushed with pride and determined to do his best. He already had an idea for the new job; one of his mum's mates was away on holiday and the house would be empty for a while. It was worth checking out.

In Bottomfield Close, Wettenham, Leigh Purslipp was enjoying a night off duty and spending the time watching a film on the television with his wife Elaine and a couple of cold cans of lager.

Elaine had been worrying of late and considering her rather delicate position regarding her accidental pregnancy. That morning while doing a batch of ironing with the television tuned into a shopping channel,she had had an idea. It was quite an audacious plan but, given her circumstances; pregnant by boyfriend, desperate for a baby which her husband could not give her and an appointment with the fertility clinic in the offing, she thought that she might just pull it off. Even if it went all wrong and Leigh refused to accept what she had done, it would be just the one marriage destroyed, rather than two. Not that she wanted her marriage destroyed, it seemed to make her feel better about the whole damned mess if Trevor's marriage could be saved. And she would still have the baby. Even so, nerves made her slightly hesitant in broaching the subject and she had had a fortifying glass of sherry in the kitchen before joining Leigh on the sofa to put the plan into action.

The film was just finishing and, before Leigh could switch channels to watch something else, she plunged in.

"Leigh, love – would you consider artificial insemination if you were – er – sterile – you know – if we couldn't have a baby 'cos you couldn't – you know?"

Leigh, in a show of male strength which rather increased Elaine's worry levels, crushed his empty can of lager. This had nothing to do with what his wife had just said, Leigh always did that when he had finished a can. He belched and said, "What? Let you have another man's kiddy? Put some bloke's sperm inside you? It'd be like he come around and shagged you himself. No. Not a bloody chance. It's got to be my kiddy or none at all."

Elaine put on a soothing tone, one which a parent might use to an upset child, "It's not like that, Leigh – it's very clinical, very impersonal. A doctor puts it in with a turkey baster thingy. I've seen it done, love. The sperm donor wouldn't even be there."

"Will you not listen? No! I will not have it." Leigh was feeling a little angry. Not just at his wife's suggestion but at the implication that he was infertile, a fact he was unwilling to face or even accept as a possibility.

"But, Leigh, love. How can I have a baby if you won't think of doing it like that. I've got feelings too, you know. I really want a baby, I have to have one` and I don't want it to break up our marriage." Here Elaine took out a tissue from the box kept by the sofa for when she watched a weepie on the television. She sniffed loudly for effect and dabbed her eyes.

"How do you know you'll have one anyway? Why's it my fault? You always reckon it's me and we haven't even got around to having any tests yet so you can't be sure, can you? How do you know for certain that it's not you? Go on: Tell me that."

Although equipped with the necessary proof, Elaine dared not rise to his challenge. She remained the upset and broody hen.

Leigh picked up another can of lager from out of the mini-cooler which was on the floor by his side of the sofa. It clicked and hissed angrily as he opened it.

Elaine looked down to the carpet and applied the tissue again while moaning in a semi-fearful, semi-apologetic way, "I've already done it. I've already been and got myself inseminated." This, she felt, was not really a lie. She had omitted the fact that it had not been done artificially but that was purely for self-preservational purposes.

Leigh, if angry before, was now incandescent, "You've done what? Why? Why the bollox wasn't I consulted on this before you went? Don't I bloody matter?", he shouted. Then in an explosion of realisation, "Are you telling me you're bloody pregnant?"

Elaine, despite having tried to prepare herself for Leigh's outburst, was frightened. Although they had had rows before, stand-up face to face screaming rows when she had been on the point of throwing whatever came to hand at her husband, just to try and make him see her point, Leigh had never hit her. Now she feared he might. She flinched as he waved his arm in furious bafflement.

"Yes, I am. I just thought I'd save us all the trouble and embarassment of the fertility clinic. You know, get it done, get it over with. Then just say it's ours."

By this time Leigh was painfully aware that, if Elaine was pregnant, then it must have been he who was having the problem. Therefore, his thinking went, if I say nothing, it won't get out that I've got non-functional knackers. People will think it's mine. Unless, of course, it doesn't look anything like me.

"What if it's bloody black?" Leigh was now worried that it would be obvious to everyone that the baby wasn't his.

"They know the background of all the donors. There's no chance of it being wrong, racially, I mean. No-one will be able to tell, honest." There were still doubts in her mind whether she could carry this off. Leigh had gone quiet while he absorbed all this information but there was no telling what he might do. Right now, he looked like a dormant volcano.

"I think I'll go up to bed, now, love. I've got a bit of a headache coming on." She leant over to kiss his cheek before retreating to the relative safety of the bedroom and he pulled away, out of range.

Leigh didn't say a word as she left, he had a lot of thinking to do.

Chapter Nine

ANOTHER JOB

*Lay not up for yourselves treasures upon earth
where moth and rust doth corrupt and where
thieves break through and steal.*
(St. Matthew)

Craig Devant had a date. For the two years of unwanted
bachelorhood since Lucy, his wife, ran away with Harvey
Bredgold, a man who was now not so much an erstwhile
friend as a newly acquired enemy, there had been no
woman in Craig's life.

Craig was a burnt-out star of the world of popular music
– a brown dwarf if you like, an oddly apt description since
he was something below average height and sported
a permanent, chemical tan. In the '70s, he had been a
member of a progressive rock band called Pneumatic
Doorknob. "Prog Rock, Psychedelic and Hippy Shit" was
how their oeuvre was described by an ex-member during a
press conference convened to discuss the band's break-up.
The break-up was ascribed to musical differences but in
reality, they had run out of creative steam and most of the

group members had quite lost interest.

It had been the fashion back then, when the group first formed, to name yourselves using a conjunction of two unlikely words such as 'Iron Butterfly', 'Fat Mattress' or 'Electric Prunes' so, at an early rehearsal, long before they were booked for their first ever gig, they had thrown around some suggestions for their identity and Pneumatic Doorknob was chosen, partly because it was clean and partly because it sounded trendy. Often, when members of Progressive Rock bands were asked by the press about the significance of their name, they could come up with a credible explanation but Craig's group had none. They had just gone for the sound of it. There were no sexual connotations or hidden meanings, they protested, it was just a name.

Thanks to the writing skills of Jeff Morley, the drummer and the organisational skills of Craig himself, they became quite famous. They acquired a manager along the way, one Harvey Bredgold, who was at that time handling several other minor groups from the area and who showed himself to be useful, via his contacts, in arranging some venues for them to play. They were talent-spotted and signed to a leading British label for three years during which time, they made two hit singles, two complete flops and two poorly selling albums before finally fading. The two hit singles earned them appearances on 'Top of the Pops' and, as a consequence of the publicity from being seen on the television, a good deal of money besides. After the flops, the record company declined to renew their contract and they disbanded. An apathy had descended on the group and all of them could think of better things to do.

Craig had been sensible while the group was earning good money and had invested in a large house and an extensive portfolio of stocks which he had been advised to buy by his father who was well versed in such things. Being financially independent after the break-up of the group gave Craig the opportunity to continue playing music for his own pleasure and in his own way. It no longer mattered that he wouldn't be paid much for it, if at all. The music was his passion and his life hung from the frets of a guitar. He and another ex-member of Pneumatic Doorknob, Doggy Daniels, had come together to form a duo which tried to bask in the dim light of their defunct group's fame and they billed themselves as 'Air Latch'. They were not allowed to use or specifically refer to their old name, Pneumatic Doorknob because Harvey had copyrighted it and his solicitor had sent a rather unfriendly letter when they first set out as a duo and billed themselves using the old name.

Calling themselves Airlatch was a sneaky way of referring to the original band without upsetting either Harvey or his lawyer.

Airlatch's last gig had been in the Black Swan in Port Regis. It was a depressing, badly constructed public house which had seen better days and a much better clientele. It smelled of stale tobacco smoke, flat beer and urine. However, it still had enough regulars to be considered a lively pub.

In the audience had been a woman who, as a teenager, had been a groupie. This is a species of female fan who is so besotted with a pop group or even a number of pop groups that they follow them to every gig that they possibly can with the specific intention of bedding their favourite pop idol or, failing that, one of the subsidiary members. Or all of them if circumstances allowed. One of the groups which Maureen Treagle had followed was Pneumatic Doorknob. There had been two memorable occasions when a member of the echolalic backing group had been unable to appear and Maureen had stood in and on stage along with her heroes. That she enjoyed their music as well was a bonus for her.

Maureen had eventually grown up and settled down, putting her groupie past behind her. There were still times when, ironing the children's clothes, perhaps, while listening to the radio, a record from one of 'her' groups would be played and drag her memory back to those hectic and irresponsible days of which she never told her family. Now, the children grown up and her husband dead from a combination of drink and driving — he'd been drunk when he stepped in front of a car driven by a young, sober driver who had been going a little too fast— she was alone again. She had gone along to the Black Swan with Patty, her neighbour, with the express intention of seeing Airlatch as she knew them to be ex-members of Pneumatic Doorknob and she liked nostalgia. It's fortunate that nostalgia is so pleasant an affliction since it seems to attack everyone at some time during the life-span. As with the common cold, it would be a remarkable individual indeed who wandered through their three-score and ten without being hit by it.

After the gig, Maureen had introduced herself to Craig who, amazingly, remembered her and the date tonight had been the end result. This was nostalgia hitting Craig, too. Doggy Daniels had also remembered Maureen but said nothing to Craig. After all, he was a mate.

Craig is a dog-owner, a Rottweiler called Monty and, every morning, he takes his pet, not so much for a walk as for a shit. At eight o'clock, for Craig prides himself on being an early riser, he pours a cup of coffee and takes it and Monty for an amble to the end of the road which runs parallel to his house and then ambles back. Outward bound, the dog seems to look pensive as though something was troubling it but on the return leg looks relieved because Monty knows that to crap on the street during the walk is good doggie but to do it within the grounds of Craig's house is bad doggie and often a painful experience. Nor will there be another chance that day. Craig is not keen on serious walking for either the dog's or his own benefit and views the grounds of his home as large enough for Monty to get all the exercise he might need. Not surprisingly, Monty lacks the initiative to set himself a keep-fit regime and so lies by his kennel suffering from aching boredom. The highlight of Monty's day, aside from feeding time, is the arrival of the postman or any other stranger with business at the house. Monty's tactic, not one studiously thought out but somehow innate, is not to run barking madly after the unwary visitor but to stroll quietly up and sit behind him while he knocks at the door. If he is let in, then Monty strolls back to his kennel and waits for the time when the visitor comes out again. He then trots over to the front gate and snarls when approached, daring that person to leave. If there is no answer to his knock and the visitor turns to leave, he is confronted by a growling Monty. It would be a brave man to ignore this dog. We cannot give Monty any credit for having a sense of humour as it is difficult to discern whether the dog is amused by these goings on. Craig often has to rescue the visitor saying affably, "It's all right, it's only his game. He wouldn't bite anyone." You could certainly qualify as naïve were you to believe this.

At night, Monty is taken indoors where he has free range of the lower floor. All the doors are lightly sprung and will open in either direction with a push; partly for Monty's benefit and partly because Craig removed all the doorknobs to deter guests from asking whether they were pneumatic. Craig liked a good joke as much as anyone but this one had worn so thin that you could see anger through it.

Craig finished dressing in readiness to take Maureen out. He had decided against the velour loons and flouncy, floral shirt as being a bit too retro and chosen instead a pair of flared black corduroy trousers, a pale orange shirt, a scarlet neckerchief and black leather jacket. He wanted to impress rather than entertain. Stylish rather than theatrical. Whistling the flip-side of Doorknob's first single, he headed for his car in the garage.

Maureen watched excitedly as Craig drove up in his Audi saloon. She hoped the neighbours were watching.

She greeted him at the door with a kiss and he escorted her to the car in as gentlemanly fashion as he could muster.

"Where are we going?" she asked.

"I know a lovely pub cum restaurant just outside a place called Wettenham. It's in the country – bit of peace and quiet, you know. I did a gig there a while back and got to know the manager. He'll look after us."

It had been noisy in the dining room, a brash country band had been hired to entertain the diners and, through enthusiasm rather than talent, had greatly reduced conversational opportunities.

After the meal, Craig and Maureen left the dining area and found a table near to the bar where it was a little quieter so that they could chat together about the old times and maybe even make some plans for some new times. The banquette on which they sat lay alongside a wall and served as seating for two tables which each had two chairs facing. On the other table was a young couple also quietly chatting. This night had seen Wayne splashing out and treating Kerry-Ann to a proper sit-down meal as a change from the usual stand-up fish and chips which normally was Wayne's idea of taking a girl out for a meal. The reason for this was that it was Kerry-Ann's birthday and she had demanded something special.

"I remember that tour to promote your first single," Maureen cooed, "I really fell for you, then. You had a big, red guitar which you played. That bit sort of sticks in my memory."

Maureen probably didn't recognise the phallic significance of the red guitar at the time although she did find herself wondering whether the guitarist was well hung. She found later that he was just average in that respect.

"I've still got that guitar." said Craig, proudly. "It didn't cost much in them days but it's worth a bomb, now. There's a black one, as well, which a mate reckons would fetch forty-two grand."

Because of the occasion, Kerry-Ann had let restraint fly out of the window and had chosen the most expensive items on the menu; grilled lobster and chips followed by chocolate pudding and ice-cream, all washed down with numerous vodka cocktails thus putting an enormous strain on Wayne's finances. Consequently, money was foremost in Wayne's mind when the gentleman on the next table used phrases like 'worth a bomb' and 'fetch forty-two grand'. This grabbed his attention and Wayne faded out Kerry-Ann's prattle and faded in Craig's boasting. Money had been mentioned. Valuable items, too. He needed to find out where this bloke lived so that the team could pay them a visit. When to visit was going to be a matter of luck because nothing the man said gave away his habits like when he went out to work and the times he was likely to be away.

Suddenly inspired, Wayne leaned towards Craig and asked, "'Scuse me, mate. Did I overhear that you're a musician, in a group and that? I know someone who's looking to whatsits, book a turn for a party, like."

Craig was a little irritated by this young man's intrusion but he remained polite and confirmed his status and, taking out what looked to Wayne an extremely fat wallet, took out a red business card and handed it to Wayne. "Give us a call on that number."

"Thanks, mate."

Wayne was quite pleased, the card had the man's address written on it besides his e-mail address and two telephone numbers. He put the card into his coat pocket and broke Kerry-Ann's look of puzzlement by telling her that she looked really pretty tonight.

Kerry-Ann had expected Wayne to be a little peevish after spending so much on her, she knew how close with his money he liked to be so she was pleased when he remained quite even-minded although distracted – just not hanging on to her every word. But then, not listening to everything she said was a trait she had noticed before in Wayne.

As the evening closed, the two couples went their separate ways.

The relationship between Maureen and Craig quickly grew with the nourishment that each provided and he found himself, some nights, a guest at Maureen's house. An overnight guest.

Wayne had reported Craig as a find and watched him for long enough to know that there were occasions when Craig's house would be left empty for the whole night. Having discovered where Craig spent these nights, it became easy to check whether the coast would be clear for a raid.

The team, on constant alert, received word from Robbie, via Wayne, that tonight was the night. Wilf told Beryl a little lie about where he was going and she didn't believe a word of it but she let him go without argument. Robbie and Annie had a row about his disappearing for the evening after having promised to take her out for a drink but he was confident that, once back in the funds, he could buy back her favour.

Monty fretted on those nights when Craig left him alone. He was, by nature, a sociable dog and when feeling forlorn on those lonely nights, would wander through the ground floor rooms of the house, sometimes settling in a favourite spot for a minute or two and then, whining quietly, he would get up and wander about again.

Alone again, Monty had entered the kitchen which often boasted some very interesting smells. This was almost a doggy way of settling down with a book. Even with his head pushed part way under the cooker, he was still able to hear the noise of someone trying to open the front door. Monty snuffed his nostrils clear and sat on the kitchen floor with his ears pricked up. Company.

Wilf and Robbie had all the information about the house that Wayne was able to give them. This did not include the dog since Wayne had never seen Monty. So, as they prised open the front door, each was still confident of a profitable night.

Over to Robbie's right were a pair of swing doors with round windows in them rather like the ones seen in restaurant kitchens. Rightly divining that beyond those doors lay the kitchen, an unpromising room as far as burglars were concerned, Robbie motioned to Wilf to search the rooms over to the left whilst he checked upstairs. Wilf nodded, pushing through into a large room, a sort of sitting room or lounge which, to his trained eye, contained absolutely nothing valuable apart from the very thing he was looking for, the red guitar!

As Wilf had pushed through the door into the lounge, Robbie had reached the top of the stairs and Monty had pushed an inquisitive nose through the kitchen doors. He padded over to the bottom of the stairs and sat down to await the arrival of one of the visitors.

Wilf had checked around and found nothing to add to his haul and so, grasping the guitar by its neck, he walked out to the hall to wait for Robbie to finish upstairs. He could hear a rumbling noise which, at first, he couldn't place. Then, in the gloom, he spotted Monty and realised what the noise was. Wilf froze, unsure what to do. He clicked on his flashlight and saw just how big and fierce the dog looked. It was an unnerving experience. As yet, the dog didn't look as though it would attack but he didn't fancy pushing his luck. So he stood where he was until he heard Robbie walk across the top of the stairs. Robbie had found nothing in the first bedroom he'd checked and was about to start on the second when he heard a loud whisper from the ground floor.

"Robbie!" Wilf hissed, "There's a big bastard dog 'ere. What shall I do?"

"Where is it?" asked Robbie.

"At the bottom of the stairs. I don't like the way it's growling."

"Has it bitten you?"

"No."

Relieved, Robbie came down the stairs to see what he could do. He felt confident with dogs and he believed that he had a way with them. As he reached the penultimate step, Monty shifted his attention from Wilf to Robbie and increased the growl to the teeth-showing stage. Robbie's confidence evaporated.

"What we gonna do?", inquired Wilf.

"Try moving towards me but slow."

"What for?" Wilf liked to be clear about instructions he was given, especially when his well-being was threatened as a consequence.

"Just take a couple of steps – just see what the bloody dog does."

Wilf took two grandmother's footsteps and the dog turned its teeth towards him.

"Do you fink I could beat the dog to the door?" Wilf asked. Doing a runner was the main thrust of his plan.

"No, you couldn't and, even if you could, how the bollocks am I going to get out, you dozy sod?"

"You could run up the stairs and climb out of one of the windows."

The idea did not appeal to Robbie but he thought about it all the same.

Monty decided for them both. Since Robbie was still on the stairs which, unbeknown to him, was forbidden territory to Monty, the dog launched himself at Wilf, snarling in such a way as to make it clear to Wilf that he was about to be attacked. With commendable timing, the result of a strong sense of self-preservation, Wilf clubbed sideways at Monty's head with the guitar. The blow felled the dog and snapped the neck of the instrument. Monty lay sprawled in an ungainly heap on the carpet.

"Shit and derision! You've bloody killed it!" shouted Robbie.

"Well, it was going to bite me." said Wilf, horrified at the sight of blood on the dog's head.

"Bollocks to this lot," said Robbie, "We're going home."

"What shall I do wiv this?" Wilf asked, holding up the wrecked guitar.

"Chuck it. It's no bloody use now, is it?"

Craig was whistling as he walked from his car back to the house. It had been an enjoyable evening with Maureen, an enjoyable night, really. This thing with Mo' (his private pet name for Maureen – even she had never heard him use it) was getting – whoa! There's a song there.

He stood, thoughtful, in the middle of his garden while the words struggled to free themselves from the grip of his muse: This thing with Mo' is getting too big for me; I'll have to go and beg her down on one knee – the tune and words flurried in his mind like busy autumn leaves; he felt compelled to rush into the house, grab his guitar and start to put the words and emerging music onto paper. Could be a hit.

He unlocked the front door and pushed it open. What he saw drove the hit single far, far away, never to be recalled. A broken guitar lay at the bottom of the stairs next to a brown stain which looked like dried blood.

Where's Monty?

The dog often slept on an old cot mattress on the kitchen floor where his water dish and food bowl were placed. Craig barged the kitchen doors open wondering what could have happened and saw Monty, whimpering on his bed with a torn ear and a cut on the side of his head. Blood had stained the mattress where he had lain down. The dog looked at his master with a mixture of fear and sorrow, gave a solitary wag but made no move to greet him.

"Bloody hell, dog. What's happened?"

The dog added a weak wag to the last one and wouldn't tell. Then his eyes slipped away from Craig's curious gaze, it was enough for the dog that his head hurt inside and there was a wound which he could not reach with his tongue to lick. To be able to lick a wound is comforting to a dog. Pondering these problems was as much as Monty's intellect could cope with. The added load of his master barking at him in an unintelligible manner was too much.

Despite calling in the police, Constables Clough and Purslipp who were sympathetic but useless, and despite a subsequent visit by a pair of detectives; the female of the duo sharp and inquisitive, her partner all eyes and world-weariness, Craig never did discover who it was broke in, nearly killed his dog and broke his second-favourite guitar.

The insurance company paid up, even for Monty's vetinary bill but money couldn't buy a replacement for a beloved guitar. Sentimental value has no place on an assessor's list. The guitar was repaired but would never be playable again. It was for display purposes only.

There was a sort of replacement, an object of affection which deflected the feeling of loss Craig felt over the red guitar. Maureen moved in shortly afterwards.

And they lived happily ever after.

The team went back to their separate homes in rather a disgruntled way.

"What a farce!" Wayne would say from time to time. Farce was a word quite recently resident in Wayne's vocabulary and, with a vague idea that it was synonymous with cock-up, he found it handy to describe the evening's events.

"What a farce!"

"Do shut it, Wayne" This was as much as a tight-lipped Robbie would say during the trip back other than an acknowledging grunt as the other two left for their homes.

"Do you fink I killed the dog?" asked Wilf. He was as much concerned with the dog's welfare as with the failure of the job. He couldn't bear the pressure of guilt that thinking about the dog's death brought him.

Neither Wayne nor Robbie felt either qualified or bothered to answer him.

* * *

Leigh and Ellis were aware of skulduggery in the area but not unduly concerned since it was in the normal run of things. They had no reason to suspect that there might be a specific gang involved because there was no evidence to support such a theory. They could have speculated but, at this time, they were parked up by the motorway discussing Leigh's problems.

He had begun by explaining to Ellis what Elaine had

done, how she had gone behind his back to the fertility clinic and been artificially inseminated. And how upset he had been when Elaine had told him about her pregnancy.

"So, lemme get this right. She reckons you can't make her pregnant – and that's without the tests you was supposed to have – and, to save you getting embarrassed just in case she's right, she's gone, on her own, and got herself a baby."

"Yes, that's about it, mate." Leigh looked worried and tired as though he had lost some sleep recently. This was because he had lost some sleep recently, either worrying about how the baby would turn out or being angry with Elaine for doing it without consulting him. He had taken to sleeping alone in a spare bedroom and their relationship was very cold. They barely spoke to one another and, usually, when in a similar situation in the past after a monster row, she would be very pushy, making sure that Leigh knew that she was in the room and that, as far as she was concerned, he was in the wrong and she very much in the right. This time, it was like sharing a room with a mouse. He was beginning to feel that for once, he was in the right, he was the moral victor. That didn't make him feel any better, though.

Ellis wore a look on his face which reflected his concern. He didn't like what Leigh had told him and was deeply suspicious of Elaine's actions.

"I don't think she's allowed to get artificially inseminated without your consent. I'd check up if I was you. What she might have done is tell 'em that she's a widow or a lesbian or something. Anything to hide the fact that she's got a husband."

Leigh turned quickly from gazing through the window of the car to face his friend, surprised at his thinking something which had never occurred to him before.

"Bloody Cow! Why would she do that?"

"Dunno, mate. You could go and check with the clinic.

Pretend it's police business or something. Or even do it straight. Just tell 'em what you know and see what the deal is."

A doubt had crept into Ellis' mind as to just how Elaine had really become pregnant. He kept it to himself. If Leigh was going to find out, it wouldn't be from him. Besides, he wasn't completely sure. Just very suspicious.

* * *

In Christina Farron's room, in her mother's country cottage which sat on the Welsh border, there was a photograph of Henry Pym-Hughes. It was kept in a closed, brown, leather-bound frame which could be opened like a book and placed, the photograph visible, on a flat surface. Christina kept it usually closed and in a drawer as her mother had a waspish aversion to it. Once, when she had accidentally left it out, she had found it swept into the waste-paper basket. That had been a bitchy gesture which Christina didn't need repeating. She looked at it wistfully, sometimes, when alone and when she needed a reminder of how the man she regarded as her father looked and perhaps also speculate on what life might have been like had she grown up with him.

Today, the photograph stood open on top of the dresser and what had prompted Christina to set it there had been the receipt of a wedding invitation from Angela Poindexter who was about to marry her Dad.

Tim Farron, her biological father, the man to whom her mother had last been married was, and always had been, distant from her. There had never been a warm relationship and she had arranged to avoid him whenever possible. Thanks to him, she had enjoyed her schooldays, spent near Bristol in a boarding school and later, in Sheffield, in university. This had greatly reduced the time she had had to spend near Tim – she never had called him Dad except when she was little. When, at around the age of ten, she had stepped in to take her mother's side during a blazing argument, he had turned on her and slapped her. Since then she had refused to accept him as her father and had called him Tim. On his part, it was as though he objected to her presence, that he would have preferred it if she had never been born. Christina never gave him much to object to, she had cut him out of her life, airbrushed him from her history.

Tim and her mother eventually split up, partly because of Sophia's erratic behaviour near a sherry bottle and partly because of her affairs – "They don't mean anything, darling." she would protest to Tim. Meaningful or not, Tim became disenchanted with her and they went their separated ways.

Christina had stayed in touch with Henry by letter alone because her mother would not countenance any meeting between her daughter and her first husband. Soon she would be old enough to decide for herself and this invitation presented itself as the ideal opportunity.

She looked into the mirror on the dresser top at which she was sitting at a slight angle. Daddy would recognise her, despite not having seen her for such a long time for she had been occasionally sending him photographs slipped inside her newsy letters.

There was no resemblance to him, though. She could never be mistaken for Henry's daughter no matter how she wished that was so. Hers was tawny hair, tumbling around a long, sometimes mournful face with finely cut features, all of them angular.

But she felt a stronger emotional bond between herself and Henry than between herself and her natural father. No love lost there. None to lose.

Christina missed Henry, missed having his paternal care, missed his love.

And now, he was re-marrying and Christina had every intention of being at that wedding. It was a perfect time for a reunion. She wouldn't tell Mummy, though. Mummy would do all she could to prevent her going, to the extent, if necessary, of having one of her turns, a piece of theatrical hysteria to which she would resort when things weren't going her way.

No, she must rely on subterfuge. She felt a wave of excitement and began to plan in her head what to take with her.

Chapter Ten

MISUNDERSTANDINGS

Love built on Beauty, soon as Beauty dies.
(John Donne)

Under normal circumstances, being the happy soul that he was, an end of shift drive home was done to music with Leigh singing loudly along to some favourite rock numbers on the CD player. This morning, with that tiny shard of doubt which Ellis had planted now growing spikes and edges and getting ever larger, Leigh's face was set by anger. Deep down, he knew what really had happened with Elaine and her pregnancy but he needed to confirm it, had to hear it from her own lips. There was no predicted event after this, no thought for any future, things would go however they might. There would be confrontation –so what? He just wanted to hear the truth.

He parked the car outside the garage, too impatient to put it away and walked sadly to his front door.

As he stood in the hall taking off his coat, he could hear Elaine working in the kitchen. Other than that, it was quiet. Usually, she would listen to the radio or even watch the tiny portable television she had in the kitchen, the one he had bought for her as an anniversary present. Evidently, her mood was out of the ordinary, too. It felt a little like a showdown.

Leigh's first words to her were direct and to the point, bushes were not beaten, no shillies were shallied and no hums hawed.

"You've been having it off with someone, haven't you?" he said.

Elaine was startled, unprepared. "What?", she said, playing for time.

Leigh moved closer as if this would make his words more audible, his point clearer.

"You've been seeing another fella and he's been seeing to you. Who is it?"

By now, Elaine had subconsciously worked out that her chances of brazening things out and calling his bluff, if bluff it was, were zero. Perhaps Leigh had found out from someone else – not Trevor – someone who had seen them out together and then gone and told Leigh. She felt fearful that things could turn violent if she tried to lie to him outright. But she could lie about her motives, that might soften the blow, shift a bit of the fault his way.

"Yes, I have." Ersatz shame made her look down and not directly at her husband, " I was so desperate to have a child that I went with another man just to get pregnant by him. I'm sorry, I didn't mean for you to get hurt." There were no tears this time, just dry defiance.

"Well, who the bloody hell is it. I want to hurt him. I want to show him just how pissed off I am!"

Her voice was levelled by the coldness she felt inside, "I'm not telling you, Leigh. I don't care what you do, I'm not telling you."

"Well, you realise that's me and you finished, don't you? You can't stay here with that bastard in your belly. You'll have to leave."

Elaine was resigned. So now it was just her and her unborn child. "Just let me stay long enough to sort myself out.

I promise not to be too long about it. I'll go as soon as I can."

Leigh found that he couldn't answer, he was choked with the disgust he felt for her. He turned and went straight upstairs to his bed in the spare room and quietly closing the door on the world, he lay on his pillow and wept.

* * *

Gerry spent the day following his date with Toni feeling quite delighted with life. There was a smile attached to his face which had ambitions of becoming a silly grin. After locking up the shop and making his way home, Gerry sat in the armchair next to the telephone holding the slip of paper which bore Toni's number, rubbing it between his thumb and middle finger. He was uncertain whether to call immediately or leave it for a day. Was he being pushy if he rang now? Or would it seem as though he wasn't really bothered if he left it a short while? His train of thought was broken by the tinny ringing tone next to him. He picked it up quickly, the question, 'Is it Toni?' forming in his mind as he said "Hello?"

"Gerry, it's me, Monica. I really miss you and I would love to see you again. Can we arrange a meeting?"

All her nervous gabble had disappeared. She spoke quietly, almost hesitantly and something in the tone of her voice removed the initial snappishness which Gerry had begun to feel. He didn't have the courage to tell her about Toni. Something, a lack of backbone perhaps, would not let him be firm enough with her and make her understand that he did not want anything more to do with her.

"No, Monica. Look, I'm tired, I've had a long day and I really don't need this conversation now. Will —?"

Monica had hung up. Just as he had been about to to ask her not to call her again, Monica had broken the connection. It was almost as if she'd known what he was going to say. She didn't want to listen to a brush off.

He tried to imagine what she was feeling right now;

what was going through her mind. Why was she behaving this way? More importantly, why did he care?

* * *

The woman was free. At large as Charley had put it. They had nothing on her and the investigation was looking very shaky.

Danny had put a lot of thought into this case and now he had an idea. He did not dare discuss it with anyone, he had to do this on his own and not even breathe a word of it to Charley. Not unless he cracked the case, of course. He would cultivate the woman's acquaintance – not as a police offficer but as an admirer – and slowly gain her confidence. Maybe then she would give something away. An idea had formed. He would go to her house and introduce himself as a writer who wanted to use the old house as a setting in his novel and would need to photograph the place – inside and out – to help him describe the scenes. Better make it a love story; not a mystery and suspense thing otherwise she might get suspicious. Perhaps then, he might get the opportunity to find a clue to what was going on.

* * *

The telephone rang again. He let it ring until the answering machine chipped in. He listened for the caller to speak but the line went dead. He supposed that it was probably Monica again. Well, she knew he was in so she must realise that he didn't want to speak to her. The woman was quickly becoming a nuisance and brooding about her had made him feel angry. All thoughts of Toni had gone out of his head and the smile had gone from his face and he was in no mood to do any more writing. He read over what had been written that evening, it didn't take long, he hadn't felt very inspired and switched off the computer. Grabbing his coat and notepad he headed for the local. It was raining as he left the house and even this seemed to be Monica's doing.

The evening turned out to be a pleasant one and, despite Gerry's initial reluctance, sociable. Dave Belloe had been there and bought him a drink because, as he told Gerry, Dave was celebrating his wedding anniversary. Mrs Belloe was nowhere to be seen and Gerry considered it wisest not to ask picky questions when the man was so obviously in a good mood. They had been invited to make up a foursome in an ad-hoc darts match with two other regulars of the pub with whom Dave was on nodding terms. Gerry had drunk a little more than he would have done under more normal circumstances, he'd come last in the darts match and the only solid food he'd consumed had been two steak pies and a packet of crisps. Still, it had been a bloody good evening and the smile that Monica had stolen was back again.

As he nearly hung up his coat before preparing for bed, Gerry noticed another message had been recorded on his answering machine.

"Oh, piss off, Monica!" he said exasperatedly, "Leave me alone, will you? Mithering cow!"

The woman was maddening him. Something would have to be done.

The night brought dreams of chattering teeth. Some were false, clinking madly at him like surreal ice cubes from within the confines of a tooth glass; some were disembodied, surrounded by a fuzzy, indistinct border which was sometimes lips and sometimes fur or hair. They were all Monica's teeth. He knew they had been hers when he woke in the depths of the night – the clock's hands were too blurry for him to see the time – but he needed the wakefulness to push the teeth away from that part of his mind which was in charge of generating dreams. He didn't want to go back to sleep unless some other, pleasanter thoughts were there. He switched on the reading lamp and rolled out of bed in order to empty his bladder and then, back in bed, to prepare his mind for rest without any unwelcome visitations. He settled on his back, switched out the light and started to think of animals beginning with the letter 'A', trying to name five before going on to 'B'. It was a trick he'd been told by a friend some years ago to help him sleep through a worrying period. Three or four letters generally did the trick. When the alarm woke him at five o'clock that morning, he suddenly remembered – Dormouse! That would have made five! The trick had worked, there had been no teeth for the latter part of the night.

Downstairs, as he made tea, he rewound the answering machine to reset it, thought better of it and listened to the message which had been placed while he'd been out. Something jumped in his chest as he heard Toni's voice. She was disappointed not to have caught him in but would he please ring when he could.

Shit! Damn that Monica! If she hadn't called me, I could have spoken to Toni last night. That woman is blighting my love-life with her pestering.

That morning, in the shop, as often happened, Police Constable Purslipp stopped in for papers and cigarettes. "Bugger me, it's like a lighthouse keeper's Christmas party in here. What's up with you?" This was Leigh's blustering reaction to the mood of the shop as reflected from Gerry as he slumped over the counter, morosely reading a magazine.

Gerry looked up from the Agony Aunt column from which he had hoped for a little guidance. "Oh, hi, Leigh, can I ask you for some advice? You might be able to help me here, you being a police officer and all. There's a woman who is bothering me. I think she might turn into one of these stalkers, you know? What should I do about it?"

Leigh seemed to consider the question and then said, "After what's happened with my marriage, I have to warn you that I no longer consider myself to be an expert on women."

Gerry interrupted, "Yes, I was sorry to hear about that. How is Elaine?"

Leigh ignored the pleasantry, " I'll do my best. Is she good looking?"

"Yes, to give her a fair appraisal, I'd say she was quite attractive."

"Can she cook?"

"Yes, she's actually quite a good cook but that's not the point."

"Oh, yes it is. What you want to do – and this is strictly amateur advice, mind – is to get round there, give her a good tommying, let her cook you breakfast and, take my word, things will sort themselves out."

Gerry didn't follow Leigh's logic, he thought it might be based on Leigh's over-developed interest in the opposite sex. He also thought that it would probably have the wrong effect on Monica and give her the wrong signals.

"I can't do that, you don't know the woman. Besides, there's another one waiting in the wings and I don't want her finding out about this one. What I need to do is dump the first one in favour of the second."

"Two bloody women! You don't need my help, mate. Get in there."

Leigh left feeling as though he had been a great help to Gerry despite recent events in the Purslipp household. And slightly envious, too.

Gerry phoned Toni as soon as his morning stint at the newsagency was over, apologising for not having been in but not giving her the real reason for his absence.

Toni had wanted to thank him for the lunch date which she had found unexpectedly enjoyable and to suggest an evening out in the near future.

"Yes, a wonderful idea." said Gerry enthusiastically, "Where shall we go? I won't suggest an evening in a pub, that's probably a bit predictable. Do you have any ideas?

Where would you like to go?"

"I have two tickets for a Stoppard play at the Playhouse in Steadmore and we could perhaps have supper somewhere afterwards."

"Can't find fault with that. What time shall I pick you up?"

"No, it's easier for me to pick you up since you're on the way to Steadmore from here. I'll be there at seven tomorrow evening, all right?"

Once again, Gerry was conscious of being steered away from discovering her address. Undeniably, it made sense for her to come to his house but she still wasn't letting on where she lived.

I'll find out eventually, he thought. Then, an image probably gleaned from the television flashed across his mind of stars and starlets in expensive clothes stepping from expensive cars into a theatre and he realised that he had no idea of what was the proper dress for such a place.

"Is it posh? What should I wear? I don't own tie and tails."

"Don't worry." she laughed, "It's informal. A suit will be fine. Sweater and jeans would not. That, by the way, is my dress code, not the theatre's."

It was a novelty for Gerry to be picked up by his date. By a quarter to seven, all ready to go, he was pacing his front room and making frequent checks of the road outside and of his image in the mirror, shooting his cuffs, worrying the knot of his tie and straightening his collar. Toni arrived promptly and Gerry was out of the house to meet her before she had had a chance to get out of her car. Seeing his eager charge down the pathway, she refastened her seat-belt and patted the seat next to her.

"'Hello, are you looking forward to this evening?" she asked as he sat alongside.

Gerry hesitated briefly and admitted, "Yes, I am. I'm

actually feeling quite excited. Like a big kid being taken out for a treat."

He noted but did not comment on the glamorous blue jersey dress which she wore. Compliments didn't fall easily from Gerry's lips. It was a fault which Carol had often had reason to criticise.

Toni smiled indulgently and headed for Steadmore. Gerry inhaled the peculiar but attractive melange of leather, violets and dog. He felt exhilarated.

"I haven't been to Steadmore Playhouse since I was a child. It was Puss-in-Boots but I can't remember who was in it. It just remains a fond childhood memory."

"That's sad." Toni remarked, "I love the theatre and I should find time to go more often. Perhaps we will, now?"

Her glance seemed playful but had an underlying seriousness to it which was lost on Gerry. The subtle facial vocabulary of womankind was a closed book to him.

The play was enjoyable, the time spent sitting next to Toni in the near dark was constant pleasure but for Gerry, the most memorable part of the entire evening was that, as they left the brightly lit foyer and walked into a soft drizzle that made the darkened streets shine, Toni slipped her hand into his. This prolonged contact was confirmation that she now felt comfortable with him. It seemed such a natural act even though she had probably thought quite carefully before doing it. A tiny part of Gerry on detachment as an outside observer saw the two clasped hands and marvelled that it had happened here and now.

"Where are we going now?" Gerry asked, "I'm not really familiar with Steadmore."

"For a curry." she said, "I just love Indian food and, as I can't make it at home, I like to eat Indian when I'm out. I'm assuming you like spicy food. Is that all right?"

Curry sounded just fabulous.

Red plush wallpaper, subdued lighting, soft sitar music and dark-suited Indian waiters floating over a thick, crimson carpet. Gerry wondered whether the décor reflected the management's taste or what they thought might be the expectations of the customers. The service and food, however, were fault-free and both he and Toni appreciated the intimate surroundings, they could talk quite unselfconsciously.

Toni was falling in love – this day her prince had come – but she hadn't wittingly accepted the fact yet while Gerry, if pushed hard, might have admitted that his thoughts might be wandering in a similar direction. There was a lot of eye contact along with the conversation and Gerry found himself wondering what it might be like to live with her. Then came attempted images of sharing life; an argument - - what would she look like when her temper was frayed? An evening at home sharing a bottle of wine before retiring. How about holidays? Where would they go? He would go wherever she wanted to be taken. Yes, he thought with some satisfaction, he could imagine himself and Toni together. Wonder what she looks like first thing in the morning?

Toni noticed the concentrated look. "What are you thinking about, have you gone off somewhere?"

"I was trying to imagine what you would look like when you're angry."

"Frightening. Why?"

"Just a writers' thing." he lied.

To redirect the conversation, Gerry suggested they go out somewhere the Saturday following. Toni swallowed hard as though there was some difficulty with her food and explained that Henry was to be married that day and she would be spending the weekend as a guest of Angela's, Henry's bride-to-be. She would phone him on the Monday and tell him all about it but couldn't really take him along, it was too soon to drop him into the family circle. She looked at him, expecting disappointment at not being invited or anger because she had been evasive.

He smiled, Gerry was quite happy with this arrangement, he wasn't too fond of weddings, anyway. The ones he'd been to had been dreary affairs with long periods of unutterable boredom broken only by the entertainment provided by the wrong people having had too much to drink. He was about to tell her the tale of Carol's uncle Edwin's antics at cousin Elizabeth's wedding but stopped himself. Perhaps Toni would be too sensitive to appreciate a graphic description of how uncle Edwin had urinated on the groom's shoes.

"I'm not sure whether to be pleased or not at your evident lack of disappointment." she said.

At the end of the evening, Toni drove him home and, as he unbuckled his seat-belt, she pulled his face towards her and kissed him.

"I really enjoyed the evening." she said, "I'll call you on Monday, I promise."

There was something in her manner which made it clear that to pursue that kiss in search of more would be useless. It had left an impression on his labial nerves which was pleasant to recall and he moved his lips reluctantly as he bade her goodnight because he didn't want the feeling to wear off too quickly.

* * *

The following day when he spoke of his date to Meera and Bob, Gerry could not remember what he had eaten at the restaurant. Meera was behind the counter and reading a newspaper and, without looking up, said that whatever it had been, it couldn't have matched her standard.

Bob manoeuvred Gerry a little way from Meera, hoping that she could not hear his question.

"Did anything, you know, happen?" A man-to-man question.

"What do you mean – happen?" asked Meera loudly, still reading.

That had been the question that Gerry was about to ask and so he said nothing, allowing Bob to attempt an acceptable answer.

Bob coloured, "You know – I was just wondering whether Gerry and – thing – had – did –."

Gerry saved him after enjoying the spectacle of his embarrassment for a little while, "Actually, yes. She kissed me and wants to see me again." Gerry smiled and Meera scowled.

* * *

In order to completely fool her mother over the plans for Henry's weddding, Christina rang Louise, a friend she had been close to while at university. She explained the situation and then asked Louise to ring back at an arranged time so that her mother could answer it, issuing an invitation to stay at Louise's home over in Derbyshire for a few days. A birthday celebration would be an ideal reason to make the call – it wasn't necessary to actually have a birthday, Louise pointed out.

Sophia, suspecting nothing, relayed the telephone message to Christina.

Soon afterwards, she left for Cabley Hall where Henry had asked her to put up for as long as she would like to.

Henry met Christina at Port Regis railway station. It was an emotional reunion and a dispassionate observer would have found it an exacting task to choose which of them was the most affected. Indeed, the said observer would have found it equally difficult not to shed a tear of joy himself. Henry was almost too overcome to drive.

"Before we go on, I need to ask something of you," Christina began, "I don't know what to call you face to face although I do know what I want to call you the same as I did in my letters. You never said I shouldn't so, may I call you Daddy?"

Henry's eyes welled with tears. These were feelings he hadn't experienced for such a long time and he had lost the ability to control it. He pulled out a big white hanky from his coat pocket and wiped the tears away.

"Please, darling, I wish you would."

There was a lot of catching up to do on the journey and the car was filled with shiny eyed chatter as they made their way to Cabley Hall.

Toni and Angela were waiting in the drive as they rolled up and Henry proudly introduced his daughter to his sister and his fiancee.

Henry's wedding went well. None of the events which Gerry would have supposed unavoidable at weddings occurred and, outside the church, the family group was photographed; not just by the photographers hired for the purpose but also by one or two representatives of the press. This, after all, was a society wedding.

Toni often found herself imagining the scenes she was witnessing but with Lady Antonia in the role of Angela and with Gerry in Henry's place. In between, she was having to come to terms with the absurd fact that she was falling in love with Gerry. How, after all these years, was it possible? Ludicrous! She grew wistful. She was so far away that she failed to notice that David Carrough, a cousin of Angela's, had put his arm around her waist as they posed. David misinterpreted her acceptance as a come-on and later, at the wedding breakfast, tried to follow up his success by trying to become more friendly. Angela had mentioned to him in the invitation that he was being invited as a single male in order to make up a twosome with Henry's sister. David had come with the impression that it was all settled, that he had only to introduce himself and the lady would be his for the evening if not for longer.

David asked Toni for a dance and, out of politeness, she accepted although she was not in the mood to dance at all. Also, it seemed to be a duty to dance at ones brother's wedding. David was encouraged and, during the second waltz, allowed his respectability to crumble a little and his hands to wander. Toni simply cut the dance short and left him on the floor. He had hoped to leave the celebrations with a woman but Toni's unfriendliness unsettled him and he left her to search for loose bridesmaids.

Henry noticed her, sitting alone, chin on cupped hand, watching the bride dancing with the best man.

"Come on, sis. You should be happy for me. Shall we dance? Guy has stolen Angela from me for a while."

Toni danced with her brother and thought about Gerry.

"You seem a bit distant, old girl. Something the matter? Has that David chap said something to you?"

"No, it's not him. He's just not my type. There is something on my mind but I don't think you'd take me seriously if I told you, anyway."

"Is it this new man you've been seeing?"

"Sort of." Her hesitant manner made Henry curious.

"He's not running you around, is he? I can find ways of dealing with him if he's going to hurt you in any way."

"Oh, stop being so protective, Henry, I'm not a vulnerable little girl any more. He's not likely to hurt me, really."

Henry understood from Toni's manner that it would be wiser not to pursue the matter any further but his concern remained. So did his determination to deal with this man if he dared put just one foot wrong.

On that Saturday morning when Toni's new, dark-blue, wide-brimmed straw hat was being jostled by other hats of an equally pugnacious design and by one or two grey silk top-hats, too; their owners trying to get ever closer to the bride and groom with each successive photograph, Gerry found himself being jostled in a completely different environment. He was crossing supermarket trolleys with other Saturday morning shoppers. Their impatience fed Gerry's demeanour with irritability until he could feel his nerves at breaking point. He could see the whites of his knuckles as he gripped the trolley's handle.

Having bought everything he needed and contained his temper while navigating through other, less focussed shoppers, he headed for the check-out. Gerry always seemed to pick the wrong queue. No matter how short his queue for the till was, people joining longer queues adjacent to his would be through before him and on their way home before he got to unload his trolley. Being used to this, he'd grown philosophical about it and tended to attach himself to the nearest check-out and just wait patiently. Sometimes he would check out the clientele for potential characters for a novel or imagine what their private lives might be like. Today, unfortunately, patience was in short supply and he spent the time frustratedly. It was with a feeling of relief that he picked up his credit card and pushed his reloaded trolley to his car. As he picked up speed to a fast walking pace, a woman thoughtlessly stepped in front of him and he could not prevent the trolley hitting her a glancing blow on the hip.

Why do women do that? he thought angrily. They should know, as inveterate shoppers, that trolleys do not steer well and have no brakes whatever. Would they step in front of a bus with similar specifications? Admittedly a trolley is unlikely to maim or kill but it can certainly take the shine off your day and make a mess of a pair of tights. While Gerry was filling his mouth with reproach to spit out at the culprit, she turned. It was Monica. Gerry coughed – the tirade gone like the contents of a waterbomb hitting the pavement and it occurred to him that she may have done it deliberately to engineer a meeting.

"Monica – oh! – sorry." he said. There was a lameness in his voice, inflicted by misdirected invective.

"Hello, Gerry." she said sweetly, "Are you doing a bit of shopping?"

Monica eyed the contents of the bags surreptitiously to check whether he was shopping for two or for one. She still had that suspicion that there might be another woman in Gerry's life.

"Yes – now, I must go, I'm in a hurry." he said, completely unsettled by her unexpected presence.

"Hasn't it been a lovely day?" she smiled, ignoring or unaware of his last remark and continuing to witter on without giving Gerry a chance to answer, "They said it would rain today and yet it doesn't look at all likely, does it? I don't think they know what they're talking about, these weather people, they just guess what's going to happen and they must get it right some of the time and we give them the credit for knowing more than we do when they probably don't. I bet if I —"

"Bye, Monica." Gerry pushed his trolley past her with a look which reflected the unpleasant thoughts he was having of her. It was not in his nature to be rude but he felt justified behaving so to Monica. He was relieved that she did not follow him.

* * *

The locker room of the police station was at basement level, a row of high-set, frosted paned windows marked the line of the pavement outside.

Inside were three rows of grey-green steel lockers with a bench between each row. The room smelled of a peculiar mixture of sweat, disinfectant and stale tobacco. It was decorated with odd pieces of male detritus, an abandoned sports sock here and an empty deodorant spray can there.

Leigh Purslipp and Ellis Clough were seated in the locker room preparing to go on duty. Ellis had seen straight away that Leigh was very upset to the point of distraction and concernedly asked him what had happened, fearing perhaps a death in Leigh's family or something equally disturbing.

Leigh realised that it would be good for him to unburden himself and explained the situation with Elaine, finishing by telling Ellis that the marriage was, as far as he was concerned, over for good.

"I dunno, El." Leigh continued dolefully, "They say that broken families make broken marriages. My parents were divorced, you know, and here am I doing exactly the same."

"So, was you brought up in a single parent family, then?" asked Ellis.

"Not really, I was twenty when they split up – me Dad was giving next door's one – and I'd already left home by then but you get my meaning, right?"

Ellis opened the flask of coffee which Sandra, his wife made for them both every shift and poured out two cups. It felt time for a coffee.

Leigh went on, "It always seems to me that coloured families do a better job of staying together than white people. So, what's the secret of a tight family life? You being of the black persuasion, as it were."

Ellis looked sideways at Leigh with heavy sarcasm crossing his knitted brow, "I'm no scientist, mate, but I believe this black skin is a result of genetics. No-one persuaded me to become black. In fact, if you take a black mother and a black father, chances are that you'll get a black child."

Leigh looked back at his partner, not sure whether he was serious or just having a dig at him.

"You know what I mean. I'm just not expressing myself well is all."

"Yes, I know. And I'm just trying to get your mind out of that sad rut it's in. Is it working?"

"Yes, a bit. I'm sorry, mate. Let's get saddled up, it's time."

In the row of lockers just behind Leigh and Ellis was another member of the force, one Trevor Mittman. Any other bobby would have ignored the conversation going on nearby but Trevor was interested and listened carefully. He determined to contact Elaine, this might be a lucky break for him.

Chapter Eleven

LOSING YOU

But misery still delights to trace its
semblance in another's case
(William Cowper)

Toni rang Gerry on her return from the weekend's activities.
They discussed the wedding and how it all went. Gerry
had been thinking over Toni's reluctance to disclose her
address and it occurred to him that he might shame her
into it if he invited her to his place

"I'd like you to come over and spend the evening at my
house." he said, "We could watch a film or listen to music
and I will attempt to cook us a meal. Would you like that?"

Toni would. She didn't care very much what they did
so long as they did it together. She very much wanted to
spend more time with this man. But that was not put into
words when she agreed to Gerry's suggestion.

"Dress casually, I shall be in jeans and tee-shirt." he
added.

Toni arrived clutching a bottle of wine and dressed at the formal end of casual, wearing jeans displaying a better pedigree than Gerry's, a white woolen sweater with a soft floppy roll-neck and a string of pearls rolling around inside. She gave Gerry a peck on the cheek by way of a greeting and instructions to chill the bottle. Gerry noticed that it was a Montrachet, a wine he had never tried before, he wondered whether it would be as good as the New Zealand Chardonnay he normally chose.

As he turned to put the wine in the fridge, he heard Toni giggle.

"What's amused you?" he asked.

"Are those jeans new?" she asked, a smile on her face.

"Yes, why?" He had bought himself two new pairs especially for his renewed social life, "How can you tell?"

"There's a label you missed." She leaned forward and peeled off a sticky label from the back of the leg which had Gerry's waist measurement and inside leg printed on it.

Gerry coloured, partly from embarassment and mostly from the touch of her hand on his thigh. This intimate touch was a new sensation and very welcome.

"Do you like Buster Keaton?" asked Gerry, changing the subject hurriedly.

"I don't believe I've ever seen a film of his. Are they good?"

"This one is. It's called 'The General'. I've seen it dozens of times, I never tire of it. As it's silent, you can watch while I cook and it won't prevent our chatting from time to time."

"Would you like some help in the kitchen?"

"I'll shout for you if I do. It's only pasta; there's not a lot of preparation and little likelihood of failure. I've practised pasta."

While Gerry was in the kitchen, he could hear Toni laughing at the film. He smiled to hear her enjoyment. He felt relaxed and happy. Maybe he could ask her shortly about a visit to her place.

Later, the meal over, they sat together on the sofa, a second glass of wine at their sides and listened to a Haydn C.D. on Gerry's stereo. Toni moved a little closer and nestled her head on Gerry's shoulder. He took this as a prompt to put his arm around her. He smiled to himself but she must have glanced up and seen it.

"Why are you smiling?"

"I've just been transported back nearly forty years to the back seats of The Gaumont in Wettenham. I was on my first date with a girl called Beryl Nevin and I put my arm around her then just like I put my arm around you. I was as nervous as hell when I did it, I thought she'd throw it off."

"Did you feel nervous just now?"

"No. It felt natural." He pulled his arm in a little, giving her a sideways hug. That sweater felt warmly expensive. Its contents felt that way, too. Toni settled back down to listen to the music, sharing his grin and sipping her wine from time to time.

When the C.D. ended, Gerry moved to change it but Toni put down her glass, reached round, pulling his right shoulder down to prevent his getting up and pulling his face closer to hers and kissed him. It was a long, sensual kiss and the lack of background music was forgotten while they enjoyed this new proximity.

Beryl Nevin never let me get this far, thought Gerry. He could feel the beginning of an erection and he felt a little embarassed, unsure whether Toni's advances had intended that effect. I mustn't push – I must try not to lead this farther than she wants to go. Control yourself. These thoughts had no success with his arousal and a slight feeling of panic invaded his breast. It would be unthinkable to repeat the clumsy gropings which had been a feature of his early intimate embraces with the successors to Beryl Nevin.

Toni pulled her head away a little, looked at him with

a new, wild gleam in her eye and said, "Take me to bed, Gerry."

Later, they lay together in Gerry's bed, shoulder to shoulder, just absorbing the feeling of each other's nakedness from the warmth of the points of contact. Her right leg lay carelessly across both of his.

"Did you expect that to happen?" Toni asked, an impish smile on her lips.

"No, I wasn't really sure that our relationship was strong enough yet to go this far. You're more forward than Beryl Nevin was."

She smiled and said, "I didn't expect it, I intended it because I have reached the conclusion that I'm in love with you. I'm not going to ask you whether you love me or not, that's for you to say whenever you're ready to." She reached for his hand and gave it a hard squeeze.

Gerry remained silent for a while. He was fairly sure that he did love her but he couldn't tell her now. It might ring false. Soon. He would tell her soon.

"Shall it be your place next?" he enquired. A double edged question. He felt a slight squirm of discomfort and her answer did not come straight away.

"Gerry, there's a very special reason why I can't tell you where I live. When I'm at liberty to do so, you will understand my reluctance. Can you trust me?"

With this last, she rolled toward him and raised herself to look into his eyes.

Gerry was disappointed and more than a little suspicious, thinking that perhaps he'd got himself a married woman who was having a fling but he mustn't let her see that. She was too good to let go, married or not. Even so, he felt a little troubled.

"Yes, of course I can trust you", he lied when what he really meant was, I suppose I've got no option. Then he put his arms around her, pulling her down and kissed her as though it were a means of proof when he was really denying her the opportunity of seeing the truth in his eyes.

* * *

Well, she'd fallen for it. He had wormed his way in, using his novelist story as a cover and she'd taken in every single word. She had been a big help, too, giving him all sorts of historical information about the house. Even allowed him to take photographs of some of the rooms. Then he had invited her to dinner as a thank-you for all her help and she went for that as well. This was too easy.

Over dinner Danny had broached the subject of the murders – merely introducing it as a conversation piece and pretending not to know that she was a suspect. He feigned shock when she told him. She was innocent, of course. Aren't they all?

The trouble was, Danny had begun to believe her and worse; he was falling for her! He really fancied this woman, there was something about her which made little scratches on the surface of his heart. She had begun to occupy a sizeable chunk of his thoughts during the course of a day, too.

* * *

Trevor Mittman knew when it was safe to ring Elaine, he'd been well coached because neither of them wanted to be found out by Leigh. And if Leigh found them out, then Trevor's wife Susan would find out, too. That would have been disastrous for both of them. Care was the watchword.

Trevor had a plan. The result of the plan would have meant that both Leigh and Susan would become aware of what had gone on between him and Elaine but far too late to do anything about it. He still loved Susan but Elaine had the advantage of newness. There hadn't been time to get fed up of sex with Elaine.

"Elaine. Hi. It's Trevor. I overheard Leigh and Ellis

talking in the locker room. You're pregnant, aren't you? And Leigh knows it's not his so it could only be mine, right? He says you and him are splitting up so I want to help bring it up. You and me, Elaine. We could run away together – set up home somewhere – Wales, maybe – start a new life with the baby. What do you say?"

While Trevor had been waffling along with his offer of a permanent basis to their relationship, Elaine thought of a lie. One which would rid her of Trevor and perhaps make him stay with his wife.

"It won't work, Trevor. Don't leave Susan for me. And what about your son? Doesn't Mark matter?" She sighed in exasperation.

Before Trevor could say any more, she added, "And besides, it's not your child. You mustn't ring me again. Goodbye." On this last word she hung up before Trevor could come back with any persuasive argument.

She left him stunned and a little hurt. As the click of the cut-off sounded, Trevor could only wonder who the hell it had been. Surely if there was a third man, he would have suspected something? And anyway, how was she so sure whose the baby was if she was sleeping with three men?

Well, understandably she would have discounted her husband but – another man! What a slutty cow she turned out to be!

Elaine turned away from the telephone feeling a little traumatised but not upset enough about breaking off with Trevor to muster a single tear. Her mind had already been made up. She had spoken to her mother down in Berkshire and she would be going back to live with her until she could become independent again. Her and baby. Mum was quite pleased about being a granny at last.

* * *

One of the perquisites of running a newsagency is the range of free reading material available during quiet periods. When Gerry was still a child, this had been the only aspect of such a job which had appealed to him, the privilege of getting to read the new Beanos and Dandys without having to pay. He noticed that his father didn't take this advantage, having no interest in the comic book rack but he never stopped Gerry from his enjoyment. Later, as an adult, Gerry realised that those revered comics of his boyhood had no appeal for grown-ups. All the new Beanos and Dandys lay unread on the shelf.

The magazine which Gerry had selected to leaf through during his last half hour before shutting up shop for the evening was the recently delivered 'County Life'. A van belonging to the Port Regis based magazine group which owned 'County Life' had, that afternoon, dropped off three bundles of magazines for Gerry to sell. He always made a point of looking through them all for articles of interest to him although he rarely found much in this particular magazine. The page he was looking at had a selection of photographs from the wedding of Lord Henry Pym-Hughes to Mrs. Angela Poindexter. It was merely the surname of Pym which had increased his interest to one notch past boredom. After all, society weddings were in a world greatly separated from his. In the largest of the photographs, he noticed a woman who bore a startling resemblance to Toni next to a cheerful looking man in a grey topper who had his arm around her waist. Without thinking, he dropped his eyes to the list of names printed below. This woman was one Lady Antonia Pym-Hughes, the sister of the groom. Gerry started to put several ones together and arrived at a sum which shocked him. It was Toni! And some bugger hanging on to her in a very possessive manner! Maybe he's her husband.No wonder she didn't want him to find out where she lived. She was probably too ashamed or frightened to introduce him to her family. He felt anger well up inside of him. Bloody aristocracy! Was she having him on? Stringing him along as a bit of rough, no doubt.

I'll phone her right bloody now and have it out with her. Absorbed and angry, he did not hear the customer come in and was alerted only when a female voice asked for a copy of 'The Wettenham Chronicle'. He looked up and his jaw failed to match the speed of the rest of his face as he recognised Monica. Gerry tried to treat her off-handedly as he would any unfamiliar person in his shop so, without a word, he passed her a folded copy and asked for eighty pence. Monica gave him a pound.

As he gave her the change she spoke, "Gerry, is there any chance that we could make it up again?", tears glistened in her eyes as she added, "Is there anyone else?"

Gerry could feel his irritability growing and he snapped at her, "Yes. There is. I don't give a shit if you have a problem with that because right now I have a problem with it myself and another one with you. Will you please piss off?!"

This last was delivered almost in a shout and a boy who had just entered the shop in the hope of getting himself a paper-round left very quickly, trying to convince himself that he could probably manage quite well on the pocket money his mother gave him.

Monica's feelings for Gerry turned to disgust as she saw the ugly face of his temper and this slowly settled down into a burning, strengthening hatred. She turned away, watering the feeling with her unshed tears and left the shop. She now knew that her suspicions had been correct and that Gerry would never be hers. It hurt her.

Gerry felt a little guilty for having upset Monica but he pushed it aside. At least the break must have been made now. She must realise that I'm not interested in her. He went to close up the shop at the front before telephoning Toni, he did not want any disturbances. Inside, he was seething with fury. Women in general rather than one in particular were the focus of that ferocity.

"Hello, Gerry." Toni said as she answered his call.

He could hear a horse snickering in the background

and the atmospheric sound suggested she was inside a building so he guessed he'd caught her in the stable.

"I've just seen a photograph of you in 'County Life'. What's going on?"

"Oh, Gerry. I was hoping to tell you everything myself. There's never a good time for these things but now you know who I am, we must talk about it."

"I'm bloody furious about this, you know. I think that you're taking me for a fool. Who was that bloke with his arm around you? Is that your husband or another stupid boyfriend?" His temper had been soured by his contretemps with Monica and he knew he was being sharper with her than was necessary.

"Gerry, it was no-one, I never even noticed what he was doing. He was just a guest."

"Yes and I wasn't. I wasn't good enough, I suppose. Well, I've had enough. Don't bother ringing again. Goodbye!"

What have I done? Gerry thought as he put the phone receiver down. Bloody Monica! Wound me up to such an extent that I've broken off with the woman I want. He banged his head on the counter to punish himself for sheer brainlessness.

Toni was so startled by his outburst that she stared at the telephone for some seconds after Gerry hung up. Then the tears came and she cried inconsolably. She had not planned it like this. How was she to have known that he would spot the photographs. She would not have taken him for a man who would normally read 'County Life' — but that was snobbish. He's a newsagent!. Of course he would handle a publication like that.

"Stupid, stupid, stupid!" she said aloud.

She had given so much of herself to this man. He could have been her future husband. Now, nothing. Just like that. One phone call. And all because of a silly misunderstanding. She upbraided herself for not having been honest with

Gerry right from the start. Henry would have disapproved but so what, at least she would still be with Gerry.

That night, Toni slept badly and the next day was listless and uninterested in what she was doing in the stables. Sally sensed her mistress' mood and kept away, Grundy knew something was wrong and pushed his muzzle into her hand when he could but was ignored each time. His sympathetic wagging went unseen.

Every now and then she would cry, "So stupid!" and there would be fresh tears. Several days were to pass before she felt close to her normal self and every now and then, a sad recollection would stroke her mind and she would think back to what had been lost.

Gerry spent the following day feeling shocked, as though some part of him had been amputated. One or two customers asked kindly after his health as they noticed that he didn't seem to be his usual ebullient self. They received a reluctant and uninformative reply. Later in what was the most miserable week he had spent in a long time, both Leigh and Ellis came into the shop. Gerry looked up from the newspaper he was almost reading and asked, "Both of you? Who's looking after the car?"

"Oh, we had bright idea," said Ellis with a grin, "we locked the doors. Some of the bastards will nick anything with wheels if they get half a chance – even a milk float."

Gerry looked puzzled. "Yes, but who would nick a police car?"

"Kids." Ellis explained, "We always get the car back again eventually but it's bloody embarrassing. We'd get the piss taken unmercifully by other bobbies if we let that happen. And it ruins your promotion prospects."

Leigh changed the subject and indicated Ellis, "I've brought him in to show him how a man looks when he's running two women." announced Leigh, a touch of vicarious pride in his voice.

"Well, you'll have to look elsewhere. I don't have one, now."

"How have you managed that?" Ellis asked.

"Easy. I told one to piss off and the other one, the one I really wanted, I fell out with on the phone 'cos I was pissed off with the first one and I felt a bit jealous as well. It's a long story."

Ellis and Leigh were intrigued and questioned Gerry about what had happened. No-one noticed that three customers had come in, singly, seen Gerry being interviewed by the police and sneaked out again.

At the end of the explanation, Leigh said to Gerry, "You've got one option, mate. Eat shit."

"What do you mean?" Gerry didn't really understand the advice.

Ellis explained, "You are going to have to go to her and apologise, man. Get down on your knees and beg for forgiveness. That's the only way to get her back."

"Yep." Leigh agreed. There was a professional air to Leigh's comment as though he spent his life dishing out successful advice to the lovelorn and this was despite feeling somewhat lovelorn himself.

"Bit of a snag," Gerry pointed out, "I don't know where she lives. So I can't go to her."

"Got her phone number?" Ellis enquired.

"Yes."

"Ring her. Don't matter about going down on your knees that way 'cos she can't see you." Ellis had the look of a teacher explaining the obvious to a stupid pupil.

"O.K. I will. Soon as I get home, I'll do it."

"Good lad." said Leigh, "Let us know how you got on."

* * *

Had Gerry been asked to choose an adjective to describe his state of mind, he would have picked turbulent. Visually, the sort of image an author might paint to put this idea of turbulence more clearly would be to liken it to looking into a washing machine in action. Rather than undies and sheets swirling around in a frothy lather, there would be half-torn pictures of Monica and Toni, with soggy self-reproach tumbling between them in a tepid, grey turmoil. A constant and annoying humming noise would be heard in the background.

After locking up the shop for the evening, instead of making for home, Gerry took a walk, hoping to soothe the seething mental mess. He walked through streets, through an industrial estate, and round about a public park seeing no-one or anything. He pushed himself to walk harder, to punish himself, to tire out his mind to get everything to slow down so he could think more clearly. There was a picture in his mind of Toni, laughing and tousled which kept crumpling up and he urged himself on to smooth it out. From time to time he was forced to stop in order to get his breath back and take his bearings and it wasn't until nine-thirty that evening he felt once more in control. Almost. He had made up his mind what he must do. He must grovel – apologise – try and explain his muddled thinking and what made him behave the way he did. It would be pointless trying to explain Monica and how upset he'd been after speaking to her. Also, it might look as though he was trying to shift some of the blame when, really, it was all his.

What remained was up to Toni. Would she accept an apology? Would she have him back? Should he buy her some flowers? They are supposed to have some magical effect on women; make them more receptive to excuses or lies. Bunch of roses or whatever and they're like putty, so they say. He remembered then just how hungry he was, set a course for home which included, en route, a fish and chip shop. Flower shops were all shut by then and so were not a consideration. He pushed himself forward again with renewed vigour.

The smell of warm, damp chips, vinegar and curry sauce put him in a better mood. There was no-one but himself being served and he took the opportunity to get a bit of free advice while he was there. The woman behind the counter was friendly looking but with a hard edge to her face, possibly due to over indulgence in cynicism.

"What are the best flowers to buy a woman if you want to tell her you're sorry?" he asked her.

"Flowers? I'd prefer chocolate or a bottle of vodka, me. Bloody flowers ain't much good. Roses, I suppose." She laughed harshly and added, "Day I get flowers off my old man will be the day I'm buried. Bastard."

Gerry ignored most of her advice and walked homewards, more slowly, now, munching on a meat pie and chips as he went.

He let himself into the house and, still with greasy hands and mouth and wiping what he could remove onto the side of his jeans, Gerry hurriedly reached for his journal. He wanted to put in what he thought before the mood evaporated. When he had finished, there was a dark, greasy smudge on the page which made that part of the paper almost transparent. He thought that it would serve more forcefully to remind him of this evening when he re-read this:

' I'm bloody stupid. There is no other way of putting it. I've behaved badly (bloody Monica) and had a row with Toni – my fault entirely, going off half-cocked like that and I may have blown any chances of a really steady relationship with her. Now, I'm not sure what to do.'

On that final note, he headed off for bed.

* * *

It took three attempts before Gerry finally and nervously got through to Toni. In between calls, he chewed his nails and walked up and down the room, cursing himself between fervent prayers that she would answer the phone. Not just that but forgive him, too. He hadn't thought about what he would say, he was going to play it by ear, deal with whatever situation presented itself. But he didn't feel confident.

"Hello?"

Her voice sent relief and renewed twitchiness through him, "It's Gerry," he said, "Don't hang up, please, I want to apologise for shouting at you. I'm sorry. There was a reason for me feeling so bad and then hurting you. Can you forgive me? Is there any chance we can start again?"

There was a silence at Toni's end as she experienced some odd sensations, too. It made her unsure of how to respond. She bit her bottom lip while she thought and a tear found its way gently to the corner of one eye. "Gerry, I don't know." Then the tears fell more freely and Gerry could hear her crying over the phone. He didn't know what to say. He couldn't cope with a woman's tears when face to face and over the phone you're denied the alternative of giving her a reassuring hug. "Are you all right?" Stupid question. Gerry knew that before he'd even said it.

"Look, Gerry, ring me again tomorrow, will you. Then I will have had some time to think it over. 'Bye."

Toni sat back on the sofa and waited for the tears to stop and then sniffed. "Yes, I do want you back but you can wait a little. Then perhaps I'll feel better able to listen to you." Gerry would have appreciated hearing that last remark but Toni had not meant for it to be heard by anyone but herself.

Gerry waited precisely twelve hours before ringing Toni again. In that time he had snapped at everyone who had asked after him and slept no more than four hours. Now, he was tired and a headache was waiting in the wings. Soon be over, he thought as he dialled that number again.

Toni was feeling more self-possessed and able to see faults on both sides by that time. She, too, felt the need to clear up the mess which had soured their romance. So, rather than immediately plonking herself on the moral high ground, she listened to Gerry's explanation without tears and then spoke calmly to him,

"I didn't mean anything like this to happen, either Gerry. Can we meet this evening at the Demsbury Arms – seven-thirty. Is that all right? I promise to explain everything."

Her quiet tone encouraged Gerry a little but he still fretted and he was unable to be better than curt as he accepted her suggestion, "Seven-thirty, then. 'Bye."

Still, he thought, I've another chance now.

That evening, still upset and a little worried by recent events Toni left her house to meet with Gerry. When she turned the key in the ignition of her car, there was just a click. This was not a normal noise. This was the noise of a car with a flat battery which was too tired to even try to start. She banged her forehead softly on the steering wheel, letting out two or three words which she would not have used in Gerry's company and was about to weep again when she remembered that she had an alternative mode of transport. She would be late but, provided the bloody thing started she would get there. In her haste, she forgot to take her mobile phone from its holder on the dashboard. It had been left there to charge and its battery was in a healthier state than that of the car.

At seven twenty-eight, armed with a bunch of roses with which he felt something of a prat, Gerry went directly into the bar of the Demsbury Arms. He had not seen Toni's car outside so it was safe to assume that she had not yet arrived. He said hello to Carol and explained why he was back there clutching flowers but did not order a drink; he was far too wound up. He wanted to settle this thing with Toni as soon as possible. He could feel himself jittering inside, he was more nervous than for the first date with her. He wasn't sure whether he'd like her explanation. But did he want to carry on with her if she was married or if she was hiding him away from her family and friends? He didn't know. Rather than pace about in the bar area, Gerry went back outside to watch the road for her arrival, first placing the roses on the passenger seat of his car. He walked a few yards along the verge in the direction of the village hall, his back to the way she would come, his hands in his pockets, his thoughts in disorganised tatters. He turned and walked back again a similar distance past the car-park entrance. He could see a good way up the lane towards Cabley, it lay straight, rising until the crest was cut by the horizon. There was nothing on it. His frustration increased with the delay. He continued to pace the hundred yard stretch in front of the Demsbury Arms for what seemed like an hour although it was only twenty minutes or so. No vehicle had been seen approaching from Cabley and just one, a Land-Rover being driven by a surly looking farmer with a black and white collie in the passenger seat passed him going in the opposite direction. Gerry stopped opposite his car and tried to call her on his mobile phone. Her phone rang but there was no-one to answer it. The tone changed to indicate that the call was being accepted by a machine and he hung up.

"Bugger it." he said aloud, "I'm off home. If she wants me, she knows where to find me."

Even so, he was reluctant to make that final move. A vehicle crested the rise of the lane and came into view. Gerry's hopes rose and then were quickly and sickeningly sunk when he recognised the vehicle as a horse-box. His head dropped and he gazed sullenly at the grass, willing himself to leave and just forget about her when the proximity of the horse-box made him look up again. It slowed and turned into the car park and Gerry caught a glimpse of a familiar tousled head at the wheel. He was overwhelmed with relief that she had finally arrived, all other thoughts flew or were shattered by the thumping of his heart. He walked slowly to the cab, his legs feeling slightly out of control, as Toni climbed down. She had evidently been crying again.

"Let's go inside." she said quietly and took his hand.

Over a drink, Toni explained, "Henry, my brother, advised me not to reveal just who I am in case my social position became the reason for wanting me. I had to wait until I knew for sure that our relationship was for the right reasons." She gave him a sniffy smile and continued, "And that man with his arm around me on the photograph was just a guest. I didn't notice what he was doing because I was worried about my hat being knocked off. He got short shrift very soon afterwards. Do you still want to see me?"

"Yes, of course I do. I'm just likely to take some time absorbing all this new information. So, do I get an invite now?" Gerry knew that this was an important question. Now she would have no excuse for not inviting him to her home.

"Yes." she announced decisively, "Now. Or at least, when we have finished our drinks."

"I've bought you some flowers but I left them in my car. And I'm sorry for making you cry." he said, almost tearful himself.

She seemed brighter now, the smile more ready. "You can follow me in your car, I promise not to drive too quickly."

Gerry kept pace with Toni's horse-box as she drove through Cabley and along a narrowing lane lined with hawthorn hedges and, every hundred yards or so, a passing place let into the edge. Normally, he hated following vehicles like these as they were slow and often smoky. Toni's horse-box fully fitted the general description but with his car windows wound up tight and in his current mood, he didn't mind in the slightest.

The lane swept left and on the opposite side Gerry could see the tops of the trees in an extensive woodland. Then, the right-hand hedgerow gave out abruptly to be replaced by a sandstone wall topped with iron railings. Through these could be seen an enormous house, half hidden by large, deciduous trees. Toni turned into the open gates and then shortly afterwards, turned off the main drive towards some outbuildings which Gerry imagined might be the stables. She stopped and Gerry pulled up alongside.

"Welcome to Cabley Hall." she said.

"Wow! You live here?" He had had no idea that she lived in such a place. He was overcome by the presence of the building sitting quietly in such opulent grounds as it had no doubt done for hundreds of years. Stateliness; that was the word. Like an old lady in expansive green crinoline. He sat in the seat of his car just looking around him, trying to appreciate the grandeur of the place, trying to imagine himself rolling up the drive to escort Toni out for the evening. Toni came to the door and impatiently hauled him out of the car.

"Make love to me, Gerry." Her eyes sparkled as they pleaded.

"What, here?" Gerry's brain wasn't quite set up for intelligent questions.

"No, here." was the reply as she took his hand, opened a side door into the horse-box and pulled him firmly in.

It was a warm smell; farmy, horsey, prickly and dry; really quite pleasant. There was a pile of fresh straw thrown down in one of the two stalls and this was where Gerry was led. Toni clasped her arms around his neck and wrestled him to the enveloping comfort of the stalks.

Afterwards, Gerry sat picking bits of the straw from his clothing and watching Toni dress. "I've never made love in a horse-box before." he told her.

"Neither have I but I have always wanted to ever since

I was a teen-ager. It seemed such a romantic place to do it. But, on the whole," she added after a little reflection, "I much prefer bed." and began to dust herself off.

"Now for the grand tour. Give me your hand."

"I bought you some flowers," he reminded her, "They're in the car."

"Really? Why?"

"To say sorry. It's what people do, apparently."

"Bring them with you into the house, I'll find something to put them in."

Gerry looked down at his rather dishevelled person and said, "I can't possibly go traipsing round that house dressed like this."

"Of course you can," she reassured him, "No-one is in to see you."

They linked hands, swinging them happily like two children in on a secret, Gerry's other hand self-consciously holding the bunch of roses as they walked towards Toni's house. It seemed to him that there was no comfortable angle at which to hold a bunch of flowers. As they neared the porticoed front, Gerry somehow expected a butler to open the door to receive Toni and to sneer at him but it remained firmly closed. He could see signs of neglect everywhere; the wrinkles on the old lady's face only becoming visible with proximity. He noticed, too, that there was no letter-box let into the door. How odd, he thought with not so much mail in mind as newspaper delivery.

Toni steered him around to the right and into a conservatory tacked onto the side of the house at its far end. A wet, muffled barking greeted their entry and two labrador dogs welcomed them; a fat old bitch with a greying muzzle and a younger, livelier male whose tail seemed to have quite destructive potential as it swept powerfully from side to side.

"This is Sally and her son, Grundy." said Toni as she knelt to pet them. All four went through the side door into the kitchen. Evidence of dog was all around. In both the kitchen and the conservatory, paintwork had a scuffed and dirty look up to about two feet from the tiled floor level while the area above that, in comparison, looked clean and fresh. Two large dog-baskets with food and drink bowls were placed untidily across the far wall of the kitchen while on the right, an old-fashioned range greeted them warmly. Toni threw her coat across the unpainted wooden table and announced, "Come and see the rest, the dogs won't follow, they are not allowed past the inner kitchen door."

Gerry dropped the roses on top of the washing machine and followed obediently.

The tour finished in the library and, as Gerry looked about him, taking in the thousands of volumes stacked on shelf after shelf, he could hear, in his mind's ear, the strains of an opera aria being mastered by Caruso.

"So, how do I match your criteria?" Toni asked.

"Perfectly," Gerry said, amazed, "It was only a shot in the dark but – I must say – I love it, I love everything, I love you, I really do. And, no, its not for what you represent." he added, indicating by a double, all-embracing arm gesture the whole of his surroundings, "It's you. Let me take you away from all this."

Toni laughed and insisted on showing him her bedroom for a second time.

Chapter Twelve

THE RECTORY

There are two tragedies in life. One is not to get your heart's desire. The other is to get it.
(George Bernard Shaw)

From a distance, Angela Poindexter could look mousey and indistinct, melting into the background and more easily ignored than noticed. Proximity brought to your attention the forceful nature of her personality and you became more directly aware of a woman beneath whose gaze whole regiments of blood-thirsty Cossacks would quail. Her eyes, under the concentrated brow, would quickly assess anyone within range and, taking a dim view of fools, was furiously impatient with anyone less direct than she liked them to be. A stranger, on first encountering Angela for whatever reason would describe her as cold eyed and haughty but once better acquainted with her, he would find there was a good deal of warmth in her no-nonsense manner and gently chiding wit. Provided, of course, that he was neither one of the aforementioned Cossacks nor a fool. It was these admirable qualities which had attracted her to Henry Pym-Hughes.

Once Angela and Henry had decided to marry, they began house-hunting and eventually found an old rectory in the village of Grange Leigh which suited them both. It was a picturesque village, a few miles north of Steadmore and whose buildings were half-timbered frames sitting on sandstone foundations. The main street on the sides of which most buildings sat was uncertain in both level and direction and the houses, cottages and shops had been settled on whichever level and orientation was suitable in its particular position. This gave an untidy and badly planned effect to the village as though the builder either did not possess or was not acquainted with spirit level or plumb-bob. A few trees, seeming to have grown accidentally, dotted the footpath which threaded its way down the street's southern side The adventitious appearance of almost everything in the village was also one of its attractions, bringing to it a variety of folk in search of a life less ordinary.

The rectory, off the main road and built by someone at least familiar with the rudiments of architecture, was decorated and furnished prior to the date of the wedding but the hiring of staff was deferred until after the honeymoon in Malaysia. In the meantime, Henry and Angela thought it necessary to employ a house sitter to look after the place during their absence.

Outside the church of St. Thomas the Unwieldy in Grange Leigh stood, in common with many parish churches all over the country, a noticeboard. It was a wooden structure with a silly and purposeless wooden-tiled roof. In front of this noticeboard stood Miss Gladys Knight, a middle-aged spinster of the parish. Her spinsterhood was not due to her largely unprepossessing appearance for, after all, love is truly blind but rather to her wildly independent spirit. She had no interest in men or indeed in fellowship of any sort. She was happy with her own company. She was often happiest, late at night, after consuming five or six cans of lager, a secret habit of hers. So secret was it that she ignored the local off-licence and bought her beer in bulk from Steadmore, waiting until dark before she unloaded her car. This undercover method was meant to hide her habit from her neighbours but this clandestine trade had been spotted often enough and most knew Gladys' habits.

Gladys was reading the advertisement for a housekeeper which Angela had placed on the notice board. She had already read the one which had been placed in the newsagent's window and was not only familiar with the wording, but was determined to apply for the situation. She was merely reassuring herself that the two positions were actually one and the same.

Those traces of grace and femininity still residual in Gladys served only to establish her gender in the eye of the beholder. You were never likely to hear her singing snatches of song such as 'Who's that pretty girl in the mirror there?' or 'Mirror, mirror on the wall'. In fact, songs of any sort were unlikely to be heard in her vicinity for hers was not a musical soul. A heated discussion or a Parliamentary debate on the radio were her preferred entertainment. She loved the sound of discord.

When Gladys knocked on the door of the rectory to be greeted by a mildly surprised and instantly wary Angela, she was wearing a washed out blue baseball cap from the rear of which an untidy hank of rusty, greying hair protruded. A yellow sports shirt covered a heavy bosom which nowadays rested thankfully on the platform provided by her paunch, the lower slopes of which, combined with the upper elevation of her buttocks, forced her navy-blue shorts to a jaunty angle. This also prevented the lower hem of the shirt from ever having proper contact with the waist-line of the shorts, presenting the onlooker with a fashionable but unpleasing bare midriff. Grey woollen socks were rolled down onto her soft walking boots, the toes of which seemed to peer back up at the wearer in a sort of disbelief. These were suede, rubber-soled lace-ups of the type you would imagine an indoor hiking boot to be. Not that there are many houses where an indoor hiking boot would be of much use.

From the back pocket of her shorts, Gladys produced a short curriculum-vitae and two references; one of which was from the magistrate who lived at the other end of the village, the other, less verifiable, was from the previous tenant of the Rectory who was deceased. Angela was too polite to comment on Gladys' peculiar wardrobe but she did notice, from the smell, that Gladys was a smoker. Apart from that, there was no reason for Angela not to hire Gladys. Besides, time was short and there had been no other candidates. Angela impressed on Gladys' mind that she must not smoke in the house and that, if she must have a cigarette, it had to be smoked in the garden.

Gladys nodded dutifully.

Gladys was, by nature, bone-idle. If something could look after itself, as her philosophy went, then it would be silly to interfere. She did not realise that, in consenting to house-sit, thus abandoning her own home for the time being, she was agreeing to the unspoken suggestion that her house and its contents were less of a temptation to burglars than Angela's and therefore less in need of continuous habitation. In truth, Gladys could not have complained for the suggestion was an accurate one.

Gladys moved into the rectory the day after Angela and Henry left for tropical climes and treated herself to a nose around. Angela had shown her around the house before leaving but there were rooms and cupboards which demanded closer inspection. First to be checked was the kitchen and, in particular, the fridge. There was room enough for at least a dozen cans of lager and they were taken from the boot of her car and placed there to cool. She had brought enough beer for a week at the most but it would be all right to leave the house for essential shopping. Angela had prepared a spare bedroom for Gladys' occupation and after unloading a small pile of her favourite videos and a few magazines into the living room, she took her bag upstairs. Once there, the bedrooms were checked. The master bedroom caught her interest and she walked around the wall peering at the pictures which were hanging there. Then she tested the bed by bouncing up and down on it. It met with her approval, it was so much better than the guest bed which she was to use but she thought better of moving in. They might find out.

That evening she arranged an armchair in front of the television, placed a table next to it on which she put a newspaper to protect the table's surface from beer rings and, on top of that, an ashtray. It would be all right if she was careful, kept the house aired and observed the no-smoking rule just before they came back. With a gory gangster film on the video and a cold can of lager by her side, Gladys prepared to enjoy her assignment.

Two days before Angela and Henry were due back, Gladys decided that it was time for a quick dust-around and a swish-about with the vacuum cleaner. During this rather desultory house-cleaning session, Gladys stopped for a quiet smoke in the passageway between the kitchen and the dining room. She opened a window overlooking a field beyond which lay woodland and the effect of this view on Gladys was pacific to say the least. It would have been difficult to guess what may have been going through her mind and it is probable that she may have undergone a partial mental shut-down, a blank state of consciousness and was smoking in automatic mode.

Her cigarette finished, she sucked the ash and cigarette end into the vacuum cleaner and closed the window without giving full attention to her actions. Tonight she had decided to go back home. She was missing her own place and 'er and 'im would be back soon so it would be all right to just leave things to look after themselves for that short while.

That night was the one chosen by the team to pay a little visit. This had not been a critical choice. Any night during the time that Gladys was staying there would have been right for she was such a deep sleeper, helped to undisturbable depths by the alcohol she consumed, that she would have slept through a burglary and any ensuing police raid.

Robbie, Wilf and Wayne had met up again in the Irish Hand to discuss the continuing success of Robbie's grand plan. It was working like a dream. The punters were coughing up just as planned so as to minimise the fuss that they would have to endure by involving the police and the insurance companies. They parted with the ransom money like lambs. Not one person ever tried to put one over on the threesome.Robbie seemed to have the talent of pricing the demand just right. Cutting out the middle men was proving to be a very lucrative way of doing things.

The team's subsequent ventures had gone as successfully as the Stillwater job. They never made mention of the attempt foiled by that stupid dog, that was part of learning the trade. Mistakes are often made early in successful ventures. Robbie had realised that he needed to pick the mark carefully and even more precisely, although he was willing to admit that there was an element of luck in finding the right object, taking away what was most highly treasured. Knowing a little about the mark helped and Wayne had been instructed to discover as much as he could about personal details. For instance, in that old girl's place they'd done last, it was a wedding album; nothing else. Not that she had much else barring the cash for the grandchildren's inheritance. What's that? It was only a grand. She couldn't raise any more and, anyway, bollocks to the grandchildren, such was the thinking behind Robbie's logic, they can work for a living same as I do, not sponging off their gran.

The hand-overs had gone smoothly, too. They picked a fresh meeting point each time, they didn't like the idea of re-using the old places too quickly. It had to be dark, away from street lights so no-one was recognised. This generally meant the countryside and so this was another responsibility that Wayne had taken on whilst out spotting for them.

That last handover had seen just Robbie and Wilf manage it for themselves, Wayne had been indisposed. Wilf had had the brilliant idea of putting on his growler face-paint, the grey make-up he wore when performing with Borborygmus. Wilf explained to Robbie that, not only would it frighten the punters just that little bit more when they saw him but it would add to his anonymity.

"Works a bit like a stocking face-mask, Robbie, they won't be able to describe my features to anyone wiv it on. Plus, it don't snag nor run." was how he put it.

Robbie agreed but declined to follow his example. He had a niggling doubt but couldn't quite put his finger on the flaw in Wilf's thinking.

The punters were just too frightened to play hero - - they'd no idea how many confederates were around, unseen – too dark, wasn't it? Moreover, they were so glad to get their precious belongings back, they were almost pleased to hand their cash over.

"So, Wayne, where've you been? Have you found anything for us?"

Wayne planted his pint pot on the beer mat and folded his arms.

"You know Geoff Biddon, does domestic security work – fitting cameras and alarms – that sort of shit? Well; he had me doing a foreigner with him up north of here."

Wilf knew this Mr. Biddon, a man responsible for

teaching him a lot of his present skills.

"Place called Grange Overy." Wayne continued, "There's two or three villages up there called Grange something or other – and I'm in the boozer on me lunch break on the last day of the job and there was this old, fat bird in there talking to the barmaid. Just chattin' and you can't help earwiggin' a bit. Anyway, she's supposed to be looking after the rectory in Grange Leigh, a couple of miles away because the owners have buggered off on whatsit, honeymoon. Place is empty. I've been for a gander and it's posh enough to be worth doing."

Wayne drained his glass and banged it down on the table to illustrate his point, "Empty as that glass!"

"Right.Sounds good. Where's this fat bird go of an evening? Does she go home?" said Robbie.

"No, she's house-sitting and sleeps in but she's a bit of a piss-head by all accounts so we wouldn't wake her."

"Fair enough. The sooner the better we do this one 'cos all honeymoons must come to an end. Tomorrow night O.K. for you two?"

Wilf and Wayne nodded.

"I'll be round with the van for ten – your round, Wilf."

While Wilf busied himself at the bar, Robbie was digging further for possibly useful details from Wayne's brain. He knew that Wayne had odd bits and pieces of unconnected data bouncing around inside his head and with the right bait, an intelligently directed question, things that even Wayne was not aware of could be fished out. Thus, Robbie discovered what other properties overlooked the Rectory, where they were and what the chances were of doing the job undisturbed.

By night, the rectory looked quite unpleasant from the outside, a feature which neither Henry nor Angela was aware of as they hadn't seen their future home in the dark. The stone griffons which stood atop each gatepost; a shield in one claw and a sword in the other, sightless eyes fixed on a future no human can see, had, when silhouetted against a clear night sky, a rather threatening posture. A breeze shuffling through the nearby wood and coming out to ruffle the heads of the rhododendron bushes in the rectory garden produced for the stranger an unsettling noise. The house seemed to frown down upon you as you approached and Wayne, who was very nervous and rather wished he hadn't chosen this place, jumped as a pheasant screeched indignantly from the wood, its repose having been disturbed by an ambitious fox.

They had left the van parked in a lay-by on the outskirts of the village to walk quietly and unnoticed to the rectory. Wilf was quick to pick out for Robbie the easiest point of entry, a window at the back of the house which had been latched carelessly. None was worried about his movements being caught on camera since none could be identified and, besides, if the punter played the game, the tape would never be seen by anyone else. They relied on signals rather than voice for communication. Over the weeks since they had been working together, Robbie had even devised a signal which said, "No, you dozy bastard, the other way!"

The job was easier than they expected. Wilf had previously been detailed to check upstairs looking specifically for jewellery while the other two remained below. He checked only the master bedroom and a second room furnished as a study. The third bedroom showed signs of recent occupation but was of no real interest and the fourth bedroom was completely bare as Henry and Angela had not yet started to decorate it. It never occurred to Wilf that the house-sitter was missing.

Robbie, meanwhile, collected a dozen paintings from the walls of the entrance hall and the library. These were strapped together in two bundles by which time Wilf had rejoined them, clutching a shopping bag which contained something quite weighty. He signalled to Robbie that upstairs was done and then brandished the bag as though by doing so, he could guess its contents.

"Let's call it a night." Robbie signalled, "We've got enough."

He quickly wrote out a note and left it on the table and, as he did so, his eyes were drawn to a figurine standing on it; a ballerina crafted in what looked like silver, poised on one leg, the other pointed backwards and her hands clasped under her chin in a supplicatory gesture. It felt awkward in his pocket but it had called out to him.

Two days afterwards, Henry and Angela arrived back in Gatwick and drove home to the sickening discovery that they had been burgled. There appeared to be no damage to their remaining property, no signs whatever of vandalism, just missing items and the note. Angela dropped into a chair and wept, all the strength had dropped away from her, she felt heartbroken. The first suspect was Gladys. She, supposedly, had been on the premises at the time of the break-in. Henry called at her home and found her in. He asked her to come to the Rectory immediately and Gladys, thinking that she was about to be praised for her efforts and perhaps be given a bonus, arrived some time later. It became apparent during the rather tearful interview with Gladys that she had had nothing to do with and, amazingly, was not even aware of the robbery. Because, as it transpired, Gladys had broken her contract with them by leaving the house empty for the last day or so of their holiday, Angela was not prepared to pay her for her time. Henry, even irritated as he was with Gladys, persuaded Angela to pay her just the same. Gladys took the money sniffily and went back home, certain that none of it had been her fault – she'd no idea why they were picking on her.

Henry was angry with these unknown housebreakers but he was confident that they would be brought to book, he would have caught them on his security cameras. It was just unfortunate that the telephone link to the local crime response unit had not been set up yet but he had remembered to put a tape into the recorder. After reading the note once more, Henry became thoughtful. Perhaps it can be resolved without much trouble. These people were probably not aware of what they had stolen and were surely just amateurs. Had they been art thieves, the mix of what had been taken would have been different. The choices made by this gang were plainly random, just grabbing at whatever looked pricey.

Also, three of the paintings did not officially exist. They were hidden heirlooms, a means of avoiding some of the crippling death-duties normally incurred by wealthy families and had been passed down through two generations without ever having been insured. One, a Sickert, had been given gratis, by the great man himself, to Henry's maternal grandmother who had considered herself a patron of the arts. Two other canvasses this same grandmother had rescued from a pile of paintings about to be destroyed by Whistler who had wanted to make room in his studio. Henry's grandmother passed them on to Henry's mother before she died and now Henry owned them. Or, rather, had owned them.

Henry went to pour two brandies and settled down to watch what the cameras had seen. The rather grimy pictures showed three young men wandering confidently around the house, looking at his valuables and selecting some for removal. They were careful not to break or disturb anything which hadn't appealed to them but seemed to know, more or less, what was valuable enough to be worthwhile stealing. Not a single distinguishing feature was shown by the cameras except fleetingly, when one of the men put the statuette of the ballerina into his pocket. This man was dressed in denim and had very short hair. Even so, Henry doubted that he could recognise the man if he saw him on the street.

Monica, meanwhile, was seething. She had not nurtured her anger against Gerry enough to destroy any keepsakes she had of him and his photograph, or an enlargement of the one he had sent her complete with a facsimile signature and framed in silver, still stood on top of the television next to the stuffed pink rabbit. Whenever Monica felt frustrated about her unhappy relationship with Gerry, she glared at the photograph and it seemed to help somehow. Another woman would have flung it angrily into the bin once it became obvious that the affair was dead. Whether it was a sliver of hope that stopped Monica from following the common example or its use as a memoir of romance, not even she could divine. She knew that there was another woman. Some tarty cow who wouldn't be able to look after him, to care for him the way that she could and would if she had the chance. Well, maybe she ought to do something about it. Something that would bring that Gerry Fledding to his senses. But what? What could she do? First, she must find out who this woman was and where she lived. She went out into the kitchen to make up a flask of coffee and cut some sandwiches and left a note for Wayne, telling him that he would have to get himself a take-away that night.

When Monica took up this sleuthing, she went to great lengths with her personal appearance, especially with her make-up, applying it with great care as though she was out on a date and hoping to impress some lucky fellow. She understood that wearing perfume was not appropriate but she dabbed some on anyway, it made her feel better.

Monica parked in a side street which gave a partial view of the front of Gerry's house, enough to see anyone who came or went and there was less likelihood of being seen by Gerry. She saw him come home from his evening stint at the newsagency and he didn't go out after that.

At eleven o'clock, Monica decided that it was safe to go home, she knew what his movements were likely to be for the early part of the morning. She would pick up the surveillance again when he got back home later in the morning. She would telephone Mrs. Wardle and tell her that she was too sick to work. Tummy bug. That's the best thing to have for sick leave.

* * *

'Danny! We've re-arrested that woman — her from the park.'
'Donna?'
'Yes. That's her. How come you're on first name terms?'
'We're not – I mean, I got it from the file you showed me. What have you got on her? Is it new evidence?' he asked these questions hurriedly to cover the confusion he felt. It mustn't appear that he had become friendly with the woman.

'Yes, the knife has been found, the one used in the first two jobs. A stiletto — buried in the park and it's got her dabs all over it. She even admits to owning it. Says she uses it as a letter opener and someone must have taken it from her house. Yeah, right. Like we believe that.'

Danny did believe it. He was now convinced that Donna was innocent. He must try to help. But how? Who on earth could be trying to frame Donna and why?

* * *

As Gerry showered and changed before going to Toni's place for his introduction to horse-riding, his feelings were mixed. He felt excited and happy at the prospect of spending more time with Toni but an apprehension born of his fear both of horses and of making a fool of himself was chipping at the edges of the good feelings. No man likes to look silly in front of a woman he is trying to impress.

Perhaps it may rain, he thought. He peered hopefully up at the sky from his bedroom window. The sky was a pale blue beneath which was a large flock of irredeemably fluffy clouds, folding, refolding and spreading in an attempt to become even fluffier as they passed across Gerry's view. A light breeze ruffled the feathers of a jackdaw perched on top of the street lamp across the road.

And then again, it may not, he thought. Come on, move yourself and get it over with.

Monica had parked in her usual place in order to watch Gerry's movements after his morning shift. She had parked there so often that Gerry, had he been asked about the little yellow car, might have supposed that it must belong to a resident. She followed him carefully as he drove south-east, surmising that he was making for Demsbury again. As Gerry approached the village, Monica swung into the turn-off for the village hall and parked. Just to make sure, she got out and walked round to the Demsbury Arms to check for Gerry's car. The car-park was empty. Bugger! He must have driven straight past and gone elsewhere. Monica ran back to her car and blew gravel and dust at the village hall as she raced off to try and catch up with Gerry. There were really only two lanes down which he could have gone. One led back, circuitously, the way they had come and the other, to Cabley. Monica urged the little car up the rise to catch up with him again. Through Cabley she slowed, looking to left and right to see if she could spot Gerry's car but failed to see it. Now Monica felt a little panicky. She felt that she might have lost him but drove on hoping to see him again. She was forced to slow again by the nasty left-hander just before the big house. Looking over to her right at the house, more from nosiness than anything else, she spotted his car parked at the front. Gerry wasn't visible; the only person she could see was an old man on an old ride-on mower who bore no resemblance to Gerry at all. This, evidently, was where he had come. The big house, probably, was where the new woman lived. So, it was money that had lured him away. Well, money can't buy everything. He would find that out soon enough. Monica realised that to spend time waiting outside this house would likely be non-productive so, after mentally criticising the external paintwork and the curtains at the bedroom windows, she drove sadly home.

* * *

As Gerry turned into the gates of Toni's home, he noticed a figure dressed in black moleskin trousers, black waistcoat, a collarless striped shirt and a panama hat who was driving a venerable petrol-powered mowing machine. The man was perched on a backless seat suspended over the roller which served as the rear wheels. Two long, wide handles stretched back from a sick, smokey engine by which the driver steered. Hung from the front of this machine was an enormous grass box which would have become very heavy when full.

Why British Racing Green? Gerry thought. Is it ironic?

As Gerry passed the mower, The driver half stood and took his hat off to him in a gesture of greeting. Gerry waved back.

He parked the car in front of the house and went around to the side entrance and let himself into the conservatory where he was welcomed by a cautious Sally and an effervescent Grundy. Toni came out to complete the picture and her attentions, Gerry felt, were preferable to those of the dogs although, it was always nice to be made to feel wanted by whomever or whatever.

"There is some old buffer doing laps of your paddock – is that the right word? – on an ancient ride-on mower. Who is it?" Gerry asked.

"No. Grounds." Toni corrected, "That's Kelps, the gardener. He comes in at odd times whenever anything needs doing. I pay him a sort of retainer and he turns up and keeps the vegetation from rebellion. He's not so old,

216

either. He's your age or thereabouts. He just dresses in an old fashioned way. When I was younger he was what was referred to as a young fogey and he has never let go of fogeydom. From a distance he looks about seventy-odd but when seen up close, he looks like someone got up like an old man. I've known him for years and, do you know, I have no idea what his christian name is. A long time ago, he used to be married but then his wife died, I think it was 'flu, I'm not sure but he has never found anyone to replace her. He's a lovely man – lives in Poast. You pass it as you come here."

Gerry remembered driving past the four or five houses which represented Poast. They stood alongside the old road to Demsbury which had been straightened in that area, leaving Poast in what looked like a lay-by.

Kelps had spent all his life in Poast and his working life in the surrounding area as hired casual labour. His various accomplishments had made him popular with all the farmers locally and, even in winter, he was never short of work. His way of life and his occasional confrontations with poachers and illegally camped travellers had made him physically strong and capable.

He had begun work as a part-time handyman cum gardener with the old Earl, Henry's and Toni's father while still a young man and had hung on to this facet of work because, from it, he gained the most enjoyment. Something about the care of a large garden, something about pressing his personal seal into a small part of the English countryside appealed to him greatly.

He had married his first love, a girl named Susan whom he met at the county fair when he was just eighteen and had made their home together in the Kelps' family abode, living side-by-side with Kelps' widowed mother.

When he lost his wife to influenza just two winters later, Kelps hit the bottle for a while and those who knew him supposed that the shock had deprived him of the will to live but gradually, with the support of his ever-patient mother, he survived the tragedy. The experience left its mark, giving him a thin, pinched, blood-shot face with a sad look which remained there even while he smiled.

"Anyway, bad news, I'm afraid.", Toni continued, " No horse riding today. Would you believe Henry has been burgled? He rang me a short while ago and is a great deal shocked by it all. He and Angela are driving over as we speak. Angela feels that she can't sleep in the rectory tonight so she and Henry will stay here until the shock wears off. Would you like a coffee?"

"Please." said Gerry absentmindedly. He was pondering the news and the consequence that he would meet Toni's brother under rather unusual circumstances. He had always imagined a staid family gathering, a dinner party or similar event where Toni would introduce him as the favoured suitor to the rest of the clan. Today, he didn't feel ready to meet prospective in-laws. Even the pleasure of a cancelled riding lesson didn't improve the mood.

"Go and sit in the library while I prepare some."

In the library, Gerry found an easy chair which faced one wall of books, a pleasing panorama for one of his tastes and a sight which encouraged contemplation. There were aspects of the plot of his novel which needed sorting and this was as good a place as any in which to resolve them. He felt satisfied that he would not be making a prat of himself on horseback today. The idea of getting up and scanning the shelves to see if any masters of his genre were present to offer help and advice occurred to him. Then again, the shelves might only contain dusty tomes of professional interest to lawyers or accountants and would prove disappointing to him. Mulling this decision had rather led his mind away from current events and he didn't hear the door open as a man dressed in a checked woolen jacket of impeccable cut, light brown slacks and brown brogue shoes let himself in. He stopped, close to Gerry's chair and put his hands in his pockets at which time, catching the movement in his peripheral vision, Gerry noticed him.

"Hello." said Gerry, rising to his feet and putting forward his right hand.

"You must be Toni's pet peasant, am I right?" said the newcomer, firmly shaking Gerry's hand in greeting, his smile underlining the humour intended in his opening remark, "I'm Henry, Toni's brother."

Ah! thought Gerry, he wants to take the mickey. Let's see how he thinks on his feet. "Yes, I am." he said, putting both hands back into his pockets and looking Henry in the eye. He had no intention of giving any further information yet nor of rising to his bait.

"So, what is it you peasants do in your free time?" Henry asked in seeming innocence.

"We sit around plotting your downfall, why?"

Henry was pleased with the other's reaction. That remark of his could have caused anger in someone with no sense of humour – or someone too thin-skinned to think straight. Gerry's retorts were good ones and he mentally applauded him. He admired anyone who could appreciate badinage.

The two men stood facing the other each with a suppressed smile on his face, each trying to draw the other one out. An instant rapport had formed; one of those infrequent instances where two strangers find themselves intellectually attracted to one another, both on the same plane of thought.

"Not been very successful, yet, have you?"

Nice one, thought Gerry. "No," he countered, "otherwise you'd be tugging your forelock instead of pulling my pisser."

"Touché. If nothing else, you have a sense of humour. I'm very pleased to meet you."

"Pleased to meet you, too. I had imagined that we might meet for the first time at an arranged dinner party or something of the sort. You surprised me turning up like this."

Henry smiled wryly, "We'll arrange for the dinner party at a more convenient time. Has Toni told you the bad news?"

Gerry nodded, "Yes it must be a big shock coming home to find you've been burgled."

"Yes, it is. I left Angela, my wife, with Toni in the kitchen to help with the coffee. They'll join us shortly. Look, I'll show you the note they left. You may be able to help."

Gerry read: 'We have kidnapped your paintings and some of your wife's jewellery. You can have them back for £5000. We will contact you with the details of the ransom. Don't bring the busies if you want to see your stuff again.'

He handed back the note. "That's a novel use of a word – kidnapped paintings. What sort of paintings have they taken?"

Henry explained the value and provenance of the artwork and added the reason for three of them being uninsurable.

"There was also a statuette taken. They don't mention that. I wonder if they have any intention of returning it. It isn't listed in the note. And what does he mean by 'busies'?"

"The police." explained Gerry. "The way I see it, you'd be better paying up. I realise that would mean they get off scot-free but I can't see an alternative.If you do call in the police, there's no guarantee that they'll be caught and you have a promise there that you won't see your belongings again, anyway."

"I think you're right, you know." agreed Henry, "But we have to try to at least make things awkward for them somehow."

At that moment, Toni and Angela came into the library bearing a tray of coffee and cups.

"I like him already.He'll probably do." Henry told his sister.

Introductions were made and here Gerry felt just slightly out of place – not unwanted but not quite fitting. It was possibly because his was the only working-class accent. He may also have been the only person in the room with a job. But there was no similarity to the man behind the Job Centre desk. It was difficult to reassure himself. Angela seemed to reinforce this feeling. She seemed remote, off-hand with him; almost as if she felt embarrassed to be seen hob-nobbing with his kind. Give her the benefit of the doubt, thought Gerry, she's probably too upset to be her normal self.

After the formalities, Angela dropped back into the conversation she and Toni had been having as they came into the room, it was a finely detailed litany of what the thieves had taken from her bedroom. Henry sat quietly, hunched forwards on his chair, fingers interlaced between his knees and watching, rather than listening to, his wife.

Eventually, Henry said to Gerry, "Well, what do you think the first move should be?"

"Wait – at least for the moment." suggested Gerry. "I've seen hostage handovers on news programmes on television. I imagine that this will be run along the same lines. When they have contacted you and presumably set up a meeting place to do the hand-over, perhaps we might come up with something else. We at least have a breathing space in which ideas might turn up."

"Shoot the bastards!" said Angela pointedly and unhelpfully. From her lips it sounded almost a practical suggestion, such was the authority her voice carried. Gerry found himself trying to imagine ways in which it could be done until his sensible part realised the futility of the project.

"Yes," said Henry patiently, "We don't know who it is we're supposed to shoot just yet – besides, I believe it is close-season for burglars."

No-one else could better Gerry's proposition and, despite the beautiful, dry weather outside, the atmosphere in the library continued cold and damp.

When, unenthusiastically, the afternoon trudged towards three o'clock, Gerry had to take his leave in order to relieve the Jamiesons at the shop. He felt almost grateful to have to go, the burglary had cast a shadow over everything. As he shook hands again with Henry, he said, "You must get in touch just as soon as they contact you – Toni knows my number. Maybe we can come up with some means of thwarting them."

"Thank you." said Henry sincerely. He knew that Gerry was as clueless in this matter as he was but it was reassuring, nonetheless, that there was someone else on his side.

* * *

The evening was cool and pleasant and Danny was thinking hard about Donna's predicament as he strolled his beat. Crossing the open square formed by the magistrates' court, the council offices and two adjacent rows of shops and fast food establishments, he saw a figure approach. Danny quickly recognised Dean Thompson, a minor miscreant with no scruples; it was possibly even a disadvantage to be scrupled in Dean's line of work. However, he wasn't currently wanted to assist anyone in their enquiries so Danny was civil to him as Dean had been known to pass on the odd bit of helpful information. Especially when encouraged to do so in the right way.

"Evenin' all." said Dean, introducing a humorous note to the conversation.

"Hello, Dean. What's happening?"

"Don't know nothing me but I have heard one or two of the lads discussing these murders. Benjy, he's as queer as a concrete parachute but a nice bloke, he reckons they haven't

got the right one. That blonde piece didn't do nothin'."

Danny's heart leapt when he heard this piece of unexpected news but he wouldn't let Dean see how much it meant to him. Dean might expect favours in return.

"Any ideas who did?" Danny asked as casually as he could manage.

"Nah." Dean scuffed his trainers along the paving stones as though trying to wipe off dog crap, his hands stuffed into the back pockets of his jeans. His boredom was showing through.

"O.K., where can I find this Benjy and what does he look like?"

"Any chance of borrowing a tenner? I'm a bit short until me Giro comes in." Benjy's hopeful whine was annoying but Danny knew that this was his way of announcing the cost of the information he had. Money and knowledge changed ownership.

* * *

To the Rectory, Grange Leigh, was delivered two days later an unacceptable number of junk mailings, two utility bills and a small, type-written envelope. Henry, suspecting that this missive might be from the burglars, opened the latter first. The message, also type-written, described a car-park near the derelict Wettenham railway line as the meeting place, the time to be eleven p.m. and reiterated the earlier instruction not to involve the police.

Still, thought Henry, it might be a good idea to view the place in daylight to get the lay of the land and to see if any ideas occurred to him.

It was not an inspiring place, looking dismal and forlorn, merely serving to depress him further. It looked as though they might have to take whatever chances presented themselves as they arrived.

The only possible valuable card in what was a poor hand – and this was no court card – was a gut feeling that this group were not the sort to carry fire-arms. There had been no mention of that sort of thing in the notes. Perhaps they relied on physical prowess and the psychological weight of people's innate fear of the criminal fraternity. If he were to turn up with one or two others and a couple of shotguns, it could turn the scales against the thieves. Perhaps they might not expect their victims to be armed, Henry mused. I must ensure that Gerry knows which end of a shotgun is which before we go. Kelps is handy both with his fists and with a twelve-bore and I know he would jump at the chance to assist us in this sort of game.

A vague outline of a ghost of a plan was forming in Henry's mind as he drove home from the proposed meeting place after giving it a once-over to familiarise himself with the area but it was Toni who gave it some substance. Henry called her and explained that a team of four consisting of himself, Gerry, Kelps and Toni would go along. Angela was to be left behind to pace the floor because she was rather emotionally fragile at the moment and was unlikely to be an asset to them if things got hectic. Marisa promised to keep her company. Toni was to drive Henry's car and the male members of the team would provide the muscle.

Toni said, "Let's capture them!"

"What?" enquired Henry, unsure whether he had heard his sister's suggestion correctly.

"We'll capture them!" she repeated with no loss of enthusiasm.

"If that were possible, where would we put them? There's only room enough for one in the boot of the car and what on earth are we going to do with them? That is, provided we are not out-numbered by them."

"We won't take the car, we'll take the horse-box. There's room enough for half a dozen in there. We must remember to take plenty of rope."

"You still haven't explained what we would do with them even if we could carry it off."

As Henry was saying this, another idea was slowly forcing itself to the surface of his consciousness. Perhaps he had a use for their burglarious talents. Wouldn't need a whole gang of them, though. One or two would be enough.

While this inkling was germinating and developing into a solid plan, Toni answered, "We'd give them a taste of their own medicine, that's what!"

Henry's own plan had distracted him too much to pay full attention to the second part of his sister's idea otherwise he might have made a discouraging comment or two.

"First things first. We have to get Gerry and Kelps in on things and make sure they know what their role is."

* * *

Some forty miles due north of Port Regis in an old people's home in the leafy suburbs of the town of Wednesday Market, an event occurred which would have an adverse effect on the team's plans. On the morning of the day set for the hand-over of Henry's paintings, a Mrs. Mathilda Capstick, a widow of ninety-three and grandmother to Robbie Benson, was preparing to start her day. The first several minutes of it were quite normal; things happened expectedly and actions were according to habit. After rising from her bed she went over to the curtained windows and, before drawing them apart, pushed her head between them to peer secretly at the day and its contents. Mr. Ethers was taking his customary pre-breakfast stroll in the grounds, prodding the garden into wakefulness with the rubber tip of his walking stick and flicking out the weeds which the council gardeners had overlooked.

Mary from the kitchen was emptying a small container into a larger one, a sour look upon her face as she eyed Mr. Ethers. The look was caused by the contents of the small container rather than by any disapproval of what Mr. Ethers was doing.

Mathilda turned away and dressed herself, said good morning to the picture of Arnold, her late husband, tidied her hair and fished her teeth from their overnight soak, put them in and inspected the result in the mirror before going to the bedroom door and making her way to breakfast.

She was only part way downstairs when she had a dizzy spell, took a purler and arrived at the foot of the stairs much more quickly than she was accustomed to. Mathilda missed breakfast, having died about half way down. Her number had come up and the good Lord had called it in. It was a relief for Mathilda's soul which had patiently waited sixteen years for this moment; that being the length of time that her beloved husband had predeceased her.

Robbie's mother, Mathilda's only daughter was informed of the tragic news and, once her initial grief was over, press-ganged Robbie into transporting her, post-haste, to the scene of her mother's demise.

"But Mum, I've an important job on tonight with Wilf and Wayne. I can't let them down!"

Robbie's mother knew how he supported himself or, at least and unlike Wayne's mother, knew that what he did was outside the law. but she asked no questions. It would put her in a dilemma if she knew exactly what he did. No mother willingly offers her son up to the law saying, "I believe he can assist you with your investigations, officer." She preferred suspicious ignorance to guilty knowledge. She wasn't prepared to let Robbie cry off just because he'd got illegal things to do, she put her foot firmly down and impressed upon Robbie the importance of his mission.

In the end, Robbie was forced to call Wilf to explain the situation and to pass on last minute instructions and advice on the meeting with the punters. He was confident, Robbie told Wilf, in his and Wayne's ability to effect the hand-over with no problems.

"Can we not cancel it?" asked Wilf naively.

"Cancel?" shouted Robbie. "It's a handover, part

of a carefully planned operation, not a bloody dental appointment. It will have to be done on time."

He left it with Wilf to inform Wayne of the new arrangement.

Wilf left a message with Monica for Wayne to come out to Robbie's lock-up with his van where (and this bit was not told to Monica) they would load up and make their way to the meeting point as Robbie was not going to make it. Apart from Robbie's, or rather, his grandmother's mishap things proceeded smoothly. Monica passed on the message to Wayne having first written it down to avoid confusion or forgetfulness, Wayne started out to meet Wilf in plenty of time and, despite Robbie's absence, both felt confident in their respective abilities to to clinch the matter. Neither doubted that it would go as smoothly as the other hand-overs.

Gerry had a feeling that events in the near future might clash with his job at the newsagency. That afternoon, when he called in to take over from Bob and Meera, he asked whether they would be willing to run the place for a couple of days.

"I've got something important on over in Cabley and I might not be able to make it back in time so I would be really grateful if you could stand in for me."

"No problem." said Bob who had already performed this service for Gerry once or twice in the past.

Meera smiled and asked, "What did you say her name was?"

"Ah." Gerry judged that an explanation was called for. "Yes, there is a new woman in my life. Her name is Toni but what I shall be involved with shortly more concerns her brother. So, yes, I shall be seeing Toni but not on a romantic footing – if you see what I mean."

Meera beamed and said "Yes." in such a way as to convey a certain amount of disbelief but with lots of approval.

Chapter Thirteen

THE RANSOM

You think this is cruel? Take it for a rule, no creature
smarts so little as a fool
(Pope)

In 1925, the Western County Railways Committee elected
to construct a spur line from the existing Port Regis-to-
London line to serve Wettenham, some ten miles away.
There was a demand for both a passenger service and an
agricultural goods service along the length of the spur and,
until the 1950's it was a profitable line. By 1960, the profit
had disappeared as it was found expedient to service the
farms' needs with lorries and the passengers opted for the
convenience of private car ownership. The popularity of
the line dwindled and so the decision was made to close
it. It lay derelict for many years, the former owners of its
land seemed uninterested in claiming the land back and
then someone had the bright idea of turning it into a linear
park. A flat ribbon of countryside for the use of walkers,
cyclists and horse-riders. Its stations were sold off as
desirable residences and car-parks were attached here and

there to make it easier for those former passengers and their descendants to walk where the line used to run. Now, instead of the clanking of buffers there was the clip-clop of horses and the majestic chuffing of steam engines was replaced by yapping dogs and squealing children.

In one of these car-parks, a little used one approximately mid-way along the track, Robbie had arranged to meet for the drop. It was lit, rather poorly and one-sidedly, by the lamps along the minor road which passed it, the sick, orange glow deepening the shadows. It was tastefully decorated in the way that the great British public likes its countryside; strewn with litter and dog faeces. At its entrance, a rusty barrier stood sentinel, pointing vaguely to the sky and if you craned your neck, you could make out the words written on a metal plate about half-way up the barrier: 'This car-park closes at dusk'.

It may well have done at one time but now, it was open all day and all night, the barrier stuck through disuse in an almost upright position. The only two vehicles to be seen in the area were an irreverent looking Skoda van belonging to Wayne Prough and a blue horse-box which was Toni's.

The latter arrived first and Gerry and Kelps secreted themselves on the shadowy side, near the rear of the vehicle and watched as Wayne's van entered the park. It never occurred to Wilf and Wayne that a horse-box was an odd choice of transport for the punters. Odd enough to cause suspicion had they thought about it. Toni remained in the cab of the horse-box, its driver's side window open, while Henry went to speak with Wayne, allowing him to venture into their territory. Wilf, complete with grey face-paint which he fondly hoped would make him not only unidentifiable, but terrible to behold, remained in the van but watched the proceedings. A high-pitched beeping noise sounded from his pocket; someone had sent him a text message. He pulled his mobile phone out and read a message which Beryl had sent: Pck sum mlk up on way bck xxx Byl. This message from his wife distracted Wilf from the proceedings outside and he began to tap out a reply.

"So where's the money? Your gear's in the van." Wayne said curtly. His tone and body language, borrowed from a favourite American gangster film, belonged to someone who thinks they have the upper hand. Henry, in pantomime, patted the pockets of the checked gilet he wore. "Bugger!" he swore, "It's in my jacket in the box; hang on, I'll get it." He turned and walked up the ramp into the back of the horse-box.

Wayne, hands in pockets, followed him and stood at the base of the ramp as Henry returned, waving a convincing looking large brown envelope. Gerry, unnoticed by the texting Wilf and unseen by Wayne, crept behind the latter and then pushed him hard so that he stumbled on the base of the ramp and fell flat on his face, his hands only just reaching the wooden slatted surface of the ramp before his face did. Wilf was still busily texting his beloved when he heard Wayne's cry and so was a little behindhand in his reaction.

Gerry knelt on Wayne's back, fist in the nape of his neck and shouted, "Hands behind you. Now!"

Kelps meanwhile, taking advantage of the surprise Wilf was feeling at the present time, had run to the Skoda and slammed the door as Wilf was opening it in order to shout his disapproval at the un-sportsmanlike behaviour of the punters. In times of stress like this, logical thought takes a back seat and there is never an opportunity to ponder the stupidity or inadvisability of one's actions. The sudden meeting of Wilf and the van door had the effect only of increasing his surprise and of re-seating him. In this state he noticed the twin barrels of a shot-gun pointing at his head. He put his hands up. Wilf considered that that was acceptable conduct in these situations.

Wayne, also no hero, nor in possession of any of those qualities which might help to make one, obeyed Gerry's command. His wrists were tied with a length of cord and

230

then Gerry climbed off him and ordered him to stand. He struggled to his feet and looked about in amazed anger. Toni had by then arrived from the lit side of the horse-box holding another shot-gun. Wayne's mind was doing its best to race but it was genetically disadvantaged. Mostly it was shuffling through a sequence of half-remembered films where the hero is captured by the bad guys in similar circumstances in order to get a few tips which might help Wayne to regain his freedom. It was a slow process and meanwhile he was herded into one of the stalls of the box, thrown down onto a pile of straw and his ankles were bound. Wayne's mind, by this time, had established that he was the goodie and that the others were the baddies. It never occurred to him to consider that the opposite might be true. The straw smelled of horse shit. By the end of the journey, so did Wayne. He tried a form of escape he'd seen to work successfully in the cinema at some time. He stood up and tried to chafe his bonds through against a vertical strut of the stall. Unhappily, horse-boxes when driven at speed are not the most stable of platforms on which to practise this manoeuvre and, hampered as he was by the rope around his ankles, Wayne fell over. After two attempts and having been twice thrown back to the floor, Wayne was trying to think of an alternative method of escape.

Wilf's fate was a little different. Once Wayne was out of action and Henry was satisfied that there were only the two of them to deal with, he went over to Kelps' side and told Wilf to get out of the van. Wilf sprawled out, his hands still up or, at least they would have been up if the rest of Wilf had also been upright.

"On your feet and put your hands down." Henry shouted.

Wilf complied dejectedly, feeling that valour was overrated.

"Are you all right?" inquired Henry of Wilf, noticing

the grey face paint which, under the pallid sodium lighting from the distant street lamps, did not have the terrifying effect on the casual observer that Wilf had hoped for. It made him look quite ill and this was why Henry was being so solicitous.

"What djer mean?" Apart from having failed to deal adequately with his current situation, Wilf felt as right as normal and did not understand Henry's question.

"Never mind." said Henry, accepting that perhaps the man usually looked this way, " I have some questions for you."

It had the potential of being a painful interview, Wilf could tell so he answered his interrogator's questions with something approaching honesty, keeping half an eye on Kelps who was stood to one side with the gun hooked over his arm. At the end of it, Henry understood most of the situation and that the brains behind all this was Robbie the Burglar. An apt name. Wilf was instructed to walk home and to pass the message to Robbie that the scam had not worked this time and that not only was there no money forthcoming, he, Henry, demanded the return of the statuette which was missing from the returned belongings. Henry gave Wilf a mobile telephone number by which to contact him.

"And don't tell the busies!" Henry added unnecessarily as Wilf turned to go. Wilf scowled and shot Henry a filthy look as he left.

Wilf felt annoyed and angry with himself at having been duped and with those people for having taken Wayne although he would, under questioning, have admitted to some relief that it was Wayne rather than he who was in their custody. He understood that the job had blown up in their faces and the immediate future of all the members of the team rested with these posh bastards. Fancy bringing guns! I mean, that was not playing fair! He headed for

Wettenham, it being nearer than his own home and hoped that Wayne's mum would either let him crash there or maybe even run him home.

After some painful and smelly miles for the terrified Wayne, the horse-box and its cargo arrived at the destination and the ramp was dropped. Wayne had no idea where he was except that he was in the sticks, in the dark and in the shit.

Henry was enjoying himself. He'd driven the horse-box as fast as he dared back to his old home. Toni sat at his side hanging on tightly and saying nothing. In his side mirrors, Henry could see the headlights of Wayne's van as Gerry, with Kelps riding shot-gun as it were, tried to keep pace with him. The lights were readily identifiable as Wayne's as one of them would switch off from time to time, leaving just the dim glow of the side light. It seemed to wink at him.

Henry stopped the horse-box near the stables and went round to let out 'Chummy' as he'd begun to think of his captive. It was a word absorbed into his vocabulary from a dimly remembered police drama which he'd once seen on television.

Wayne was marched at shot-gun point into the stables and made to sit in an old armchair to which he was firmly tied. A powerful light came on, shining directly into his face. Under its glare, he could see the posh bloke on a wooden chair which had its back turned towards him. The posh bloke leaned forward on the chair back and looked at Wayne. To his left and visible only as a pair of beige jodhpurs with a shotgun across them, the rest being hidden in shadow, sat the bird. The third bloke was stood next to her. Wayne had only counted three people in the car-park. In the darkness, he could hear horses snickering and stamping. Wayne had never been fond of horses and his recent experience in the horse box had only made matters worse. Things were getting a bit melodramatic for him, not that Wayne would have employed that particular word. Fright'nin' would have been his choice. Far too many scenes from thriller movies crowded his brain and his mind could hear the shrill whine of a dentist's drill.

"Right, sonny," the posh bloke began, "We've reclaimed those belongings of ours which you brought with you. Where is the rest?"

"I don't know about any other stuff." Wayne whined.

"There's a missing statuette. Can you think of anyone else who might know?" asked Henry quietly. He wanted Wayne to corroborate Wilf's story.

"Robbie would know." Wayne answered before he could check himself.

"So you and this Robbie burgled my house and you don't know what was taken?"

"I was never in your house. I stayed outside watchin' out. It was Wilf and Robbie who did the nickin'. I never seen what they took till tonight." Wayne's compliance was fuelled by his very real concerns for his personal safety.

Little by little, Henry worked with Wayne, winkling information from him until he knew the whole story.

"Where can I find this Robbie, then?" he asked.

"I don't know where either of them live." whimpered Wayne, "I only ever see them in the Baltimore. Or the Irish Hand. The Baltimore is Robbie's local"

"What are those, public houses?"

"Yes, why?"

"Where's this Baltimore?" prompted Henry.

"Baltimore Oriole; Dock Road – Port Regis. Wilf knows where Robbie lives. It's somewhere near there.Can I go home now?" Wayne felt that his helpfulness deserved a reward.

"No. You've been kidnapped, just like our property. You'll be returned when all of our things are back safe.

You're being held to ransom."

Wayne's eyebrows met in the middle to discuss their suspicions.

"That's illegal, that is. I know my rights." Wayne almost shouted.

"We are aware of that. Burglary is also illegal. We won't tell the police if you don't. You'll be looked after, meanwhile co-operate with us, behave and you'll soon be home."

Henry stood up to leave and Gerry stepped forward, "What's your name?"

"Wayne – Wayne Prough." he said reluctantly.

Gerry started at the name but covered himself, saying "Right, a Wettenham lad are you?"

Wayne nodded. The game was up; he'd had enough.

* * *

Benjy had been helpful. Danny knew who he was looking for but couldn't do anything about it. He wasn't in a position to be able to arrest this new suspect without some sort of justification. Time for a bit of snooping, he thought.

Coppers on the beat have an intrinsic reason for wandering around in the dark. Even if surprised on someone's property, any old tale would do for a cover. The copper is always believed, I mean, he's the goodie, isn't he?

Danny had watched the woman come out of The Roseate Kitty club by the railway station and climb into a Ford Mondeo to drive home. A check on the Police National Computer got him further details including the woman's address. Not quite on his beat but he was going to nose around anyway.

* * *

When Wilf finally arrived at Monica's house she was, not surprisingly, in bed. It took a few minutes of knocking before she put her head out of the window to find out what was going on and a few more before Wilf could make her understand that it was important, it concerned Wayne and he wasn't going to discuss it on her doorstep. Several more minutes passed before Monica made her way downstairs as she had to make herself look respectable before she opened the door to a strange man. Seeing Wilf close up across the threshold rather took Monica aback.

"What's up with your face?"

"Ey?" inquired Wilf.

"Your face," Monica reiterated, "You've got something on it. What is it?"

"Oh, it's face paint," explained Wilf irritably, "Do you want to know about your Wayne or not?"

Her previous knowledge of Wilf was only of having seen him in Wayne's company just once so she was reluctant to let him in. Wilf insisted that he was not about to pass on the news – bad news, he might add – about Wayne's predicament until she did. Monica's reluctance evaporated once she understood that her son might have a problem and she ushered Wilf in quickly whilst checking whether she was being watched by her neighbours. It was past midnight and she need not have concerned herself as most of these worthy people were fast asleep and those who were not had no interest in Monica or her activities.

Wilf sat on the sofa and Monica placed herself on its arm at the opposite end.

"Wayne's been kidnapped." Wilf began, reaching the nub of the matter immediately.

Monica started and clutched the neck of her dressing gown, "What?" she said, "Where is he? Is he all right? Who's taken him?"

"Let me explain." began Wilf, "We did a job – a burglary – me, Robbie Benson and your Wayne."

A stifled syllable, possibly beginning with a 'W' escaped from Monica's lips then, "You mean to tell me that my Wayne's been burgling?"

When Monica's face took on a horrified expression, anyone seeing it could have been forgiven for mistaking it for a terrifying one. She didn't mean to do this and probably wasn't aware of its effect as she wasn't the sort of person who practises gurning or grimaces in the mirror. She was just trying to convey the shock she felt on hearing this unbelievable piece of news about Wayne. Wilf was, nonetheless, unnerved by it and consequently unsure of whether to continue or to flee. Wayne's mum looked as though she was about to attack him and bite him. The walk back to Port Regis was looking like an attractive way of passing the remainder of the evening. Any activity which took him further away from this fearsome and angry woman was preferable to sitting within range of her. The pink fluffy rabbit perched on top of the television set, had it been asked and also been capable of giving an opinion on which of the two humans in the room looked the most frightening: Wilf, setting out to look fearsome in grey face-paint and Monica, who owed her alarming visage to an accident of genetics, would have picked Monica without a second thought.

"Go on." demanded Monica as she realised that Wilf had stopped his story and was staring at her with a strange look on his face. She hoped he wasn't getting any ideas. A woman on her own isn't safe.

Wilf went on as ordered,"Well, the idea was to nick stuff and sell it back to the owner. Less fuss that way and everyone's happy. The police are kept out of it, the punter gets his stuff back and we get a wedge of cash."

Wilf noticed that Monica's lower jaw was slowly rising back to its normal position just below the top. He felt a little easier as the teeth went out of sight like a drawbridge closing on a portcullis.

He continued, "Well, this last job, the punter turned up team-handed and wiv shot-guns."

Monica's lower jaw started its slow descent again and Wilf hesitated. Fascination was taking over from fear.

"Tell me they haven't shot my Wayne!" she cried.

"No. no, he's fine. No-one got shot. Erm, Robbie wasn't with us 'cos his gran's died and they forced Wayne into one of those trucks that they carry horses in. I've been told to get hold of Robbie and get him to meet up with this posh bloke who's running fings or they won't let Wayne go. No idea what's going to happen – we certainly can't involve the law – I'll just have to see what Robbie says. I fought I'd better tell you first so you would know where your Wayne was."

"Well, where is he?"

"I dunno, that posh bloke's taken him somewhere."

Whilst he had been talking, as an alternative to watching Monica's face, he had been slowly scanning the room and its contents. There was no professional interest in this, it just made a change from facing Monica. His eyes lighted on the photograph on top of the television set.

"Ey! That's him!" Wilf pointed and got up to move closer to the photograph of Gerry. He turned to Monica, "Are you in on this?" he asked, puzzled.

"That's who?" asked Monica, also puzzled.

"That's one of the blokes who's got your Wayne."

"Are you sure?"

"Yes, missus – he's the one who drove Wayne's van off – took it wherever they took Wayne probably."

A combination of intuition and recently acquired knowledge brought Monica to a realisation. "I know where he is! He's at that big house!"

Wilf didn't argue or ask for a little more detail on this discovery, he just wanted to go home. He could tell that Monica knew something that he didn't. The photograph proved that but it was adding an element of confusion to the matter so perhaps it was better not press her for details of her involvement.

"Any chance of a lift home, then, Mrs Prough?"

"None at all, you can come with me."

This nonplussed Wilf a little, his plan had been that he

would accompany Monica but only as far as his home.

"Where?" Wilf asked – clarification being his aim.

"To get my Wayne back."

"No chance, I'm not going nowhere near that posh bloke's place – he's got a gun."

"Well, you can bloody well walk home, then. Goodnight." And in true melodramatic fashion, she indicated the front door with a stiffly outstretched forefinger.

Wilf left, grateful, at least, that she hadn't forced him to go with her for he found her almost as frightening as the posh bloke with the gun. Shortly afterwards, Monica also left and with the intention of restoring her only son to the expansive bosom of his family.

Fortunately for Wilf, Wettenham boasted an all-night taxi service. Unfortunately, he had only five pounds about him. It had seemed pointless, when setting out, to carry more than that when someone was supposed to be handing over five thousand pounds later that evening. He'd only stuck the fiver in his pocket in case they needed petrol money or something.

The taxi offices were in semi-darkness. A sleeping figure could be made out in the dark corner and there was a sign on the door which said: 'Open. Please ring the bell for servise.'

Wilf thumbed the bell-push and there was a movement from the dark corner. At last, the door opened and an untidy looking man with several day's growth of beard looked out.

"Yeh?" he asked tiredly.

"I need to get to Port Regis," said Wilf, "but I've only got a fiver. How far can you get me for that?"

"You've woke me up for a bloody fiver?" asked the man in a tone of voice which indicated that he wouldn't normally stir for such a negligible amount.

"Yes. It's all I've got." apologised Wilf. He'd had enough

of being frightened by people for one night.

"A bloody fiver? I don't normally turn out in the day time for a piddlin' little fare like that and what the bloody hell's up with your face?"

Wilf, by now, was beginning to regret having put the face-paint on.

"Face-paint. You really don't want to know."

The taxi driver stared for a moment as though trying to work out whether he really did want to know but then thought better of it, "Well – I'm awake now – I'll drop you off at the end of the motorway, will that do you?" His voice was calmer but it was evident that if it didn't do then Wilf could find alternative ways of getting to his destination. "I'm buggered if I'm going any further."

"Please." Wilf said, at least, that was most of the way home. He could figure on getting to bed before it got light if he hurried. And then he would have to deal with Robbie.

As an afterthought, the driver asked, "Does that stuff come off? I don't want grey paint on my upholstery."

Close to the motorway interchange where the grumpy taxi driver dropped Wilf off – for he refused to go any further, even with a promise of immediate payment of the balance of the fare at journey's end – is a lay-by. Edged by tall hedges, at night it is thrown into deep shadow and is a favourite stopping place for courting couples, youths wishing to pursue their experiments with illegal substances and police patrol cars in need of rest and recuperation. It is probable that not all these types would be found there at any one time in that lay-by at night. Their needs being different, they tended to avoid one another's company. So, this evening, the sole occupants of the spot were Constables Purslipp and Clough. Their car pointed towards the well-lit interchange area so that they were afforded an uninterrupted view of what went on over there.

"Are you coping all right now that Elaine's gone?" Ellis

asked. Leigh had been uncommunicative, even surly this evening and Ellis wanted his friend to talk about things instead of brooding over them.

"It's a bastard. I can't stop in the house long except when I go to bed. When I'm off duty, I'm up the pub or the cinema; anywhere there's lights and people. I'm not sorry she's gone, though."

"Perhaps you could come round to mine and Sandra's one night." This was a very kind offer of Ellis' although it was more of a gesture than a profound desire. A moody Leigh sobbing on the sofa was not what either he or his wife would wish for.

There was a short silence. Leigh may have been pondering Ellis' offer and Ellis may have been wondering how to worm out of it but when the taxi pulled up to let Wilf out, Ellis' interest was piqued.

"There's a funny thing." indicated Ellis.

"What's that." Leigh had been digging around in the butty box which Ellis' wife had made up for him and he had not noticed the incident. Sandra had made the assumption, based on personal experience, that a man without a woman was helpless and therefore, in a kindly gesture, had made up a packed meal for Leigh as well as her husband.

"That taxi has just dropped that bloke off. Wonder why? There's no houses near so what's his game? Doesn't even look as though he's about to hitch a ride onto the motorway. Damned silly time of night to catch a lift."

"Should we call the police?" Leigh asked with a grin on his face, the first of the evening.

"I think we'll have a word with him – see what he's up to – clear up the mystery as it were."

Wilf was walking across the motorway bridge with his back to the police car so, as it approached, all he was aware of was a vehicle coming up from behind. He was so pissed off with life just at that moment, he couldn't summon the interest to look around. Not that he could have run very far if he'd known who it was. His heart sank a little deeper when Ellis and Leigh drew up alongside and he wondered what more could go wrong with the day. Events had drawn him ever deeper into some sort of nightmare and he longed for it to be all over.

"Where are we off to, sir?" asked Leigh, employing the constabulary 'we' as he climbed out of the car.

"Off home, why?" offered Wilf.

"So why have we chosen to walk rather than have the taxi take us all the way?"

At this point, Leigh had come close enough to Wilf to spot the face paint which looked leaden under the motorway lights.

"Ellis, come here and look at this! I'd be obliged, sir, if we stayed just where we are." This last to Wilf who looked nervous enough to attempt flight.

Ellis rolled out of the driver's side and wandered over to Wilf who was becoming worried by their attention. His gloom had made him temporarily forgetful about the face paint and didn't understand their reason for scrutiny.

Ellis looked closely at Wilf and asked, "What's the matter with your face, sir?"

"Oh, that!" relief washed over Wilf, "It's face paint." He didn't elaborate, he thought his answer would explain everything.

"Face paint?" There was a note of disbelief in Ellis' tone.

"Yes, face paint. I'm a growler."

"Sorry, sir. We're not clear on that. You're a what?"

"A growler. I sing wiv a deaf metal band."

It was evident that neither of the officers were familiar with 'deaf metal' which is how they heard it from Wilf's squirreling lips and he was obliged to explain about his group and what they did. This was a convenient cover story for Wilf's actual activities that night and the real reason for the disguise and so he felt happy to invent a gig ("A what, sir?") from which he was returning home but lacking the full fare, the taxi dropped him off where he did. Further explanation was required for the direction he was taking and by the time the two officers were satisfied, half a very long hour had gone by and Wilf was feeling more tired and more desperate to get back home to his bed.

* * *

Monica found herself once again outside the gates of the big house just two days after following Gerry there. She tried the gates but they were chained and locked. Through the bars she could see a few exterior lights which were illuminating the front of the house and a building nearby which looked like a stable block where there was a parked horse-box and a white van which looked very much like Wayne's Skoda.

After Wayne's interrogation, Kelps had been set to guard him while Henry and Gerry unloaded the van and carried the pictures and bag of jewellery into the house. Angela was overjoyed to see her belongings back and carefully checked it over before acceding to Henry's suggestion that they all get some sleep: Toni to her room, Angela and Henry to his old room and Gerry on the couch. Toni had thoughtfully provided a blanket and a pillow and it was a long, comfortable couch and Gerry was too tired to care very much where he slept.

Monica explored the perimeter wall of Toni's house looking for an easier way in than climbing over those gates.

Over in the woods, two male tawny owls recommenced a conversation which had been interrupted by the rude intrusion of daylight some hours before.

"Tu – Whik." said the first, by way of an opening gambit.

"Tu – Whik." countered the second.

There was a period of silence during which a badger was heard to cough as the first owl considered the import of the second owl's remark before adding, "Tu – Whik?"

No doubt Monica would have loved to stop and listen to the end of this fascinating exchange but the duties of motherhood bore her on. A little further and Monica discovered a fallen coping stone leaning handily against the wall, forming a sort of step. It had been dislodged during a storm earlier in the year by an overhanging bough as it moved restlessly in the wind. Kelps had been meaning to repair this defect but he didn't consider it an attractive job and he found it easy to defer. By standing on this coping stone, Monica was able to hoist herself up to where the stone should have been. Once she had pushed herself off the top and onto the grass inside, it occurred to her that she had no way out. Still, never mind, the important thing was to rescue Wayne.

Kelps, meanwhile, confident that Wayne could not escape, had succumbed to the warmth of the stable and dozed off. Earlier, he had switched off the internal lights as he could see enough by the weak gleam from the outside lamps penetrating the stable windows and he leaned a chair back on the wall, the light switch within easy reach and the shotgun across his lap.

Wayne had seen something like this in a Western where the sherriff's deputy, who is supposed look after the mistakenly arrested hero, falls asleep leaving the keys just where the hero, with the aid of his belt or some such thing, could drag them to his outstretched fingers and regain his freedom, tiptoeing out of the sherriff's office without disturbing the deputy.

It was a wooden, two-storey building. On the ground floor, of one room only, about one third of the floor space was covered by a steel cage, divided into two cells, each with its own door and within, there was no place a person could be and not be visible to someone in any other part of the room.

The outer cell was unoccupied and the inner's solitary inmate was a man called Wayne. It was a frame-up. The sherriff needed him out of the way so's he could get to Miss Kerry and force her to sign over the ranch to him. There was gold under that ranch and the sherriff knew all about it. Wayne had to find a way out and stop him.

Slim, the deputy, was sitting at the sheriff's desk, leaning back in the chair and with his feet on the desk. His hat had slipped over his eyes, Slim was relaxing.

The man called Wayne could see the keys thrown carelessly on the edge of the desk. They were on a big iron ring. He slipped off his belt, rolled it up and, keeping the lead end in his hand, flipped the buckle towards the key-ring. It caught in the ring first time and slowly, so's not to disturb Slim, Wayne gently pulled the keys towards him. When they were about to drop to the floor, Wayne realised that he had a problem. If he pulled any more, the keys would clatter to the floor and likely wake Slim. Got to take a chance. He flicked the belt and the keys towards him with a violent jerk and caught them with his free hand before they hit the bars. Slim stirred in his sleep.

The man called Wayne stood still for a moment, listening. Then he refitted his belt, let himself quietly out of the cell and out of the door. The first sound he made was a loud, piercing whistle which brought Shadow, his night-black pony, trotting up to its master. He swung into the saddle and clicked a command. Shadow surged forward into the darkness. Now to save Miss Kerry.

Wayne could not see any keys and, besides, he was tied up. Struggling did not seem to help so he sat quietly and thought about what he could do. Wayne eventually began to doze himself. Actually, doze is probably the wrong word where Wayne is concerned. If there is anything in the world which Wayne can be trusted to do properly, it is sleep. If you drew a metaphorical line between doze and coma, Wayne's condition would be a long way from the former and not too far from the latter. His was deep, black, dreamless sleep completely undisturbed by his present situation. It always took a lot to wake Wayne.

Monica made straight for the stable because that was where Wayne's van was parked. There seemed to be no-one around, the house was quiet with very few internal lights left on and so she crept around to the stable windows to peer inside. The owls had, by now, gone quiet. Either the conversation had palled or they were taking an interest in Monica's doings.

Moss Trooper and Ezekiel grew a little restless as they sensed the presence of an intruder; one stamped quietly and the other whuffled. It was only a human; nothing to worry much about. It had been an odd night for both of them; lots of strange people doing strange things so a little more would hardly make a difference. Neither Kelps nor Wayne was disturbed by the noises the horses were making.

Monica could see a figure in a chair sitting motionless near one of the empty stalls but there was no-one else visible. It looked a little like Wayne but she couldn't be sure. She tried the door and found it unlocked. Inside, it was much darker and her eyes had difficulty adjusting to the lower light level. The horses still made nervous noises but they were doing it quietly as though trying not to wake anyone.

Monica crept forwards to the figure in the chair which had been visible from the outside. She could barely make out anything now, it was so dark.

"Wayne!" she whispered.

She crept forwards again and fell over Kelps' outstretched legs. She gave a little cry of alarm as she fell but Wayne slumbered on. Kelps woke and put on the light which illuminated the doorway.

"Who are you?" he demanded of Monica, looking past her to check on Wayne.

"Have you got my lad?" asked Monica, who still hadn't positively identified her somnolent son.

Around about this time, something long buried was stirring in Kelps' heart. This woman, whoever she was, was bloody attractive. He could fancy this one and no messing. A silly grin started to form on his face, the first one there for many years. It was foreign soil for silly grins and it had difficulty maintaining a foothold but it hung on tenaciously.

Something similar was happening inside Monica's bosom. Her errand of mercy had been pushed aside into the box marked 'Pending' as she drank in the sight of this delectable male form before her with such a winning smile on his face.

"Oh!" said Monica ineffectively.

"Hello." said Kelps through the grin.

"I, er –." was the closest Monica could get to explaining her reasons for being there before becoming quite distracted by this wonderful man. He reminded her a little of her father.

Wayne slumbered on.

Kelps decided that the diem must be carpe-d forthwith, laid the shot-gun down on the chair and wrapped his arms around the uncomplaining Monica.

"I've been looking around for someone like you." he said.

Monica kissed him fervently and said, "Oh!" again but with more feeling and a little more sensuously than the last time.

"Oh." added Kelps. Their conversation held, for the casual audience, about as much interest as that of the owls.

Then he took her hand and led her to a bale of straw

where they sat side by side and whispered informal introductions to each other. Kelps had his arm around his new-found lady, she held his other hand while her spare hand nestled on his thigh. Such a nice thigh, she thought. They kissed each other from time to time. Just short, tentative kisses which kept the pressure of passion from reaching dangerous levels.

Discomfort had made its way to that part of Wayne's brain where physical complaints are registered and with a request for the body to move into a more comfortable position. The request was granted and Wayne tried to roll over and found he couldn't. As he forced himself awake to find out why he could not roll over, he looked over at Kelps who was sitting next to a woman who – "Mum!" he shouted.

Monica didn't even look round.

"Hush, baby – mummy's busy – go back to sleep."

Wayne did not go to sleep but he kept quiet. Something was going on and it looked as though his mum had everything under control. She had come to rescue him. Good old mum.

Dawn arrived and the owls went to roost. They had had a very fruitful night, having caught a number of small rodents and they felt content. There would be something more to discuss when the following night came.

Kelps, who had gone so far as to reveal his christian name to Monica, still sat by her side quietly chatting. They, too, were content. Wayne sat patiently waiting for his mum to pull a master stroke and disable this man and set him free although it did seem to him that she had let one or two chances go by.

The stable door opened and Henry walked in.

Oh no! thought Wayne, she's blown it now.

"Morning, Kelps. Who is this?" said Henry vaguely indicating Monica.

"It's this lad's mother. She came to rescue him," he

nodded his head towards Wayne, "but we started to chat and time rather got away from us."

"How do you do." Henry said to Monica, apparently satisfied with Kelps' explanation. "I'm Henry Hughes and I'm responsible for your son's condition. If you'd like to come to the house where there's fresh coffee brewing, I will explain everything to you."

Monica was reluctant to leave her new friend but Kelps promised to join her in the kitchen just as soon as he was relieved from his post.

"What about my son?" she added as an afterthought.

"For the time being, he must remain here. You may understand why when you hear what has been happening." Henry gallantly handed her out of the stable.

Later, after the embarassment of seeing Gerry again had dissipated, after the whole story had been explained to her and after she had been introduced to Angela and Toni to whom she curtsied ever so slightly upon hearing the title, Monica agreed to leave Wayne in their custody until they had sorted out the matter with Robbie Benson. After all, Wayne needed time to consider the error of his ways and she would prefer this was done informally here than in the rather more regimented atmosphere of a correctional establishment.

"Can I go and have a word with Wayne first, before I go?" asked Monica.

Henry agreed.

She marched into the stable where Wayne was seated but untied and talking to Gerry. The errant son felt a sudden joy, his saviour had come. Freedom, any second now. Then he saw the grim set of her face and understood that perhaps she knew of the dark side of his life and that he was in for a bollocking. Still, grin and bear it, he thought, Be home soon.

"Have you been thieving?" Monica asked angrily, "Tell

me the truth, now, I'll know if you lie to me."

Wayne could never figure out how his mum did that. Whenever he fibbed to her, she would smack him and demand the truth. He was compelled to be honest with her.

He told her everything and, during the account, he noticed a couple of tears reach his mum's eyes. She wiped them away quickly, trying to maintain her angry look but Wayne had seen them and he felt guilty and ashamed. When he had done, she ordered Wayne to be co-operative, to stay where he was and told him that he wasn't welcome back at home until they had done with him and when he had promised to get himself a proper job.

Now, she had a man she could look after and she didn't want a thief in her new family. She liked everyone she had met today but she liked Hemingway Kelps best of all.

* * *

Another favourite place for a nocturnal visit by Constables Purslipp and Clough when looking for rest and recuperation, somewhere to enjoy a coffee and a chat was a public car-park half way along the old Port Regis – Wettenham railway line. It had to be visited in the dark because daylight showed the ugly side of the place and at night, there was often someone who would leave quickly at the sight of a police car. That was always fun.

What Leigh and Ellis were completely unaware of was that two days beforehand, this place had seen Wilf and Wayne receiving their come-uppance from Henry's vigilante party. The two policemen had been up by the motorway that night – interviewing Wilf for part of it.

Also, that very afternoon had seen Heavy George and his partner out for a stroll together.

Something happened to George when out in the country. He was no longer an intimidating or threatening presence. His demeanour improved along with the density of the greenery around him and he assumed an avuncular look. Sometimes, familiar birdsong would give him a gentle face with en-suite beatific smile. Violence was never further from his mind than at times like these.

Today had begun happily for George but things took a bad turn. George had not the smallest suspicion that Brian, his main squeeze, had been planning to bring their relationship to an end. Dusk was falling as they stood together on the old cinder-covered bed of the railway, the encroaching trees arching verdantly overhead, and Brian told George that it was over, finished. They would no longer be partners. George was stunned. Then, as he watched Brian walk away, tears began to fall. These were the first tears for many years to visit his face and they were hesitant tears. George was so overcome with grief at losing Brian that he'd forgotten that it was Brian's car which had brought them here and he, George, was left stranded. He could just see Brian in the distance, turning into the car-park. George shouted, was heard and ignored and so he began to run. His frame was not really suited to running. His was a body which blocked out sunlight, that threatened retribution, a physique which intimidated but never moved speedily for any protracted length of time. In essence, George had treated his body less like a temple and more like a betting shop. Even so, he made it to the car-park only to discover it empty and Brian gone. This last finding was too much for George's put-upon heart. This does not mean put-upon in terms of sympathy or charity demanded of it for these terms were foreign to George. His heart had suffered the shock of losing a loved one and then, in a stunned state, been called upon to pump blood rapidly around George's corpulence as he ran to Brian. That extra little push when George saw the car gone was just too much and his heart stopped. Wrapped its hand in. Folded its arms and refused to beat another beat or pump a single ventricle-full more. George dropped like a stone at the edge of the parking area, hitting the ground with his shoulder and rolling onto his back just under the base of a rhododendron bush.

Two minutes later, Brian came back, feeling bad about leaving his ex-partner stranded. He had relented and turned back to pick him up although nothing George could say would change his mind about breaking up. There was a new prospective partner in the offing about whom he did not want George to know.

When Brian discovered George's lifeless form, instead of trying to revive him with the kiss of life, he panicked, got quickly back into his car and drove home where he sat and fretted, not knowing what he should do. Eventually, after Eddy, his new boyfriend, came around, he started to forget all about George.

The car full of youths who next entered the car-park didn't spot the corpse under the rhododendron bush. By then, it was fairly dark and they had no intention of getting out of the car, anyway. They had come for a smoke and a drink and a laugh. They left as Leigh and Ellis arrived, the patrol car had been spotted slowing for the turn into the car-park and the lads thought it best to leave right then. They had each promised himself an early night anyway.

Ellis drove in and reversed into a parking space. As he came to a halt, he felt the rear wheels come into contact with an obstruction. It felt soft.

"Some bugger's been fly-tipping, I think, mate. I've just backed onto a rubbish sack."

"Won't have damaged the car, would it?" asked Leigh.

"Nah." It wasn't a fully convinced reply.

"I'll check it." offered Leigh and took a flashlight from the door pocket and got out to investigate. The beam illuminated a crumpled herring-bone overcoat and dark trouser legs ending in brown brogue shoes.

"Shit, Ellis, it's a body!"

Ellis opened the driver's side door to hear better what his partner had said as he wasn't quite sure he had heard right.

"A what, man?" he asked.

"A body – a bleedin' corpse – some bastard's dead here." That more or less encapsulated the information which Leigh wished to convey to Ellis.

Although he hadn't, by then, realised it, Leigh had achieved his ambition albeit not quite in the way he would have liked.

"What we going to do, man?" asked Ellis.

"We're police officers, we're supposed to know what to do!" Leigh's voice had an edge to it induced by a sort of excitement. "First off, pull forward so's you're not actually parked on the body. It doesn't look respectful, otherwise."

"I've not run him over, have I?"

"Just move the bloody car, El!"

A closer examination of the lifeless and now extremely heavy George revealed no chance of resuscitation and no indication of foul play and that the most likely cause of death was cardiac arrest. A couple of muddy scuff marks on George's coat which might have raised concern were simply tyre marks from where Ellis had almost reversed over him.

Leigh called an ambulance.

"Hey!" said Ellis, a burst of realisation lighting up his face, "you've done it, man!"

"Done what?" Leigh was slightly suspicious.

"Achieved your ambition. It's a body, innit?"

"Piss off, El. It's no bloody murder, just some fat old bastard whose ticker gave way. No big deal."

Ellis had a look for himself with his own flashlight. He wanted to see a dead body that he wasn't related to. As he shone the beam on the corpse's distorted features, he realised who it was.

"Hey! It's Heavy George. Come and have a look."

Leigh looked and had to agree. It sort of took away the shine from his discovery that Ellis had identified the man. A local reprobate with form, too.

"So, that's 'Miss' Chevis Yardley's minder who's gone to meet his maker. That'll put a smile on some villains' faces. Let's go and have a coffee while we wait for the ambulance crew. I feel quite cheerful, now."

Chapter Fourteen

THE RAID

The robb'd that smiles steals something from the thief
(Shakespeare)

"Now that the situation with the charming Mrs. Prough has been resolved and she is on our side," (here Monica blushed a little), "I have something I wish to share. While we were driving back from the drop-off point, an idea started to form." said Henry as he sipped his coffee, "Suppose we make use of these villains. They may be small-time but I think they have the necessary talents to do what I have been thinking of. And now, of course, we have a strong bargaining position with young Wayne in our custody and," he leaned forwards to place his cup on the table in order not to be hampered by it should forceful gestures be required, "with his mother's approval." He nodded towards Monica whose blush deepened a little.

"What are you thinking of?" asked Angela, too impatient to allow Henry's dramatic pause to remain unfilled.

"I'm going to get Wayne and his friends to steal back that miniature that was taken from you."

Toni remained silent, she felt too distant from the emotional side of what was going on to have any sort of reaction to her brother's idea. Angela, however, her hand in front of her mouth, was shocked at the nerve of Henry, coming up with a plan which was quite plainly illegal and this feeling was somewhat jumbled by excitement at the prospect of having her property returned and serving one on Robert's parents for the mean thing they did.

Gerry had been able to spot a flaw which he thought that perhaps Henry hadn't seen and which he thought should be pointed out, he pushed up his hand to gain attention as a child would in school, "Surely, once they realise it's gone, they'll call the police, won't they? And it won't take a lot of detective work to come up with you as the prime suspect."

Before Henry could counter this, Angela threw the argument away with, "No, they wouldn't dare call the police, especially if that is the only thing that goes missing. Don't you see? It's not theirs, it rightfully belongs to me and if the police smell something funny – and I'm sure they would in that situation – they might ask a lot of awkward questions. Ma and Pa Poindexter cannot afford a scandal. Believe me, they'll say nothing."

"Well, thank you for that, Angela." said Henry, "That's one problem out of the way, I can only see one more at present. I think it's essential that the house should be empty when we take the miniature; if we were spotted by the inmates, it may cause a certain amount of alarm. How can we guarantee that they will be out of the house on the night of the job?"

"Could someone invite them to a party or dinner, something like that?" Gerry suggested.

There was a short silence while the rest pondered Gerry's idea and tried to develop it into something practical. Then Angela thought of a plan, "Ma Poindexter loves opera. Her husband can take it or leave it but if she goes to the opera house, he goes too. Also, they're both quite keen on Shakespeare and will put in an appearance if there is anything being staged nearby."

Angela had picked up this information from Robert's occasional reference to his parents. Robert, knowing that his mother and father disapproved of his choice of bride and that she wasn't welcome at their home, rarely mentioned his side of the family but he had still spoken of them from time to time and Angela always listened to what he had to say despite her lack of enthusiasm for the subject.

"That's it." Henry said delightedly, "I shall send them two tickets for the opera. Port Regis is far enough away to give us time to get the job done. Who knows? They might even make a night of it and get a room at a hotel."

"You would have to send them anonymously or they would be suspicious. But even that is suspicious in itself." Henry nodded his acceptance of Toni's objection and he became thoughtful. At length he said, "Possibly, but I can't see round that one just yet. Leave it with me for a while, I shall think of something."

Gerry was astonished at what was unfolding around him. Notwithstanding that he was new to this world he found himself in and was barely acquainted with the people around him, he was now party to a burglary plot! Life had certainly become a little more exciting since he put in the advertisement.

* * *

Leigh hadn't been entirely truthful with Ellis. Once the anger had subsided, he found that he missed Elaine more than he would have imagined. There were times, at home, when he would start to say something; mention some trivial piece of news perhaps, look up towards the chair in which she usually sat and then stop himself as he saw its emptiness.

There were times, sitting alone watching a television programme, when he would suddenly weep. Unbidden tears would blur the screen and he would wipe them away on his shirt sleeve. Yet he didn't want her back. If she came back tomorrow, he thought, I'd send her away again.

It would be like packing in cigarettes, something he had unsuccessfully attempted twice already, it would be uncomfortable, painful even, but he would get through it. There would be someone else one day, maybe quite soon. Someone to take her place.

Meanwhile, Leigh had discovered that he was a natural in the kitchen. He had always left cookery to the woman in his life. This had been part of his upbringing – his mother had always said that a woman's place is in the kitchen, cooking for her man. But, with no Elaine and no desire to visit the chippy or takeaway every time he needed feeding, he had cooked himself some rice and vegetables one evening. Encouraged by the result, he rooted out the few cookery books which Elaine had left behind (the excitement of discovery pushed back any nostalgia) and, over a weekend, nurtured the talent latent within him. Between meals, he tackled the housework. Piece of piss! What do they complain of? The washing is practically done for you, vacuuming takes a matter of minutes and the only serious consumer of time was shopping. Leigh found that he liked to shop. It was almost therapeutic. It was certainly a relaxing thing to do.

* * *

"But they had guns, Robbie – what could we do?"

Robbie banged his fist on the table. "Shit and destruction!"

They were seated in the Baltimore Oriole and Wilf was trying to persuade Robbie that the foiled hand-over had not been down to any failure on his and Wayne's part but because they had been unprepared for what he saw as an armed response.

"And it wasn't no fun havin' to walk all that way home.

And the scuffers stopped me. Good job I fought of a story. And Wayne's mum went potty. I've no idea where she is now, she went to look for him."

"Why did you go there? To Wayne's house."

"Didn't fancy walking all the way home, did I? I fought Wayne's mum might give me a lift after I'd passed on the bad news but she practically frew me out and buggered off to find Wayne. She seemed to fink she knew where he was."

Robbie was angered by Wilf's tale of how the ransom went wrong and of Wayne's capture. And worse, just how easily the two were duped by rank amateurs! His mind felt feverish, scratching away at the dirt of his subconscious, looking for an idea which might give them back the upper hand. This was a factor never considered in his plans, the punters turning up with guns, getting heavy and playing the vigilante. It wasn't playing right, those were not the rules. Punters don't have guns, punters don't fight back otherwise where would burglary be? It'd be a waste of time if everywhere you turned up for a bit of quiet thievery and they all had guns. He almost snarled through his teeth as he turned to Wilf and asked, "So, I've got to phone this bloke. What for?"

"He's going to set up a meeting wiv yer. Some way of sorting fings out so the coppers don't get called. I don't know!" Wilf's voice had taken on a dejected whine.

Reluctantly, Robbie tapped out the number Wilf had given him on the keyboard of his mobile phone.

"Hello? Henry Pym." said Henry, not recognising the number which came up on his mobile phone screen when his phone rang in response.

"It's Robbie Benson – Wilf Hevard asked me to ring you. – What's it about?" Robbie was not keen to prolong his conversation with this clever bastard who'd knackered up his job and got Wayne into the bargain. He disliked him intensely on principle alone.

"So, you're Robbie the Burglar, are you?" the cool, cultured voice of Henry asked.

There was a grunt of admission from Robbie.

"You know the Demsbury Arms? In Demsbury village?" the voice asked matter-of-factly, patently unaware of the ill will pouring into the phone from Robbie's end.

"Yes." Robbie confirmed curtly.

"You and Wilf – and no-one else – are to meet me there at twelve noon tomorrow. I have a job which will employ your peculiar skills for which the payment will be the return of Wayne and the non-involvement of the local constabulary. I will explain the details tomorrow. Do you understand and do you agree?"

"What if we turn up team-handed? What're you going to do? We could have you easy and you know it." Robbie's blustering had little effect on Henry, "You know that the ultimate outcome would be bad for you, Wilf and Wayne. I trust that you aren't that stupid." His voice had a smooth and confident tone which irritated Robbie.

"Yeah. O.K., then." Robbie was loath to co-operate with anything suggested by this man but he couldn't yet see a way out. Who was he anyway? Ordering people about. Thinks he owns the bloody place.

"Tomorrow, then – and bring that ballerina with you; I'm rather fond of it and I want it back." said Henry and cut the connection.

"Bastard." said Robbie, offering this as a precis of the conversation he'd just had. Then, realising from Wilf's puzzled expression that a little more detail would be helpful, enlarged upon his last remark.

"Bastard wants us up the Demsbury Arms to tell us about a job. Wouldn't say what it was. Won't let us have Wayne back until we do it."

"At least there's a job in it for us." said Wilf unhelpfully.

Robbie ignored him, he became thoughtful, chewing his bottom lip as he tried to see a way back on top. There was nothing. Luck would have a large part to play in the near future. His face became determined, "Right – we'll go along with him as far as we need to. Once the chance comes up, we'll stuff him. I want to come out of this in profit."

For Wilf, this plan still lacked clarity and a certain amount of fine tuning but, since he could not improve on it, he was happy to accept Robbie's suggestions.

* * *

Wayne, having given his guarantee not to escape, which may not have been as copper-bottomed as his mother's guarantee of what would happen to him if he misbehaved, was given a room in the house. He was very impressed with what he saw about him and had given the place a professional appraisal; albeit more to pass the time than for future reference. He was determined to accede to his mother's wishes and go straight. After all, he had plans for his life ahead; honest employment at something or other and his mother had threatened to tell Kerry-Ann everything if he just once strayed. If Kerry-Ann found out what he'd been up to, she'd kill him and then pack him in. And probably hand him over to her father to finish him off, most likely. No, Kerry-Ann might just agree to an engagement if he showed her that he could hold down a steady job. That would be one over her dad, too.

Then, to kill the boredom which he was beginning to feel, Wayne went out to help Kelps.

Kelps, having warned Wayne that he had better keep his eyes off his job, gave him the task of clearing out a flower bed and re-planting it with summer blooms in order to occupy him. Here Wayne found himself happier than he had been for a long while. It was so nice to work outside; to see a result in what you had just done and to make a difference to the surroundings. This was evidently his métier and he told himself that once he was allowed to return home, he would get himself a job with a landscape gardening firm or similar. Digging his fingers into warm, dark soil or holding living bulbs – baby flowers as he thought of them – gave him a good feeling. Even the tedious jobs, lawn edging or weeding the gravel paths, gave him time for reflection and the world seemed to slow down and match the natural pace of his mind for the first time he could remember.

* * *

Outside the Demsbury Arms on the following day at noon, a warm insistent drizzle of the type that often mars the perfection of an English summer day dropped lazily from the dove grey haze above, seeming not to care whether it hit the ground or not. It was a very mellow drizzle. It was a drizzle which had been designed to dampen – spirits or clothing – but not to wet things.

Inside the pub, the atmosphere was drier and very tense. Henry and Gerry had left the womenfolk at home to worry and fret and were frustratedly awaiting the arrival of Robbie and Wilf. Kelps had offered to join them as extra muscle but Henry thought this unnecessary and thanked him anyway.

Eventually, a large, white Transit van turned into the car-park and reverse-parked angrily outside, its nose pointed towards the exit as though already keen to be away again.

"They're here." remarked Gerry, pointing out a fact with which Henry was already familiar.

Robbie and Wilf marched in with a bravado which belied the nervousness they were both feeling but which only Wilf would have owned to. This was not Wilf's honest streak showing, just an awareness that his anxiety was probably obvious to all.

Robbie instinctively knew that these two men sitting at a table by the window were the ones he was supposed to meet and walked towards them followed by Wilf whose last remaining trace of swagger had left once he realised he was back in the presence of the posh bloke with the gun.

Henry rose and greeted them both with a warmth which felt genuine and then disarmed them both by making introductions, inviting them to sit and then asking what they might like to drink.

Robbie had been prepared for hostility and had come in with his mind at battle stations. One wrong word from either of these two and he would have waded in flailing. Henry's politeness wrong-footed him and only made him very wary.

When the four had each a glass in front of them, Robbie opened the conversation proper by asking what the meeting was all about.

"First of all, hand over the ballerina." Henry asked.

Robbie pulled a dirty cloth bag from inside his denim jacket and pushed it reluctantly towards him. Henry pulled it out of the bag to check it for damage and then, satisfied, put it into a hold-all at his feet. Facing Robby, almost ignoring Wilf, Henry explained what the job was to be.

"My wife used to own a miniature – a small painting – which was repossessed by relatives who felt that she had no right to it. Unfortunately, she cannot prove that it is rightfully hers but she would dearly love to have it back. I want you and Wilf, here, to go and steal it and bring it to me. Nothing else may be taken from the place. Not one thing. Once you have completed your task, we will release your friend, Wayne and the three of you will be allowed to go on your way with the added proviso that you never again work in this neck of the woods. Is that understood?"

"I understand," said Robbie, "but I'm not sure that I like the terms. Is it O.K. if me and my mate discuss the job privately?"

"Of course." said Henry, gesturing with his right hand, palm up; a dismissive wave.

"Bar." ordered Robbie, curtly, to Wilf.

"Yeah, I need some crisps, as well." Wilf said and got up

from the table to join him.

Blind to the importance of the move away from Henry and Gerry, Wilf's first act on reaching the bar was to order a packet of cheese and onion flavoured crisps.

"Bugger the crisps! Listen, I'm getting an idea. Did you hear what that posh bastard wants us to do?"

Despite Robbie, Wilf had by now been handed his crisps by Carol, paid for them and was noisily opening the packet. "Yes. He wants us to nick...."

"Shush, you dozy sod. Don't tell everyone!"

Wilf stuffed a few crisps into his mouth, partly to shut himself up and partly to listen better to what Robbie had to say.

Carol busied herself washing glasses that did not need to be washed and tried to look uninterested as she strained her ears to listen to Robbie. She had no idea of the connection these two had with Gerry and his charming friend but they didn't seem comradely.

"Now, listen." said Robbie, in a loud, angry whisper, "Posh Bastard wants us to nick something for him. Not a proper job – just one thing. But – how's he going to know that's all we've got? I bet that we won't be allowed to carry no bags to put anything in so wear your poacher's jacket; you know, the one you wear when you go shopping with Beryl. And I'm going to do a note. One that'll drop Posh Bastard and his mate right in it and I'll drop it somewhere when we're in there."

Wilf wasn't in full possession of the torrent of facts which Robbie had just let go and his face showed this.

Robbie summarised. "Just remember to put your shoppin' jacket on for the job – O.K.?"

Wilf nodded and cheese and onion flavoured crisp fragments dropped onto the surface of the bar. That they were to do the job for the posh bloke and that he must wear his shopping jacket was now clear. Then they turned to rejoin Henry and Gerry.

Carol was puzzled. Gerry mixed up with thieves? What on earth was going on? Whatever it was, Gerry must be told as soon as possible that those two weren't going to play fair. She still felt a sort of loyalty towards Gerry or, at least, if forced to pick sides, she would have picked his rather than go along with the two characters she had just overheard. But – how to let him know? She'd no idea of how much time she had. She tried to attract his attention with a few grimaces and failed. Waving her arms and shouting, she felt, might give the game away. She realised that she must wait for an opportune moment.

Wilf and Robbie re-seated themselves and Robbie announced, "We've discussed it and we'll go along with it for Wayne's sake but I want to make one small demand. We want fifty quid for expenses and it's a deal."

Wilf looked suprisedly at Robbie, he didn't recall any mention of a fee while they were at the bar.

"Done." said Henry. He and Robbie shook hands. Robbie's dislike of Henry was so intense that he felt his hand was unclean after the shake. He wiped it roughly on the leg of his jeans but there remained an overwhelming urge to wash it.

"Now that's sorted, there's a couple of details we need about the actual job. First, will the place be occupied?"

"I am in the process of arranging that the house will be empty that night. That's not something you should worry about."

Gerry looked at Henry with folded arms and the air of a man in on the secret. His role today was minor and, subconsciously, he wanted to puff it up a little. He didn't want to be mistaken for just a supernumerary.

"And second," added Robbie, " What about internal alarms? What sort of system are we looking at? We don't want any unexpected visits while the job's on, do we?"

"That will be your department. This is why you have

been engaged. If I took on that responsibility, I might just as well do the job myself."

"O.K. Wilf's a dab hand at alarms and things," conceded Robbie, "Now there's just a matter of time and place and we can all go home."

Wilf was still eating cheese and onion crisps and so could only nod his agreement.

Henry would only reveal the time, date and place where they were to meet. They would be furnished with the address when they turned up.

Robbie and Wilf got up to leave. They were both relieved, in differing degrees, that the interview was over. Wilf had spent a worried time of it and Robbie had smouldered with an ever increasing feeling of antagonism towards the pricks who had his mate, Wayne, and were now pulling his string. Much longer in the company of that posh bastard and he would have happily twatted him. The van spat gravel derisorily at the pub as they left.

As soon as they had gone, Carol came quickly from behind the bar and scurried over to Gerry and Henry who were themselves preparing to leave.

"Gerry, I don't know what you're mixed up in but I heard those two men talking at the bar and I think they've got it in for you both."

"Do tell." said Henry, sitting down once again.

"Oh, this is Henry Pym," said Gerry hastily introducing him to Carol, "he's a m– friend of mine. Gerry, this is Carol. We're old friends."

Carol was impressed with Gerry's new friend. She liked his calm bearing and air of confidence. Here was a classy fellow. Wonder if he's single.

"Well," she began, waving a careless hand in the direction of the distant duo, "It seems as though they're doing a job for you – I don't want to know anything about it – and they're going to try and –" here she hesitated as though unsure of the choice of word, "drop you in it. Him in the denim says that he's going to drop a note and he told the other one to wear his poacher's jacket because they're not just after the one thing.I didn't understand a word of it at all." Her delivery had become breathless and she placed her left hand on her chest as though trying to slow herself down, "I just hope it means something to you."

Carol had her suspicions and a possible scenario based on what she had heard and moulded by her native intuition had already made its way through her mind but she wisely kept it to herself.

"Thank you for that information." Henry said, "I can assure you that what we're doing is acceptable if not praiseworthy but we would rather you kept it under your hat."

Carol did a zipping action across her mouth. It seemed appropriate somehow.

Thanking her again and adding how delightful it had been to meet her, Henry left with Gerry.

The morning after the meeting and some miles away, Mr and Mrs Poindexter were having breakfast when the mail arrived. It was Hilary Poindexter's habit, if not duty, to deal with the mail. Aubrey, her husband, read the newspaper, throwing snippets of news at Hilary just as quickly as those she threw to him which had been culled from the letters she was reading.

One envelope contained two tickets for Puccini's 'La Boheme', which was being staged at the Port Regis opera house, and a brief note which she read aloud to her husband, "'Cannot use these as I shall be out of the country on that date and so I thought of you. If you are unable to use them, I feel sure you know someone who can. I hope you have an enjoyable evening.' And it's just signed 'J'. Who do you think that could be, Aubrey?" And then, without giving him time to offer a possible explanation, said brightly, "Oh, that will be Julian. Do you remember Julian, darling? The

Pemberly boy – I say boy – he must be twenty five by now but he always loved opera. We met him at the Spring Ball last year. It must have been he who sent us these. I shall ring him to convey our appreciation. Oh, I can't if he's out of the country now, can I? I shall write to him. I have his address somewhere."

Aubrey's contribution to this conversation was nothing. He had recognised the content of his wife's rhetoric and experience had taught him that trying to comment was largely a waste of time and it wasn't even necessary to concentrate on what she was saying. If it was important or if it concerned him, there would be a recap.

"Have you seen this damned stupid idea the government has come up with, now?" he asked, pointing at the newspaper.

The letter which Hilary wrote to thank Julian for the gift of the opera tickets was received by that worthy just two days later. As he hadn't sent anyone tickets for anything and hadn't been anywhere abroad recently, nor was he planning to go in the near future, he did not understand what Hilary Poindexter was blathering on about. Nor was he inclined to investigate the matter.

"Batty old cow!" he exclaimed and threw the letter into his waste-bin.

* * *

The night was exceedingly clear, nothing suggesting cloud could be seen against the backdrop of a myriad stars. There was a partial moon, its unlit sector visible by starlight, making Gerry wonder why ancient tribes believed that the moon, on a regular basis, was eaten by some star dragon or whatever when it could be seen whole so clearly. And what's more, it was so very definitely spherical that it must raise doubt in any flat-earther's mind.

Gerry and Henry were waiting for Wilf and Robbie to

appear at the pre-arranged meeting place, a roundabout above a junction of the motorway which served Port Regis. Henry was listening to some classical music on the car radio. It helped his concentration, he found.

Constables Purslipp and Clough were off duty that night.

Robbie's van turned up five minutes late due more to Robbie's unco-operative attitude than any other factor. He still felt very bad about the job which he was to do tonight. He objected to being told to burgle a house on someone else's say-so and come away out of pocket. Especially the posh bastard's say-so. Wilf thought him grumpy. Wilf was slightly more cheerful – his mind was more on Wayne – he had had visions of his friend bound hand and foot in some dark cellar, suffering from hunger and thirst and what Wilf was doing tonight, in his view, was working for Wayne's freedom. This made the job a noble cause and worth doing because of that.

Henry got out of his car and waved to indicate their presence as he saw the van approach and Robbie pulled up behind Henry's car but made no attempt to get out. Henry went over to speak to him.

"Good evening, Wilfred, Robert, how are you?"

There was no intelligible response other than a curt nod of recognition from Robbie.

" Right, the job is in Cammonbank. Do you know it?"

Another, surly nod from Robbie. Wilf's face had an attentive look, he did not want to mess up any instruction he might be given. It was also a clean face. The face paint had been put aside for tonight's job.

"You will follow my car," Henry continued, "and we shall park on the layby just outside the village. You two are to join Gerry and myself in the car."

Robbie was a little concerned about leaving his van unattended and out of sight. He weighed up the chances of its being inspected at close range by a keen-eyed member of the constabulary who might notice that it was tax-deficient. He judged the danger to be minimal and agreed unenthusiastically.

* * *

The address was that of a terraced house which fronted the street without the bothersome buffer of a garden. All lights were out although, at two in the morning, it was quite understandable.

Danny strolled, a policeman ostensibly on his legal beat as far as any observer might be concerned, to the end of the terrace where a narrow, cindered back-alley served the rear ends of the two back-to-back streets. The wooden gates, slightly too tall to look over, were helpfully numbered although, for whose benefit, Danny couldn't figure out. All that was required to let himself into the back yard was to insert his forefinger into the hole drilled into the right side of the gate and lift the latch on the inside. The gate swung open without a sound. On his left, Danny noticed the rubbish bin left ready for the morning's bin collection. Two plastic bags were stacked next to it, one of which was a peculiar shape. Ignoring this for a time, he wandered down the path towards the back door of the house and, as he neared it, an outer lamp came on, flooding the yard area with light and a woman's voice asked, 'Who is it?'

'The police, ma'am.' Danny said, brandishing his warrant card.

He told the woman his prepared story of a roaming band of youths up to no good and how one of them had disappeared up this alley. He was to check all the back yards while his colleague stopped up the only exit. They were sure to catch him. As he spoke to the woman, he was carefully observing her every expression and movement but nothing significant caught his eye until she gestured for him to leave. Her left arm bore recently inflicted scratches. Danny left thinking excitedly

of what he'd seen and then suddenly it came to him. No watch!
It could have been ripped off during a struggle. There should
be plenty for forensic to go on if only he could find some way
of implicating her. He waited at the bottom of the alley for an
hour until it was safe, determined to see what the contents of
the strangely shaped plastic bag were.

* * *

While the four drove to the Poindexter house, Henry briefed the two villains. "There's been a slight change of plan which won't affect the overall outcome. First; Wilf will go into the house and disable the security system alone. Then he will come out through the front door and allow Robbie and myself to enter. I only need your presence, Robbie for professional advice – to ensure that I don't do anything ill-advised – er, amateurish. Do you understand? I know where the painting is kept and we will go straight to it – take it – and leave. Job done.While we are inside, Wilf will remain outside with Gerry. Do I make myself clear Wilf?"

Wilf nodded.

"You never said nothing about a change of plan," complained Robbie, "and can you turn that shite off?" He nodded towards the radio which was playing light classical music.

Henry turned off the radio. "I don't think any of us has been entirely honest. I suspect that you two harbour a secret or two which I'm not supposed to know about. Am I right?"

Henry's manner in asking this question was so friendly and disarming that Wilf nodded with a grin before checking himself and looking worriedly at Robbie.

Both Robbie and Henry ignored Wilf's mistake and Henry turned back to face forwards.

"Do I turn in to the drive?" enquired Gerry who had been quiet up until now.

"No – that'd be stupid – park on the opposite side of the street just past the gate – and in shadow, rather than under the street-lamp. Less likely to be noticed." Robbie advised.

"Right, Wilf and Gerry out first – we'll give you five minutes start. Will that be enough time, Wilf?" asked Henry.

"Could be a couple of minutes more – not much anyway." Wilf said.

"Don't slam the bloody doors!" More advice from Robbie.

Leaving the car, Gerry and Wilf turned up the drive, walking along the grassy edge to minimise the noise of their footsteps. There was no need for flashlights, it was still beautifully clear. There were few lights visible in the surrounding properties. Evidently these people go to bed commendably early, Gerry thought. He felt very excited at what he was doing. His very first housebreaking venture and, all being well, he would be basking in Toni's appreciation before the night was out.

Arriving at the front entrance; a heavy, double door sheltered by a sandstone porch, Wilf said to Gerry, "Wait in there. I'll be back soon."

Gerry had no option but to comply and thrust his hands deep into his coat pockets while he waited. He felt an urge to whistle but suppressed it. His nerves weren't standing up to this experience very well. He promised himself a stiff drink when it was all over.

Two sets of sounds brought Gerry back to full alertness. Outside he could hear the muffled approach of what he hoped was Henry and Robbie while from inside, there were noises which were too unfamiliar for him to picture any activity which might have caused them. Most likely to be Wilf doing something or other. Then the door opened and Wilf's grin stepped out.

"All done." he announced proudly.

"Search him, Gerry." ordered Henry.

Wilf's grin vanished. "Why?" he complained.

"We're just making sure no-one operates outside the rules, is all." Henry told him.

Gerry checked Wilf's coat, including a thorough search of the rather spacious inside pockets. He was amazed at the depth and number of these. At the bottom of one of them he found a china figurine.

"It's all I had time for." Wilf said apologetically to Robbie who said nothing.

"Where did it come from?" demanded Henry, angrily.

"Off the table in the hall."

Henry took it from Gerry and then said, "Right, Robbie, it's our turn now. Am I ready to go in?"

"Gloves." grumped Robbie.

"These do?" Henry flourished a pair of driving gloves. Robbie nodded.

"One more thing. Give Gerry the note which you're planning to drop inside the house, please."

"What note?"

"Don't try to fool about – we know some of your secrets – you have no idea of ours – just give Gerry the note."

Realising that perhaps he may have underestimated this posh bastard, Robbie handed over a crumpled piece of paper which Gerry read.

"Yes, this is it." he said to Henry.

Henry and Robbie went into the house, Henry, after wiping and replacing the figurine on the table indicated by Wilf, made straight for the music room. There was no reason for Mrs Poindexter to suspect that anyone would try to snatch back the miniature and therefore none to put it anywhere other than the place it had always hung.

This far into the house it was necessary to use a low wattage flash light which had a very diffuse beam. He stationed Robbie at the open door so that he could keep half an eye on him and so that Robbie could maintain eye contact with the front door in case of unexpected arrivals. Henry made a quick tour of the room, briefly examining the pictures he found hanging there, occasionally making an appreciative remark to himself when he found a worthy piece. Eventually, on the opposite wall from where he'd started, he found what he was looking for. It looked exactly as Angela had described and he lifted it carefully away from where it hung. Turning, he spotted Robbie casting about, probably for something small and easily carried – his instincts had overcome his fear of Henry. He had found it frustrating to be standing in the house of wealthy people in the dead of night and under instructions not to take anything. Fortunately, Henry caught him before anything fell into his hands.

"Out, you scoundrel!" Henry hissed, "You could never be a gentleman."

Robbie really never had ambitions of gentility so he wasn't offended. He did feel somewhat thwarted, though.

The rest was straightforward: Robbie was instructed to drive the van home by himself and Wilf, who Henry rather liked and trusted in a slight way, was taken in the car to Toni's house. A blindfold had been considered but the confusion of unlit lanes was thought enough to disorient anyone trying to remember the route. Especially Wilf. Besides, Wilf was honour bound to stay away from the property.

They drove up to the front of the house and, after being greeted by a worried Angela and Toni, went to fetch Wayne who had been drinking tea in the kitchen. Wayne had a big grin on his face and looked, Wilf thought, surprisingly well for a hostage. He had half expected a dishevelled and dirty Wayne to be pulled out from a shed somewhere, still tied up to prevent escape but his friend looked more like a departing guest as he made cheery goodbyes to those on the steps. Rather than worry about it, he welcomed

Wayne back and the pair drove off in Wayne's van. On the way, Wayne explained his new situation and that he would, from now on, not be working with the team. He was going straight. His mum had said.

Gerry, thankful the adventure was over, kissed Toni farewell and waved to Henry and Angela as he, too, drove back home.

* * *

Danny took the bag back to his car, threw it into the boot and ripped it open immediately. The item which had caused the odd shape was a large wooden crucifix of the type that you might see wall-mounted in a religious institution. It evidently made a formidable weapon because there was blood splashed all over the top end, covering the image of Jesus. Two or three hairs could be seen stuck to one of the arms of the cross. He was careful not to touch them.

Danny pulled out his mobile and called Charley.

'I'm not kidding, Charley, I've found the murder weapon used on that last one and I reckon that this is the woman who has done all three!'

Charley sounded incredulous, 'Where did you get it, Danny? How come everyone else missed it?'

Danny gave him a short explanation, promising the full version when he met with him at the station.

'I'm bringing it in.' There was a grim but satisfied smile on Danny's face.

* * *

In Cabley Hall, most of the household slept late the morning following the raid and so missed the beauty of the dawn. Almost as clear as the previous morning, the sky was as fully azure as the advertisements claim. One or two tiny clouds moved unhurriedly across it, propelled by a light breeze but these were reconnaissance clouds rather than anything which might threaten rain.

Driving to his newsagency after a very short nap on his sofa – he didn't dare to risk the comfort of his bed – Gerry was tired but happy. Too tired to really appreciate the loveliness of the early morning but happy that things between himself and Toni were working out. But Gerry was fed up with being a newsagent. He was considering retirement. Selling newspapers was beginning to pall and, in the light of what had happened to him recently, it was not a surprise. It was time for a change; a big life-style change.

Angela was awake but unable to see the morning. She lay on her side, her back to the window and smiling happily at the reclaimed miniature which she had propped up on the bedside table and, behind her, she could feel the warm bulk of her hero husband, his front to her back, as they lay like spoons. Henry was still fast asleep. She could hear birdsong, too, as the blackbirds chortled their greetings. It was an enchanting morning for Angela.

* * *

Wayne's first action as a free man was to call round to see Kerry-Ann at her home. The door was opened, to Wayne's relief, by her crotchety mother. Kerry-Ann had an exceptionally grumpy father and Wayne was rather frightened of him. Kerry-Ann's mother, by comparison, was sweetness and light.

"She's not happy with you – I'll get her." said Mrs Graves bluntly, closing the door and leaving Wayne alone on the doorstep. There were raised voices to be heard from inside the house where mild discord had broken out but soon the door was re-opened by the love of Wayne's life.

"Where've you been, you bastard? I was waiting for you last night to pick me up from work. I thought we were going to the chippy together."

Kerry-Ann was definitely cross, her mood falling

somewhere between her mother's current ill-humour and her father's permanently vile disposition and Wayne felt that it was unjustified. She should be showing concern for what he'd been put through.

"I was kidnapped." said Wayne lamely, playing the sympathy card.

"You were what?" Kerry-Ann asked and a small explosion in her face made its way out as a snort from both mouth and nostrils.

"Kidnapped." Wayne put his hands in his pockets. He was disappointed that she had not fallen on his neck weeping with relief that he was now rescued.

Kerry-Ann laughed and turned back towards the interior of the house to shout, "Wayne says he was kidnapped."

"Not by aliens, was it?" came the voice of her rather credulous mother.

"He is a bloody alien." said another voice, a little farther away but still too close for comfort, belonging to Kerry-Ann's peevish father.

"Look – I'll tell you later – are you coming out?" Wayne was a little unnerved by the knowledge that her father was in the house and his valour, ever at a low ebb, receded further.

"I'll get me coat." Kerry-Ann said.

* * *

Hilary Poindexter's view of the morning was marred by puzzlement. She and Aubrey had enjoyed a splendid evening at the opera, thanks to Julian's kindness, marred only once by an intrusive mobile phone, the male owner of which, she was satisfied to note, had been clapped around the ears by the lady seated next to him wielding a rolled up libretto. They had stayed overnight in an hotel and, after a leisurely breakfast, made their way home. What caught Hilary's eye almost as soon as she walked into the house and the cause of her bewildered frame of mind right now, was that a china figurine had been moved from its accustomed place on the mantle-piece to the hall table.

"Have you done that?" she asked her husband who was struggling in through the door carrying an overnight bag.

"Done what, dear?"

"Have you moved my Regency beau from the mantle-piece?"

"Why on earth would I do that. I wouldn't dream of re-arranging things in this house or any other for that matter because you would simply return things to their proper place. It would be a pointless exercise."

"Hm."

What a triumph of expressiveness the English language is that this short syllable uttered by Mrs. Poindexter not only indicated concurrence with her husband's remark, dissatisfaction with his reaction to her question but also continued puzzlement. The idea now making its unwelcome way into her consciousness was that someone had been in the house while they had been away. The questions Who? and Why? disturbed her. Hilary's next thought was of her jewellery. The night at the opera had only required a pearl necklace, pearl earrings and a mother-of-pearl brooch. There were two diamond brooches and several other quite valuable items in a box by her bed. Or, at least, that's where they should be. She hurried up the stairs to her room, ignoring her husband's query on what to do with the bag and, to her relief, found her jewellery box untouched. Still suspicious, she checked around the room but could find no signs of intrusion. She went back downstairs, instructed Aubrey concerning the overnight bag and went on a tour of the house, an activity in which she was well practised as it was one she indulged in each afternoon when the daily, Mrs. Crellin, was finishing her work. A shock hit her when she entered the music room. She noticed the gap on the wall immediately. The miniature had gone! Her first instinct to ring the police was quelled. Another – to call her husband was put on hold. Another suspicion was creeping into her head but first, she must finish her tour of the house. The kitchen, the room least likely to be burgled, was last on her list. Aubrey was there making coffee and he was curious about his wife's behaviour.

"Whatever is the matter, dear?"

"We've been burgled." she said, almost tearfully as she sat at the kitchen table.

Aubrey's first thought was of his golf clubs. Had he been asked to draw up a list of household items which he would most miss should they have been burgled or the house burned down, his golf clubs would have been top and all of Hilary's belongings somewhere near the bottom. "What have they taken?" he asked quickly, "I haven't noticed a thing wrong."

"It's funny," she said, accepting the cup of coffee he put in front of her, "nothing has been taken except the miniature which I got back from Robert." She sniffed, her dead son's memory renewing her grief.

It was ill-advised of Aubrey to voice his thoughts and, had he considered them properly, he would never have done so for fear of the consequences.

"Which you stole from Robert's widow."

Here, Hilary's tears showed and two of the brave ones rolled, one from each eye, down her cheek. These were tantamount to an admission of guilt. She knew that Aubrey was right but she remained convinced of her moral right to that painting.

Aubrey immediately regretted saying what he did. Unfortunately, you can't rewind real life and so the words remained said.

"I take it, then, that you have decided not to call the police." Aubrey said, as kindly as he could. He felt a little moved inside by his wife's tears. Genuine ones were not frequently seen but, despite their rarity, Aubrey had spotted that these were the real thing.

She shook her head. She really meant to nod but her thoughts, a little scrambled, confused the response.

Aubrey understood anyway.

Chapter Fifteen

ENDINGS

And the crooked shall be made straight
and the rough places plain
(Isaiah)

It was a grey morning, warm with a capricious wind which promised to keep any rain away and just two days after the affair of the miniature as Gerry liked to think of it. He was driving to Toni's house to resume the postponed horse-riding lesson. He didn't feel quite so nervous this day. For one thing, after the raid on the Poindexter's house, horses, by comparison, didn't seem quite so fearsome. Besides, he was a little pre-occupied with the final chapter of his novel. He wasn't sure how it might end and there was also a half-formed plan regarding Toni. He'd spent some of the night awake and thinking of her. Rather a pleasant way of spending time, usually, but now he was coming to the cliff edge of their relationship. Should he jump? He was very sure of his feelings towards her. He loved her. Of that he was absolutely certain. He was also positive that he would like to spend more time with her. Like the rest of his life.

One aspect which jarred, which was refusing to fit into any sort of place, like a part from a different jig-saw, was the social gap. Could he cross it? Could he cope with life at her end of the social spectrum? And, more importantly, were he to ask her to marry him, would she accept? He was forced to consider this social gap from her perspective. Was she willing to pair up with a peasant? And although these thoughts tumbled around his mind, they weren't yet large enough to cause worry. There was plenty of time. No rush. No problem. He decided that he should play it by ear. First things first – riding the damned horse.

He turned into Toni's drive and saw the dogs break into a run as they spotted his car. A little touch like that made him feel very welcome. Provided that it was understood that it was a friendly gesture on their part which prevented you from climbing out of the car once you had opened the door. Their combined greeting had pushed him back onto the car seat and Grundy was about to climb in with him. Gerry was laughing too hard to protest much.

"Grundy! Sally!" Toni shouted as she came to the door, giggling at Gerry's predicament. Freed from the exuberance of the dogs, he brushed dog hair from his clothes and joined Toni in the kitchen for a coffee and a briefing before they made their way to the stable.

While being introduced to the horses, Gerry noticed several things; horses can be as pushy as dogs when their curiosity must be satisfied, they seem incapable of producing a friendly face in the same way that dogs can – their teeth somehow contribute to the worrisome feeling that they want to bite you – and he noticed some letters and numbers seemingly tattooed on the horses' skin.

Toni explained that these were indelible identification marks which deterred thieves as they couldn't sell a stolen horse to an honest customer with these marks visible.

She poo-pooed the idea that horses don't look loveable. It was simply a matter of reading their facial expressions differently and not using dogs as a reference point.

Then came the coaching; how to mount, to set off, to stop; instructions which Gerry understood to be significant but, to him, alien since his modes of transport had been so far exclusively mechanical. What bothered him was the knowledge that horses can think and make decisions which may or may not be in accordance with a rider's intentions. Toni did her best to reassure him by impressing upon him the fact of his superior intelligence.

"Ah," said Gerry, " but they have a superior malevolence to make up for the lack of I.Q."

After a little more than two hours in the saddle and, by now, thoroughly enjoying himself, Gerry, mounted on Ezekiel, was on a woodland ride, trotting alongside Toni on Moss Trooper. The advantage, Gerry found, of being on a horse's back is that you can't see its face, you won't try to imagine some form of threat from the animal if you can't look into its eyes.

Toni's mind had gone back to a moment a few weeks earlier when she had been on this ride alone. Then, she had wished for someone to share the feelings she had for this woodland paradise. Now, almost unbelievably, her wish had been granted and here he was! Gerry needed a little more practice before he could ride naturally – be tall in the saddle rather than floppy – but it would come.

"Stop here." she instructed, when they reached the remembered spot.

Gerry, recalling how he had been told to bring a horse to a halt – an instruction he'd insisted on mastering first of all – stopped Ezekiel alongside Moss Trooper. Both horses snickered, possibly sharing an in-horse joke about the new rider.

Toni looked around her, appreciative that the place still felt magical and what was more, with Gerry's presence, it had gained somewhat in that commodity. Summer was preparing its grand entrance and Spring was about to bow out. The smell of blossom had given way to a loamy smell with its promise of heavy fruitfulness. The birds sang fitfully when not more usefully employed in trying to reduce the insect population.

"What do you think?" she asked.

"Of what?" Gerry was unsure how to answer the question.

"Of this place – this time – this day."

"Beautiful." He was reluctant to expand on this comment, he still wasn't certain what was required of him. Did she want him to wax poetical or be prosaic and suggest improvements? This was stressful; horse-riding as a new experience mixed with the never ending problem of trying to understand just what the lady in your life is saying. Not the actual words used but rather the meaning she wants to convey.

A little way away, on one of the footpaths leading to the clearing where Gerry and Toni were, the middle-aged man with the spaniel was out walking again and had recognised Toni with her horse. Since first seeing her, and on subsequent occasions, he had entertained fantasies of a sexual nature about her, imagining her falling from her horse when he was at hand to rescue her and she, being so grateful to him, rewarded him with the freedom of her body. Now he felt a twinge of jealousy to see her with another man. There was another sexual fantasy reduced to dust. There weren't many left now. There was that lady behind the counter at the post office; a notional raid which he might thwart, saving the lady's life and earning her lifelong gratitude. It wasn't much, though, in the way of erotic reverie. A replacement would be required. He tugged irritably at the dog's lead as it squatted to relieve itself.

"C'm'on! It's time to go home, I've had enough today."

"Gerry."

"Yes?"

"What do you think – ?"

Gerry was fairly sure he had heard this question a little earlier and, what is more, had answered it. While he pondered whether Toni was suddenly forgetful or whether this was a subtle form of a completely different question, Toni spoke again.

"Marry me."

What he had heard and its tone, falling between enquiry and order, unseated Gerry but metaphorically rather than literally. He took a little time to regain his composure, turned towards her and asked, "Pardon?"

"Don't make me say it again, it took a lot of courage for me to say that." She looked down to Moss Trooper's head and stroked his neck, avoiding Gerry's perplexed look.

Gerry had fully understood her the first time but it was a difficult remark to respond to. "What can I say? – Yes."

Her expression was loaded with smiles, disappointment and tears, it shifted among the firing points of these in the split second it had taken Gerry to reply.

"You mean you will marry me?" A broad grin shining with pleasure took over her face.

"Yes, of course I will." Gerry was surprised at how easily that came out.

The smile flared – she sagged back in the saddle with a visible relief then dug her heels into the horse's flanks, whooped and galloped away.

Ezekiel started – from instinct probably – and feeling no input from the rider atop him, stopped again.

"Whoa!" Gerry's rather ineffectual command was meant for both Toni and Ezekiel. Redundant in the horse's case and unheard or ignored in Toni's, it floated away.

"We haven't covered galloping yet!" he added, more for his own consolation. Two worried minutes later and Toni's horse was seen again, charging and snorting back to where she started from. Hauling Moss Trooper to a standstill, she looked across at Gerry with wild eyes and said, "I love you!" She wheeled the horse and galloped homewards.

Happily, one of the instructions which Gerry had received and remembered this morning in Horsemanship 101, as it were, was turning. He pressed his knee gently into Ezekiel's neck, pulled on the leather strap thingy (technical terms weren't Gerry's best suit) and Ezekiel figured out the rest. Home.

On the ride back, ideas began to come to Gerry about the ending of his novel. It all seemed obvious, now. What had been blank desperation became bright inspiration. He rode back feeling confident and happy, realising that, because Toni had ridden on ahead, for the first time he was flying solo. It gave him an immense and sudden feeling of pride – a feeling of independence – of being grown up, similar to his first solo outing in a car or the first time of setting up home outside the parental sphere of influence.

Back at the stables, Toni was already grooming Moss Trooper. She smiled at his arrival, a smile Gerry didn't recall seeing before – it had a hidden element that he couldn't identify.

"You can't just park horses when you've ridden them – you're going to have to learn how to remove all the tack and to groom and to ensure that they have feed and water. Then we're going into the house for some rampant sex."

That was it – the smile had been wicked. But Gerry had no objections to raise against her suggestions so he just got on with seeing to Ezekiel.

Later, tired after grooming and energetic sex, over coffee in the kitchen, Toni asked, "You did mean it when you said yes, didn't you?"

"Of course I did. Why?"

"I suppose it's because I can't believe it's all happening – I need reassurance that it is true. When I think of how we came together, it all seems wildly unlikely. The first man I pick out from a Lonely Hearts page and I get lucky straight away. A bit like winning a lottery."

There was short period of silence when Gerry felt that comment was unnecessary and Toni considered her thoughts.

"Are you one for long engagements in which you might contemplate the rashness of your decision or do you want to rush headlong into madness?" she asked.

"Oh, headlong every time."

"We have to careful about setting a date – we don't want to clash with Monica's wedding, do we?"

"Monica? And Kelps?" This piece of news was both fresh and unexpected.

"Yes, Monica will be moving into Kelps' house in Poast and Wayne will become a tenant of her old house. He has a job lined up in Steadmore with the council on the Parks and Gardens division. And I've no doubt that we will be invited. And we shall reciprocate, of course."

Gerry felt a mental swirl of images and opinions. He was grateful that Monica was off his back but she was hardly out of his life. He found the thought of Monica dressed in white repellent but at least he wouldn't be the one stood next to her. I do hope Kelps has the fortitude to cope with the food and sex. Not that any of it would be bad – it would be good but probably in too great a quantity. Gerry didn't envy Kelps at all but still, it takes all sorts.

Now seemed a good time to explain to Toni his involvement with Monica, "I have to tell you something which I think you should be aware of. When I put that advert in, you weren't the only woman to answer it, you know."

"I did think that was likely to be the case." Toni assured him, "How many were there?"

"Only one other woman sent a reply to me and I had a meeting with her. It was a bit of a dog's dinner really; I knew we weren't suited but she couldn't understand that. She was positive that I was the man for her and it took a lot to shake her off. I felt as though I was being stalked at one point."

Toni's eyes widened, "Do go on."

"It wasn't a pleasant experience. It felt like harassment, she just would not let go. Do you know, I even asked police advice?", said Gerry, referring to the informal questioning of Constable Purslipp and his unhelpful answers.

"Really? And what did they say?"

"They weren't very sympathetic and I can't repeat the advice they gave me. Needless to say, I didn't follow it. Anyway, she's no longer a problem and I shall be eternally grateful to Kelps for taking her off my hands."

"Monica!" Toni yelped.

"Yes, Monica."

Toni covered her face with her hands as she giggled at the image of Monica stalking her Gerry.

Gerry ignored her laughing at him and went on, "About the wedding, can I leave the date and place up to you, Toni? I shall make a point of being there, of course, but things have been happening a bit fast just lately. Not just about us – it's everything and I don't feel capable, at the moment, of organising anything."

Toni nodded, "That's fine, leave it to me."

After another short period of contemplation, Gerry was pricked by a sharp concern, "Will it be a big society do?"

"Monica and Kelps?" asked Toni innocently, a snigger on her lips, "I wouldn't think so. Probably something small and informal. I'm trying to picture Wayne in a suit."

"No – our wedding. Morning suits, toppers and what not. Half the county's top drawer braying down my neck."

"Of course, Gerry darling. It's expected. We're talking something like two hundred and fifty guests on the big day. Cathedral wedding – bishop officiating. The bishop of Port Regis was a good friend of Daddy's, so he'll insist. We'll have the do here, a couple of marquees in the grounds, a concert orchestra – just a small one – buckets of champagne. Why do you ask?"

She watched Gerry's face sag. He was quite obviously not brave enough to protest but it was plain that the picture she had just painted for him was a little frightening. Then she laughed.

"I'm sorry, Gerry, I was kidding. You should have seen your face. A quiet registry office ceremony with a few close family and friends. I wasn't kidding about the marquee, though. Just one, where we shall have the wedding breakfast, speeches, champagne and whatnot. And possibly a band. People like to dance at weddings, you know." There was a pause and Toni, as though recalling an omitted aspect of the arrangements continued, "Do you mind terribly if we didn't go away anywhere? For our honeymoon, I mean. It's just that it might be awkward getting someone to see to the horses and the dogs. I would worry, too, if I had to leave them."

"No." said Gerry, "I hadn't really thought of a honeymoon so I won't be disappointed not having one. I think that the big change in my way of life will be enough to think about."

* * *

'Clever you,' Donna said proudly, 'I'd no idea that that woman even fancied me, let alone was stalking me, too. Those other women were just acquaintances and she must have seen me in The Roseate Kitty talking to them and become consumed with jealousy. Well, I'm glad that's all sorted out now.'

'Will you be going back to The Roseate Kitty?' Danny asked tentatively.

'No fear.' she said, 'Anyway, I'm not truly a lesbian, I was just bi-sexual and experimenting with my sexual leanings. On the whole, I prefer men. One man in particular, in fact.'

'Who?' Danny asked even more tentatively.

'You, you ninny.' Donna laughed.

* * *

Heavy George's funeral took place in St. Bruno's in the Wood in a suburb of Port Regis whose graveyard overlooked the river estuary, a place with which George had no links whatever. It was a sparsely attended affair and the church was made echoey by the lack of mourners.

By far the most numerous contingent was the pall bearers, eight in number, chivvied into service by Chevis Yardley and his new minder, Preston. At least two of these were not sorry to see George go and were, therefore, not mourners in the strictest sense of the word. The chief mourner was Heavy George's mother, a formidable looking woman who had developed her worrisome demeanour during the years of her son's upbringing, in particular, his adolescence. She was very upset by George's death.

There were two other attendees, not in the congregation, who stood some distance away as the coffin was lowered into the damp earth.

Leigh Purslipp was one, there for unofficial and professional reasons. He wanted to see faces. He was aware that George was known to the police and therefore that his associates would likely be untrustworthy too. Some of the faces might be well worth remembering.

Near him, stood Brian, racked with guilt from having been instrumental in bringing about George's premature burial and tearful to see him go.

"Know him, did you?" Leigh asked Brian as an informal way of starting a conversation with the aim of finding out what this man's connection was with George. He was also curious to know why he stood apart from the main party.

"Yes, I did. A lovely man. Kind, gentle. A really lovely man who will be greatly missed." Brian pulled out a large white hanky from his pocket, dried his eyes and then blew his nose.

Leigh didn't quite understand or agree with Brian's sentiments nor did he get to discover what he was to George. Gentle. That was a word few others who knew

George would have chosen.

"Strange do, altogether," he said to himself as the funeral group broke up and the sexton's men began filling in the hole, "Shouldn't have thought that all these people would be sorry to see George go. Bit of a waste of time really."

The last remark referred to his own effort in turning up.

* * *

On the morning of Monica's wedding, just outside Edinburgh, a coach broke down. It wasn't a minor mechanical hiccough which could have been cured by some roadside recovery service but a fractured connecting rod which, as it broke, caused considerable collateral damage to the rest of the engine.

This incident should not have had repercussions as far south as Monica and her plans except that the contents of the coach was a group called 'Central Reservation', a tribute band which owed allegiance to not one but several bland, inoffensive and unexciting singing groups of the recent past. The group had just completed an engagement in a small dance hall on the outskirts of Edinburgh and were heading south for their next gig, a wedding in a small town called Wettenham. The manager of 'Central Reservation', one Roland Utledge, realising that the chances of arriving on time were negligible, telephoned the booking agent, Harvey Bredgold and explained the situation. Harvey panicked and, looking through his available acts, discovered just one gigless group on his books and promised Roland that he would sort things out.

He then rang Monica to explain: "Hello, Mrs Prough, this is Harvey Bredgold. The group which was supposed to come and perform at your wedding tonight can't, in fact, make it. They've been unavoidably detained by a breakdown in Scotland."

Monica's reaction to this news was uncharacteristically

wordless but Harvey could sense the disappointment at the other end of the line. Before there could be any tears or shouting, things with which Harvey found it difficult to cope over the phone, he hurriedly added, "I do have another band free for tonight, they're a local group and they will be only too happy to be there."

"What sort of music do they play? Is it popular music?" asked Monica, a little concerned that they might not match her first choice for entertainment.

"Oh, it's very popular, it's a sort of rock and roll which they specialise in but they're talented lads, these, they'll play a bit of rock, a bit of this, a bit of that, they can turn their hands to anything." Harvey was sweating with uncertainty, he knew that it was a downright lie but he thought, once the wedding's in full swing and they've all had a few, no-one will notice that 'Borborygmus' weren't your usual wedding-oriented pop-group.

"Oh. Oh, all right then. It won't cost us any more will it?" Monica was relieved but still watchful.

"No, it will even be a few quid cheaper. I'll send you an amended bill. O.K.?"

"Well, thank you for ringing, goodbye."

Harvey hung up. The pressure was off.

Monica became Mrs. Kelps in Wettenham church that afternoon and the guests all made their way to Demsbury village hall which had been hired for the wedding breakfast. It was quite a large room with a low stage or dais at one end and most of the other end was furnished with chairs and tables. A temporary bar complete with bored looking bar-man stood to one side. Quite soon, the hall was abuzz with the congratulations for the couple, increasingly loud chatter and the sounds of food and drink being served and consumed.

The band arrived as the speeches and toasts were drawing to a close.

Their appearance made an audible alteration to the

background conversational hum. Whereas themes of discussion had concerned the several aspects of the day's events such as sartorial criticism of some of the other guests and, occasionally, a comment on a recent football match, a number of the wedding party began to compare reactions to the group on the dais. To a man, 'Borborygmus' was dressed in black denim or leather. The instrumentalists wore black and white 'corpse' make-up and sported a good deal of chromium plated personal jewellery, predominantly spiked. The singer wore a long leather coat which brushed the floor as he moved about, no chrome whatsoever except for a huge pair of earrings and grey face paint which gave him the look of someone not yet interred but fully qualified for the privilege.

As the band set up, they appeared slightly nervous, possibly because they have never performed at a wedding before and none of the guests looked as though they would fit in comfortably with the usual audience. Their normal venues were brick-lined, below ground and full of young people wearing clothes similar to theirs. In Demsbury village hall, the members of 'Borborygmus' stood out a bit. In fact, the only other person wearing as much black as they were was the groom and he looked way too old to appreciate death-metal rock.

As Wilf introduced the first number, one penned by the drummer and called 'Put my fist in your face', the revellers came out onto the dance floor in couples. When the band began to play, the dancers froze as if playing 'Grandmother's footsteps'. Then, slowly, they began to ebb away from the band and towards the far walls and clumped into nervous groups for protection. All except for a nephew of Monica's who stood on the dance floor with a big grin eating into his face. He was a Goth and a fan.

The vocal style of the death-metal is almost canine, the lyrics delivered in a deep barking sound, accompanied by the occasional yelp, for emphasis, which would, although articulate, be difficult to follow, even with a lyric sheet in front of you. What the singer was trying to say would remain a secret known only to himself.

At Gerry's table were Henry, Toni and Angela. Their conversation stopped as soon as Wilf's song started and the foursome's attention was instantly drawn by horrified curiosity to the group on the stage. Some seconds later and Gerry broke the silence with, "Good grief, do you recognise the singer, Henry?"

Henry concentrated on the contorted features of the front man with the microphone pushed into his face and admitted failure, "No, who is it?"

"He's one of the gang we met with at the car-park. Don't you recognise the grey face-paint? He doesn't look quite so ill under these lights, does he?"

Henry couldn't find much in the way of appropriate comments, "Good Lord!" was the best he could do.

Happily, most songs within this genre are short and forty two awestruck seconds later, Wilf had finished and was taking a bow.

This was when Henry decided to intervene.

As Henry strode to the dais where the band stood, sorting themselves out for the second number, one composed jointly by Wilf and the prolific drummer and called 'The Devil's Entrails', Wilf noticed his purposeful arrival. It briefly flashed through his mind that this was someone with a request. Then that happy thought was roughly shouldered aside by brutal recognition trailing a little fear. "Bollocks!", he thought, "it's that posh bloke wiv the gun." Wilf quickly noted, with some relief, that this time there was no gun in the crook of Henry's arm but his confidence didn't fully return.

But Henry's mission was neither vengeful nor belligerent. "Good evening." he said, politely, "The guests find that this sort of music a little difficult to enjoy. Could you please play something more gentle which might encourage them to dance rather than cower over there like that?" He waved his arm in the general direction of the other guests who were looking at Henry in the manner of maidens threatened by dragons who see Saint George bent on rescue.

Wilf knew the answer to Henry's question but still looked around at the other band members enquiringly on the slim chance that he was wrong. There was one shaken head and two sets of shrugged shoulders.

Then, turning back to Henry and trying to look disappointed, he said, "Not really."

It should be noted that the principal guests, Monica and Kelps, the bride and blushing groom, were oblivious to any of this, being completely wrapped up in each other's company. They continued to sip white wine and talk softly to one another. Actually, what Kelps did mostly was to listen softly to what his new spouse was saying. But he was a happy listener.

On stage, the bass guitarist, a bright lad who was quick to assess the situation, one Scurge (his spelling of his nom de theatre and not a name his parents were familiar with) McCluttney remembered that, in his van which the group used for transport, was a box of crap vinyl (Scurge's term for old long-players) and an old record player which had belonged to a recently deceased aunt. This collection had been willed to Scurge's mother who, not having any use for this bequest, had charged her son with the responsibility of dropping it off at some handy charity shop. Scurge had forgotten this errand in the excitement of getting a paid gig. His suggestion that the record player could be wired up to the group's amplifiers and that Wilf could do a spot of Disc Jockey work was seized upon gratefully. Henry suggested that, while the rest set up the equipment, Wilf might like to visit the gents' and wash his face. When he came back, some of the colouring had been pushed back into his hair-line, contrasting strongly with his blond hair and looking as though he was a bottle-blond who needed a refresher. Those of the group not involved in the playing of records were invited to spend the rest of the evening as guests. This time, the group were the ones not enjoying the music as the strains of Herb Alpert drew the dancers back onto the floor.

* * *

Wilf and Robbie both felt that, with the team broken up and with things, in general, not having gone their way, they should return to their old haunts and habits.

Wilf had fallen back into his old routine gratefully but Robbie was still dissatisfied.

One morning, walking aimlessly along the length of the market in Port Regis which was in full swing, he found himself on a convergent course with Chevis Yardley with his replacement minder in tow. Robbie recognised this baleful presence as Preston, an ex-employee of a debt collecting agency which had had to reluctantly dispense with his services owing to the number of police investigations which Preston's enthusiasm tended to initiate.

Some people, when they smile, have a reassuring or welcoming air which can put you at your ease. They communicate the pleasure they feel on encountering you and make you feel good in their presence. Preston had a smile like a bashed-in dustbin lid which produced feelings of discomfort in the mind of the beholder. You would experience misgivings and a longing to be elsewhere.

"Morning, Robbie." said Chevis, warmly. "You haven't been seen around the market very much, lately. Have you gone straight?"

"No. – It's–"

Without allowing Robbie to finish what would have

probably been a weak excuse, Chevis continued, "Word is, that you and Wilf have gone independent. Is that true?"

"No – We–"

"You don't get holidays in this job, do we Preston?"

Preston's face crumpled some more but he said nothing. It was a sort of crumple of agreement.

"You're an essential part of this market, a small wheel on which us bigger wheels depend, understand?" Chevis' tone had a threatening edge and Preston's grin widened in a sideways crumple.

"We (the word implied Preston and all that Preston was capable of) would like to see more input from you. Can we expect a little more effort in the future?"

"Yes." Sullenly, like a small boy promising an angry parent better behaviour.

"Good boy." Chevis said, prodding the air with his cigar as he and Preston continued on their way.

* * *

Gerry had spent the morning thinking about his immediate future. If he was to marry and settle down, he could retire as he wanted to. The sale of his house and business would provide a good lump sum with which to enter into marriage with Toni. A sort of dowry, as he liked to think. It didn't suit Gerry's personality to live with and off Toni, even though she was wealthy enough to support him. It wasn't acceptable to be thought of as a kept man. He was considering advertising the business when it occured to him that Bob and Meera might want to take over. They wouldn't appreciate a new owner, their jobs would be in jeopardy if that happened and they might just jump at the chance of newsagency ownership.

When they arrived, shortly before eight o'clock, laughing together as they entered the shop, he challenged them both directly.

"I'm about to get married —."

Before he could finish, Meera let out a delighted squeal and locked his neck in a jasmine scented hug.

"Oooh! It's the new woman – we thought something was going on – will we get to meet her – When? When is she coming? When's the wedding? Can we come?"

Bob stepped in to calm his wife a little, "Give the man a chance, Em, he's going to tell us if you let him."

"Yes, I think, to everything." Gerry continued, now freed from Meera's embrace, "It's the new woman, Toni, her name is, and you will both meet her at the wedding because you are invited. There's something slightly more important to discuss – afterwards – after the wedding, I mean, I won't need to work here anymore so I'm thinking of selling up."

Meera's grin diminished slightly as she considered the consequences of Gerry's plans. Before she could settle on the darker effects, Gerry asked them if they were at all interested in becoming the new proprietors and received another bruising but fragrant hug from Meera.

"We'd love to, Gerry. It would be a dream come true for us. Since we won that money, we have discussed buying a little corner shop for ourselves but were reluctant because – well – we like it here and we didn't want to do the dirty on you."

"That's excellent. And convenient. I'll discuss terms with you before I go home and sort out the legal bits."

Later that evening, Gerry finished his shift and locked up the newsagency and went quickly home to change before calling to collect Toni. They were going for a celebratory meal at the Demsbury Arms. Neither of them had felt like going further afield for anything more lavish. Besides, the place had romantic associations since that was where they had both first met.

"You must watch where I go as I'm driving – I have a

tendency to take wrong turns and get lost if I'm talking to someone in the car." said Gerry as they left the creaky gates of Cabley Hall behind them.

"I'll keep quiet if you'd like me to." suggested Toni, who was wearing what she referred to as 'haute équipe' or, as Gerry preferred, casual.

"All right, if you don't mind. It's just that I've been thinking a bit at work today – about us. We'll discuss it at the pub."

Oh no, thought Toni, he's reconsidering his commitment. If he suggests a long engagement or anything which might delay the wedding, I shall –. Here she couldn't think of an appropriate course of action. This last remark of Gerry's had lopped the top off her happy feelings, leaving them stumpy.

"Now that you've said that much, you'll have to tell me. I can't wait until we're sitting at our meal. What have you been thinking?"

"I'm assuming that I shall be coming to live with you rather than you to live with me. I suppose that much is fairly obvious – you'd have nowhere to put your horses at my place – and that's all right with me but it did occur –"

"Left here." Toni prompted, feeling a little relieved now it seemed as though he wasn't trying to back down.

"Thank you." Gerry said as he turned. "The thing is – would I end up with a title when we get married? Not that I want one – Lord, no – I was just a little concerned that it might be compulsory."

Toni couldn't answer him immediately. She had a fit of the giggles. "No, darling, you won't have to take a title. I do love you, though."

There were problems crossing the social divide, Gerry thought, and the more you consider the move, the more problems there seem to be. Still, so far, none was insuperable.

"There is one other matter – I'm going to sell the

newsagency. I don't suppose you would have any objections to that, would you?"

"No. I hadn't even considered that side of things. What would you do with all your spare time?"

"Well, It would mean that I wouldn't be coming into this marriage empty-handed. That's the main thing. The money from the sale of shop and house would be what I would bring – It's difficult, this," He didn't want to use the word 'dowry', it didn't seem right for what he was trying to explain, "Into the kitty, I suppose. I'd like to write novels on a professional basis and that money would be enough to support me for a few years. Marrying you has given me a golden opportunity to do something I've only dreamed about. Is that O.K.?"

Toni smiled, "I'd be happy whatever you do as long as it's with me by your side." She hugged his arm as tightly as she dared, remembering that he needed it for driving.

As they entered the Demsbury Arms which was still relaxing in an early evening tranquillity, Gerry put his arm around Toni's waist in a rather proprietary fashion and steered her firmly towards the bar and the smiling Carol. More than anything, he wanted to show off his new woman with a metaphorical foot across her neck and a metaphorical shotgun across his shoulders and who better to start with than a woman who knew him, both socially and biblically.

"We're getting married." he announced proudly.

"Good for you, it's about time you settled down properly." Carol grinned.

"Don't tell me that you and Carol have a history, too." said Toni, intuiting a good deal from Carol's remark.

As Gerry issued a hesitant confirmation, Carol asked, "What do you mean, 'too'?"

"I've only just discovered his affair with Monica." said Toni, playfully.

"Who's this Monica?"

"Another flame. You'll likely meet her at our wedding. You're invited, of course. I will send a formal invitation through the post, later. Will you come?"

"I'd love to. I want to see him," nodding towards Gerry, "taken into control."

The metaphorical foot and shotgun both disappeared in a metaphorical puff of smoke.

* * *

Little by little, Gerry had moved his belongings to Toni's place. She had suggested he do it this way, rather than move in all of a sudden. There was little of his furniture which he wished to retain and the overall effect of his move into the house was minimal. He had set up his computer and writing paraphernalia in the library, a perfect place in which to write. The ending of his first novel had been completed in that room and, after spending some time polishing it with repeated readings, he switched on the printer and made a typescript copy and clipped it into a rigid, black binder. He carefully wrote the title onto a sticky label and stuck it onto the front. That was it! That's a book! That's my book. He thought wistfully of how it might look, published in hard-back and sitting on one of those shelves. His mind wandered a little in the paradise it had made; crowded signing sessions in big city book-shops, book-tours around America, film-rights and then, squashing the dream, Gerry pushed himself up from the chair and went to find Toni.

He found her in the kitchen preparing the dogs' food. "I've brought this for you. It's a sort of wedding gift from me." he said, kissing her on the back of the neck, a gesture which she loved.

Toni took it, puzzled. She read the title on the sticker, 'The Pussy-cat Murders'. "Oh!, you have finished your book. Am I to read it?"

"Yes, if you would. It's just the typescript of the whole

thing. I thought you might enjoy it. Ninety seven thousand words wrung directly from my soul. You could be the only one to read it."

"Won't you submit it for publishing?"

"Well, I'll cast about to see if there is someone daft enough to want to accept it but I have no experience in that sort of thing. I'm not sure how to go about it. I enjoy writing, though. It's a good hobby but I'm not yet confident enough to think that it merits being dropped onto the reading public. I'm thinking of taking a more professional approach with my next one. I'm looking upon this as a practice run"

"Well, let me be the judge of that. I shall read it as soon as I have a little time."

* * *

In contrast to Monica's wedding, that joyfully noisy affair in which the groom blushed more deeply than his bride, in which bouquets, rice and confetti were hurled with careless abandon, in which much was eaten and drunk – far more than the modest guest list might have suggested, Gerry's and Toni's union was a subdued occasion. Gerry felt very uncomfortable in his new suit and longed for the ceremonials of the day to be over. Toni seemed overawed by everything, as though it had all been completely unexpected. On the groom's side, Bob and Meera Jamieson, Carol with Sammy the vet were the only guests. There were a few more from Toni's side but the numbers were made up a little by mutual friends. Monica and Kelps brought a shiny Wayne and a wide-eyed Kerry-Ann along and Marisa brought her son who was deeply hostile to the whole idea of weddings and was further infuriated by the discovery that, Wayne notwithstanding, he was the only child present.

Later, in the marquee, Henry, who had been best man, made a long speech outlining the events which had brought his sister and Gerry together and expressed his relief that, despite his initial misgivings, everything had turned out well. Everybody thought, but no-one said, that Henry's speech was far better than Gerry's. Gerry had made an attempt to write something which sounded spontaneous and which contained no awful jokes but a sprinkling of wit. He was pleased with the result and when he rose to give the assembled guests the benefit of his literary skills, he could not find it. So it was with genuine and nervous spontaneity that he stuttered out his thanks to those who deserved it before he faded into speechless panic and then sat down. Toni clutched his arm in sympathy and waited for the watery applause to die. When he was settled, she handed him an envelope, "My wedding gift for you."

She kissed him as he took it.

Gerry opened it up and read it. It was from a firm of publishers, Brasken and Mardean, who were offering to publish his book and wanted to meet with him.

"Wow! How did this happen?" He grabbed her and hugged her, filled with gratitude and excitement.

"When I read your typescript, I rather enjoyed it and so I telephoned an old school chum, Phoebe Brasken, and persuaded her to give it a look over. I thought she might just do me a favour. She read it, liked it and you're in!"

Gerry immediately stood up and banged on the table to attract the attention of his guests, "They want to publish my book!" he announced, "To 'The Pussy-cat Murders'!"

That statement received a louder applause than his speech although most of those assembled had no idea what he was talking about. They understood that it was good news and should be drunk to.

With relief, Gerry welcomed the end of the wedding breakfast and thanked and waved away the guests. When all had left, both he and his new wife were very tired and ready for bed. It wasn't Gerry's first night sleeping in his new home but he still couldn't quite shake off the feeling of being a visitor.

"I'll call you when the bathroom is free, by the look on your face, you need to freshen up. You look half asleep and that will not do tonight." Toni said.

"I'll have a bath; that will do it."

After a short soak: too long and he would have fallen asleep, Gerry climbed out, dried himself and spent some time inspecting his face and the top part of his body for removable defects; long nose hairs, bits of wedding cake sticking to his teeth and other deflators of passion.

Toni called out,"What are you doing in there? Are you all right?"

"I'm anointing my body with aromatic oils and unguents." he called back.

A pause: then the door opened and a fluffy head poked through the gap, "And what would they be?"

Gerry looked at her and smiled – he felt intensely happy right now, "Pile cream, Muscle Balm and mentholated chest rub." he smiled.

"Well, just don't get them mixed up, will you? We don't want to spoil the mood."

As she withdrew her head, Toni must have pushed the door a little because it swung slowly open and Gerry caught sight of her, naked and walking back to the bed. It was a lovely bottom; a broad, flattened, horse-rider's bottom. It swayed with dignity and he loved it. He realised that this was the first time he had seen her naked from this distance or angle. Other times they had been close together, entwined, even. Shit, she's good, he thought; referring more to her repartee than her retreating backside. His penis cared little for verbal sports and began to stiffen.

* * *

About a fortnight afterwards, Gerry was taking a turn in the garden and spotted Kelps emptying the mower of grass clippings.

"So, how are you getting on with Monica, Kelps?"

Kelps put down the barrow he was pushing towards the midden and removed his cap to mop his forehead with.

"Wonderful, sir. Wonderful cook – wonderful woman if you know what I mean."

"Do you not find her – chatty? I thought you preferred the quiet life."

"It's true, I'm not one for conversations so it suits me that she does the talking for both of us. I just close my ears to her when she's in full steam – if you know what I mean."

"Yes, I do, Kelps – I do."

* * *

Well, I've done it, Gerry thought, I've drawn a nap hand. He sat back in his chair and surveyed his surroundings. On either wall were more books than you could shake a librarian at. Behind him, the sun, on its way to streaming through the window and warming his back had illuminated a huge swathe of autumnal countryside. In front of him, on the table which was the centre-piece of the library, his computer was set up and running his favourite word-processing software. With the promise to publish his first novel, Gerry had received an advance to write the sequel, the first lines of which were already up on the screen:

Detective Inspector Danny Craven was never one to sit on his backside. He was not content to wait at his desk for a job to be brought to him; he was out on the prowl, as he had been when still a mere Constable – and looking through his old haunts. It was a familiar beat. In a town like this, he thought, crime is never far away.

It would be nice if there were happy endings all round but life doesn't allow that sort of thing. Two years afterwards, Gerry and Toni were still happy and Gerry was almost as succesful in his horsemanship as he was with his books which sold locally in small numbers. Henry and Angela were also enjoying well earned contentment and from time to time would meet in either the hall or the rectory for the sort of dinner party which Gerry had imagined would be his introduction to his new family.

Kerry-Ann dropped Wayne in favour of a sales representative named Edward Spears who had used to call in to the chemist's shop from time to time. Kerry-Ann was impressed as much by his manner as by his job which, to her, was far more up-market than Wayne's calling. It had more syllables than gardener or council worker and, in addition, there was a company car.

Wayne was philosophical about the split and quickly forged a new relationship with a young lady who worked in the council offices and to whom he had been introduced by his mum.

Annie became pregnant and used her condition to pressure Robbie to go straight and, after a course in adult evening classes, he became a gas fitter. He missed the excitement of his old life and was severely tempted several times during the course of his work, a little like an alcoholic would be when working behind a bar. He carried a picture of his son, Robbie junior, in his wallet and looked at it whenever he weakened and felt the urge to relieve a customer of a few belongings.

Kelps came downstairs on the morning of his third anniversary to find his beloved sitting in an armchair talking animatedly but incoherently to the stuffed pink rabbit. He had never liked this particular ornament but had allowed Monica to display it in the living room. Now, it seems, it had taken his wife away. On the advice of a doctor, he had Monica committed and Kelps went to see her from time to time and listen despondently to her babble and walk with her, the rabbit tucked under her arm, around the grounds of the mental institution. He missed her cooking most of all. Sometimes he was accompanied by Wayne, dutifully visiting his mother but Wayne preferred to stay away.

Toni suggested that she and Gerry might visit Monica and Gerry refused outright, saying that he had been terrified of the woman when she was considered sane and that there was nothing which could drag him into her vicinity now that she was round the twist.

Toni accused him of being unsympathetic and joined Kelps on one or two of his visits.

* * *

It was late at night and in a lay-by on the Wettenham – Steadmore road, a police patrol car was parked. Constables Purslipp and Clough were whiling away the quiet period before the end of their shift.

"You might find this surprising, El, but I've not had much luck with women lately. There's no second Mrs Purslipp on the horizon. I feel the need for a new soul mate. I'm bloody frustrated."

"You should try 'Lonely Hearts', mate. They reckon it's easy pickings there. Stacks of women. Give it a try."

"What? Out of a newspaper?"

"Newspaper, magazine, whatever."

"I might. See how it goes."

There had been a period of silence such as friends can enjoy without the need to fill it with conversation and Ellis broke it with an emerging thought, "Remember that bloke who used to run the papershop, Gerry Whatsisname? Well, he wrote a book called 'The Pussy-cat Murders'. Have you read it?"

"No." Leigh said, interested, "I seen it for sale in the paper shop. Is it good?"

"Not bad. He needs a bit of advice about police work,

though. Some mistakes in the details here and there. I'll lend you my copy if you want."

The End